Ra

qntm

Originally published serially on Everything2, 2011–2014, and on Things Of Interest, 2011–2014 and 2018.

Copyright © 2011–2014, 2018, 2021 qntm.
All rights reserved.

Cover illustration by Alexi Vex.

ISBN: 9798735007937

CONTENTS

Thaumic City	1
Sufficiently Advanced Technology	9
From Ignorance, Lead Me To Truth	24
Magic Isn't	31
What You Don't Know	45
Ragdoll Physicist	68
Broken 'Verse	85
Thaumonuclear	96
The Jesus Machine	109
Space Magic	123
The Seventh Impossible Thing	144
Daemons	165
Abstract Weapon	180
Death Surrounds This Machine	191
Zero Day	192
ॐ	204
Bare Metal	213
Hatt's People	232
Deeper Magic	249
There Is No Cabal	265
Protagonism	284
Scrap Brain Zone	308

Inferno	322
From Darkness, Lead Me To Light	338
Direct Sunlight	351
Abstract War	364
Everything Is Real	380
Why Do You Hate Ra	397
Last Thursdayism	415
Akheron	429
All Hell	442
From Death, Lead Me To Immortality	457
Machine Space	465
It Has To Work	480
This Can't Happen	496
Free	504
Continuity	514
Thaumic Sky	524

1
Thaumic City

"Nottingham has enough pubs and clubs", say the local police. If you wanted to get around every last one of them it would be a year at a brisk trot before you were starting to visit establishments more than one mile from the centre of the city. Pick a Friday or a Saturday, any Friday or Saturday of the year: the establishments will be rammed and jumping and the streets bustling with people in their most tightly-wound and elaborately crafted drinking costumes. It's almost Christmas but the cold season has not added much to the average number of layers. Multicoloured decorative illuminations span the alleys and narrower streets: yellow curlicues and red stars and inexplicably five-pointed white snowflakes. Orange light spills out onto the street from the pubs. Floodlit trams cruise past, bells ringing at stumbling people in the way. Officers with cars and vans and fluorescent visibility jackets hold a largely pre-emptive presence on various likely streets. Quite frankly, it's a quiet one.

Laura Ferno and her three compatriots— and that's how she thinks of them, herself plus three, there is no question in her mind as to who is the first among these equals— stumble across the Square towards Iris, ratted on vodka-and-vodkas, largely insulated from the cold by the invisible effects of booze. There is a saying. "Drink through it." "It" is usually clear from context, but in this case the interpretation seems to be "life".

Laura is the shortest and darkest and cleverest of the four. "You're so clever!" Diane and Sandra tell her, all the time. She denies it, and tries not to show it. Highly polysyllabic words give her away, though. Diane is snarky and insufferable when not handled with the greatest of tranquility, and adorable and sweet when she wants something. Sandra is the oldest, and is practical and maternal and overweight. She prefers beer and has the greatest capacity for it. Natalie is Laura's twin sister. They are very nearly identical. Or, to put it another way, they are not identical. Natalie is a little quieter, that's it. The four study at opposite ends of the country now, but just for tonight and a few more days they're all back in town, and painting it.

Iris's neon sign casts neon light over the frankly preposterous queue outside the establishment's front door. Every step closer reveals more people in this line. "It never ends!" Sandra says. "We're going to be waiting until Christmas."

"How much is it to get in?" asks Laura.

"Five fifty," say two others simultaneously.

Laura rummages through her purse. "I need to stop and get cash again."

"What did you get last time?" asks Diane. "A fiver? Did you find— excuse me— the only cash machine in this city which dispenses single fivers?"

"I'll cover you," says Natalie. "You can buy me a drink once we're inside."

"No no no. I can't, I don't have cash."

"Well then use a card!"

"I— okay, why are we going to Iris anyway? It's crap and you can't see anything and it's *so* expensive. It's *so* expensive."

Sandra: "Because the music's good, and dancing, and it's Diane's friend's first day behind the bar so he can get us a discount."

"Well, I don't even know him, and I hate Iris anyway."

"Overruled!" Laura is dragged forward by several limbs.

"If overruled I will not queue! If— if dragged in I will not pay! If someone covers me to get in I will not drink and if someone buys me a drink I will still not drink. Seriously, I'm trying to— hey— keep a cap on my entertainment budget. It was one cash machine visit per outing, no cards—"

"Come on!"

"Oh, come *on*, it's only—" Natalie turns around and looks at the big clock overlooking the square. "One. Five to."

"There's a night bus at one. I'm going to try to get the night bus at one. I'm going. Take care!" There are some hurried hugs, but Laura manages to extricate herself and hobble off within a few moments.

*

Crossing the Square takes a little while because her shoes were made for looking good at the expense of comfort, convenience, durability, mobility, price and so on. Her boyfriend never wants to know how much they cost, and yet, like a car crash or gripping slasher flick, can't look away when she reveals the hideous truth each time. (Where is *he* now? In another city, staying with his family for Christmas. Probably drunk out of his skull with his mates at their local, or, by this time, in bed with half of a sloppy, cooling pizza from the Exchange, taking a good run-up for tomorrow's hangover.)

It's sixty seconds to one and she has a long zig and then zag to take to get to the top of the hill where the bus stops are, but there is thankfully a shortcut, a narrow and steeply-stepped (but usually quite well-lit and friendly) alley which cuts off the corner of the triangle, so she takes that instead. It's well-lit because the Slouch is halfway along it and usually completely filled with people. Of course, she remembers a little too late, the Slouch got closed down a couple of weeks ago because some stupid woman took drugs and almost died on their property. It'll be back, but there are legal proceedings. In the meantime, for the moment, this is quite a dark and empty passage.

A couple of men come around the corner and start coming down the steps. "'Scuse me!" she chirps, moving to slide past them on the side. They don't move. How irritating. One of them reaches into his jacket. The other already has both of his hands free.

"Her," she hears a third man utter some yards behind her.

Oh shit.

It would be nice to say that all the alcohol in Laura Ferno's system leaves her at this point and she gains laserlike, crystalline clarity and the following happens in slow motion. But, though armed, she is drunk off her face.

A momentary pause to elaborate on what she's wearing. The key word here is "rings". The high-heeled, high-impracticality shoes have been touched upon already. The black leggings, black skirt and black top are inconsequential. Resting comfortably around her neck, though, is a very fine silver necklace made from thirty-seven components, each a unique three-dimensional elongated silver shape linked to the next with wire; this is much more significant. Decorating her ears are large silver earrings in equally complex shapes. Around her left wrist are four silver bangles and one golden bangle, all slightly different sizes, each custom-made by a different craftsperson, but engraved with the same complicated repeating and interlocking design, reminiscent of Korean text but illegible in any human language. These five are independent, but amplify each other. Around her right wrist are three more bangles, these ones relatively commonplace items bought "off the shelf", albeit a specialist and extremely expensive and obscure shelf. These three interlock and (in ways which may become apparent) interact with one another in useful ways. On her left index finger, left thumb and left middle finger, three smaller rings with similar designs which control the bangles on her right hand. On her left ring finger, nothing (but ah, one day). On her right index finger, no rings, but an intricate tattooed design circling the base of the finger where a ring would sit.

That covers everything not concealed in her purse. The three thugs — no, four thugs — aren't mages. They haven't realised that Laura Ferno is bristling with openly-carried thaumic weaponry. Even with just the tattoo this would have been a bad idea.

Laura turns as fast as can be expected given the events and alcoholic content of the preceding six hours. Thug Three's Maglite, the four-D-cell kind, lands on her head with a *bop* like a coconut and she yelps and drops to the ground. She rolls and hisses at the pain for a moment or two. Her purse falls off and is kicked away down the steps. That much of the scene goes exactly as the four thugs anticipated. Then Laura's had enough time to remember her emergency phrase and form a few syllables.

"Dulaku surutai jiha, twenty you em!"

She flails her right hand at her attackers and they recoil with hot pain as large amounts of hard infrared and microwave radiation wash over them like water from a fire hose. The thermal output is invisible, but immediately felt on the face and skin. The first one she hits recoils instinctively, hands across his face, cheap plastic jacket bubbling and beginning to melt in places. He runs for it, escaping down the alley steps and into the Square. The one with the Maglite takes the thermal energy in the face and throws himself back against the wall, clutching his eyes. The third ducks with surprising speed.

And the fourth sees it coming. He shields his head with his heavy leather jacket and lurches forward in front of Laura, managing to deflect her hand upwards where it's relatively safe. Her hair begins to singe and the wall starts to scorch. But before he can get hold of her other hand (and before her hair can catch fire) Laura has managed to pronounce "Kafa'u six kay dulaku!" and a quantity of directed linear momentum has erupted out of that hand like a fist into his sternum, hurling him up and backwards into the wall and along it and down into the street beyond. Even if the buses miss him he'll break a leg or two. He won't be back.

"Get her arms!" shouts Three, but there's nobody else still in the game. He cannons into her from below and pins her right hand to the wall, pointed sideways this time. But Three's too slow to get her left hand either—

maybe he thinks she needs to say the whole spell again to carry it out a second time?

"Sedo!" she says, and another invisible piston smashes Three against the far wall of the alley. *CRACK* go several parts of his body, and several parts of Two's body too, who was curled up on the ground right behind him. Three drops from the wall like a ragdoll and rolls down the steps. Laura manages to find her footing and slump down against the wall. "Thono," she says, which switches off her thermal lance. It's over.

Alcohol and junk food from earlier in the evening swirl in her gut and she throws a lot of it up on the steps. It makes her feel a lot better, for a moment; then her brain becomes clear enough to process what just almost happened.

There are no badass quips.

With a jolt she realises that Two is still moving, groping his way up the steps towards her. But he's moving slowly. He can't see— his face is visibly burned. Laura yelps and scoots up a step, pulling her feet out of Two's reach. Something blurry and primal and red-hot in the front of her brain demands that she kick his head in while he's vulnerable, or blow it off with another kinetic pulse. *Stamp on it, kill the spider!* But she reins that instinct in for just a second, just long enough to scrabble to her feet. Standing up steps from the pathetic burnt creature, a less impulsive component of her vodka-blunted psyche manages to wrench control back. *Get out of there,* it tells her instead. She stumbles backwards and runs up the steps, towards the bright lights and the buses.

CCTV, that's why.

She staggers up the last of the steps and out into the street. There are already several curious heads peering down at her, wondering what just caused a man to be thrown out into the middle of the traffic. There's a pair of police officers hurrying in her direction, one of them radioing details in. "I need some help," Laura explains, staggering forward. "Um."

"Easy, easy!" says a man, catching hold of her as she's about to blunder into the road. He's a bus driver, very tall and much older and friendlier-looking. He manages to hold her up. "Easy. What the hell just happened?"

"I think some people attacked me," says Laura Ferno. She feels a stabbing pain in her stomach, and shivers. "I need to sit down." The man helps her over to the nearest bus shelter, but all it has are uncomfortable anti-seats, barely horizontal planks. The best Laura can do is lean against one for support.

One of them ran away, she thinks. *The one with the torch is— he's still in there. But he can't see. He won't get very far. I hope. One of them* — she looks around through the scratched plastic window of the shelter and focuses on the far side of the road — *is a pile of thug in the gutter. He might be breathing. I don't care. And the one with the knife is wallpaper.*

That's right, thinks Laura Ferno. *He had his hands free because he was carrying something. And then he didn't— he could have grabbed both my arms—*

But he only used... he only used one hand—

Way down at the far end of the street, a siren starts wailing.

"Is your hand okay?" another strange voice asks her. She can't see who's talking. And then there's a gasp. "Let me look at you. You're covered in blood, honey."

"My hand's fine," says Laura, and collapses, bleeding out slowly from a hole near her kidney.

2
Sufficiently Advanced Technology

"Stab wound" is a really amazing phrase to suddenly be forced to consider from close, personal range.

Laura Ferno wakes up the following afternoon with a belly wrapped in bandage, a mouth tasting like sun-dried vomit and two distinct hangovers: one from the alcohol, and one from the anaesthesia. She spends a restless and irritable Christmas in hospital, forced to keep still so as not to tear her side open again. She is discharged shortly before the New Year, with a sizeable antibiotics prescription and instructions not to drink alcohol while taking them, which only makes her angrier. After a month and a half, her doctor gives her permission to be physically active again, and doesn't bother to set up another appointment. And then the physical injury is totally in the past. Laura forgets about her scar for months at a time. It should be over.

But this is the United Kingdom, and a muggee can't straight-up kill a mugger in self-defence and simply return home to unified rapturous applause. Very large, very serious questions have to be asked, questions to which "But he was trying to kill me!" doesn't qualify as an acceptable answer.

When her solicitor first explains this to her, Laura sits there in the chair unable to actually comprehend what he is telling her, incapable of even a bewildered "Huh?", let alone a full sentence of rebuttal.

They are found guilty, of course: the two-and-a-half people who were left after she'd finished with them. They go *away*, very quickly. But there is a serious chance that she has broken the law in turn, by *having been a victim of attempted murder.*

"No. That's not how it is. You've broken no law. That's something you're going to have to keep a firm grip on. It's just going to take a little time and effort and preparation and training to get to the point where a court of law is convinced. It's going to take some reasoning. Let's talk about your weapons."

"They *aren't* weapons," says Laura, but then immediately realises that this is exactly the reaction that her solicitor is trying to draw out.

"If they're not weapons, what are they?"

"They're tools. I improvised. They are, at best, improvised weapons."

"Go on. Convince me."

"...I'm not a Marine. I'm not a spy. I'm not a gun nut. I don't walk around carrying weapons. I'm a mage. Which, in case you're not clear on this, is a classification of scientist. I'm studying for a degree in thaumic engineering and I spend a lot of time in the lab. In the front ten pages of any thaumic engineering textbook, you'll find a summary of the basic tools that are required to get anything done in magic. That accounts for ninety percent of what I carry. This equipment is advanced and unusual for a random woman in the street, but it's completely standard for a trainee mage anywhere in the world. Most of it was purchased 'off the shelf'. Some of it, I built myself in class. *For* class. And ten years from now, B&Q is going to stock this stuff alongside the power drills. Convinced?"

The solicitor nods. "Next question. Does a kitchen fitter typically carry his power drill with him when he goes out on the lash?"

Laura glares at him. "I carry *my* tools everywhere I go. I'm wearing the same equipment right now." She rolls up her sleeves and shows him. "It's how I dress. Ask anybody."

"Do you have a licence to carry or use magic amulets in public?"

"I don't need one."

"Why not?"

Laura shrugs. "Magic amulets aren't restricted."

"Why not?"

Laura thinks about this, looking into the man's eyes and trying to figure out what he's trying to make her say. "Ah... Because this hasn't happened before."

The solicitor smiles. "Yes. The complicating factor. This is what makes this case a little less straightforward. Magic is... subtle. And it's a little bit new. Now, all things being equal, that would be the end of the case. You were attacked, and you defended yourself using equipment which you had available to hand, equipment which you were carrying legally. It would be no different if you'd defended yourself using something else that had never been used before, like a... a bottle of toilet cleaner, or a stuffed swordfish.

"But tell me about the other ten percent of what you carry."

"I'm... *very* good at magic."

"How good?" The solicitor has a completely straight face. He doesn't want modesty. He wants a straight answer.

She inhales. "I'm ahead of all of my classmates. I'm ahead of all of my lecturers. I'm ahead of all the theoretical or applied magic textbooks I can find. I have performed experiments and demonstrated results in the lab which, to my tutors' knowledge, are both completely original and highly significant. The only thing stopping me from pursuing a bachelor's degree in theoretical magic simultaneously with my applied course is university policy, and the only thing stopping me from claiming two separate PhDs right now is the speed at which I can type. As for my equipment..." She slips all five bangles off her left wrist and selects one of the silver ones to hold up. "I made this myself. It's called a Veblen arbitrator. I can't explain to you what a Veblen arbitrator does without going through about six weeks of technical jargon, but in industry these are generally expected to be the same size and weight as a grand piano. And cost. And twice as difficult to use properly. Nobody else on Earth has one like this, and nobody else on Earth has the spell I use to drive it. The same is true of most of what I carry in my purse. And yes, I did use this when I was attacked."

He nods. "Okay, Miss Ferno. Now answer this question. If you're that good at magic, why didn't you defend yourself non-violently? Or at least non-fatally?"

"Do you want to just go with 'Laura'?" says Laura, primarily to buy time to phrase her answer.

"That's fine."

"I'm thinking."

"This isn't a trick question. There's a correct response here. I want you to find it."

She counts off on her fingers. "Three reasons. Because I didn't have time; because, advanced as my equipment is by lab standards, it's still experimental and unpolished; because I was improvising and because I'm a mage, not a witch. Well, that's four reasons. The heat spell I used was created in the lab as an exercise for me to see what was possible. I've used it a few times in the lab to heat metal for metalworking, but my supervisors discourage me from doing so because, as should be plainly obvious by now, the spell is incredibly dangerous when wielded by hand. If the technique were to be used in industry, it would probably involve mounting the generator/arbitrator in a static assembly with some manual controls, or maybe combined into some sort of blowtorch-like tool. In either case a visor would be used. As for the kinetic spell, that was, believe it or not, written over the course of a weekend about six months ago when I was helping a friend of mine move house. It was supposed to help move furniture. It didn't work very well for that purpose then, and it doesn't work very well now either, because it's too, uh, 'blunt'.

"Both spells *could* have been used non-lethally or even non-violently. Unfortunately, I didn't have the two weeks' preparation available that I would have needed. I had about five seconds. Honestly, it's a miracle that I was able to cast *anything* given the circumstances. We have a saying in our field: 'Magic isn't'. It doesn't 'just work', it doesn't respond to your thoughts, you can't throw fireballs or create a roast dinner from thin air or turn a bunch of muggers into frogs and snails. It's incredibly hard, even for me. It's getting easier, but it's not that easy. Yet."

The solicitor says nothing for a long while as he finishes typing out notes.

"How much of this did you already know?" she asks him.

He ignores her: "If I consult an independent expert in thaumic engineering, will he or she be able to corroborate your statements about the standard range of tools carried by a trainee mage? What about if I ask a selection of actual trainee and professional mages across the country?"

"Yes."

"If I read every thaumic engineering textbook published in the last five years will the majority of your equipment really appear in the front ten pages?"

"Maybe the first fifty pages. And only the entry-level ones. In the appendices for most of the rest."

"If I ask all your friends and relatives and other people on your course, will they all confirm that you wear magic rings as jewellery almost every day they've ever seen you, including formal and informal occasions, in and out of the lab? What if I look at photographs of you taken over the past year?"

"Yes. Yes, almost certainly."

"Almost?"

"I take them off when exercising. And when I'm sleeping, obviously."

"Will your instructor confirm the story about writing the thermal spell in the lab and will your friend confirm the story about writing the kinetic spell for a move?"

"Yes."

"I'm going to take a guess and say that you've played the events of that night through in your head about a hundred thousand times since they happened. You've spent the last month and a half thinking about different things that you could have done. Is that true?"

"Yes."

"What should you have done?"

Even having answered the previous question truthfully, Laura has to stop and think for a long moment. All of her alternative outcomes were predicated on chance: she could have taken a different bus, worn different shoes or worn her rings on opposite hands; she could have kept hold of her purse, or ducked, or evaded the first grab; she could have slurred either or both of the spells, or tripped and passed out and bled to death on the steps.

She could have never taken up magic at all.

"There's nothing else I could have done."

"I'm going to talk to your tutors and your sister and the people who know your capabilities best. I'm going to ask them what they would have done, and what you should have done. Will they give the same answer?"

"Yes."

Laura's solicitor smiles broadly.

And that's exactly how it goes.

Surprise witnesses don't appear. Unexpected damning evidence isn't introduced. All hope isn't lost right at a critical dark point two-thirds of the way through the trial and victory isn't triumphantly clawed back in the middle of act three. It's lengthy and gruesome and tedious and involved and expensive and unpleasantly detailed and at times it seems like it's never going to end. But she wins. She straight-up wins.

She wafts out of the court, as light as a feather.

*

Now it's the day after she was cleared and Laura is having coffee with her sister at the bottom of a skyscraper chasm in the London Docklands— or, as

Laura thinks of it, The Future. This specific Future is the utopian, ultra-clean, ultra-stylish future, with brushed white stone, shiny metal railings and advanced semi-automated mass transit on elevated rails. It's the Future where litter and crime and unattractive people aren't permitted and where, impossibly, everybody makes substantially more money than average.

Laura finishes her thought with: The Future, in other words, that invariably has an ironic, hidden dark side to it.

It's a bright November day, but too cold to be sitting outside, from where one whole side of the tallest building in the United Kingdom would be visible. Laura and Natalie are okay with this.

Aside from her clothes, Natalie Ferno is almost the mirror image of her sister. She's fractionally taller, though well within the error bars introduced when either or both of them wear heels. She's a little lighter of the hair, a little narrower in the cheeks, wears substantially less jewellery as a habit and talks a lot less. But her clothes actually have colour and that's what sets them apart. Laura Ferno blends in with all the white stone and grey concrete and black suits. Natalie is visible: today, she wears mainly orangey-red.

"You're paranoid," Natalie tells Laura.

"I'm not paranoid," Laura tells Natalie. "Just because a court says something is true or false doesn't make it true or false. Courts are not the arbiters of reality. And I don't mean the court that just said I defended myself legally. Even though *they're* about to go ahead and revise their opinions of what constitutes 'legal' because I just showed them something scary that any idiot with a workshop can do if they know what words to say."

"And what the words mean."

"Magic is perfectly safe, it's not a crushing revelation that you can kill someone with magic. You can kill someone with anything. Rocks, trees, clouds, plants, ants. I don't know. Marbles. *Clover.* If it's hard, it can split a head open; if it's soft, you can suffocate on it. You can kill someone with magic, so what? That elevates magic from the level of, well, *magic*, i.e. *fairy stories*, to the level of something that actually exists. And you can kill someone with fairy stories! Probably. Some fiction is bad for you. Almost certainly. I can't think of any examples offhand.

"Anyway just because the court says magic is a dangerous force that suddenly needs regulating because nobody completely understands it— that is to say, the *court* doesn't completely understand it, much like it doesn't understand the internet, fax machines, GPS or... or the offside rule— doesn't make it so. And if they do pass a law which says I can't carry regular equipment with me—"

"You'll put it in a bag, like everybody else," says Natalie.

"No. No, I will keep carrying my so-called *arsenal* where people can see it," (Laura is waving her arms around while she expounds on this topic, and the bangles are indeed where people can see them and hear them jangling) "and people will look at me and they will *know* that I am not a woman with whom to fuck. And other women like me will wear similar-looking stuff and they'll scare would-be whatevers away with fakes. It's a deterrent. But anyway, I was talking about the other court. I'm not paranoid. Despite that ruling, and despite the fact that those *wannabes* went away for half as long as they should, that was a hit."

"It was not a hit, Laura."

"They recognised me! The blind one said 'Her.' I mean, the one I blinded. And they kicked my purse down the steps because they knew it was full of enough clatter that I could have gone through them like a food processor, which it was. They wanted my weapons. And don't look at me like that, I know I just won a major case on the basis that they're tools, not weapons. You know what I mean. They wanted to steal and adapt and use them as weapons. They wanted something that doesn't need to be mounted on a truck to work."

"They picked you at semi-random because you were in the wrong place and they took the purse out of the equation because they thought you might have pepper spray or something. Laura, if they knew who you were, and they wanted the flamethrower et cetera that you were carrying, don't you think they knew you'd just have to say 'dulaku' and take them out?"

"Ah, but they thought I was drunk."

"You were drunk!"

"But not drunk enough! They knew I was too dangerous to confront at any other time, but they thought I was drunk enough."

"This again."

Magic is more complicated than pointing a hand and reciting words; one has to think one's way through the spell while saying it, in order for the effect to "catch". It is not unlike performing advanced mental arithmetic. Vodka, naturally, dulls the ability to do this. Laura has made a great deal out of her evident ability to cast reliably under extreme pressure after consuming a quantity of alcohol that, at best, could be described as above the recommended daily allowance for women. Natalie has refused to rise to challenges to meet or beat what Laura has begun to term her "record".

Natalie says, "Here is my take. And here is the court's take. They were unlucky."

"*Unlucky?*"

"Yes! Unlucky for them. Admit it. Mugging a person at random and finding that they're armed, in this country, is effectively unheard-of. Even if you were specifically targeting mages, the odds of encountering one as battle-ready as you? You're off the charts, if not unique. Nobody carries as much junk on their wrists as you do. I'm a mage and I don't carry as much junk on my wrists as you do."

"That's just because you work with theory. Wait." A completely new expression crosses Laura's face.

"But I still—"

"I said wait a second."

Laura puts her hand flat on the table and thinks for a moment. Natalie takes the opportunity to finish her coffee and chew some more oatmeal muffin. She stares out of the window at flowing people. It's pushing towards dusk. She should probably be moving off home to get some dinner started.

"What do you carry?" Laura asks.

Natalie holds up both hands, revealing bare wrists and ringless fingers.

"What about in your purse?"

"Nothing. Sometimes a linker." A Kaprekar linker is the magic equivalent of a Phillips head screwdriver or a USB key — a keyring-sized object, indispensible for a huge variety of elementary tasks and never available when you need one. Laura has one on her necklace.

"What is your current project?" asks Laura. "In your coursework or off the clock. Is it a physical object? Do you carry it with you? Is it important? Is it valuable? Who knows about it? Can you tell me about it?"

"Nothing, no, no, no, no, nobody and no."

"You can't tell me about it."

"Because I'm not working on anything!"

Laura takes the first bangle off her right wrist and holds it out to Natalie, who gingerly accepts it.

"And this is?"

"Just read the runes while I find the driver dot," says Laura, taking off her necklace and sorting through its various elements.

"This is the top component in a field extruder," says Natalie, reading the engravings on the interior side of the bangle. So far, nothing she has seen is unusual. "So what?"

"This." Laura finds what she is looking for, and laboriously unthreads a small metal bead from somewhere near the middle of the necklace. She hands it to Natalie as well. It has a hole drilled through it and more engravings around its equator. These engravings are much finer and much more unusual. "Keep this somewhere on your person. In your purse isn't good enough, it's too detachable. On a necklace is fine, but an earring would be ideal. I'm sure you can think of something." Natalie's ears aren't pierced.

Natalie picks the bead up in her other hand and says "Zui eset." Invisibly, a small amount of mana jumps out of her thoughts, into the bead, on to the bangle and back into her mind, now carrying a little information about where it's been and what it saw on the way. She examines the echo with interest.

"You'll need to charge it every day before you go out," says Laura, threading the rest of the elements back onto the necklace in a precise order. "S.O.P. is to turn it on and just run away. The full spell takes about forty minutes to set up initially, probably longer for you because you don't enunciate as fast as I do, but once you've bound it to—"

"I don't think I need you to tell me."

"You can figure it out?"

"No, because *I don't need this.* When did you make this? I don't need defensive magic. This is... `zui eset`. This is..."

It's a personal shield. Not a sturdy one, and not a perfect one, but a substantial improvement on bare human skin. It coats the skin like a thick duvet and repels objects: knives, fists, maybe even bullets. For a while.

What it is is revolutionary, but Natalie doesn't want to give her sister the satisfaction of seeing her impressed.

Laura continues, "It's lightweight. It's reactive. Invisible by default so that you can see through it. Try it out a few times in an open space before you carry it in public because the extruded field behaves *really* strangely at the point where your feet touch the ground. Don't use it sitting down. It can't and won't cut anything at extrusion time. Once you're fully enclosed, it contains enough air for about eight breaths, so try not to suffocate. Emergency deactivation, you say 'zui ixuv ixuv', or you can bind your own word, or just take the bangle off and drop it. And don't use it in the rain."

"In the *rain?*"

"Falling raindrops register as incoming projectiles and wear the charge down."

Projectiles. Natalie turns the bead over in her hand a few times. Talking Laura out of her paranoia was going to be an easy enough task when she sat down at the table. It was going to be an exercise in logic, persistence and patience. Now Laura's reflected all her own shaky reasoning back on her and reinforced it with some frightening and believable logic of her own. Natalie gets it now. Paranoia, defencelessness.

She gets what it's like to feel the need to carry *equipment*.

"When did you build this?" Natalie asks.

"I've been working on it since the attack. It's not mature by a long way yet, but once I've got another driver dot of my own machined, I'll keep working on it and let you have the progress."

"I'm not working on anything," says Natalie. "I mean, *anything*. I'm really not. It's raw theory, the most abstruse thing you could ever imagine. Nothing with immediate practical value. Or even foreseeable value."

"I know," says Laura.

For a long while neither of them say anything. They sit and finish their coffee. Natalie lays the bead down in front of her and watches it, as if it might bite her; as if it might not be on her side.

"You've scared me," Natalie says, not looking up.

"I know," says Laura.

*

The interior of Canary Wharf Tube station is as tall and long as a cathedral, and is as much The Future as the rest of this square mile of London. The hall is sprinkled with LED signs, automated gates, security cameras and beeping contactless pass cards. The number of people waiting or arriving or leaving is large, but manageable, but visibly rising, like a tide.

Laura and Natalie are heading in opposite directions, so they stop for a moment in the wide No Man's Land between platforms.

"You are so far out beyond the pack," says Natalie. "I'm there, but you especially. You've seen some things which could happen if you let them happen. I mean, if you *distribute* what you've come up with. I'm saying that what gets mass-produced is a function of what people know exists and what people know is possible and what they can understand. And a lot of those *prerequisites* are already out there because of you. And I know you can take them further. And I'm saying, don't."

"Don't?"

"I'm not having the firearms argument with you," says Natalie.

"Have we ever had that argument? Do we even know that it would be an argument?"

"I'm saying... Thanks for the spell. Thanks for the 'metal'. But stay with defensive magic, Laura. Just do the future a favour and prioritise that over... whatever else you want to do. Over catharsis. That's my train. I have to go."

"Be safe," Laura calls after her as Natalie hurries towards the platform.

On the train, Natalie Ferno finds a seat and sits, turning the tiny metal bead over in her hand. She quickly decides that she is too likely to lose it and puts it away. But she puts the bangle on.

And she spends the whole journey, through both changes and the walk home, checking over her shoulder.

3
From Ignorance, Lead Me To Truth

The first magic spell is spoken by a 90-year-old retired Indian physicist named Suravaram Vidyasagar on 1st June 1972. It is one hundred and seventy-nine syllables long, comprising equal parts Upanishadic mantra and partial differential equation.

The effect of Vidyasagar's spell is nothing at all. He has discovered what will later be called "uum", the empty spell, which expends no mana and fails to rearrange the universe in any externally detectable way, but which then — crucially — returns to the dispatching mind and *tells it so*. Vidyasagar immediately notices the curious reaction to his new "differential mantra". He repeats it several times. Each time, he receives, in an almost-non-existent part of his brain, a tiny almost-thought: a thought so faint and difficult to get a grip on as to be a tiny elementary dream: "Success!"

Vidyasagar is confounded. The result is completely unexpected. Later, many will call it dumb luck. "Luck" can certainly be made to stick: future research will show his choice of wording to be at once exceedingly unlikely and exceedingly close to the ideal phrasing for the effect that it brings about, while it will become equally clear that the effects and events which follow were never Vidyasagar's intention. But "dumb"? Vidyasagar is at worst a mediocre quantum physicist, which leaves him merely two standard deviations above the global mean in raw mathematical capability. He is honest and upright, workmanlike, dedicated, competent, attentive and methodical.

After his retirement and the death of his wife, Vidyasagar has been using meditation to exercise his mind, and to keep its contents well-ordered and stable. The mantras that he has devised are lengthy mnemonic poems which map out events of his life, spiritual and ethical teachings to which he abides, stories he has learned, equations, particle interactions and gauge theories, essays and jokes, and even personalities of people he has known. Has it been working? At this point, even Vidyasagar himself is not certain. But it is a simultaneously stimulating and relaxing use of his abundant time, which has been enough to keep him at it.

"So!" he says.

An inexplicable observation. With no idea what he has discovered, or even if he has truly discovered anything, Vidyasagar follows procedure. He tries combinations. When he speaks the words too quickly or too slowly or in the wrong frame of mind, or if he skips more than a few words or rearranges phrases or loses his train of thought midway through, he receives no such acknowledgement. Some rephrasings are legitimate. Some pronunciations result in clearer and more powerful successful nothingness. He takes notes. He charts patterns. He extrapolates predictions.

He obtains a satisfactory degree of certainty about his result. Then, he seeks independent confirmation.

*

Suravaram Vidyasagar's son Rajesh is 59 years old and also a physicist. He collaborated with his father for decades prior to the latter's retirement, and has continued with his own very closely related work. After Suravaram explains his observations, during a long weekend of unbroken rain, Rajesh considers them for a moment and then tells him that they are trash.

Suravaram is a naturally soft-spoken individual, unperturbable. Seated at the other end of the table, his eyes widen and he stiffens noticeably; for anybody else, this would be the equivalent of throwing his glass through a window in fury. "Are you sure you've fully understood?" he asks.

Rajesh has the carefully-typed paperwork spread out in front of him on the table. He gathers it all up into a pile and shoves it away where he doesn't have to look at it. "Dad, listen to me. I remember a time... it must have been thirty or forty years ago, I can't believe how long ago... we were at the lab and some visitors had arrived and they heard we were father and son physicists. One of them was an excitable young man. He had a boneheaded collection of ideas and he couldn't help but explain it all to us. He thought he had married together science and religion. He had no grasp of physics and he was so far from correct that neither of us had the faintest idea where to begin to explain how or why he was wrong. He thought matter was simply a hardened form of energy. He thought that that *meant something*. That it was *useful*."

"It was a party," recalls Suravaram. "Dr. Mishra's retirement party. Or perhaps Dr. Khurana's. We were encouraged to bring our families."

"But I distinctly remember that after we had got rid of him, you turned to me and said, 'That was your first fool.' My first quantum idiot. And you had run into a few of them by then, but later quantum theory began to gain traction and publicity and nobody understood it and it happened more often, to me and to you. Letters and telephone calls and visits from crazy people, friends of friends and often strangers. And after a while it got that I could tell who they were from just a sentence. Just one sentence. And now I read this..." Rajesh lets the fragment hang.

Suravaram regards him with only the faintest irritation in his expression.

"How do you think you would react?" Rajesh asks him. "A man comes to you and claims that spoken mantras have literal power. You'd dismiss the claim out of hand, wouldn't you?"

"I would," says Suravaram, softly, "unless that man was a competent physicist with a strong track record of rigour. And he was my father."

"A strong track record of what? Is there a Vidyasagar particle? A Vidyasagar equation? If I go to a man in the street, or even a random quantum physicist, and I ask them what the name Suravaram Vidyasagar means to them, what will they say? What have you *done*?"

"It is fair to say," says Suravaram, "that I have relatively few important results to my name."

"You spent your whole life investigating phenomena which nobody else had investigated because nobody else thought they were important, and what did you find? That they weren't important! You collected leftovers off the ground, tidying up where others had already been, because you never had the skills or the intellect that you needed to build something really significant from scratch. And now you're at the very bottom end of your lifetime, looking back at your accomplishments, and there's not enough to them, and you know you'll never live long enough to see the real advances in computing hardware and particle accelerator technology. You're worried you're going to miss the real thing when it really happens. This is the threshold. Everything's going to happen, for real, starting now, and you're not going to be part of it. So what I think has happened is that in desperation, you've invented a whole new alternate science that you can be the king of."

"It's not a science," says Suravaram. "It's not a theory or even a hypothesis. Or even a claim. It is nothing, so far. It is just an observation that I cannot be certain is repeatable."

"You're seriously suggesting that the recitation of mantras can have a physical or measurable effect. What you're suggesting overthrows—"

"I am not," says Suravaram. "I am asserting nothing. Least of all about physics. It could be a psychological effect or a biological effect. I don't know yet. You are reading things that I have not written. You are having an argument, but it's with somebody who isn't me."

"You're blurring the line between science and, and *magic*—"

"I am not. I just want you to repeat my experiment."

Rajesh glares at his father and then at the paperwork. "... No."

For a long moment there's no sound except roaring rain. Suravaram stands up and stalks around the room, inspecting trinkets on shelves. He should be using his cane, but hates to do so in front of people who knew him before he needed it. He reaches a window, and stares out of it into the vertical water.

"I am a scientist," he says. "Since before you were born, I have never not been a scientist. I am not disappointed with my life. I am proud of my limited accomplishments, because they were obtained rigorously and with great care. It's true that there is no Vidyasagar particle. But you are also a scientist. And your name is also Vidyasagar. So?"

Suravaram turns around, pausing for just long enough that his son feels like he should respond, but then interrupts him: "And you are also much nearer the end of your scientific career than the start of it. And you are also, very soon, going to miss a great deal of the future. So? I think it's you. You're arguing with yourself."

"I'm not frightened of *my* lack of accomplishment," says Rajesh.

"No," says Suravaram.

"I'm not frightened of upsetting all of physics," says Rajesh.

"No," says Suravaram. "You're frightened of making a fool of yourself. Just like I am."

Rajesh fidgets. He fumbles for the piece of paper with his father's first mantra on it. "I... I suppose I could try reading the words out loud—"

"No," says Suravaram. "It must be honest. You must make an honest effort. You must believe the words you're saying, and follow through the mantra in your mind without losing your train of thought, or it will not work."

Rajesh looks into his father's eyes and says, "But I don't believe it. Not a word of it."

And the rain keeps pouring.

*

Suravaram Vidyasagar dies less than a year later, believing that "uum" and whatever else it signified is dying with him, if it has ever been real. Rajesh Vidyasagar reluctantly revisits his father's work soon after this, predominantly in order to obtain closure. It works first time.

Before the end of 1973 he has discovered a second spell, "eset", which emits small amounts of mana into the world and records the echoes bouncing back off nearby thaumically-aligned materials and architecture. Before the end of the following year, he has devised a third spell, "kafanu", and an arrangement of static materials — almost a tonne of mostly tungsten — that allow him to move a physical object with words alone. Rajesh Vidyasagar thereby becomes the world's first mage.

Much later, once Suravaram's historical significance has been recognised, a popular myth is widely reported, that his final words were "I do not know what I have begun."

4
Magic Isn't

When a man and his love interest first encounter one another in an adversarial setting, it's supposed to go like this: he proves overconfident; she proves overwhelmingly more competent; she decisively gets the better of him, with embarrassing and hilarious results; this impresses him (and anybody else who happens to be watching) while demonstrating that she's sassy and capable and can take care of herself.

But this is a little too early in the lives of Nick Laughon and Laura Ferno, and neither of them can really take care of themselves yet. It's their first year at university and it's their first Beginner's Bojutsu lesson. Every time she lands a blow on him they both drop their bo staffs, and every time he tries any kind of clever spinning move (while the instructor, who would disapprove, is not looking) he loses his grip and ends up hitting himself in the stomach. The whole lesson is awkward stances, heavily telegraphed moves and clumsy falls. Fortunately, stage one in any martial art is learning to take a fall. And stage two is learning to not feel like an idiot for falling down over and over again.

Nick has turned up for the class because a group of his friends have taken it up. After the end of the lesson, he invites Laura along to the pub with the rest of his gang. She, it transpires, has already been invited to the pub and is already coming along. In fact, she already knows everybody in the gang except Nick. This is because apart from Nick, all of them are thaumic engineering or theoretical magic students. They've all been taking elementary magic theory together for the last week and a half.

Huh.

So Nick, a mere English student, trails along behind their animated and highly technical conversation, listening in, bewildered. He watches Laura's bracelets jangle as she waves her hands around as she talks. She puzzles him. Most mages, including all of his mage friends, are male. And magic rings and the other small metallic tools of the mage's trade really *are* tools. Every mage he knows wears at most a few small rings hooked on a keyring or on a carabiner on a belt loop, with the rest in a rucksack or an actual toolbox. He's always thought of them as washers and gaskets and nuts and bolts. He's never considered them as jewellery.

It dawns on him why mages would be interested in bojutsu, and he feels stupid for missing it. Magic rings are less than half of the picture. A mage-in-training is a person who intends to spend most of his or her adult life waving a magic staff around for a living and a magic staff is a six-foot-long metal pole for propelling and coercing mana into the right shape.

Nick Laughon is 18, middle-sized, wavy-haired and fresh-faced. It's mid-evening in early autumn, hence dark and cold already, but he wears shorts in every weather and season. He cycles everywhere. When he's needed somewhere that's inaccessible on wheels, he runs there. Things that can't be run through, he climbs over. He is constantly reading and seemingly constantly eating, replenishing burnt energy; all of his books are full of dropped crumbs. He loves movies and music and beer and sport and learning new things that he didn't know before. He has almost no definition beyond what he loves. It's almost as if nothing bad has ever happened to him. His personality is pure, sharp and golden.

Laura Ferno is 18 and fiercely intelligent. When Nick pulls up a stool next to her and finds his way into her conversation, she gives him the impression of a girl caught at the instant of launching herself out of the starting blocks of her life. She intends to make history; she intends to learn literally everything there is to know about magic over the next three years, and then continue at the same pace of discovery for the rest of her life. Whether she has the talent to accomplish any such thing is not for Nick to judge, having known her for all of three hours, but she has determination and confidence. She talks at length about Montauk battery theory, magic-driven casting, the Three Open Problems and her mother, a gifted mage who taught Laura everything she knew. Laura has designs on the future.

So they drink Greene King IPA and gin and tonic respectively, while the evening and the conversation get comfortable and settle in for the long haul. It's the beginning of something, although it's not obvious to either of them that this is the beginning of anything. Later, she'll scale back her ambitions — a little — and he'll get a better grip on reality and how badly it sometimes works. And the relationship will grow patiently, like the good kind of record, the kind that doesn't sound good until the third or fourth listen. By the time either of them realises that they should have been counting from somewhere — Nick will realise first, but Laura will be the one who brings it up — neither of them will remember what day this was.

*

Precisely six months later they're in the pub again. Nick still hasn't succeeded in bringing Laura around to the real ale point of view. He'll eat or drink anything, regardless of what it used to be, what it was cooked in or whose plate it's on. People with the audacity to express *preferences* come off to him as wimps and he refuses to stop teasing Laura about her refusal to drink a real drink.

So it's the same two drinks, and so far tonight it's just the two of them; others may turn up but arrangements have been lazy and confused. In fact it's pretty much just the one of them. Nick feels like he's the only person who qualifies as "in attendance", because Laura's spent the last five minutes fiddling with the manual controls on the television mounted in the upper corner of the lounge, trying to find the channel showing today's Shuttle launch from Florida. She is maniacal about Shuttle launches. Today's has been relatively simple to catch, but NASA's operations adhere to no working day and even if they did it would be five hours removed from Laura's, so every few months she skips lectures or supervisions or bo lessons, stays up until two or gets up at four, whatever is necessary to be near a television at the right time.

"This is it," she says when she finds it, sitting back down and getting ready for the show, still not "in the room" in any real sense. There's no sound, but the rocket on the pad is visibly hissing with anticipation, venting steam and liquid oxygen vapour. The countdown is paused at T minus twenty minutes. It's a routine built-in hold. Laura has the whole sequence memorised from cryo tanking to MECO. If Nick watches her eyes carefully during the countdown, he can almost see the big banks of lights flicking from red to green.

"I still don't get it," Nick says. "Is this a magic thing? Isn't this the fiftieth Shuttle launch there's ever been and haven't you seen them all?"

"Fifty-six recorded, one in person, thirty-eight on live television," says Laura. "Soon to be thirty-nine. The full set."

"Is this a magic thing?"

"First-generation Shuttles predate any kind of serious magical modelling capability," says Laura, "so they left the whole technology on the shelf for safety reasons. They didn't understand it well enough back then. I mean, magic is pretty predictable now, because we have some solid theories about how magic moves and we have simulations that can model mana flow in three dimensions properly. But this was back in the late Seventies. It would stun you how low-tech these things are. You know how — you must know this — your wristwatch has a more powerful microprocessor in it than the Apollo Lunar Rover did?"

"My wristwatch, or any wristwatch? This is pretty sophisticated."

"I mean yours. Probably not so much an eight-quid Casio. But it's almost the same deal with Shuttle computers. You'd be stunned. But it makes sense because of how fanatical about safety you have to be when you fly space rockets with people on them. I think they have a saying, or if they don't have a saying then they should, which is 'If it ain't broke, fixing it can endanger the mission'. If it ain't broke, don't... don't kill people."

"Which is why there's a Space Shuttle II now," says Nick.

"Yesssss," says Laura. "Which is about ten percent lighter because of thaumic heat shielding, and also because it has ring-and-sigil attitude controls, and... a bunch of other stuff which they didn't want to retrofit into an existing orbiter."

"Has there been a Space Shuttle II launch yet, and if not..."

"Not for another few years," says Laura.

"...Are you going to watch those launches too?"

"I don't know," says Laura.

"You never answered my first question," says Nick.

"Which question?"

"My first question. Because space travel is cool and all, but you nearly missed an end-of-term exam last year."

Laura doesn't answer.

"Are you waiting for another Atlantis disaster? Because that was our generation's 'do you remember where you were' moment. You want to see a Shuttle blow up live?"

"No," says Laura, staring into her drink. And adds, "I've already seen that once." Here goes nothing, she thinks.

There's a pause.

"You saw the Atlantis disaster live?"

"Yeah."

"Wait, TV live or live live?"

"We were there," says Laura.

"You were there? You and your family?" Laura nods. "You were what, fourteen?" Another nod. "Wait. Wait." Nick realises there's something important here. He does some mental arithmetic.

Laura stares, holding her glass in both hands, eyes defocusing. She's been working up to telling him this for how long? And she still doesn't have more than the first few words worked out.

"Was that how your mother died?"

The countdown starts ticking again. Nineteen minutes, fifty-nine seconds.

"I don't know."

Fifty-eight. Fifty-seven. Fifty-six.

*

It's December 1993 and the Space Shuttle has never failed. As a super heavy lift launch system, the Shuttle program has a mind-boggling quoted probability-of-mission-failure figure of 1 in 60,000. The actual figure will later be discovered to have been closer to 1 in 60, with the difference made up by carelessness, lax safety culture and systematic managerial overconfidence. This overconfidence has arisen predominantly from the Shuttle's flawless track record. The Shuttle program is broken and unsafe. It is unsafe largely because everybody thinks it *is* safe. It is about to fail because it has never failed before. Tomorrow's headline will be: "LOST".

At 10:08:08 on 17 December, T+45.5 seconds into Shuttle mission STS-77, a large chunk of ice is pulled into Space Shuttle Atlantis' fuel system. The ice is there because the fuelling system was accidentally exposed to air while the External Tank was being filled. Two of the Shuttle's three main engines are destroyed instantly. The flight controller immediately orders "Abort RTLS", Return To Launch Site. At this point in the mission, Atlantis is still attached to two much larger Solid Rocket Boosters. Once triggered, SRBs cannot be shut off, so they are left to run out and detach as normal at T+123 seconds. Then the orbiter and External Tank, still mated to one another, pitch forward and fire their one remaining engine in the opposite direction, cancelling out their forward and upward velocity and accelerating back along the flight path. The plan is this: achieve a satisfactory course and trajectory back towards Florida; roll upright; disconnect the External Tank; and glide in to land at a dedicated landing strip at the launch site, which is ready for this exact eventuality. This is an insanely risky plan with many variables, chief of which being that whatever knocked out the first two SSMEs could imminently knock out the third. However, it is the best and only plan conceivable, and it has been prepared for. An RTLS has never happened before in reality, but it has happened ten thousand times in simulations: the pilot and six crew are as ready as any humans could ever be. If anything could work, this is it.

At T+181 seconds, Atlantis' last engine goes dark. A second piece of ice has been pulled into the turbopump system, which is now gutted and haemorrhaging liquid oxygen and hydrogen into clear air. The vehicle is 22 miles up and 31 miles downrange, still travelling directly away from its landing strip at well over a thousand miles per hour, upside down, with no motive power and freefalling like a thrown rock. The mission is now over. There are no more abort modes. There is no pulling out of the trajectory, no chance of crossing the ocean to a transatlantic abort site, and no crew bailout capability. In another minute, Atlantis will reach peak altitude. Around five minutes after that, it will crash into the Atlantic. Everybody on board will be killed. And everybody watching on the television and everybody listening on the radio and everybody watching from the ground is going to stand there while it happens. Except one.

"Doug," Rachel Ferno says to her husband, and surprises him by kissing him as he turns to look at her. "I love you," she says. "`Kasta anh sukudat mirsii.` Kids!"

"Rach, what are you—" Douglas Ferno begins, then stops, distracted, as the five pieces of Rachel's two-metre-long magic staff jump out of her rucksack and screw themselves together in mid-air. This apparently simple trick astounds him. He's seen his wife do a lot of magic, and he's seen the staff a million times, but he's never seen her assemble it except by hand, laboriously, taking at least a minute each time. He's a treasurer, no mage, but he knows that a spell like this takes about a month of writing and a month of practice, because of the laundry list of failure cases that have to be handled. How do the pieces know how to exit the rucksack? How do they pick a spot in the air to assemble at? How long should the assembled staff wait to be collected? What if there are only four pieces, what if half of them are stuck behind a wall?

Laura and Natalie are teenaged, and don't pick up on her urgency when Rachel hugs them both at once, one with each arm, and says "I love you," again. She tries to cover her bases by inflecting somewhere between "I love you: see you in a little while" and "I love you: goodbye forever". "`Eset kasta oerinuum OOLO,`" she adds, which starts her oxygen supply. It's not tuned properly: it blasts her hair downwards like an invisible localised hurricane. Her clothes flicker in the gale and the grass under her feet splays out in all directions. But there's no time for corrections. Here are the components that do matter: "`Sedo oerinuum INKEH sedo MOMEH. Kasta esduq jachta!`"

Douglas Ferno doesn't recognise the phrasing; the words just wash over him. Laura and Natalie fare worse.

They have enough basic magical knowledge to understand that what their mother is doing is either nonsense, or so far beyond the modern magic state of the art that it might as well be... well, whatever comes next. Rachel Ferno has just initiated a pair of high-throughput transduction spells with almost fractal complexity. The patterns of mana radiating off her are incomprehensible. More than that, they're as bright as a sun. To a tuned mind, they're blinding. Who can handle spells that advanced? Who can imagine them?

Rachel Ferno's feet rise a few centimetres from the ground. She moves her hands around, something like sign language, distributing virtual controls to points in space where she can reach them. She's building a virtual cockpit. And she's just using hand signals and finger and thumb rings to do it. *She's not even saying any words now.* "Mum, what are you doing?" cries Laura. She and Natalie can now see luminous manifolds of mana closing up around their mother, like ornate armour.

Douglas Ferno can't: he reaches for his wife but is stopped by the invisible force field. "Rach, what's happening?" And he's right to be confused, because the smallest, simplest force fields in the world require a portable module the size of a motorcycle to project, and they categorically *cannot* be curved. Nothing she is doing is possible. "Rachel!"

Rachel reaches out with her right hand and collects her staff from where it was waiting, suspended in air. "Here goes nothing." As she touches it, there's a single pulse of real light, like a camera flash. Then she's airborne, following the exhaust trail out to sea and the plummeting orbiter.

*

Of course there are witnesses. It's impossible to watch a Shuttle launch from a good spot without company; the Fernos' spot is a crowded park in Titusville. That Rachel Ferno has disappeared, the police are prepared to believe. That she disappeared out at sea, during a Shuttle launch? The coastguard take the notification seriously and a search is begun. But even the people who watched it happen — *even the people with photographic evidence* — don't believe that she flew away.

A human being doesn't show up on radar. A human being in the air at 40 miles' range is too small a speck of dirt to show up on the video footage.

At T+318.9 the venting liquid oxygen and hydrogen finally ignite, blowing up the External Tank. The crew compartment of the orbiter survives the explosion and hits the Atlantic almost intact, though it and its occupants are pulverised on impact.

Seven bodies are recovered from the crash site by NASA.

*

(Nine minutes.)

"That's *it*?"

Laura shrugs.

"So what happened? ...Laura, what happened?"

"We don't *know*! We stayed in Florida for a month, waiting for information. And they never found her. The police, the coastguard, NASA. If NASA were looking for an eighth body, which is doubtful. We don't know what happened. We don't know for sure that she tried to save the Shuttle. We don't even know if she's actually dead. She's been missing for... well, not long enough. In another few years we can declare her legally dead. Does that answer your question?"

"Christ," says Nick, and takes another long pull from his pint while he thinks. And once he's done that, he says, "No. It doesn't.

"You loved your mum. But when you talk about her she always sounds as if she was half-teacher and half-rival. She taught you everything you know about magic — you and Natalie — and you were well on your way to catching up with her and then eventually surpassing her. No problem. Then just at the moment when you were starting to be a real match for her, she pulled the rug out from under you both. She did seven or eight completely impossible things right in front of you, things which she had never bothered to try to explain were *possible*, and then she flew away without telling you what she'd done or how she'd done it. She left you with no idea how much else she was holding back, or even who she actually was, because in that last second, she—"

"It was like she'd dropped the mask of mum-slash-wife," says Laura. "'This is who I *really* am. I'm a fucking Titan, I'm a cloaked thaumic witch-goddess and I can do anything. Goodbye.'"

"She was like an actual magician—"

"—never revealed her secrets," says Laura. "That interpretation had occurred to me too. But — and I'm sure I've covered this — magic is the worst-named field of science in the world. It was a lousy, stupid nickname for some genuinely new physics, and it stuck, and now everybody hates the man who coined it. Including himself. Magic isn't magic. It is a field of science. You *do not sit on results*. Not results like that."

"So you don't follow the launches because you're scared of another launch failure and want to be the one who stops them from happening," says Nick.

"No."

"And you don't follow them because you miss her."

"No."

"Although you do miss her."

"I do."

"And you definitely don't secretly want to be like your mother."

"God, no."

"So I don't get it. She made you *angry*. This is nothing but a big bad memory. What do you want?"

"...What I want is for us to go into space right now," says Laura. She takes off a few bangles and spins them idly between her fingers. "Just us two. We could walk out the door and it would take about ten minutes to get there, straight up. I just need the right words to say. I want autokinetics, air UI, the fluid pump spell she used for O_2, non-vocal casting, DWIM, dynamic shielding, and whatever it is she used for a mana source. To begin with. I want it all and I want to be the first person to go into space without a vehicle. Today, if possible. And more after that.

"Magic's not the Force. It's not mystical, it's a gauge theory. It explains observations. It is, at its root, a collection of dry and unpalatable nonlinear partial differential equations which are known to be not totally accurate. Magic does not speak to us or obey our commands. Getting magic to do anything, let alone what you want it to do, is close to impossible without insanely complex equipment. The equipment itself couldn't be built prior to around 1981, and prior to 1990 computer-aided design and manufacture weren't sophisticated enough. That's to say nothing of the mental gymnastics. You know that people on my course are supposed to spend at least twelve hours a week meditating?"

Nick does know this. He also knows that Laura gets away with less.

"Magic is difficult," she continues. "It's harsh and expensive and obtuse. Magic isn't magic."

"...But it should be," Nick concludes.

"Yeah."

"It's not likely to happen today, Laura."

"This week, then."

Nick shakes his head. Laura shakes her head too. She knows what she's asking for.

Their glasses are both empty. "Another?" Nick asks.

"In a minute," Laura says, pointing.

On the television screen, because she knows what to look for, Laura can see the launch pad sound suppression system activating, dumping a thousand tonnes of water onto the pad just before liftoff in order to protect the orbiter from acoustic damage. In the pit underneath the Shuttle's engines, a shower of red sparks erupts, burning off any lingering pockets of flammable hydrogen before the engines themselves fire. In the absence of an on-screen timer or an audible commentator, Laura is counting to herself:

"Nine. Eight. Main engine start—"

They start, all three of them, bright red at first, then white, then ramping up in a matter of seconds to a temperature where the hottest part of the flame isn't visible. The whole launch stack pitches forward slightly, reacting to the off-centre thrust, then gently leans back towards vertical. All that's left now is for the SRBs to ignite. "Four. Three. Two. One."

5
What You Don't Know

Dr. Dan Czarnecki arrives at the lecture theatre thirty seconds after the lecture was supposed to begin and stalks down to the front through a noisy cloud of conversations-in-progress. He throws his leather briefcase at a chair, grabs a marker pen from the nearest shelf and begins scrawling a board-wide equation on the far left whiteboard. His handwriting is appalling, even worse on the board than it is on the heavily photocopied notes he sometimes remembers to hand out. Today, the marker pen is running out. Czarnecki realises this halfway through the equation, glares at what he's written, glares at the pen, caps it and hurls it overarm into the waste paper bin at the other end of the wide, mainly circular stage. The bin is metal, and there's a sharp and satisfying *tang* as it catches the pen. Czarnecki finishes the equation with a different colour. Only then does he turn around and start removing his gloves, hat and coat.

This is also the point at which he will start speaking, regardless of how many people in the room haven't managed to shut up yet. But they've shut up by now, because at the speed Czarnecki works, not listening for more than half a minute is a recipe for irreversible, eternal confusion.

"If you have the slightest recollection of what's happened to you in the last five-and-a-half weeks you'll recognise this as Vidyasagar's First Incomplete Field Equation, which I showed you on the first day of the course. You will also remember that when I showed it to you, I told you it has three errors in it. I corrected the first error right away. Can somebody tell me what that was?"

Czarnecki's tone of voice indicates that he wants this answer fast.

"Pi should be two pi," shouts a voice from the mid-left of the theatre.

Czarnecki adds a "2" to the equation. "Reflectivity," he clarifies. "Full-blown fully-accounted 5D thaumic flow is self-interfering. Good good. Vidyasagar's First Incomplete Field Equation was derived correctly, but derived from partial observations and inaccurate assumptions. When it was shown to disagree with the first 'real' uum casts, Rajesh Vidyasagar corrected one of his assumptions and revised his work. Good. This equation was for some years known as Vidyasagar's Completed Field Equation.

"The word 'Completed' was dropped and replaced with the words 'Second Incomplete' as a result of the Shelburne-Sharma experiment, which you duplicated in microcosm in the laboratory last Friday afternoon. At that time, all we gathered was raw data. Partially that was due to a shortage of time, but mostly that was to give you a chance to collate the data and draw a conclusion.

Does anybody have a conclusion? Does somebody want to put their hand up and admit to having done some work last weekend? A vague stab will do. A guess?" Czarnecki starts snapping his fingers rapidly. He paces around the stage. "Come on. Come on, come on, come on! Not you."

Czarnecki's class is attentive and blank, but he singles out one girl at the front on the right. Czarnecki makes a deliberate habit of calling everybody "you" even though he has picked up just over a third of the sixty-five or so names. In his view, it is fairer if he pretends to not know any of them. But everybody knows Laura Ferno.

"Okay. Will somebody whose Veblen arbitrator didn't bleed out on Friday, and who therefore at least collected good data, and who has since had access to graph paper or an electronic substitute thereof, please summarise their observations for the benefit of the class? Come on. Who actually *made* graphs? Anybody? Yes! So what did you see? You?"

Czarnecki seizes on a student at the back of the class who has hesitantly raised his graphs in the air. From this distance the graphs look good: for one thing, at least five different plots are visible.

"They disagree," says the student, whose name is Mathis Schröter.

"What disagrees with what?"

"The measurements predicted by... Vidyasagar's Second Incomplete Field Equation... and the actual measurements don't match onto one another properly. There's a difference between them. But—"

"Characterise that difference for me."

"I... I don't know how. It's a five-dimensional vector field embedded in three-dimensional space, I can't visualise it. I couldn't slice it right."

Student Mathis Schröter is evidently in the dark. Czarnecki relents and calls on Laura. "You. Go."

"What, me?"

"Always you, who else?"

"I didn't actually have my hand up."

"Why not?"

"Because I don't know the answer."

"I thought you knew everything."

"My results were garbage."

Czarnecki strides forward, picks up Laura's results and skims the raw data for a moment. He is surprised.

"Garbage. Fine." He hands the paper back and returns to the board. He writes "$+ S_{t,\tau}$" on the end of his equation. Then he moves to the next board and essays a complete definition of S, a lengthy triple integral. While writing, he narrates: "The missing term is called the Sharma transduction tensor, also known as the thaumic flow transduction potential: the amount of nearby matter and energy which is enchanted and/or arranged in a mystically significant way. Flowing electrical lines will contribute to this factor. So will static or charmed magic rings, static or charmed staffs, electromagnetic waves, large electrically neutral masses and, in the smallest quantities, all other mass-energy in the universe out to an infinite range, give or take the inverse square law. It counts anything which could affect thaumic flow at that point in space or which could in turn be affected by that flow. The S-tensor is a statement of two critical facts: firstly, that magic can be created, shaped, collected, stored, transmitted and released using real, physical equipment; secondly, that magic can in turn be used to apply real, measurable effects to the physical world. The necessity of the S-tensor is the proof that magic is an interacting component of the real universe, whatever the real universe is, and not constrained to a co-located 'bare' universe of magic matter and magic energy. In short, magic is real. Precise measurement of this tensor led to the creation of the first reliable magical machinery and spelling. Congratulations, after five-and-a-half weeks of tensor algebra you have been handed on a platter what it took Indian physicists six years to derive from scratch. Welcome to thaumic physics, you are almost ready to begin.

"The third error took longer to find. Why?"

There's a pause, because this is a puzzle. While he waits, Czarnecki starts putting his staff together. His staff is split into six pieces of varying sizes, enabling him to construct any of two dozen different lengths using different combinations, but today he screws all six together for a total length of exactly two metres.

"Because it was a lot smaller?" somebody guesses.

"So how much magic do you think it takes to demonstrate that error under laboratory conditions?"

"A lot," says the same person.

"You, you and you, well volunteered," Czarnecki says, picking out three students in a row from the front. One is a gangly fellow with large glasses and long, scraggly hair. One is a broad-shouldered man wearing a scruffy blue shirt. The other is Laura — shortish, dark-haired, uninspiring. None of them had volunteered. "Come on. Come up here, come on. How are your mana levels? Good? Good."

The stage is larger than most, big enough to embed a seven-metre E-class magic ring in the floor. Czarnecki wheels a piece of machinery out of a corner and kicks the power switch on at the wall. The machine is a Veblen pump. It has the dimensions of a pair of upright pianos placed back to back, but it looks more like an enormous tower PC case, with the side missing and the interior filled with small magic rings and runes and tubes instead of circuitry and disk drives. Specifically, it looks like the old kind of tower — manufactured an optimistic white, but now faded to a depressing creamy beige after a few decades of use. It's a little beaten up, and could really use replacing, but as long as it continues to serve the fairly menial purpose that it needs to serve, that will never happen. On the side of the machine are some rolls of hose with more magic rings tying off the ends. Czarnecki unwinds a few turns of hose for three of the rings and hands them out to the students. He directs the gangly student to stand at twelve o'clock on the rim of the magic ring in the floor, the shorter one at eight o'clock and Laura at four. The three of them trail long hoses over the floor ring's interior.

Czarnecki invokes a few presets just to get the machine started. Then, "Mister Noon, would you provide me with a continuous steady flow of zeta-formatted mana, please?"

It's a moment before the tall student realises he's being spoken to. "My name's Jeremy," he says.

"Zeta load. Ring. As much as you feel you can part with while leaving your brain stable. Thank you in advance for your cooperation. Don't worry about overspill, I'm acting as buffer. Mister Eight O'Clock, the same amount of iota-class. Shout if you need reserves and we can work something out." As the stockier man starts his spell up, Czarnecki interrupts him with a clarification: "When I say 'the same amount', I mean tap into Noon's link and make a stabilising connector first."

Mister Eight, whose name is Benj, constructs and recites a rather longer mantra than Noon's. He mis-speaks a few times and has to stop himself, erase syllables from the floating stack and resume from mid-word. Perfect diction is desirable in a mage, as it gives an impression of professionalism and competence to observers, but it's totally unnecessary. In practice, one can get away with anything short of a genuine speech impediment. Constructing an industrial spell invariably takes a hundred times longer than speaking it, and unmatched floating syllables will hang around for the best part of half an hour before dissolving. So every mage learns up front to be methodical rather than reckless; nobody cares if the last and least important step in the process takes a few attempts to get right.

There's a hum now, something of a discordant buzz. Magic is silent, but the machine isn't. "And Four: mu."

"Same amount?" asks Laura.

"Yes, but you'll probably find yourself forced to synchronise with the others whatever you do."

Laura says a series of words which, in sequence: identify her simplest collector-spell, written years ago but still in regular use; prime it to slurp up a certain blend of ambient mana from the invisible clouds that surround her (and every mage, and every other human); associate the collector with her True Name and assigned mu band; and kick it off, like opening a keg tap. She feels her reserves ripple and start to spiral out of her. The mana emerges from her skull into air, seeks out the magic ring in her hands and bolts down into the machine with the rest. Harmonic effects from the two other flows interfere with hers until they settle down into synch, amplitude-modulated at a natural rate of a few kilohertz. *Zoontch* goes the machine as it spins up a gear.

So far so standard. These are the three most common "brands" of mana and this triple-phased feed is typical of the type used to power heavy chemical engineering equipment in industry. Three mages is two more than a real employer would be prepared to employ for this job, but these are the early days for this class and that kind of multi-tasking takes practice. Even the quantity is short.

Laura softly adds some modifiers to her collector which widen its metaphorical maw by a fifth, letting more mana through. After all, the experiment calls for a lot of raw mana, right?

Thanks to symmetry, Eight and Noon's feeds increase correspondingly in lockstep with hers. Eight and Noon feel the feedback and look at her quizzically; Czarnecki doesn't appear to pick up on the change. Laura shoots a look back at them which says "We can do better than this," and applies the same modifiers a second time.

Unperturbed, Czarnecki strolls into the magic circle and installs a small but heavy metal bracket in the circular slot that exists at the centre. Into the bracket, he plants his staff vertically like a flag pole. He says a few magic words of his own, which add the staff to the half-built thaumic system and turn it into the core of a real live "lightning machine", an almost purely thaumic machine designed solely to vent/waste raw mana in a safe way. "Magic effects wash over you," he explains. "You're all feeling this by now. Those of you at the back of the room feel less than those at the front. There's a mild physical equipment response if you know what to look for and there's a mental reaction if you know how to think. These are S-tensor effects. But the reaction is fuzzy. It's like trying to figure out where the Sun is in the sky with your eyes closed, just by feeling which half of your body is warm. I count at least ten conventional senses. And this eleventh sense will indeed allow you to perceive things which cannot be perceived with the conventional ten. However..."

He leaves the fragment hanging, strolls back to the corner where the equipment is stacked up and picks up one last piece of equipment. This is a magic ring as wide as a hula hoop, but substantially heavier and ornately machined. He adds more words to the standing spell, these words completely new to the watching class. This charms the ring. Then he holds it up, pointing it at the class as if it were the frame of an invisible painting. In the empty frame, *behind* the frame, as if the window were augmenting reality with its own version of events, there is now visible evidence of flowing magic: sharpened streams of white mana linking the core staff with the rings at Noon, Four and Eight, creating what, from above, would take the form of a brilliant magnesium Y. Smaller light effects appear in the gaps between the streams, fluctuating in the air like shock diamonds. Czarnecki moves around the stage, pointing the magic window in different directions, making sure that everybody gets a look.

"Magic is lossy," he says. "Mana transferral and transduction are lossy. These waste emissions are in the chi-band. You have been told two facts in total about chi-band thaumic emissions, what are they?"

"There aren't any," somebody says.

"They don't do anything," somebody else adds.

"You were told that chi-band mana will cheerfully waft through a few metres of solid lead. You were also informed that chi mana is *extremely rare*. The logical consequence of which, is what? Come on." Czarnecki lays the ring down. "Why is that useful?"

"It means you can—" Laura begins, then stops when Czarnecki whirls around to face her. But he glances back at the class, sees that nobody else is about to jump in, then gestures for her to carry on. "It means you can use a Kovachev oracle like that one to see inside a machine," she says. "While it's running. And you can see how it's working and whether it's working, which means you can diagnose and debug a thaumic system."

The doctor turns back to the audience. "Chi emissions exist almost exclusively as waste products from magic expenditure. Up until now you have been measuring thaumic effects using gut feeling, inertial reactions in Kaprekar linkers and odd bits of old-fashioned, low-accuracy, manual, mechanical devices. Your results have been usable. But the instruments you've used are from a generation now thankfully past and no longer suitable for the needs of modern magic. An oracle scoops up chi particles, transduces them into photons as they pass the mouth and multiplies the photons to make an effective virtual retina. We can now render magical activity into hard numbers at great distances, through solid rock and metal, quickly and reliably and repeatably. You've been sitting there for nearly six weeks thinking 'When is he going to get to—?', well, here we are. *Diagnostic power.*

"Divination is *the* core skill of a mage. Oracular spells are numerous, complex and powerful. It's possible to waste arbitrary amounts of time refining them, up to and including your entire professional career. Right." A minor alarm has gone off in Czarnecki's head: whole minutes have now passed without him writing something on the board. He kills power to the oracle ring and props it against the wall. He scribbles out the third correction and its definition on the whiteboard above. "This is now Vidyasagar's Third Incomplete Field Equation. This is a name coming from modesty and cynicism. There is no third error yet, but historical trends suggest we're due. This year or next."

The three trainee mages are still happily running their machine. Czarnecki stares at them for a moment, while still writing. "Are none of you going to speak unless spoken to or are you all in trances? Nobody wants to sit down and take these critically important notes?" That gets a tiny bit of a laugh from the class, but no reaction at all from the 'volunteers'. Czarnecki frowns. He rolls the ring out again, crouches and powers it up while looking through it. He sees the same brilliant white triple flow: stable, minimal harmonics. "`Kzarn oppol we xa oerin xa`," he says, switching it over to a different mode which could be called 'Is there something wrong?'

Then he stands up, strides into the magic circle—

*

It's the freezing cold wind which wakes Laura up, not the approaching footsteps. She breathes in once, still lying on her side on the dark glassy ground, then rolls upright and stands. The world is deep glass, a horizontal featureless plane. Not some purified fibre optic blend, transparent to a mile depth, not volcanic obsidian, just regular glass: dirty, and deep black at a metre's thickness. Only the faintest red colouration is detectable. It's a land designed to shatter underfoot and slice your footwear and feet with the pieces, unless you tread softly or wear fat boots which distribute your weight. Or you can just fly. It's night. There's a full Moon and a glittering three-pointed Milky Way, both of which reflect dully off the ground.

The wind is so cold it's razor-sharp. Laura is wearing... well, just *clothes*, suitable for a temperate to cool climate; indoor clothes and an indoorsy sort of shoes. But she can do better so she moves through an ill-defined blur which summons something warmer, something in the vein of heavily layered robes, with gloves and a hood.

She moves around vaguely, in blips; now she is a mile away to get a different look, now she is back in place, now she is a mile up. She can't go any higher. It is still all glass. The air is still icy on her face. There's faint yellow glow all around the horizon but she knows she could wait and wait and the Sun wouldn't rise. She could try to wait, anyway.

Zhzzzzzz.

It's a fuzzy place, but this fuzziness is all normal. It's an unhappy place, but that's okay.

She still hears the footsteps.

"Laura, take my hand, this is—"

Familiarity. That's okay. But Laura doesn't remember where the familiarity is coming from. The memory of her asking him "How do I know you?" appears in both of their heads, without any sound having been transmitted.

The man is a fixed size, older and bearded. He wears dark brown trousers and a boring blue jumper and his dark brown hair in a dated style. Laura knows these colours even though there's no real light. This oddity passes her by. "What are you wearing?" he asks in return. Her clothes are shifting, inches thick and layered and elaborate. They would take an hour to don and remove if they existed, but they haven't actually been designed or put there. These are just the impressions he receives when he concentrates on her. The name of a thing is the same as the thing.

His name is Dan, Laura remembers. He is her... her... they know each other.

"Do you remember what happened?" he prompts her.

"I don't really know."

There's a buzzing, a locusty *zhhrhzrrzrhzrhz* as if from a very quiet badly-tuned radio.

Laura blips them across the country in mile bursts, which seems to startle the man. He stumbles around as the geography of the dark glass changes. First it's big glass cuboids with rounded corners, in neat stacks. Then they're in a valley with huge sharpened black glass peaks rising around them. There's a crunch as they land. Why does he stumble? Laura stands him up. Now triangular polygon surfaces, like crystal landscape from some antique videogame. Now a mosaic of tiny hexagonal glass tiles. Dan begins to find his mental footing and starts rippling between locations himself, but he doesn't quite know how he's doing it yet.

"We don't have a lot of time," he says. "Laura, two more people are stranded here. Can you find them? `Kzarn eset`." Bright colours seem to pour out of his mouth as he speaks the magic words, but he frowns at the results and waves them away, like bad breath. They aren't what he wants to see. "`Kzarn eset. Kzarn uum`. This is loco." Now he has a staff in his hand and is trying more words. Elementary charging words, then collector spells and other simple things. The magical equivalent of *Three Blind Mice*. There are thumps and crackles and sparks. Laura watches and listens with interest. Bigger and more convoluted magical machines dance into existence, hook together and fade out over time. None of it seems to be giving him the results he wants.

"What are you doing?" she asks.

"Laura. Jeremy Willan is here somewhere. Can you find him?"

Saying things and doing things are the same thing, so now they have also found Jeremy. He was found because he was trying to be found. There was no flare, just something that he and Laura mutually made happen. Jeremy is in another part of the world on the glass shore of the glass ocean. He is young, about Laura's age, much taller. The glass is greener here, but the sky is still pitch dark and it is still cold and odd. The horizon is a fraction lighter and there is a faint *hzzh* on the wind.

"Are we okay? What is going on?" Jeremy asks. He's shivering.

"Why is he cold?" Laura wonders out loud.

"I'm cold," Jeremy says. "I don't know."

"Just be warm."

"I don't know how. I can't get anything to—"

Laura tries to make him be warm but it doesn't work.

I don't feel well, Jeremy has now said. He seems to be icing up.

Dan catches up with them both, out of breath from figurative running. "Do either of you know what happened to Kazuya Tanako?"

"That's not any of our names," Jeremy says, angry. "Why don't you bother to remember our names? Stop calling us 'you' all the time!"

"I do know your names," says Dan. "`Dulaku, tolo, ennee`." Again, nothing.

"I'm so cold. We shouldn't be here."

"Kazuya Tanako isn't any of you. He was one of the greatest mages of all time. He died when he was just 25 and *this is how*. We need to locate Benj. Jeremy, do you remember what happened? Magic doesn't work here."

"Are we in trouble?" asks Jeremy, teeth chattering.

"Do you see shelter? Water? Food?" says Dan. "Do you feel *welcome*? No equipment, no rules. We need to locate Benj."

Laura stops trying to heat Jeremy up, and instead shows Jeremy how to warm himself. Jeremy makes himself some clothes and now he is warm. This is good!

"Laura, where is Benj?"

Laura tries to point, but Benj doesn't want to be found and resists being pointed at directly. But that is a naive way to hide. By feeling the strength of repulsion, Laura can guess his direction. Blip blip blip.

It takes them a long time to reach sight of him, and then it feels like they're running on the spot while he runs on the spot too and runs away. They spend a long time looping around, running and not getting anywhere. Delays and delays.

Jeremy builds a new Benj instead, who just stands there with them, blank. That's better. "I get it now," Jeremy says. The real Benj keeps running away and soon is gone.

"No, he should be Benj," says Laura. "Not just look like Benj."

She does something and Benj wakes up inside the Benj body. "Hello?" he asks.

Jeremy wonders why Benj was running away. From what? Dan checks his wristwatch, but all he learns from it is that he is still wearing a wristwatch. The light on all horizons is brightening. He glances at the sky and does some brief trance work, muttering odd syllables which just drip onto the floor like paint, but which may possibly prepare his mind for a rough re-entry. "Did you ever see a man get hypnotised to forget the number seven exists, then try to count to ten?" he asks nobody in particular. "Derive the existence of seven from first principles and talk to me about thinking outside of the box. Let's try the falling reflex."

A cubic mile of glass below them disappears. They plummet into the chasm; then it slams closed, a tectonic movement of broken glass crushing them to shreds.

ZHRZHZZHRRRHRHRZZZZ

*

—kicks his staff out of the bracket and breaks the spell in half, scattering mana backwash over the three trainee mages like hot coffee.

All three of them fall, rings dropping out of their hands. The magic circle is too wide; Czarnecki can only catch the person nearest to him, who happens to be Jeremy. "Stay where you are," he advises them. "Don't get up, just sit down here and wait. You," — now he points at the student on the far left at the front row of the class — "go to that red telephone on the wall, dial eight zero four zero and ask for Dr Neal Marek to come down here. Everybody else, please stay in your seats for a second. You can all leave once Dr Marek has arrived, I don't want him struggling through all of you on the way in. We're finished for today."

Ten minutes later the lecture theatre is empty except for the five of them. Czarnecki has attached a segment of his staff to the Veblen pump and is flaring off the accumulated mana, prior to a proper shutdown. It's taking longer than it should. "This is a lot of energy," he says, partly to himself. "Three or four weeks' rent for a basic mage. At a guess."

Dr Neal Marek is about fifty-five, with a full grey beard and thin-rimmed varifocals. He is the deputy head of department. He has already had some words with Czarnecki, and he has already taken some notes in a fat A4 hardback notebook. Now he focuses on the three students, seated in the otherwise empty front row. They aren't actually in shock, but look like hell. "Tell me exactly," he says.

"I don't remember anything," Benj begins. "I just woke up falling on my face. Must have fallen into a trance while casting. I've got nothing."

"Laura committed us to too much mana," says Jeremy.

"Benj, how much mana do you have left right now? All bands."

"Nothing," says Benj.

"Running out that fast could easily have sent you to sleep. Basic exhaustion."

"I don't remember anything."

"That's normal, don't be concerned about it. Jeremy?"

"I'm tapped too," says Jeremy. "I can tell it's going to be a few days."

"And Laura?"

"I used a collection multiplier," says Laura, and recites the spell in regular words. Marek nods and takes some notes. "I used it several times."

"How many times?" Marek asks.

"I... don't remember."

"Do you mean you lost count?"

"...Yes." Laura slips a pair of thick grey rings off her right arm and hands them over to Marek. "I use storage. Most nights before bed I unwind all the mana I've got left into these rings. They're modified Montauk sinks. They're paired, like electrodes of a battery, so try not to touch them together too much. They'll take any type of mana. They're not as full as they have been historically. At one point I had to wear them on opposite wrists to keep them far enough apart. But I use a lot of mana for coursework and practice these days, so..."

Dr Marek tucks his notebook under an arm and inspects the two rings, pinging them thoughtfully.

"Because it's just a waste to leave mana ambient," says Laura, to fill the silence. "Every second it sits there, it's doing nothing. So I save it, why would anybody not save it?"

"Very interesting. I can't tell how much energy they contain without direct inspection," says Marek. "But this is the equivalent of a few tonnes of TNT."

"*Tonnes?*" says Benj.

Laura hurriedly interjects, "Sure, but, you see, it's impossible for all of that to be vented at once—"

"And that's *now*," Marek continues. "Not before."

"I don't— I didn't do anything wrong. The demonstration needed a heavy concentration of mana. What happens when you run out of mana? You *run out*. The experiment *stops*! I didn't do anything! Why did we all end up in my dream?"

"I don't remember anything about a dream," Benj repeats.

"There was this big dark planet," says Jeremy, "like a big— marble. I can't remember. We were all there."

"The more I think about it, the more detail slips away from me," says Laura.

"It wasn't a dream," says Marek. "For one thing, whether you remember it or not, you were all in it together. For another, I've had it before. Laura thinks it was her dream— she's had it before. So have other mages. It has several different names. 'Tanako's world' is as good as any. As for what it actually is: we, mages collectively, do not know. To the extent that it's a dream, it's a bad one. To the extent that it's a world, it appears to be fictional. All we do know is that magic is incredibly complicated, magic heavily involves the human brain and the human brain is even more incredibly complicated. The best theories say it arises from training our brains the way we do. All of us do essentially the same meditation exercises, which means we have a lot of common mental ground. And so some sort of link occurs."

"But how come we've never heard about it?" Jeremy asks.

"Because you haven't been doing magic for long enough. You were going to hear about it in your third year. It's right here." He flicks through his notebook and produces a high-level schedule for the whole Thaumic Engineering syllabus, a 16-page paper booklet. He opens it to the relevant page and hands it over to Benj. "It's not a secret. Three years from now, I hope you'll all be qualified to help us pursue the question. Or, better yet, we'll have an answer before then."

Benj hands the syllabus to Jeremy. Jeremy reads it, and hands it to Laura. She reads it.

"Is it dangerous there?" she asks.

There is an unsettlingly long pause. Marek glances over his shoulder at Czarnecki. Czarnecki is completely expressionless.

"Yes," says Marek.

"Kazuya Tanako died of a stroke. Did he die... there?"

"Yes."

"So I'm having dreams that could *kill me*?"

"No. Not unless you're habitually sleeping inside a hundred-kilothaum Dehlavi lightning machine. And even then—"

"But he *put* us in a hundred-kilothaum Dehlavi lightning machine today!" cries Benj, pointing.

"Again, no."

"If he knew the experiment was dangerous why didn't he warn us beforehand?"

"Because Dr Czarnecki wasn't following procedure."

"What?" says Czarnecki. He looks up, suddenly angry and embarrassed.

"He should have made sure that none of his students had brought dangerous foreign objects into the system.

He should have paid closer attention to his students while they were casting. He should have realised that something was wrong sooner and, yes, he should have warned you up front." Marek says all of this without even turning around.

"About what? What the hell, Neal? You're doing this in front of them?"

"There was more than one mistake made today, Dan. I want all of us to understand all of those mistakes."

"*She* got them into it! That ring-couple is close to undetectable! I don't have to listen to this."

"Actually, you do. That machine needs draining safely and it isn't going to do that by itself and it'll take a little while."

There's a heated pause.

"One of the purposes of the experiment," Marek continues, "was to— safely— demonstrate, ah, 'low-energy high-energy magic', and introduce some of the safety concerns associated with it. If procedure had been followed, it would have been perfectly safe. As for what Dr Czarnecki did right: while he was setting up the experiment, he verified that all the raw mana held by everybody in the room combined couldn't have crossed the threshold of danger. That's by the book. When he did realise something was wrong, he quickly determined the problem and was decisive in resolving it. And he got all three of you out of Tanako's world very quickly, which is a testament to his skill."

Czarnecki glowers.

"Benj, did you notice that you were running low?"

"I did. It happened fast, though—"

"Were you told to say something if that happened?"

"I— yes."

"Then you should have said something," says Marek. "Jeremy, did you notice when Benj dropped out?"

"He didn't fall over or anything..."

"His eyes would have closed and he would have been visibly unsteadier on his feet. Like a sleepwalker. Also, Laura would have taken over his iota supply when it dropped."

"I didn't notice any of that."

"Then you should have paid closer attention. You also should have said something when Laura started using unwarranted collection multipliers."

Jeremy holds his hands up, the gesture that means "Fine".

"Laura—" Marek begins.

"I should have paid closer attention to Benj and Jeremy. I shouldn't have—"

"Shut up."

Laura shuts up.

"Laura, you *know* what you did wrong. What are these?"

"They're modified Montauk sinks—"

"Where did you get them?"

"My mother taught me how to manufacture them."

"Did she teach you how to use them?"

"...Apparently not," Laura concedes.

"Did she warn you about high energy magic? Did she warn you about Tanako's world or how to break out of it?"

"No."

"How often do you bring your own equipment to labs?"

Laura is silent, but Czarnecki speaks: "That must be why your results from Friday were gibberish. Equipment that advanced is designed to suppress exactly the kind of interference you were supposed to be measuring."

Marek summarises: "You brought foreign objects into a magic circle; you altered an experiment on the fly without consulting your teacher; you either didn't notice or ignored or *were unable to help* your fellow students when they got into trouble. You assumed you knew what you were doing, when in fact there are *things you don't know*."

"I'm done here," says Czarnecki, pulling the fragment of staff out of the machine and letting it switch itself off. Its background hum cuts out, leaving a conspicuous silence. He returns to the front of the stage.

"Accidents happen," says Marek, tossing the Montauk sinks back to Laura one at a time. "Almost every lab accident could result in fatalities if carried to its logical extreme, including this one, but in the vast majority of cases it's not a big deal, including this one. Accidents happen, they're part of the learning process. But so is learning from your mistakes." He nods at Benj and Jeremy, "You two can go. I think you've got the point. Laura: I want this lesson learned. You're going to come and see me first thing next Monday morning and pass a TES-3 practical exam."

"That's a third-year high-energy magic safety course," says Czarnecki. "She doesn't know how to pass it."

"Then you should both get to work," says Marek, making one final note. "I'll see you next week." He leaves.

There's an echoing clang from the door closing behind him, then silence. Czarnecki prowls around the theatre, putting equipment away, wiping the boards clean, and generally avoiding making eye contact with Laura. Eventually he loses it. "That was—"

"Unprofessional," Laura suggests.

He glares at her. Then he visibly relaxes, as if defused. It's disconcertingly sudden. "Thank you. I was going to say 'typical'. There's a story. I'm not going to tell it to you now. What's your university email ID?"

"ltf15."

"I'll book us some lab time and email you when I have a slot. It's going to be early in the morning. Go to the library and check out Parasara's *Thaumic Engineering Safety*. You already know section 1; read as much of 2 and 3 as you can before tomorrow."

"Understood." Laura collects her coat and bag and hurries for the door. "I'm sorry."

"No, you're just embarrassed," says Czarnecki. "You don't know how badly we're being punished for this. By Monday you'll be sorry."

"You've done TES-3?"

Czarnecki nods.

"What's wrong with it?"

"Have you ever found magic boring?"

Laura shakes her head.

Czarnecki smiles humourlessly. "You really do have a lot to learn. See you tomorrow."

6
Ragdoll Physicist

"Interesting" is the term geologists use to describe Iceland, and geologically interesting places are worth paying attention to in the same way that warzones and brand new nuclear powers are. Entire cubic kilometres of lava are seen emerging from the place. Sometimes it grows new islands. Sometimes its volcanic fissures eject so much sulphur dioxide into the atmosphere that the global temperature drops significantly, crops fail across the Northern Hemisphere and millions die from famine. Iceland is the place you go to remind yourself that planet Earth is a *machine*: very large, continuously operating, working on a time scale too long to easily observe, towards a highly uncertain end; and to remind yourself that all the organic life that has ever existed amounts to a greasy film that has survived on the exterior of that machine thanks to furious improvisation rather than any specific dispensation.

Iceland is also one of the few places on Earth, other than on people's skin, where mana is naturally occurring. It's a geological phenomenon, arising from molten rocks with just the right combinations of rare earths stirred into them. If you travel to a suitable spot and scan the horizon through a suitable oracle, you can see luminous mana radiating off the mountains and coiling into the air, like steam off microwaved pudding. There's a research centre, a smallish clutch of temporary buildings offshot from Reykjavik University. They drill holes into volcanoes and model the natural process on computers. There's a cooperation program with the UK.

So Laura and Natalie Ferno are here, along with a collection of other people from the same year and a few staff. It's a three-hour flight to Reykjavik, practically next door, but the town of Blönflói is almost on the other side of the country, so the final leg by road takes substantially longer. It's midsummer, which means noonday temperatures peak around "brisk". When the Sun is up (21 hours per day at this time of year), it casts a clean, white light uncommon in the UK, such that the grass here really does seem greener. There are sheep and Icelandic horses and dry stone walls at the outset, but as they travel, the countryside becomes wilder and more inhospitable. Grass shortens, clinging closer to the ground until bare soil is exposed.

"This isn't me," Benj says again.

"It's just culture shock," Laura says again. She's in the passenger seat; Benj Clarke and Natalie Ferno are crammed in the back between rucksacks. Benj, by his own admission, doesn't like foreign countries. Or foreign languages. Or customs, roads, buildings or food. It's like he's attached to his birthplace with an elastic cord. The further he travels away from home, the more highly strung his nerves become. "You can get used to anything," Laura elaborates. "This is day one and you'll be here long enough to get used to it."

"This isn't what I do," says Benj.

Laura's loving the scenery. Nat's quiet as ever, indifferent as far as anybody can tell. Years ago, as kids, Laura used to try to enthuse her about interesting things (sandcastles, computers, boys). She gave up when they were around thirteen or fourteen. Nat decides what she's into, nobody else does. Trying to force her into something just makes her less inclined to pay attention.

Blönflói lands on a ragged boundary where the soil, too, is starting to run out. It's a minuscule settlement, sparsely distributed yet small enough to fit entirely into a single photograph taken from ground level. The buildings are square and painted uniform white and red and pale blue; from a distance, they look like delicate wooden models. There's one huge fjord nearby and three ridges of tall, nude black mountains, but from the middle of the town looking directly to the north, there's nothing but the Arctic Ocean, all the way to the North Pole. It's more than a thousand kilometres further south than the northernmost inhabited point on Earth, but it feels like an outpost at the end of the world.

"Do you feel anything unusual?" their driver prompts them as they arrive. His name is Þór. (Nobody got his surname.) He is sixtyish, bearded, spectacled and very bulky; half of the bulk is fat, the other half is thick woolly sweaters. "Do you feel like there's more energy in the air?"

Benj and Laura generally agree. "Yeah, I definitely feel something, sure."

"Well, you shouldn't," Þór snaps. "There've been double-blind experiments. Nobody can pick up anything at this range without equipment. Pay more attention. This is a place where we do science."

The car rumbles along in silence for a little way. *He's had this discussion before,* Laura thinks. *With tourists.*

"It's nine more kilometres to the lab and three kilometres from the lab to the nearest foldback epicentre," Þór adds. "You might as well claim you can hear birds squawking all the way up there."

Nat nods.

There are fifteen students and staff on the trip altogether: Nat, Laura and Benj in the car, and the rest in a minibus following them. Accommodation is an informal youth hostel/guest house/cottage sort of place, a square two-storey building with a pointy red roof. A nice blonde lady of about forty-five shows them around the place and shows them the written list of rules and quirks. It has a lot of bedrooms full of bunks, a collection of showers, a big kitchen full of heavily used cookware and mismatched cutlery, and a beaten-up lounge with a big old CRT television. She disappears just as a welcoming party of three more Icelandic geophysicists arrives with a substantial container of local fish and other supplies. It's now well into the evening, UK time and there's a lot of hunger in the house so the four most resourceful and organised people in the building — students P and Andy, chemical mage Steve Aldridge and one of the Icelanders, Tómas — cook enough to feed an army. All of it gets eaten.

A few mages express concern about the shortage of alcohol in the house, head out and buy an amazing amount of beer. Nobody talks shop that evening; topics of conversation are sport, Icelandic customs and impenetrable late-night Icelandic television. Benj seizes on the beer, as it's something he can relate to. Laura drinks until she can't pronounce her True Name properly, at which point Natalie calmly redirects her to bed. The locals go home relatively early; the last of the students turn in at 2:45am, as the Sun is about to start rising again.

*

On day two they visit the main research building, where the establishment's second-most senior mage shows them a presentation. The subject is elementary volcanology. Spectroscopy, geology, The Local Shape Of Iceland, stratigraphy, volcanometry, geophysics, magma crystallisation, eruption types. After a short break the slides proceed seamlessly onto the topic of tools, drills, measuring equipment, vehicles and procedures. The safety section covers what to look for, what not to tread on and whom to keep in eyeshot, before abruptly ending after less than a minute. Then the magic comes into it and everybody starts paying more attention.

Exactly how the magic arises is not totally understood as yet, hence the research. The foldback points where the emanations start are kilometres deep, driven by insane magma heat and friction with the underside of unusual ultramafic rock strata. There are two major theories and a flurry of variations on those themes, some less likely than others. All the plausible ones tap into the same basic thermal equation. Research is carried out using scientific oracles, ranging from flat A4 sheets of hundreds of tiny engraved washers up to cadmium steel rings wide enough to drive trains through. The big ones are mounted on unconventional tractor-like vehicles with fat, expensive tyres.

Watching mana pour out of the interfaces and bubble upwards is informative, but what's really needed is hard chemical data, which requires dedicated deep drilling operations, which requires serious funding. More would be available if the naturally occurring mana was useful for anything. Geothermal energy is great, and thaumic turbulence modelling has come on in leaps and bounds thanks to the wealth of observations, but mana boiling out of the Earth itself doesn't belong to anybody. Sure, you can detect it, but it isn't concentrated or "collared"; it can't be used or stored by people. It certainly isn't dangerous. It's a continuously gushing oil well, except that the oil is valueless: invisible, intangible aurorae and chi-band mana particles.

In the afternoon they take their first trip up to Krallafjöll, where the magic happens. Most of the students ride in the minibus, bundled up. A few lucky ones get to ride in the mobile oracle tractor unit. The staff distribute a dozen or so monocle-sized oracles, which the students pass around, using them to study each other and the scenery. Krallafjöll is a volcanic fissure, a ridge where the local surface of the Earth has been forced upwards to breaking point, as if an axe split it from below. Lava, ash and cinders vent from the fissure, at least in theory. It's more than a hundred and fifty years since anything that could be termed an eruption took place.

The vehicles can't get far up the side of the ridge, but that's no problem. Tómas and another geophysicist, Haukur Tómasson (of no relation), use the tractor unit's two big hydraulic arms to aim the big ring directly at the core of the ridge and prime it. The ring has a huge surface area and needs specialist oracular enchantment. Haukur delivers the convoluted spells seemingly without effort or concentration. His enunciation is as sharp as anybody's and he doesn't make a single mistake. Nat and Laura are watching him alertly through a monocle as he finishes up. "`Akla orotet j'lutyu j'lu astata`," the last phrase which buttons the whole thing down, visibly depletes almost all of his available mana reserves. At his command, the big ring begins transducing all of the chi mana passing its mouth into visible photons, becoming a working holographic overlay of the ridge behind it. The image is hard to decipher at first, monochromatic like an X-ray image. After a moment to compose himself, Haukur adds false colour — well, additional false colours — to the picture.

"So, now we have a picture of the interior of the, the mountain," explains Tómas. "So, now we want to see clearly events that happen deep inside the mountain. So, can anybody guess how we do this?"

"Move the oracle closer," somebody suggests.

"No."

"Tune it to give a magnified image," is Nat's offer.

"How?" is Tómas' response.

"...I don't know."

"An oracle is a window. It is not a lens. If you want to lens light, you just use binoculars or a telescope." Tómas produces a pair of binoculars from a pocket. "It is a very strange feeling to use binoculars to look into the, the ground. But I, you get used to it."

"Would this approach be useful for geological surveys?" Aldridge asks. "I mean general geology, without magic being involved."

Haukur shakes his head. "You need the mana. The world is mostly pitch dark in the chi band. You just can't see anything. Maybe in ten years when detector spells get better."

"Is this kind of reaction visible in space?" Nat asks.

"Using a satellite?"

"No, not looking down. There are other places in the solar system with volcanic activity, where mana must be naturally occurring. Like Io. Couldn't you fit an oracle to the front end of a real astronomical telescope and see?"

The Icelanders don't answer immediately. "Has anybody tried?"

"I don't know," says Tómas. "That's not really our department."

"Astrothaumics, Nat," Laura says, poking her in the arm. "You just invented space magic!"

Nat doesn't respond.

The oracle's vision shows an upward-pouring waterfall of mana. The real topology and composition of the ridge's interior are difficult to determine because the rocks themselves are totally absent from the picture, but the behaviour of the mana flow gives significant clues. The rock is igneous, of varying granularity. Darker areas are granite. Brighter patches of mafic rock collect the flow or perturb it into lazily coiling shapes. Here and there are small, very bright vortices and thin tubes. These are underground features of uncertain crystalline structure — something naturally similar to a magic staff. Rising mana is caught inside these features and stays bound to them for minutes or hours, in a decaying orbit or on a narrow main sequence path, before escaping and bubbling upwards.

The flow is slow, and entrancing to watch. This is Iceland the component of Earth the machine.

For their next trick, the Icelanders lay the big ring almost flat on the ground like a divining pool. The students gather around it and, kilometres below, they can see the deep foldback points where magma heat is transduced into mana and starts rising through the rock. "I definitely feel this," Benj says. The ground is warm underfoot and staring into the ring is like staring into a cauldron or furnace, so a sensation of rising heat isn't unexpected, but Benj is right— there's enough randomised, unclaimed mana in the air that it can be *felt*.

The output for the whole ridge must amount to megawatts, if it could be harnessed in a useful way.

But it can't. After more of the geology lecture, the ring is turned upwards towards the ridge peaks, where magic billows into the sky in spreading clouds. The process is continuous, though varying in intensity over the course of weeks depending on the "underground weather". Nobody can spell using the natural mana; it's nobody's to use and nobody's to give away. "Perhaps if planet Earth itself said a spell," says Tómas, "something terrible could happen. But it has no throat. And the shortest known fullspell is, is a hundred and fifteen syllables? Very unlikely!"

*

By this time everybody's been standing around in the cold for too long. The enthusiastic half of the group decide to climb to the top of the ridge, take some photographs, inspect some measurement equipment and throw some spells around. They'll walk back, it's only 30 minutes and all downhill. The rest, including Laura, Benj and Nat, take the bus and the ring tractor back to the lab where Haukur Tómasson explains the speciality magic they use for deep geological inspection. At first, Laura finds the "Blönflói Book" of pre-written spells and conjunctions fascinating, but it soon becomes clear how much of a kludge their framework is. It was built piecemeal over the course of years and has never been cleaned up. Good spells are brief without being obtuse, meaningful without being waffly; they loosely couple many independent charms together for maintainability. But the Blönflói Book spells have obfuscation, pointless repetition and spaghetti-like interconnections. In many places, perfectly normal second- or third-year results are painstakingly derived from first principles in ugly, non-standard ways. Of course, the whole thing works, for a given value of "works", and that's why it's never been fixed. But Haukur's just so proud of it all. Laura soon has to excuse herself; it's the only way to avoid saying something regrettable.

Benj joins her outside.

Laura says to him, "I wish I could say these guys were underfunded and underequipped. I mean, maybe the job they're doing and the tools they're working with are harder than they're making it sound. And there must be more difficulty to geological magic than meets the eye. And their volcanometry is really impressive, I've never seen that kind of high-fidelity measurement stuff before, the outside factors that they have to take into account to get reliable numbers are *insane*. But, is this where you see yourself working? I'm torn between straight-up replacing every spell they've written with something *good*, and running screaming and never looking back. It's the kind of mess I never want to inherit."

"This definitely isn't me," says Benj.

"That's your phrase of the week," says Laura.

"I'm sticking to it. When do we eat?"

Laura checks her watch. "Not for *ever*. Is the food you? Have you changed your mind?"

"*The* food isn't, food in general is."

"Let's work something out."

They walk down to a shop in town, buy some vegetables and some fish and bring it back up to the hostel/guest house/Magic Castle. By the time everybody else returns for their main evening meal, Laura and Benj have cooked, eaten, washed up and made a decent start on the evening's drinking.

Ra

*

It's nine in the evening and the Sun is still basically up when Natalie announces that she's going up Krallafjöll herself. "I'll be back by the time it gets dark."

"We'll come," says Laura. "How cold is it?" It's getting colder, but everybody brought a decent amount of gear and the sky's basically clear. "Yeah, we'll come. I'm going to go and put some layers on and then I'll definitely come with you. Gloves! Benj, is this you?"

"Sure," says Benj.

"I'm just going to look," says Natalie. "I want to think. I want to work through some numbers. It's more than a day since I meditated."

"Sure," say Benj and Laura.

"So hang back and try not to talk to me," Natalie clarifies.

"...Sure," say Benj and Laura.

On the way up that's what happens. Natalie strides ahead with her thoughts while Laura tells Benj she wishes Nick could have come. "I'll have to bring him another year. He'd love it. He'd run around a different volcano before breakfast every day. He's a nutter."

"I thought you were never coming back."

"...I did say that. Yes." Laura falls silent, now preoccupied resolving her cognitive dissonance.

Benj fills the gap as they walk by showing her his project. At the moment it's a fat, heavy molybdenum steel ring with deep engravings. It's a base unit, a highly versatile core element of many experimental spell systems. "You take a conical force field and modulate the field spell so that it moves forwards and backwards."

"You brought that on the walk to show me? Those things weigh like a kilogram each."

"I've got this bag here."

"So what does it do?"

"What do you think it does?" Benj demonstrates. "Simple triangle wave. Two hundred hertz. `Ibra oniki opint five cee amag ennee. JULI`— wait. `Konung konung. JUNYIA two cee a ennee.`"

The ring in his hands begins buzzing, a continuous low *booooooooooooop*.

"You've made sound!" Magic is silent, to say nothing of the fact that, until very recently, small-scale non-flat force fields were impossible. "Nat, he's made sound! He's an audiomage!"

"I hear it," Nat replies, not looking back. "And stop inventing words."

"So JUNYIA's a procedure you committed in advance?" Laura asks Benj.

"Sure. `Ennee JUNYIA ixuv.`" The sound cuts out.

"Can I see that procedure some time?"

"When it's done."

Laura starts talking about the applications of sonic magic. She comes up with two dozen applications and limitations and areas for further research off the top of her head.

Benj has already thought of all of them. "Of course I have," he says. "I've been working on this for long enough."

"Encoding real recorded sounds into the spell is obviously impractical unless you want to sit there dictating pulse codes for a week. You need a recording device. And then you want to make something that can read the data it needs from somewhere. Reading from an electronic storage format is going to be amazingly difficult."

"I know."

"You need to invent a dedicated data storage format that can be read by magic. Maybe you can use an engraved ring like a vinyl record. Maybe you can modulate mana flavours and queue the flavours up inside a Montauk battery—"

"Laura, I *know*."

"Okay. Then I'm just going to stop talking."

Benj spins the ring once between his palms, deactivates it and puts it back in his rucksack for the climb. The steepest part is almost a scramble, requiring hands. Natalie leads, followed by Laura and then Benj. There's still plenty of light for now. If they're still up there when the Sun sets (around eleven PM local) they'll have a problem, Laura thinks. She starts working out illumination spells.

Nat can feel her head clearing as she climbs. It's not the cold wind. It's fresh mana rising up from the rocks underfoot. It has a different "smell", she thinks, from mana produced by people. It's less... she tries to think of a better word than "icky", which displeases her. Organic?

It's a long enough climb that they reach the top panting. The Krallafjöll ridge easily commands a view of Blönflói town and a hundred times more besides. At least fifteen kilometres of Route 1 can be seen, the Ring Road that completely encircles Iceland. To the south are rolling dark mountains leading towards the country's interior. To the north are the minuscule fishing port, the fjord and then pure, steel-cold Arctic Ocean. Nat stares into the wind and thinks, lapsing into something approaching a meditation cycle. Laura takes some photographs. As for the so-called volcanic fissure itself: other than a jagged confusion of rocks in a deep, intermittent crack at the top of the ridge, there's nothing to see. Laura was half-expecting to be able to look straight down into a pit of lava. But, she remembers, the feature has been inactive for decades. Dormant as a doornail.

"Yeah, I was going to sneak out and climb this myself," says Benj, pulling his base ring out again. "But since you're here, you're here. You need to help me. `Ibra oniki ennee.`"

"Help you with what?" Laura asks, speaking over Benj's next spell, which she almost misses. All she notices is that this time he invokes a stored spell not called JUNYIA, but QUINIO.

"I actually did solve the encoding problem," Benj explains.

The molybdenum steel ring in his hands wakes up and buzzes momentarily. Then it starts talking in a low, heavily synthesised voice. "`Ibra oniki ra. QUINIO alef a ra.`"

"Nice," Laura says, genuinely impressed. "How'd you do it? Not that that's going to work."

"Wait for it," says Benj.

"`Ibra oniki ra. QUINIO QUINIO alef a ra,`" says his speaker ring.

Laura hesitates, puzzled. "`Dulaku eset.` That's... You *can't* cast a magic spell with a voice synthesiser." Nat turns around at this point, fixing Benj with a curious eye, which he doesn't notice.

"It turns out that two things in the universe can use magic," Benj explains. "One is sentient humans. The other is magic itself."

And the base ring says, "`Ibra oniki ra. QUINIO QUINIO QUINIO alef a ra.`"

Laura backs away a step and almost trips on the uneven ground. "But... nobody cast that spell. Without a human mind behind it, it's just pressure waves in air. There've been dozens of experiments. Thousands.

Machines can't spell. *Machines can't do magic. It has to be a human being.*"

Suddenly standing right behind her, Nat takes her arm. "He's written a quine," she murmurs in her ear.

The ridge shakes. This would be an alarming development on flat ground, but at this altitude it's heartstopping. Benj falls, but gets back up again, laughing. Laura slips, Nat catches her. A few tens of metres along the ridge behind Benj, a substantial-sized rock formation dislodges and start rolling down the hill. With or without falling rocks, the incline is steep and rough enough to do serious damage to a rolling human; if he or she was careless or unlucky, they could easily reach the bottom of the slope dead.

Laura's mind is running flat out. This has happened to her before: a mage with skills beyond hers throws a fistful of new tricks in her face and she has to pick up the pieces. This time she's not getting left behind. *Machines don't have mana resources. Machines don't have Names. Where's the energy coming from?*

"Ibra   oniki   ra.   QUINIO   QUINIO QUINIO QUINIO alef a ra." The ring sounds as if it's double-tracked.

This time the ground beneath them jumps up a full twenty centimetres. Benj lands flat on his back and drops his ring, which rolls away down the hill. Nat and Laura are separated by the jolt, but Nat recovers fast and scrambles back to Laura. With difficulty, self-preservation has managed to override Laura's curiosity. She motions for both of them to get out of there, back down the side of the ridge to relative safety. But Nat tightens her grip on her sister's arm. She shouts, "This isn't you, Benj! *So who is it?*"

"I told you. I've been telling you and telling you," Benj replies, sitting up.

It's a quine, Laura thinks. She can feel that she's almost got it. *It's a magic spell which casts a magic spell which casts a magic spell. Nobody's done that before.*

"—QUINIO QUINIO QUINIO alef a ra." That's five.

"Why are you doing this?" Nat demands.

"He's using up naturally-occurring mana," Laura manages.

"This is about freedom," Benj shouts, clambering back towards the top of the ridge.

Laura swears she feels the wave rising like a tide—

And *this* time the ridge explodes, a two-dimensional curtain of lava erupting from the one-dimensional fissure above them. The explosion drives the hillside up into Laura's knees, hurling her flailing into the air.

In freefall, upside-down, she experiences a split second of perfect clarity. Over her head, the solid real world spins, completely physically disconnected from her and therefore abstract, like an expensive computer render. Under her feet is the red and black molten light show, spreading like rose petals against the deep blue sky. There must be an Olympic swimming pool of lava in the air, plus the entire side of the hill. *Hi,* says a vivid, primitive part of her consciousness, a hot black bullet-like node whom she's met once before. *Hi.*

You're going to die.

Nat cannons into her side, long hair whipped over her face. She's shouting something. And she's had her ear pierced. This, of all things, takes Laura by surprise. Nat doesn't wear jewellery; she's always said that she doesn't believe in piercings or tattoos, but there it is. A tiny engraved metal bead on a simple loop of wire through her left earlobe. A driver dot.

"—zero EPTRO zui!"

Natalie's spell engulfs both of them in a closed, six-inch forcefield duvet, a fat bubble layer coddling them like Michelin Men. They hit the hillside as a unit, bounce a little and slide a long way further, protected from the shock and friction. Krallafjöll, about a quarter of the whole mountain, is still in the air. Nat's bought them three seconds. There's no way her protective enchantment can withstand what's coming next.

"Laura, you're up!" Nat bellows. "SHIELDS!"

Laura's finally in fight mode. She dives for the shallowest possible trance state and the shortest possible spell formation. `Sedo EPTRO dulaku—`"

It's the same spell, performed with the same parameters, on identical equipment. But this one has half a year of Montauk-accrued energy behind it. There's a bone chilling instant after Laura finishes enunciating the last syllable, an infinitesimal delay. Then Laura's shield inserts itself into exactly the same physical space as Natalie's and spreads across exactly the same topology. Not inside it, not outside it, but directly reinforcing it.

And then they're drowning in rock like some drown in water.

7
Broken 'Verse

Laura and Natalie Ferno are engulfed in hellish red light underneath what might as well be a million tonnes of magma. Their world is barely larger than a pair of coffins. The noise the magma makes is strange, more of a creaking than a rumbling. The noise is pervasive and unpleasant.

Their shared multiplied force shield fizzes under load as it races through Laura's mana reserves to maintain its structural integrity. The shield only lets visible light through, which is the only reason that they haven't both been incinerated by radiant heat. They're running out of air.

About eight breaths each.

"Laura," Nat hisses. Her voice rebounds strangely inside the tiny enclosed space. "You've got to do this. I've no mana left and you're running out. You've got to do this now."

"I can't— I don't know any spells that can get us out of here." Laura wonders why Natalie is talking so quietly. She realises it's to conserve oxygen. They must have used half of it up already. The orange-red light is saturating Laura's consciousness, she can't shut it out, even with her eyes closed. She can't think.

"Then we'll write one," says Natalie, softly.

"We don't have time," says Laura. She knows that nobody can improvise magic. Not in seconds, not even in minutes.

"Then build a lightning machine," says Natalie. She says nothing else. She has exhaled deeply and is trying not to breathe.

The world shakes. Magma folds around them, pushing them in a different direction. Is Benj's spell still cascading? Laura slips her Veblen arbitrator off her wrist and turns her necklace around to find the right pair of driver dots. Of course, that shared mage dream is dangerous. They could die there. Or die here while there. But dream time is different. Not so much slower as... passing in a different direction. She inhales, closes her eyes, and chills her mind. It takes her a long moment to get there. Inside the silver ring clenched in her fist, Dehlavi's triple diamond symbol flares up.

*

In her dream Laura is strapped into the seat of Mission Specialist Elaine L. Barry, the rear left seat on the flight-deck of the Space Shuttle Atlantis, with four minutes and one second left on the launch timer. It is therefore obviously 10:02 hours Eastern Standard Time on 17 December 1993, ten minutes before the Disaster. Of course this is where she is, and of course this is when.

Even if she hadn't had this one before, there's nowhere else she could be.

There are six other seats, all occupied by men in spacesuits and bubble helmets identical to Laura's. "There's ice in the ET," she shouts at them. She doesn't have enough control over the mission to abort it directly, but she could alert the mission Commander, USAF Colonel Michael Wilcott, front row right. She struggles with her seat harness, but it's jammed. Her helmet is soundproof. Occasionally Mission Specialist Kevin Hope, in the next seat, will look over at her and pass a few words. She looks back with wild eyes. "There's ice in the ET. The SRBs haven't ignited yet. We can still scrub the launch. *You're going to die.*" Nobody pays attention to her warnings. Not a single instrument gives the slightest impression that something is wrong.

The mission starts with hard, constant acceleration, like being ground under the heel of a giant. After 45 seconds, there is a petrifying sideways lurch as the first and second SSMEs shatter, milliseconds apart from one another. There is no profanity when it happens; in fact, there is almost no involuntary reaction at all. Astronauts are built to be very, very difficult to faze. Mission Control sends the "Abort RTLS" command up almost immediately. The pilot, Soichi Noguchi, acknowledges it and the flight plan seamlessly switches tracks. An entire minute of careful preparation elapses before the SRBs disconnect and the abort sequence starts, and that minute is too long. The calm in the cabin is icy, almost supernatural. By the time the last engine expires — another loud *bang*, another lurch — Laura has had time to pass through denial and anger into acceptance.

Noguchi is fighting the attitude controls, not entirely without success. Laura wonders why. There's nothing he could do that could save the mission, and he knows that better than anybody. LOCV: Loss Of Crew & Vehicle. The orbiter tumbles like a sock in a dryer, having long since left its flight envelope. Kevin Hope, in the next seat, holds his hand out. Laura takes it.

And then there's a duller *clunk*, soft enough that she'd miss it if she wasn't listening for it. And through the centre-right window, Laura sees a woman. She's splayed across the orbiter's nose cone like a gecko, one hand on the centre-left window pane and the other spread backwards, holding a magic staff by one end. She's venting mana like a volcano, enough to make Laura's eyes physically sting to look at her. Everybody sees her. There is a fraction of a second during which she has the whole crew's attention.

And the fraction draws out and freezes. Laura focuses. It's not who she thinks.

"Nat?"

Nat waves at her. "Wake up," she mouths.

Laura's perspective shifts. She is flat on her back on cold stone, in a room as wide as a petrol station forecourt but as tall as a lift shaft. Suspended upside-down over her head like a misguided Smithsonian exhibit is the dream she was having, Atlantis at the moment before its destruction. Its nose is pointed down at thirty or forty degrees and its fat rust-coloured external fuel tank is plugged into its belly like the egg sac of a pregnant spider. She can see a static trail of liquid fuel pouring from the machine's mangled engines upwards into the ceiling. She can see right in through the cockpit window. She can see Noguchi and Wilcott at their seats.

Nat is kneeling beside her, lifting her to her feet. "Did you build this?"

Laura gets her bearings. The room is well-lit, made of sandstone, smooth and modern, like a medieval castle finished yesterday. Just like she imagined it. "I don't sleep well," she remembers. "This is Tanako's world. I came here enough times that I started to get used to it. And then I started... putting things here. For safe keeping. And then I built a thing to keep everything in, so it would all be safe. So I could find it all when I came back. Ideas, I mean. We're asleep, so ideas and memories and things are the same thing. So this above us is what this event looks like. In my head."

"External memory." Natalie stares upwards. "A memory palace. Not unheard-of." Then she frowns. Below Atlantis, but still above head height, is their mother, flying. She is caught at an instant of extreme motion, knees tucked up, arms thrown back, hair blown back, magic staff oriented horizontally across her shoulderblades. She, too, is upside-down and motionless, but clearly about to match velocities and land on Atlantis' nose cone— or else misjudge it and get pulverised.

"I— I think about this a lot," says Laura.

Nat says nothing.

Laura takes Nat's arm. She escorts her out of the Atlantis room and along a spaghetti tangle of curving corridors, which eventually spits them out onto a defensive wall. From the outside, Laura's memory palace is a convoluted half-built castle, partially fuzzed with translucent scaffolding, rising at its centre to an infinitely tall, thin spire. The wall around it is a five-pointed star with jagged bastions. The world outside is as dark as it always is, with cracked glass plains spreading in every compass direction. There's no Sun; the castle is lit with torches. In the sky overhead, a triple-pointed Milky Way hangs. Wind howls past their ears, with nothing to slow it down.

Having the idea simultaneously, they both sprout thicker clothing. Laura's design is thick, subdued and black, with a hood and scarf. Natalie's is blue and green and furry, with heavy gauntlets. Noticing her sister's idea, Nat adds a hood too. Laura, as afterthoughts, adds a hefty collection of magic bangles on one arm and an ornate magic staff as long as a pike.

Tanako's world is technically a nightmare. But the noise isn't audible yet.

Way over in the distance, perhaps five kilometres away if that's a meaningful figurative measurement, Laura can see the Krallafjöll ridge. It rises out of the ground as if some snake monster's spinal ridges were forcing their way up from below. She can see that the ridge has opened up, and that a flurry of orange and black material has erupted from it. There's a tiny white spark, which is Benj. And beyond the ridge are the slopes leading down to Blönflói village and the fjord and the ocean. She can see the whole thing, like a tiny static diorama in a box viewed through a peephole. It must be their shared mental image of what just happened, she decides. That is, of what's happening right now.

"What is he doing?" Laura asks.

Nat's extremely long and thoughtful silence is more telling than any verbal response. Eventually, she surmises: "*He* has managed to cast a quine, a self-calling spell. The spell is now casting itself without his help. He usually uses the Name of `ennee`, that's what he used for the first cast. But the second cast onwards were in another Name, `ra`. I don't think that's one of his Alternates." Two gobbets of greenish paint fall from her mouth. She wipes them up, momentarily puzzled. "Ennee. Ra. Use/mention distinction. Okay."

"Magic doesn't work here," Laura explains. "It just comes out as colours."

"His spell's using Krallafjöll's reserves of natural mana," says Natalie. "Energy consumption is going up geometrically. After he bleeds this ridge dry, he might be able to tap other mana foldback points elsewhere on the Mid-Atlantic Rift. With that much energy he could trigger a full-scale eruption."

"...You're saying that he hasn't done that yet," Laura realises. "We can still shut him down."

They have both been educated about what happens when a volcanic fissure erupts. Of more concern than the immediate physical threat to Blönflói — lava flow, ash, fumes and so on — is the environmental threat, which is potentially global in scope. The death toll would be, in Tómas Einarsson's words, "somewhere between zero and everybody in the world".

What Natalie's saying is that surviving the next ten minutes is their second priority.

"I know exactly one spell," Nat continues. "And that was it. So what have you got?"

"What about eset?"

"Alright, I know two spells."

"And uum?"

Natalie says nothing.

"...You don't know *uum*?"

"I do *theory*, Laura. Vector calculus and ring theory."

Laura rolls her eyes. She tries a few magical syllables of her own. "`A al anh a'u ay.`" She catches each primary coloured paint blob as it drips from her mouth, then tosses them all into the air. They line up in colour order, just above head height. "This is what I've got. You can show me how to fill in these gaps with theory. You can't spell, so—"

"I can spell."

"Okay. Can you paint?"

*

It could be dream logic and dream time messing with her perception, but it seems to Laura that they arrive at their finished paintings very quickly. Natalie is a very fast learner. Starting from what is clearly a skeletal knowledge of spell structure and syntax, within hours (?) she's mixing new colours and finishing Laura's thoughts for her. She has no spells of her own, but does have a seeming arsenal of heavyweight theoretical results from which Laura draws ideas. Her exact field solutions are hardcore, often too abstruse or complex for Laura to understand properly. Total comprehension is a prerequisite for a good cast, so they have to put those results aside and look at simpler ones.

Within X amount of time, maybe a few heartbeats, they're done with their montage. They have four spells worked out, which gives them some options. They work out a few plans of attack. Then they go to the edge of the defensive wall, facing out towards the ridge in the distance. Nat sits on the wall and assumes the lotus position, folding her hands in her lap and becoming a fat bundle of robes. Laura stalks about, fiddling with her jewellery and staff. She can't bring herself to sit down.

There's no more useful preparation that they can do. There's nothing left to do but worry.

"Just to be clear," Laura says to her sister, "we're probably still going to die. Nobody is going to wake us up from this, which means we're here until the dream ends naturally. My shield is still out there," she points at the ridge, "running out of mana and when it does run out of mana it's going to implode and a million tonnes of red-hot rock is going to land on top of us and we're going to die instantly. There'll be nothing left to bury, nobody'll even find our teeth. And even if it *does* somehow manage to last, then what's going to wake us up instead is asphyxiation reflex, because we're going to run out of oxygen. So I'll wake up choking to death, and *while choking to death* I'll have to save us both, and/or the village, and/or the world."

"You'll be fine," says Natalie.

"And I'd really like to know how you're justifying that statement! You're saying that to calm me down and... and psych me up but I'd— in fact, I'd like to know where this calm demeanour you're showing is coming from! Am I the only person I know who's human enough to freak out in the presence of life-threatening danger? Of *threats to life*? Am I the only person with the good sense to *panic*?"

"Would it help you if I panicked?" Natalie asks.

Laura spins her staff fretfully. "It might."

"You're not scared," Natalie informs her, without turning around. "You're just upset that I'm not scared either."

"I'm upset because I don't want to die."

"Why not?"

Laura is stunned by the question. Seven completely different reactions collide in her head, and she fails to verbalise any of them.

There's a distant rustling, like leaves, but it goes on continuously. There is a sort of clicking, grinding noise. *Kkkhhhhhhh.*

Laura prowls through her mind, trying to detect the impaired thought processes which would arise from oxygen deprivation. She breathes in once and breathes out once. She can't feel anything. "I'm worried about Benj," she says. "Do you remember that accident in the lecture? You weren't there but you heard about it, right? If nothing else I talked your ear off about the insane amount of paperwork that we had to do, right? When we were *in* the dream, last time... we tried to find him. But we couldn't. He was running away. He didn't want to be found. So... so we made another Benj and brought him back instead. It was dream logic. So who—"

"Is that yours?" Natalie asks her suddenly. Laura looks up at her and then looks at what she's pointing at. There is something else out in the glass world. If the Krallafjöll ridge is to the north, then to the east is another castle, kilometres away, on a different horizon. It is citadel-like, substantially more heavily fortified than Laura's. It's darker than the sky behind it. It resembles a Ministry from Nineteen Eighty-Four.

Many mages have this dream, Laura knows. But does that mean it's a shared space? "No, it's not mine."

Natalie uncurls and hops lightly down from the wall— a drop so far onto solid glass that it would kill a person in reality. "I think we've got time. I'm going to take a look."

"Wait. What if we wake up?" Laura calls.

"Then we wake up."

In Laura's head something is telling her that they shouldn't get separated, but elsewhere in her head something else is telling her that she doesn't know why she believes that. She doesn't want to say something if she's not sure of it so she just sits still and watches Natalie blip off towards the other castle, bypassing space in the same perfectly consistent way that they've been circumventing time. She fiddles with her clothes, reformatting them to be more comfortable. Then she experiments with her new three-metre-long staff. It is a cutting-edge piece of hardware, an oversized piece of jewellery rather than a tool, something from the very back page of a catalogue too high-end to list mere prices. It's twice as ornate and decorative as it needs to be to do the job. It's made in a single piece for better structural cohesion and drastically reduced portability, and its length ($\sqrt{3}$ times the usual) gives it harmonic performance properties worth dying for. It's wish fulfillment, exactly as practical for everyday use as a Formula One car. And since Laura's wishing, she made it out of mercury. If it wasn't a poisonous liquid at room temperature, mercury would be by far the most useful magic metal.

Wake up. Get to safety. Stop the eruption. In no particular order. Laura checks her watch; its face is, of course, blank.

"I need more information," she says to herself. Out on the horizon, she watches the brilliant white spark which marks her mental image of Benj.

The noise is getting louder. The nightmare's about to begin.

8
Thaumonuclear

The citadel is as tall as a thirty-storey building and featureless as a brick. Nat walks around it once, looking for windows and gates. Finding none, she tries imagining herself inside and then "stepping into" the mental image, which is how things usually work here. It doesn't work. Abandoning subtlety, she makes one hand gluey and uses it to pull a black stone as big as a refrigerator right out of the wall. She flings it away over her shoulder. That leaves a large rectangular slot, with just enough room for her to clamber into the dark place inside.

The wall is a metre and a half thick, with nothing behind it but a half-metre gap and an identical wall. Natalie shuffles sideways along the narrow alley until she reaches the corner, where both walls turn ninety degrees. She looks up, and can't see a lot, but there's definitely clear space above her head. She concludes that what she's looking at is a second, slightly smaller citadel inside the first one.

Everything goes dark. The outer wall has repaired itself. Something throbs in Natalie's brain, the overspill from the change to the universe. *Somebody did that.* Natalie creates a light for herself, red so as not to ruin her night vision.

The fuzzing, shuffling background noise, which, although still soft enough to tune out, has been patiently increasing in volume since they both arrived here, ceases.

That's right, Natalie remembers. *If you stay here long enough, it becomes a nightmare.*

She shuffles around the corner and along the alley a little further, just on the off-chance that there's an entrance on this wall. All she finds is flat walls and an ominous silent darkness stretching away an unknown distance. "Sedo sedo sedo sedo," she says, catching the paint as it falls out of her mouth, gathering it into a squishy ball, a water balloon without the balloon. "Eset eset eset, zui zui zui."

Then she turns around and hurls the paint blob at the eyes of the genuinely horrific, wasted *individual* which, by all nightmare logic, *had* to be behind her. She throws the paint in its eyes, not at its head, which is an important distinction. Where a normal human would have a face, it has a huge vertical mouth, opening to show two rows of fangs. Where one would expect shoulders and arms, it has rows of long feely fingers, as if its whole torso was a palm for holding things where they can't escape. Most of them are perfectly normal human fingers, merely anatomically misplaced. Two of them, Natalie discovers as she turns, have lengthened and reached out, bracketing her neck and beginning to close. There are no slavering sound effects; the thing is as silent as a spider.

And its eyes are in its neck, above the collarbone. The eyes are human enough that the thing has something approximating a facial expression. The expression is near-madness.

Nat's paintbomb obliterates its vision. As it stumbles backwards, its long fingers brush across the back of Nat's hair. She grabs a finger in each fist and squeezes, snapping them like twigs. Then she places a hand on another stone in the outer wall and pulls it into the alley as far as it will go, pulling away just in time so that the stone can crush the thing flat against the inner wall with its momentum. She grabs the stone and slams it against the crushed horror a few more times, just in case. Under this light, she couldn't guess what its skin colour is, but its blood is definitely black. And runny, like wine. There's enough of it that it must be dead.

High energy magic. High energy dreams. Natalie wonders what the concrete, real-world dangers are if one of those things eats her. Laura would know.

Natalie climbs onto the stone she just produced and looks as far as she can in every direction, casting her light up and down the alleyway and even above her. There are more things coming, making no noise but a busy shuffling. It is hard to see them but they are all permutations of human bodies, with features and spindly extremities multiplied and redistributed. They are dirty, and many of them appear to be able to climb, and they are converging on her. If it was actually happening, it would be the most frightening thing to ever happen to her.

She thumps the inner citadel wall. Its stones won't move. "Let me in! I'm real." Something picks her up around the waist and begins dragging her upwards. She can't see this one clearly, but the sensation is grotesque. She flings more paint at it, then braces herself against the inner wall to kick a hole in the outer one. The dislodged stone lands somewhere outside. A little pale light floods in, but is immediately blotted out by more malformed people flooding in from outside. They wrap her in their fingers and hold her tight. They start chewing at her toes, clothes and hair. And as one final problem, off to her far right down the alley, a brilliant green-white light flares into operation and starts moving towards all of them.

Natalie sees what the light means. It's an abstract. It's not part of the nightmare. It's an agent of something else entirely. It is a *sweep*. While she watches (out of the corner of her eye, because she can't turn her head), she sees "people" evaporating as it catches them. The green hue represents disinfectant. The white intensity represents heat sterilisation.

Natalie wonders if it'll discriminate, or just fry her too. She wonders if it'll wake her up or just kill her. Maybe it's a metaphor for the magma: it'll wake her up and *then* kill her. She screws up her eyes as the light sweeps over her and she wonders: *Tanako's world is a nightmare. I'm not scared. So whose nightmare is it?*

When she looks again, she is inside the second citadel. And inside the third, the fourth, the fifth and the sixth citadels. It is a tiny windowless studio apartment, lit dully by an uplight in the corner. There are bookshelves and a table and a bed. There are no doors. There's a man curled up in the bed, facing the wall. His hair is all that's visible. It's slightly blond and slightly spiked.

"I'm Natalie Ferno," says Natalie. "Did you build this place? How long have you been here?"

He rolls over. "You have to believe me."

"I believe you."

"He's not me."

"I believe you. I'm real. I can help you."

Benj blinks. "Can you get me out of here?"

"Yes."

*

Before she gets within a kilometre of Krallafjöll, the ground beneath Laura's feet has begun to melt. Soon she is walking over alternating sections of lava and black pan-hot rock. Smirking, she cranks up imaginary protective spells using her rings and staff. She imagines invisible iron armour and big heat sink panels like wings, all weightless. She skips straight through to her planned Mark Two defensive shield, which clings to her clothes and skin at a one-millimetre thickness, but lets cool air through so she can breathe and perspire. It's much easier to build this stuff in her head. "Do What I Mean."

While walking, she keeps catching sight of something out of the corner of her eye, but every time she turns to look at it it disappears. She has the sensation that someone is walking beside her. Not stalking. Just... accompanying.

She arrives at the nearest end of the ridge. It looks the part now: active, volcanic. Half of one side of it is missing, with lava rolling out of the wound and running downhill into a substantial pool at the foot of the ridge. The pool has swollen, and excess lava has begun to flow out of it towards Blönflói.

The whole scene is almost stopped in time, just barely crawling forward if she watches carefully, like the minute hand on a clock. At the top of the hill, Benj is still standing. It seems he's not the light source that she saw from her castle. The molybdenum steel ring which he's holding, which he must have recovered, is glowing as if white-hot. The mana radiating off it is so concentrated that it stings Laura's eyes and causes jangling perturbations in her shields.

Laura quickly scales the ridge, coming up behind Benj, who is gazing into the lake of lava gathering below them. Benj turns around and smiles broadly. And it's Benj. It's really him. The face, the body language. There's nothing about him that suggests he's anybody else.

"Neat trick. Who are you?" Laura demands.

"I'm Benjamin Clarke. We have met, you know."

"Guess again."

"I'm an animate stray thought," he says. "There was an accident. You remember. You, me, Jeremy Willan—"

"Not you. It wasn't you. It was Benjamin Clarke. Who are *you*?"

"...You, Benj Clarke and Jeremy Willan were locked into a shared trance, this world that Kazuya Tanako discovered. And you know what happens here. There are physical risks to staying here for too long. There are *things* which crawl out of cracks in the glasswork, and it never ends prettily. They got to Clarke first. So he ran away and tried not to be found. And he succeeded. You and Willan and Dan Czarnecki couldn't find him. You used dream logic to cook up a cheap facsimile of him. And you brought that home instead.

"Clarke's been here this whole time. Holed up in his castle, fighting nightmares and unable to wake up. But occasionally getting messages through." He imitates mockingly: "'This isn't me!'"

"You haven't answered my question," Laura says angrily. "What does that make you? A brain-damaged version of Benj? Jeremy built your shell, I animated it. So where are your motivations coming from? Me? Benj? Who is ra?" With the last word she spits lime green goop on the ground between them.

The "Benj" facsimile shrugs. "Everything I just told you was information you already had. I've got nothing else for you. You're not actually talking to anybody right now, Ferno. You're *asleep*."

"No. I think you're really here. That's why we've overlapped into Benj's dream. I think you've been dragged in here with us. *What are you trying to do?*"

"Look." Not-Benj points down at the lava pool. She looks. There are two figures lying in the pool, face-down. The figures are wearing familiar cold-weather gear. Laura recognises herself and her sister. Of course: give or take the heat shielding question, human beings float in lava. *Bowling balls* float in lava. It's molten rock; it has about the same density as solid rock.

Laura wonders how closely this mental image resembles reality. If she and Natalie really are unconscious on the lava's surface, they can just get up and start running — inside their shield — to get to safety. No mucking about with the highly complex, untested tunnel boring spell. That would remove one variable, leaving — by their count — three. Provided that what's she's dreaming is also real.

But as she watches, the force field protecting the figures of her and Natalie pops, and they plop into the lava. They catch fire, melt and explode simultaneously. The organic matter produces steam, which makes the lava gulp and spurt as it swallows the bodies up. Laura stares, transfixed. The reaction seems to take a long time.

"You just died," says not-Benj.

Laura grits her teeth. It is, of course, impossible that she could be dead. Impossible and deeply worrying.

"You said this was about freedom," she says.

The imposter twirls his glowing ring around an index finger. If Laura listens carefully, she can hear its deep, quiet synthesised voice still speaking its recursive spell. He says, "Do you know what's the most mana that's ever been gathered together in one location? The mana energy density record?"

"Why, set on breaking it?"

"Breaking something. Do you know what happens when you put too much mu and zeta in the same place?"

Laura takes a cautionary step backwards. Looking back, she sees that Nat has caught back up with her, wearing a shield to protect her from the heat of the lava she just crossed. In tow, sharing the shield, is Benj. The real Benj. And beyond them, in the distance, she sees that Tanako's glass world and the two castles are gone, replaced with dark mountains. *That'll work,* she realises. *We'll bring the real Benj home with us when we wake up. That might actually work.*

As far as she understands — and she likes to think that she understands a great deal — nothing special happens at all when you put too much mu and zeta in the same place. At least, in theory. But nobody's done it. How could they? There's nowhere to get that much mana from.

Laura aims one arm full of amulets at the imposter and holds her staff out backwards with her other hand. "Last chance. Tell me what you're trying to achieve. This is a dream. I can do anything here."

"So can I."

"But I can think faster than you."

The molybdenum ring is so bright now that not-Benj's fist is glowing bright red, with dark spots where his bones are. This reminds Laura of something. She can't remember what. In answer to her question, not-Benj produces a dark grey sphere from one of his jacket pockets. It is the size of a baseball, matte and smooth, and seems to be very heavy. It's so heavy that Laura thinks she would have noticed it weighing in his pocket before now. He must have just created it. It's so heavy, as if it was made of some sort of—

dense metal—

She triggers the last three spells reflexively. By the time the words "implosion assembly" and "subcritical plutonium core" have formed in her mind, the whole thing is over.

"Dulaku ragígakal!"

The first spell is a green laser powerful enough that its beam is visible in clear air. It slices through not-Benj's magic ring with a noise like two bolts being cut. The chain reaction spell cuts out mid-syllable. Half of the ring falls; not-Benj is left holding a C-shaped chunk of metal. Enough stored mana to flip Reykjavik like a pancake crackles out of the four exposed ends, and that would be the end of all of them, plutonium or not, but Laura reaches out and catches the magic with her staff, funnelling it into spell two.

Two is the heavyweight, the figurative tank, the one she could never have built without Natalie's help. With an audible *whump*, the local environment out to a range of about a kilometre and a half drops in temperature, hard. The entire fissure is instantly frozen solid, including all the visible lava, which sets into rock. That's the village saved.

Laura, Benj and Natalie all have shielding against the thermal attack. Not-Benj has shields, but not the right ones. He turns blue.

Now Laura just has to deal with the newly-liberated thermal energy rushing back the other way. With another flick of her staff she pipes it all into spell three, her old heat lance. Not-Benj might as well be standing at point blank range in front of the Sun. He simply ceases to exist; he, and his half of the ring, and his plutonium baseball. All three spells are over in a split second.

Someone faint is beside Laura. Even looking right at him, all she can see is a slight crystalline shimmer at the edges, as if he was a shell of cobweb-thin glass. He puts a hand on top of her outstretched arm and gently but firmly pushes it down, safely aiming all of her thaumic weaponry at the ground.

*

They've stumbled about a quarter of the way back to the village when they meet the Jeep coming in the opposite direction. Tómas Einarsson is driving it, with Steve Aldridge in the passenger seat. It's Aldridge who jumps out as soon as the vehicle stops and rushes over. "Is anybody injured? Anybody get burned, anybody inhale any ash, any SO_2?"

"It's fine, we're fine," Laura explains. "We ran for it and we're okay. I think there was a minor eruption and it's stopped now."

"Are you kidding me? You think you're qualified to make an assessment of that? *Get in the car.* All of you! Tómas, let's go."

Tómas has been studying the ridge through a monocular oracle. Without a word, he slots it back into his inner pocket and pulls the Jeep around to head back towards Blönflói. The road is bumpy and the ride is fast. They'll be back to the village in a matter of minutes.

"I'm not angry," Aldridge explains as they drive back. He was clearly frantic on the way up, but is now visibly cooling off. "You told people where you were going. You did nothing wrong."

"Is the village evacuating?" Benj asks.

"Yes," says Tómas. "The village is so close to the fissure that we do not take chances. The evacuation plan is very paranoid. Although, the eruption has stopped. So they will probably reverse the order in a few minutes."

"Did you radio in that we've got them?" Aldridge asks him.

"Yes. Also, this has never happened before. Krallafjöll has been inactive for a very long time."

They drive in silence for a minute. Aldridge turns around in his seat. "What happened up there?"

"We don't know," says Natalie, immediately.

"Were you doing magic?"

"We were meditating. I was meditating. The others were looking at the view. We don't know what happened."

Tómas is grinning and shaking his head at Aldridge. "It wasn't them. Everybody tries to set off Krallafjöll. It was bad luck."

Instead of stopping at the hostel in the village, Tómas turns onto Route 1 and follows several other vehicles up to the evacuation point, which is entirely on the other side of a hill from Krallafjöll and therefore — within reason — out of harm's way. There are about a hundred people there already, including all the other students and UK and Icelandic staff. They get out and gather in a sheep pasture where they can see the ridge. It's eventually revealed that since this is the first time the village's evacuation plan has been used in anger, it's being seen through to completion as a semi-live drill. There are volcanologists running around with walkie-talkies. The fissure is totally dark and silent. The air is bitterly cold but the sky is clear and starry. All they'd need is a bonfire and it'd be an event worth attending.

Natalie pulls Laura aside. "I need you to do something for me."

"Okay?"

"I need you to stop killing people."

Laura chokes. "Ah, what?"

"Benj!" Natalie shouts. Benj is nearby. He turns around. "Someone wrote QUINIO. Was it you?"

"No," he says.

"Then who wrote it?"

"I don't know. That guy."

"You killed that person," Natalie says to Laura. "You could have vented the energy upwards, away from all of us. You vaporised him and you didn't need to."

"He was threatening lives!"

"You had neutralised that threat. That makes it murder." Natalie's tone of voice isn't even accusatory. It's completely flat.

"I don't understand what you're saying. It was a dream."

"A dream that real counts as real. Any other dream, do whatever you like. But a dream with real people in it, you and me and Benj, and that much power behind it, you need to take more care. If you'd directed that thing at me, I wouldn't be here. It counts."

"It was figurative. It was metaphorical. *None of it happened*."

"None of it? The ridge exploded. You froze it solid. With a spell. And there're going to be questions about that, for one thing, but you did while asleep."

"I wasn't asleep, I was—"

"*So when did you wake up?*"

Laura blinks.

Benj says, "I don't remember waking up."

"Me neither," says Natalie. "Laura?"

Laura steps through her memories one at a time. She remembers walking home. She walked all the way back from her memory palace to Tanako's world to the fissure to reality. It's a continuous record. "...We're awake right now, right?"

"That's the null hypothesis," says Natalie. "Until you can prove otherwise, always assume you're in reality. Now, repeat after me: 'We don't know what happened.'"

9
The Jesus Machine

Grey has just put the last of the pieces together in his head when he hears the first scream from outside the shaft. The timing is uncanny. He has spent a week and a half taking photographs and drawing schematics and dispatching hesitant mana pings into likely-looking receptors in the surface of the artifact. He has observed the series of inexplicable and then unnerving and then mind-wrenching real-world effects of powering the thing up. He has spent that time patiently avoiding leaping to the conclusion. He has tested every step and ruled out every alternative. And he has, after ten-and-a-half days, for one moment, permitted himself to entertain the possibility that what he's looking at is what he feared at first glance he was looking at, and at that *instant* he hears what sounds like the world above being Cleaned, and it's almost a relief.

Magic is a science. It's a science as advanced as any other, as quantum field theory or general relativity, and there have been outlandish claims and vague or self-fulfilling prophecies and forged or questionable evidence, but there is no concrete evidence, *none*, that anybody knew anything about it until Suravaram Vidyasagar cast uum for the first time in 1972. There were no ancient astronauts. There were no real witches at Salem. Jesus wasn't a mage— nothing that he or Muhammed or the Buddha are ever claimed to have done matches up with modern magic. Artifacts from the pre-magic era are one hundred percent non-magical; magical artifacts "from that era" are one hundred percent forged. And the reason for this, which most of the world accepts, is that magic wasn't in reach then. Nobody had the knowledge of physics that was necessary, because the physics that was necessary hadn't been discovered and locked down yet. It was luck, arguably dumb: magic could have been discovered decades earlier or, equally, could have remained unknown long past the present day.

But the artifact that Gareth Grey's high-altitude thaumomagnetic survey found in the far east of the DRC, which it's taken his expedition a month to reach and dig down to, could turn all of that on its ear. It's the rabbit in the Cretaceous, the Casio wristwatch in the coal seam. It's a magic ring as big as a Stonehenge megalith, and it's embedded in rock fifty million years earlier than it could ever exist. There have been geological explanations suggested for its position, but they aren't convincing. And there's certainly no theory in the whole of human knowledge for who could have made it. It can't exist. It's beyond inexplicable. It represents a discontinuity in Grey's rational universe, a false statement which, thanks to the principle of explosion, logically implies the destruction of all reasoned thought. All statements are now false and true.

Aliens. Time travel. A practical joke?

But the thing is *huge*. Magic rings in modern engineering are of course as big as they need to be: at CERN Grey saw one wide enough to fly a light aircraft through the middle. But no magic ring is this *fat* and surely no practical magic ring weighs this much. Based on the geophysical scan (most of the object is still buried) it's thirteen metres wide and two thick, with the cylindrical hole through the middle just a metre and a half wide. If the thing's solid metal, it could weigh anything up to four thousand tonnes — assuming the metal can be identified. It could be moved. It would take an army, but it could be moved. An army isn't out of the question. An army could use it. More efficiently than anybody, in fact, Grey thinks.

The metal is shiny and silvery which rules out, oh, copper and osmium and precious little else. Except for a small, faint etched plus sign, it's smooth all over the exterior and the flat top face (again, as far as they've excavated). About forty percent of the cylindrical hole's inner surface has been uncovered. Into the inner rim, big, bold sigils are etched and there are more, smaller sigils etched into surface of those sigils, and a third iteration etched into those in turn. The writing is so dense and sharp as to be incoherent; regardless of how well-preserved the metalwork seems to be, uncovering enough of it to activate the ring has been painstaking. Grey feels dwarfed by its complexity. Way back in the Stone Age of computing, when the available resources meant that programs had to be minuscule and neatly folded and unreadably, irreducibly complex just to *fit*, let alone *run*, this is the kind of code that Grey saw and wrote. These sigils are at the same density and at the same degree of interconnectedness. Inadvisably tightly coupled and organic.

That's the word Grey is afraid of, "organic". If the artifact was grown and machined by some thrashing, senseless neural net, this is what you'd see. If the problem the thing was designed to solve was so complex that the solution wouldn't be recognisably designed at all, this is what you'd see. When he powers it up, Grey feels like an ant trying to understand the console of the starship Enterprise. And when he powers it up, it still, after N years, works.

The first time he put a jolt through it, a few insect bites disappeared from his arm. It was a whole day before he noticed.

There are more screams. The excavated shaft is a steep diagonal corridor cut into the side of a thickly rainforested mountain. The first part was easy, a thin upper layer of poor soil (as red as Mars and about as fertile), dry leaves and ants. After that it was a dangerously dusty, noisy, mechanical job using heavy machinery which was badly-maintained to start with and which had become visibly even worse for wear on the journey into the Congolese interior. The shaft is about fifteen metres long, with plenty of head room, but barely wide enough for one person to slide past another. The chamber at the bottom where the ring is being excavated is a little bigger, with room for a proper light and a camping chair. Given another month without interruptions, Grey would have had the whole roof pulled off, exposing the ring to fresh air for the first time in — depending on your hypothesis — tens, hundreds, thousands or millions of years. But Grey made them cut to the core directly. He wanted to see it. And that means he's trapped alone at the bottom of a hellishly hot, lung-scratchingly dusty hole in the ground, with no weapons beside an archaeologist's brush, a face mask and a mattock.

He blames himself for calling attention. He could have dropped the matter, let the odd readings stay odd and unseen forever and continued charting the grander topology of low-grade natural background magic on the African continent. But he wanted to see something that nobody else had ever seen before. He wanted to find buried treasure.

Grey stares up the shaft for a long moment, squinting at the light, waiting for somebody to appear at the mouth. They're here for the ring. There's no other conceivable reason for anybody to be this far into the rainforest. Which means it's as valuable as he fears.

There are two more shouts and the sound of running and the sound of bodies falling. There's no gunfire, though. He looks down at the walkie-talkie in the dust and considers trying to contact somebody up above for help, perhaps to organise a distraction. But then he counts up the screams he's heard— there can only be at most one or two of the expedition left, and they'll be running for their lives. The noise from a crackling walkie-talkie could give them away. Could he wait until dark? If he switched off the lamp down here, could he jump whoever came down to investigate? He hefts the mattock in one hand. It's balanced all wrong for use as a weapon; he'd knock holes in his own limbs by accident. Maybe he could throw the mattock out of the shaft, so that it would land elsewhere, distracting whoever is out there for long enough for him to make a run for the Jeep. How many people are out there, anyway? Surely no more than four or five. Otherwise the whole camp would have been swamped in seconds, not minutes.

Possibilities tumble. Having convinced himself that there's no way out of the situation alive, Grey wonders if he can still win by bringing the shaft down on his own head, or by destroying the artifact. But he oversaw the beaming and propping too carefully for the former to be an option, and as for the latter... it's a four-thousand-tonne doughnut of metal. As delicate as its engravings are, he'd need strong acid to do anything worse than a slight dent.

And having come to the end of that thread, having realised that he's not just dead but beaten, he remembers how far he is from home.

He exhales hard and clenches his teeth. "Damn."

"Penny for your thoughts, Dr. Grey," says a voice. At the mouth of the shaft, Grey sees the silhouette of a bald man in a dark, loose-cut suit. The man has no visible weapon. He holds onto the roof of the entrance for support, for a casual effect.

"How many of my people have you killed?" Grey demands.

"The four drivers. The two engineers. The guide and his brother. The blonde geologist and the dark-haired geologist she liked. And the fellow who carried your amulets. That's everybody." The faceless man states it as fact.

"That's everybody," agrees Grey. He hurls the mattock overarm, as hard as he can. The trajectory is long and flat enough to avoid the ceiling and walls of the shaft. Then there's a smash cut. Subjective time skips.

He's—

—flat on his back, waking up. His head is as clear as a bell. He's an early bird, but as far back as he can remember he's never woken up so cleanly, with so much clarity. Certainly not after being knocked unconscious. He detects no head injury. Gas? He sits up in the mud and squints at the light. He's still in the shaft, lying with his head and upper body in the partially excavated doughnut hole, and it's still daylight outside.

The mud, he discovers when he brushes it from his hands and hair, isn't wet dirt. It's gore. Grey recognises brain matter and chunks of skull. The other half of the doughnut hole, which is still plugged up with stone, is splattered with an entire head full of blood.

Well. That answers some questions.

Earlier, tentative experimentation had shown that the machine could resolve cuts and scars and, in one of the engineers, a years-old mild limp of uncertain origin. It was also shown to restore eyesight, which Grey found moderately troublesome, since his only sunglasses were prescription. But that was the limit. There was no chance that he was going to ask somebody, in a spirit of scientific inquiry, to deliberately break a bone and see if the machine could fix it. That would have been madness. He stands by the decision, even now, standing in the splatter pattern of his own detonated head.

So it can fix brains, from a standing start. Presumably he had to be nearby for it to record a pattern to work from. It would be impossible, surely, to put a human mind back together properly without *some* kind of "known-good" template to work from...

Grey cackles. "Impossible".

He thinks back to the smash cut and wonders how he'd detect other inconsistencies in his own memories under these circumstances. Did the machine restore his mind fully, or partially? There are other questions still open: can it do anything about mental illness? What about extreme age? What about non-humans?

There's no bullet or hole. He doesn't remember a gunshot. Not even a silenced round. Not even a weapon being raised.

He climbs to the mouth of the shaft and pokes his head out, blinking. The sunlight is so bright that it feels as if it has physical weight. Below the shaft mouth is the wide, mucky orange path that leads down to the camp site, a wide clearing littered with tents, parked vehicles and diesel generators. From where he's standing, Grey counts seven corpses. The bullet wounds that he can see look like clean chest shots. But he can't see the man. He can't see anybody living.

Quietly and with extreme caution, he sidles down towards the camp, through the trees rather than down the obvious path. If he can reach his tent, he can unlock the small metal trunk and reassemble his rifle. Then he can use it to keep his nerves subdued while he works out a plan.

"I said, what do you think?" asks the same voice, this time from behind. Grey sags, the effort of stealth wasted. He turns. The bald man is emerging from the same excavated shaft, which should be empty, but Grey is too tired to absorb this extra oddity. The man's tall and very young. Closer to a boy, in fact. Early twenties at the latest. He's young and he stands casually, with his hands in his pockets. His linen suit is loose and its jacket is unbuttoned: Grey sees no gun. He looks around and still sees no accomplices.

"You can have it," says Grey. "I don't care what you do with it. Just give me enough time to use it to bring my people back."

The youth smiles faintly and shakes his head.

Grey conceals his anger. He decides to play the boy's game, to buy time. "It's obviously a doctor. I suspected from the Red Cross symbol on its hull. It's the mechanical realisation of the abstract concept: a machine which makes people better. The most complicated medical device ever created, a million times more complicated than any medical device I've ever seen and a thousand times more complicated than the human body it's designed to fix. And... it can't exist. I can't even conceive of magic so advanced. No human can, no matter the IQ. It can't exist. I'm a mage and I know magic isn't like this."

"But what do you think?"

"What do I think about what?"

"What do you think happens next?"

"Obviously you and whoever else is with you are going to kill me and take the machine."

"What if I didn't do that?"

Grey blinks. "...We would need to get it to a laboratory," he says. "Because one isn't enough. If we put the thing at the most accessible point on Earth and formed a human processing system ten times as complicated as Mecca, and forced people through the machine one at a time, one every two seconds, for the rest of time, it wouldn't be enough. It wouldn't register statistically. It wouldn't make a dent in any of the *rates*. Which means we need to make more. Millions more. This is... it's Outside Context Medicine."

"And then what would happen?"

Grey stares into a distant possible future. "Medicine as we know it would— it would become magic. Everything we know about medicine would be revolutionised. We'd write libraries about what the machine does to people, the difference between broken and fixed people. And then we would throw away those libraries because we'd never need them again because everybody would live to a hundred and twenty without trying. If you lived inside a machine you could live for eternity. And if there's a way that the machine can reverse telomere shortening, then everybody on Earth could live forever just with periodic visits. You could have eternal youth. For everybody."

"And then what?"

"And then?" Grey concentrates. "There would— there would be no Malthusian catastrophe. There wouldn't need to be. Because you don't need food and water anymore. You visit the machine. Malnourished? Visit the machine. You come out the other side fed and watered. Food becomes a luxury item. The capacity of the planet becomes a function of physical space. Maybe if the technology can be adapted, the whole of the world could be pervaded with this restorative power. You wouldn't need to eat, or drink. Or even breathe. You wouldn't need air anymore. You'd— You'd have to rediscover death."

The bald youth reflects for a long moment, and then asks, "A likely story, do you think?"

Grey smiles darkly. "Of course not. None of it."

The youth says, "Here's what we think: A major medical research company pays for the rights to study, own and operate the machine. At great length and expense, they duplicate it. They want a return on their investment. They make eight machines, embed them in purpose-built medical establishments in world cities and sell the best medical care that is theoretically possible to only those able to afford millions of U.S. dollars per visit. When it becomes clear what the organisation is sitting on, it becomes the target of heavyweight litigation, industrial espionage and eventually overt physical attacks. A man is denied access due to perceived war crimes; another man, also a perceived war criminal, is admitted. Unrelated tensions boil over at the same time, amplifying the situation. A full European War erupts.

"But in fact, what's more likely is that the machine proves unduplicable. Its location on neutral territory in, for example, the Hague, the Netherlands, becomes the nucleus of a community of ill and dying pilgrims desperately queueing for one-time exposure to a machine which cannot physically process one in a hundred of the patients who need its treatment. A second city is founded on the streets of the first. First crime consumes both cities, then disease, then violence. In the final series of riots, the facility is stormed and the machine captured by a dozen different groups in a single week. Eventually the Dutch military end the conflict by permanently disabling the machine.

"But even that's an outside chance because, in the first place, you're never likely to get it out of the DRC unchallenged. Eight African nations including the Democratic Republic of the Congo itself become aware of the machine's existence and initiate a decades-long, interminable land war to claim it. Western nations become involved and the war in turn claims millions of lives and ends with the tactical atomic bombing by the United States of the installation where the machine is being held. Even though the machine was believed to have been rendered unrecoverably inoperable years earlier, the bombing is regarded as the greatest humanitarian catastrophe of all time.

"Except that that might not happen either. Let's say the U.S. wins the war. They capture the machine and take it to the bunker underneath the White House, where only the President, his family and his cabinet are permitted access to it. Medical technology is deliberately stalled and never reaches the pinnacle it should.

"And yet, for anybody to leave the machine unexploited is implausible. We spin more numbers and simulations and we see the machine being reverse-engineered, and the principles it applies being adapted for purposes other than the immediate, perfect restoration of living and dead humans. Mr Grey, you've seen how easy it is to heal. Can you imagine how easy it'll become to kill?

"The truth will inevitably be somewhere in the middle of all of these possibilities, but I'm sure you understand the common theme. Death surrounds this machine, like a curse. Death and leverage. The mother of all MacGuffins."

Grey imagines how easy it would become to kill. You wouldn't need a gun anymore. You could create a bullet and give it motion. You could simply "correct" a living human body to a living body with a hole in it.

"And you see," the youth concludes, "that you have to let us take it and put it somewhere safer."

"Take it back, you mean," Grey says.

"...Indeed."

"It must have been in a hell of an accident to wind up inside a mountain," Grey says. "How did you lose it?"

The young man shrugs.

"But how did you know we'd found it? I chose my crew for loyalty. Until yesterday, I didn't utter a hint to them about what I thought the thing actually was. And I know none of them satphoned home."

"Magic."

"Then who are you?"

"I can't tell you."

"But you're going to kill me."

In response, the youth nods towards the shaft mouth. "It's still a risk. You understand."

Grey does.

The youth continues, "All I can say is that we're the ones who ran the numbers. Of course, nobody can accurately predict the future, but after ten thousand high-fidelity simulations of the same events, some outcomes turn out to be more probable than others, and then when we go through our courses of action, this is the firmest recommendation."

Grey's eyes widen. He puts his hands out, mind racing, heart racing. "Wait. No, wait!"

The youth pulls his right hand out of his pocket and says "One more, please," seemingly to nobody before pointing at Grey with his first two fingers.

"How good are your simulations? What kind of fidelity? Was I a component? Could you be?" Grey delivers all four questions in about three seconds.

There's a pause. The boy doesn't lower his hand, but Grey's got his attention.

"How would the simulation begin?" Grey continues. "If you were simulating this course of action, how would it begin? It would begin with the decision being made, right?"

A longer pause.

Grey says, "It would begin exactly like this. No matter the option, no matter the outcome. The course of action to be tested is X. So they create a simulation in which the course of action selected *was* X. In the simulation, you are given the order. In the simulation, a simulation of you carries X out. And as it plays out, the *simulators* observe the results. They collect the results from X and Y and Z and stack them all together. And then pick the best one and they go out into reality and do it once, for real.

"Think about it. You, *you*, know all of the possible outcomes if nobody does anything, if nobody interferes," Grey says. "Because those runs were run. But you don't know what the other options of interference are. You don't know about the other hypotheses. About Y and Z and the rest. That's the only way that you could prove that this isn't a hypothetical, because that information is the only information that's guaranteed not to be available inside a hypothetical. And you don't have it. And this can't be the right solution because it doesn't make sense. Killing to prevent more killing? Killing to prevent a medical revolution that could save *literally every life*? This has to be one of the faulty hypotheses. And that means that you and I don't exist. *This isn't happening.* So it doesn't matter if you don't kill me."

"Then it doesn't matter if I do—"

"But the point is that X doesn't have to happen here. Make this the one where you gained unexpected self-awareness and disobeyed orders. Put your... absence of gun away. Maybe *that's* what they really want to see happen. They order you to do X but they want me to overrule you with Y so they can see how Y plays out. They want to see what happens if... you let me try to save everyone." Grey locks eye contact with the youth. Grey tries to make himself believe that he sees a flicker of doubt in there.

There is the longest pause.

"No," says the boy. "This is real."

He shoots Grey. No gun. No bullet. He just opens a hole in Grey's heart.

10
Space Magic

Rachel Ferno's burning mana so fast to stay in the air that it feels like it's doing physical and mental damage to her, as if she were consuming body parts and organs and memories as reaction mass, as if whatever it is that's finally going to match velocities with the plummeting orbiter won't even be a human being anymore but a spent propellant tank. Autokinetic effects must, on pain of burst retinas and crushing death, be applied uniformly across the whole body. She pulls what would be lethal gees to keep up with the machine's chaotic tumble, desperately fighting to stay out of its smoke trail where she can still eyeball her interception trajectory.

Virtual instruments spread out in front of her like playing cards show her relative position and velocity, her airspeed and orientation, her oxygen levels, mana levels, and her degree of concentration, but the more closely she monitors the flashing values, the closer she edges towards completely losing it, breaking the spell and then bodily breaking apart under aerodynamic stress. So she dismisses them and the shielding holds, flexing actively to stay stable at supersonic speed. Rachel rolls and deliberately loses the horizon, throwing on another twenty percent thrust. She fixes the orbiter in the centre of her field of view and pushes towards it, burning blue-hot and singing and in control. She hears music, bass waves so loud that it feels like she's riding them. She burns her life story for fuel. She burns her fingers and toes and her attachments to the ground until there's nothing left of her but purified, abstract acceleration.

Relatively speaking she hits the Atlantis nosecone as softly as a feather, wrapping her fields across the windshields and locking herself into the vehicle's motion. She feels the impact numbly, as if insulated from it by thick wool. There are seven people inside and they all look identical in the flight suits and the helmets and she can't spare the mental bandwidth to remember any of their names, but she singles out the figure in the seat in the middle row on the left. It's her daughter, having the dream again. It's the same dream. This is just a different angle.

Some messages are all medium. They have no payload. "I'm on the orbiter's exterior," Rachel tells them. "I'm going to try to save you all using magic." It's not words or sign language. She tells them this just by being there.

*

"What happens next?" Nick asks Laura.
"I wake up."
"No, the other thing."

Nick's cooking dinner. Laura's flat on her back on his floor in the next room, pouring it out like a psychiatric patient and intermittently guessing what he's doing from the smells and cookware clunks. "What happened next was the most well-observed event in history," she replies. "The thing went up like an atom bomb. Spark, fuel, liquid oxygen. It was caught on thirty-five distinct film sequences and it shows up as the terminating point on almost all of the telemetry. In fact— what happened *next* is the *only* known fact. And it's also the only part I don't get to see in the dream."

"Because you get blown up."

Laura says nothing.

"Oh, wait," says Nick. "They recovered all seven bodies? So you don't get blown up, but the explosion knocks you out. Out of the dream."

"But my point is— my point is that everything *up* to that point is... conjecture. It's fantasy, I must have pieced it together from my research. There isn't footage that shows any of what I'm imagining. There aren't voice recordings. The fact that Mum turns up at the end of it is... I don't know if she got there. I don't know if she even tried to get there. It's fan fiction!"

"You have to speak up," says Nick. "I can't hear you over the hood."

"I don't know why I keep having this dream. When I'm dreaming it, I care—"

"Do you know you're dreaming?"

"What?"

"When you start off strapped into the chair, do you recognise it? Do you remember that it's a dream you've had before? Is it lucid?"

Laura stares at the ceiling and splays her fingers out against the carpet. She doesn't know.

There's a long lull in the conversation before she pipes up again. "I smell thyme."

"Very good!"

It was an educated guess. She watched Nick buy some earlier that day. "When I'm dreaming it, it matters. Whether I know I'm dreaming or not, I treat it as real. I try to stop it. And then afterwards, after I wake up, I realise that I don't care. I have no reason to care. Because it already happened. It's in the past. I have no reason to dream this dream."

"Maybe your subconscious cares more about your mother than you do."

Laura considers this unlikely. "Maybe. All I consciously care about is duplicating what she *did*."

"'Six impossible things'."

"Six-ish. And I'm getting there. Her O_2 supply wasn't much more than a fan-shaped force field rotating at high speed. That kind of fine-grained force field projection is definitely going to become possible soon. And I've almost got the Montauk storage theory cracked. That much energy stored and released in that amount of time? It's almost definitely— well, I mean it's definitely possible, because I've seen it happen. But I've almost got it duplicated. And I'm going to guess... turkey?"

"Yesss."

"Gestural casting and non-vocal casting might be the same thing," continues Laura. "But I don't understand them. Or autokinetics. Those have been very difficult. I don't know where to look. I don't even know where to stand when I'm looking. I feel like there are empty bookshelves waiting there, you know? Whole new Dewey Decimal categories. But I'm only trying to figure out what got her to that point, or at least what could have theoretically got her to that point. Like a bug on the windshield. I don't care about what was next. Maybe the dream cuts out at the point where I stop caring."

"Okay, it's done," says Nick. He comes through with the plates. Turkey is involved, as are thyme, green salad, sautéed potatoes and a thin brown sauce. He puts plates on the table and goes back for cutlery. Laura sits up, gets up from the floor, then sits down at the table.

"What was next?" Nick calls through from the kitchen.

"What?"

"What was the plan?"

"The plan was that I tell you about my day while you're cooking, and then you tell me about your day while we're eating, so that you don't eat all of your food incredibly quickly and start stealing mine."

"No," says Nick, coming back in with knives and forks. He hands one of each to Laura and sits opposite her. "What was your mum's plan?"

"I don't know." And this revelation explodes in Laura's mind, like an airbag. Suddenly it occupies all the available space. *I don't know?*

Nick puts some food in his mouth and carries on talking: "You've said yourself that new magic takes like a day of prep, plus. That's why you need to build a toolkit. You can't improvise. So she must have had something worked out." He chews and swallows. "Or maybe she didn't have a plan, what do I know? Or a clue or a prayer. Any of them."

Laura holds her knife and fork and stares at a point on the wall directly behind Nick's head. "Wait a second."

"So potentially there's a seventh impossible thing here. When you count what her actual plan was, if she had one, there's an extra thing that you didn't even know that you didn't even know."

"But she doesn't demonstrate it. She fails. Failed. Just give me a second to think."

"Sure," says Nick. "So you're driving yourself mad. It's a jigsaw with a piece you didn't realise was missing."

Laura's elsewhere entirely.

"What was she going to do? Why can't you see that in the dream?" Nick presses.

"There's... nothing that she could have done," says Laura.

"Is there?"

Laura stares back at Nick but she's not looking at him. She's trying to remember what her mother's face looked like. She's trying to read her intentions, across a gap of years.

*

Douglas Ferno's forty-something, but looks older. Not fat, but expanding; not bald, but thinning. He doesn't care, but the degree to which he doesn't care is diminishing. A city council treasurer, he finds the routine and the rationality of his workplace soothing. He has settled into a kind of career Main Sequence, even with retirement still a sizeable distance off. In his spare time, he pursues falconry.

Raptors aren't dogs. Having found himself with the time and stability, Doug Ferno threw himself into something requiring a sustained effort across years plural to get a positive result. Raptors are stunningly well-adapted for their evolutionary niche, all talons and laser eyesight and two-hundred-mile-per-hour dives, but none of that makes them smart or friendly or obedient. Hela, his Harris Hawk, is a wild, paranoid animal. She accepts humans into her life only to the extent that they appear to be part of her successful hunting strategy. Even having been essentially raised by Doug Ferno, Hela treats him like the terrifyingly smart and dangerous apex predator he is, the same way that a man would treat a tiger who mysteriously began cooking meals for him. The instructions Hela understands extend as far as "fly into that tree over there", "fly back here to my hand" and "LOOK LOOK A RABBIT GET IT!".

Today Hela perches on a thick leather glove on his left hand, with thin leather jesses tied around her legs and the other ends held tightly in his fist. Hela is a uniform dark brown, with yellow hooked beak and a one-metre wingspan. Her feathers are delicate and brittle, like glass. She weighs about a kilogram, almost little enough to forget about.

Doug and Laura are working their way up a forest track to the largish field where Doug usually brings birds for training. Laura's carrying a mobile perch, basically an oversized metal croquet hoop, heavy enough that a bird can't fly away with it.

"I got a job interview," Laura says.

"I thought you were going to stay on for a master's," Doug Ferno replies.

"So did I," Laura says. "It's at Hatt. I think it's 'Hatt Group' in full but they just call it 'Hatt'. They're an aerospace group. They're using a lot of magic in their work. And if they're using a small amount of magic in their work that'll be ten times the amount of magic that any other aerospace outfit uses, because the industry moves like a petrified snail."

"You sent an application?"

"No."

"They phoned you out of the blue?"

"Emailed me out of the blue. Come on, Dad. They want me to come up and see the factory."

"Have they mentioned money?"

"They've mentioned hardware."

"Toys," Doug Ferno translates.

Laura grins a kid-in-a-toy-shop grin.

"How many people know what you're trying to accomplish?" her father asks. What Laura's trying to accomplish, in ten words or fewer: *An entirely magical human-rated orbital launch system.*

"Everybody knows. Everybody who'll sit still and nod and smile for long enough. As to how many people spread that word or think I'm seriously going to get anywhere, your guess is as good as mine. I guess at least one person gives me the credit. This wasn't a form email, Dad. It wasn't an artificial mail merged mailshot thing sent to four thousand people or even to four people. It was personal. Somebody sat down and decided to write to me."

"How flattering. Will you go?"

They get to the top of the track and they're out of forest onto the hillside. It's a dazzling day, the world all blue, green, orange and yellow. Laura and her father take the view in. Weather this good is a precious resource at any time of year. Hela looks around indifferently. Like all birds, her eyes can't swivel in their sockets. She has to turn her entire head to look at things. It would be impossible to tell what she's thinking, or even, with mere human eyesight, what she's looking at.

"Yeah," says Laura.

"And give up on postgrad work? Give up on a Ph.D.? Is that what you want to do?"

"If they'll let me, I'll give up on the degree."

"*What?* This close to the end? Honey, that's madness."

"What I want to do is go into space. You know how I'm making decisions right now, Dad? I'm making decisions based on what's going to get me into space fastest. You ask me where I see myself in five years? I see myself *in space*. I don't think academia's it. I think academia's going to keep me on Earth. If Hatt are going to give me the materials and the equipment, the *toys*, then I'll annihilate what's left of the theory in... in—"

"About half of an Apollo program?"

"Something like that. End of this decade."

At the near end of the field, Laura plants the mobile perch in the ground and drives it into the soil with her foot. She helps her father tie a very long, lightweight line to Hela's jesses. Doug could do it himself with one hand, but there's more than one individual being taught today. Doug sets the bird down on the perch, then he and his daughter retreat to the other end of the field, with Doug trailing about thirty metres of line behind him.

From a large leather pouch, Doug Ferno produces about one-third of a dead male chick. He gets them in bulk from a battery farm, where they only have use for the females. Laura wouldn't touch the gross tatter of chicken unless she was wearing a thick leather gauntlet of her own. She takes it with her gloved hand and holds it out straight, where Hela can see it. Doug whistles, and the bird comes.

Hela takes a lazy, low-energy path from perch to glove, almost grazing the grass at her lowest point, barely flapping her wings except for a split second of activity on landing. If the weight of the creance affects her flight, Laura can't tell. The fragment of chicken is gone in a second, gobbled up whole, even its head. Hela's hungry, which is as well, because once she's fed up, no accrued years of training and familiarity and mutual respect will move her. This is entirely about food.

Laura resists the temptation to stroke the bird's head, or to brush sticky yellow fluff off her face. Hela has absolutely no concept of personal contact. On reflex action, she would most likely gouge a hole in Laura's arm. Instead, Laura half-throws Hela back to her perch.

Doug says, "I think you're radically underestimating how big a deal getting into space is. Throw a living human being into that equation and the job becomes easily twenty-five, fifty times harder."

"Don't lecture me, Dad, do you think I haven't researched this stuff?"

"I think you *have* researched this stuff, and I think it's *lulled* you. I think you've read a lot of books and worked through a mountain of theory and you've written some pretty amazing spells. But I don't believe, and you're deluding yourself if you believe, that you're the smartest or most capable engineer in the world, and I don't believe, and you're going to get yourself killed if you believe, that you can handle a task like this on your own in five years flat. You're either going to kill yourself with stress or you're going to drop a term in some mental Vedic whatever-it-is-that-you-do—"

"Vector calculus."

"—and pancake yourself with some rogue extra force that you didn't account for. Or worse, pancake somebody else. And you'll drop that term because of overwork." Doug hands Laura another slice of chick and whistles again. Hela flies to them, as before. "And that's if you're allowed a free rein to go and work on whatever you like all day. If that's what you think Hatt wants you to do, you've lost it. That's not what a job is. Being paid to entertain yourself is very, very rarely a real job. You know things they don't, that's what they're paying for. After they've bled you dry they might just sack you, and build their magical spaceship by themselves. Did you think of that?" While talking, Doug attaches a tiny and unobtrusive radio transponder unit to Hela's tail. He checks that it's signalling correctly with a handheld unit.

He checks a few batteries, then lets Laura send Hela back to her perch.

They feed Hela a few more times, getting her into the routine.

"You need to loosen your grip on this thing," Doug says. "You have your entire life to get it right."

"I need to know what Mum was planning to do when she caught Atlantis," Laura says.

"...I don't know anything about that," says Doug Ferno.

"In five years' time I'll have everything else. I still need to work out autokinetics, and gestural spelling. But there's no way she could save it. Once she *got* there, there would have been nothing left. I need to know."

Doug Ferno's expression has dropped. So has his whole bearing. He won't meet Laura's gaze and he seems like half the man. "I don't know anything about that," he says.

"Then what do you know? Where did Mum get her knowledge from? Who taught her? When?"

"We're going in," Doug decides. He stalks back over to the mobile perch, wrapping up the creance as he goes.

"That's it?"

"I'm making a point." Doug had told Laura he was going to take Hela off the creance for the first time today. That's what the radio transponder was for, so that Hela could be tracked (as far as possible) if she flew away. It's a huge, hugely nerve-wracking moment for a falconer. It would have been a privilege to see.

"It's been too long," Laura says. "I know you don't like talking about this. But we've gone too long, not talking about this. Going on eight years. You said she was a self-taught mage. An amateur. An enthusiast. You told Nat and me the story when we were kids. You met in a choir—"

"Your obsession is problematic," Doug says.

"But it can't all be true. Not all of it. It doesn't make sense. She was secretly a whole other person. And I need to know who."

"The deal was exactly what you saw," Doug says. "The marriage was exactly what you saw. And what I saw."

There's a long pause as Doug ties Hela back to his wrist. Hela, indifferent to the human conversation, decides to make a break for it. She gets about ten centimetres and is pulled up short. She hangs by her legs from Doug's hand, mildly flummoxed, until he gently pushes her back up with his free hand.

"Who was she?" Laura asks.

Doug Ferno stalks away down the track. "I don't know," he says.

*

Then there's the other dream.

Along the corridor and through the next door on the right, after the Atlantis exhibit, is a newer room of the same size. This one has a fat rectangular slice of Icelandic volcanic fissure in it, irregular along the top but perfectly cut along all four sides, a black chunk of chocolate cake with lava leaking out of its sides. On top of the fissure there are three people. One is the raving psycho-duplicate of Benj Clarke, caught in time at the moment before he tried to end the world, with a ball of subcritical plutonium in one hand and a magic/metallic force field implosion assembly in the other. One is Laura herself, in voluminous black robes, stood a little downhill from Clarke and pointing a three-metre mercury staff at him, with her triple-spell pipeline just starting to take effect. Green cutting laser light is crawling out of the staff's sharpened tip, across the gap towards Benj's hand.

In her dreams — her *other* dreams — Laura sees all of this from the point of view of her sister, stood far away and down the hill with the real Benj.

But there's a third person there at the top of the fissure.

Since getting back from Iceland this dream has recurred as often as the other one. It makes sense to Laura that Atlantis would occupy a huge chasm in the middle of her mind. Unthreading her mother's tricks is part of the plan, a stair on the path to human-powered spaceflight, a big locked box with question marks plastered all over it. But why this too? It's a dream of a dream. Do they have something in common?

The third person is probably male, and short, barely taller than she is. He stands beside dream-Laura. His features and clothing aren't clear, because he's a hollow glass shell, glass as thin as spider silk. There's not enough ambient light to make him glisten, but Laura — real-Laura, from her transfixed perspective at the bottom of the hill — sees an outline of green photons splashing off him, reflected from the laser beam.

Everything in the room is stuck fast. Even the photons in flight. Real-Laura can't move forward to confront the barely-visible man, or even shout at him. He was part of a dream to begin with, right? Which means that the dream of the dream is as real as the original dream, right? Which means it's the same man.

And when she realises this, he looks back at her. He was stuck fast in the tableau, but then he looks around, noticing real-Laura watching him. The green light on his face changes shape when he turns. She cannot move.

And that's the moment when she also notices that the glass man seems to be helping dream-Laura with the spell. One hand on dream-Laura's shoulder. The other steadying her grip on the staff, helping her aim.

*

Hatt Group's "ancestral home" is a low office building and a factory and a runway in Norfolk, with flat greenery and canals in most directions. The offices have pleasant, modern architecture. There are glass and pale bricks, modern furnishings, an airy reception with a high ceiling and a lot of light. A customer-friendly front end. The place is a royal pain to reach via public transport.

The man who meets Laura at reception is fifty-odd but looks a lot younger, ash-blond, in a casual suit with no tie. He practically bursts through the door from the office area, and zeroes in on Laura immediately. The handshake is energetic. He is a fast-moving person. "Find the place okay?"

"Yes," Laura lies.

"You drive in?"

"No."

The man smiles in a consolatory sort of way. Evidently, he's as aware of the lousy local bus service as she is. "Bad luck. Can I get you a drink?"

Laura indicates that she has already been directed to help herself to a complimentary coffee.

The man says, "Well, I'm out of small talk. I'm Edward Hatt, let's talk about your final year project."

"You own the place?"

"I do."

"Huh," says Laura.

Hatt smiles broadly.

Laura says, "I didn't bring any of my equipment. Also, my final year project takes about an hour to cast.

And I didn't bring my notes either. And it's not finished."

"You didn't bring any gear?"

"Should I have? It's a job interview."

"We were aiming for more of an informal chat."

"Okay. ...So it's a collection of small-scale kinematic spells. The idea is that I hold out my hand and my staff assembles itself. In my hand."

While Laura's talking, Hatt goes to the receptionist and obtains a red card of some kind which entitles Laura to pass, escorted, into the rest of the building. "I'm listening," Hatt says.

"At the moment I have to hold out the first segment of my staff in one hand. The top segment, I mean. The second, third, fourth, fifth and sixth segments assemble one at a time. I use measurements of background magic so that the spell can determine how many of the segments are already assembled and which segment to move next. As each new segment connects up the background flows change—"

"S-tensor effects," Hatt observes, holding the door for Laura and waving her through.

Laura hesitates, just for a fraction of a second. "Yes. I put a continuous measurable flow of mana out into the world, and the partially-assembled staff alters that flow in ways I can pick up with other tools. Then, once the spells that detect the staff assembly progression are in place, I've also got an array of very small-scale kinetic spells to lift and guide the segments. Screwing— I mean, rotating a staff segment on its axis without translation— is a delicate operation."

"Small-scale spells always take more skill than brute force pushes," says Edward Hatt. He leads her through office corridors at a brisk pace, ignoring all of the actual offices and meeting rooms they pass.

"Right," Laura says.

"How long does the assembly take?"

"Speaking the spell takes more than fifty minutes. The assembly is two minutes at the moment."

"Are you looking at making it faster?"

"Which part?"

"Both. Either."

"The second part, sure. Like you say, though, I'm increasing from small-scale pushes to large-scale pushes while trying not to break anything by flinging a staff segment across a room in the wrong direction. It's the *skill* at speed that I need. I think I can get it down to a second. I want to be able to throw the pieces in the air and they'll come down assembled. The first part, I don't know. I can streamline the verbalisations but getting to the position where, mentally, I've got the whole thing 'juggling' reliably, takes—"

"—it takes longer the more you try to hurry. But if you relax and slow down it takes even longer. And trying not to consciously think about either of those things is worse still."

"Right. You've done some magic?"

They reach a hefty locked door. Hatt waves his ID card at a reader next to it, and motions for Laura to do the same. The reader bleeps green and Hatt pulls it open. He strides out into the place, picking up a luminous yellow hard hat from a rack and putting it on as he walks, wasting no seconds. Laura does likewise and has to jog a little to keep up.

The next room is the factory floor. It's big enough to fit a stadium. Not to function *as* a stadium, but to actually fit an entire stadium inside it without touching the sides. It has air conditioning requirements from hell. It's stacked with machinery building other machinery; a confusing, high-tech mess of airframes, engines, loaders and tiny people in overalls and hard hats. It would take a month for Laura to make sense of the layout, but after that month, Laura would know that the room contained four different production lines and components for eleven different aircraft. The place is flooded with warning signs: moving machinery, moving vehicles, falling objects, chemicals, electricity, heavy loads.

At the tail end of the big table of warnings is the one Laura was looking for. It is a black warning triangle with Mohit Dehlavi's triple diamond symbol inside it. Like the biohazard symbol and the radiation warning trefoil, it is a spiky abstract form with order-3 rotational symmetry, instantly recognisable from any angle. It means "High Energy Magic". Beside it is a rack of fat Montauk rings, suitable for throwing around an out-of-control experiment to drain all of its energy and shut it down. These look bigger than the ones Laura's familiar with from the university labs. And they look used.

"Magic's the missing link of aerospace," Hatt says. "Aerospace needed rebooting and we're doing that. We're vertically integrating our assembly lines in ways that make the rest of the industry look like a joke. Do you know Boeing ships their hulls to five different countries for assembly? I'm not talking about having multiple plants operating in parallel. A single airframe passes linearly through five different countries, having different parts glued onto it. And between countries it's on a *boat*. And magic does wild things with fluid dynamics calculations—"

"—not that magic doesn't have its own proven-generally-unsolvable fluid dynamics problems—"

"—so we do it numerically, obviously. But by 'wild' I meant 'valuable'. And magic changes the Tsiolkovsky rocket equation, and if you've spent as long as I have staring futilely at the Tsiolkovsky rocket equation wishing it wasn't such a bitch, you'd understand how much of a bitch it is."

"Actually, I have."

"To get a delta-vee of four times the effective exhaust velocity we need a *fifty*-to-one propellant-to-vehicle mass ratio! Fuck that! You know this."

"I do."

"Fuck the natural logarithm!"

"Fuck it, indeed," Laura says.

"Yes, I've done some magic," says Hatt. "This job has a lot of straight, blunt business to it, meetings-in-rooms-and-on-phones, and the more of it I do the further I get separated from the physical hands-on mage work. Which I regret. But I can stand it for as long as it's in the service of advancing science. Two things, I have realised. One, that the future isn't something that happens just by sitting still watching digits roll over. The future's something you make a conscious decision to build. Two, what you build, you can sell. Magic makes the world a lot more confusing, but I think you'll agree that admitting that there's something in the world that will never be fully understood is the exact opposite of science. With magic, we're going to cut the cost per kilogram to LEO in half. And after that, actual God-damned flying cars."

They stride on for another few minutes, reaching the far end of the factory and exiting through a door onto the apron and runway beyond. Hatt keeps walking in the same direction, now apparently leading Laura out across the concrete, away from the forest of aircraft and towing vehicles, towards nowhere. It's nowhere near as nice a day today. It's windy and grey.

"Do you get the bizarre dreams?" Hatt asks.

"What?"

"Let me show you what we're looking at," Hatt says. They stop in the middle of the runway, which, Laura can only assume, is not currently in use. From an inner jacket pocket, Hatt produces a slim black case and from the slim black case he produces a handful of thin metal cylinders, like dry spaghetti strands. Connected together they form a scaled-down magic staff, as long as his forearm and only a few millimetres thick. In other words, a wand. He has the thing assembled so quickly that Laura doesn't have time to speak. "Fib anh dulaku ANKA'U."

And—

There's a pure clear night sky above them, with a triple-pointed galaxy. There's glass underfoot. The glass is sapphire-blue and rough, as if heavy vehicles have driven over it in every direction a hundred times a day for a decade. Where the Hatt Group hangar was, there's an even more colossal building, totally made of glass, lit internally with constellations of futuristically blue-tinged flood lamps, filled with sparkling sleek black launch vehicles covered with magic runes. Where the Hatt Group offices were, there's a vast two-storey terminal building, with mass transit rails connected to all of its orifices, ferrying passengers to and from the rest of the UK.

Edward Hatt and Laura Ferno are still standing together in the middle of the runway. Hatt grins wider than ever and Laura ducks as a spaceplane shrieks over their heads, blasts their hair with reversed thrust and touches down. The machine is 737-sized, brilliant white on top, gloss black underneath, and angular like a seagull. Under its wings, instead of jet engines or rocket motors, it has red-hot glowing inscriptions and thin, comb-like distribution channels for mana. In the sky, in the direction from which the first spaceplane just came, is a column of lights, a queue of other spaceplanes on their final approach. The queue stretches out beyond the limit of human eyesight, stacked up by Space Traffic Control as close together as they'll go.

It's a future. Edward Hatt's Tanako's world. "This can't be Norfolk," Laura says. "You'd never build a spaceport at a latitude like Norfolk. It's too energetically unfavourable. You built this?"

"We will build this," says Hatt, "and there's nothing stopping us launching from the North Pole, straight up. You've seen enough of the quantum physics by now. Magic violates laws. Big, big laws. There." He points.

On the far side of the terminal building is another runway. A different spacebird of a much larger model takes off, using barely two hundred metres of 'asphalt'. Once airborne, it pulls up to an almost vertical attitude, and accelerates out of eyeshot. Laura loses track of it in less than thirty seconds. She can't tell if its trajectory is suborbital or not.

She realises that the big spacebird had windows all the way along its hull. Passenger windows. In fact, it had about the same configuration as the one that just landed, which means no discarded components. No spent fuel tank. No fuel, aside from a gargantuan quantity of magic.

"This is the Earth half of the dream," says Edward Hatt. "I don't know what's on the Moon yet, but there's definitely something there worth looking at."

"Can you do this? Even theoretically, how much of this is possible?"

"We're going to have to invent some theory," says Hatt. He says this with absolute confidence. It doesn't even appear to have occurred to him that the theory could be too difficult to invent. A fragment of paper whips past in the wind. He snatches it out of the sky.

And they're back to the grey Norfolk day.

"How did you do that?"

"Somebody lost a boarding pass," Edward Hatt says to Laura, handing her the piece of paper. It has the texture of a banknote, and a barcode of a style Laura doesn't recognise. The date on it is thirty years from now. The flight is from here to Cape Town. Duration: two hours, eleven minutes.

"You just had this in your pocket," Laura says.

Hatt puts his hands in his pockets. "Are you in?"

"That was the interview?"

"We want your finished final project. The low-level thaumokinesis. If you can complete it to your own satisfaction, you'll have shown the level of skill we need. Finish the degree too if that makes it simpler for you."

Laura holds Hatt's gaze for a while. "The thing you built in Tanako's world is no great trick," she says. "Anybody can dream that big. And I know wands cost a lot. But back there I saw mages in hard hats, doing things I actually don't understand. For a living."

"Is that a yes?"

"Send me the paperwork."

11
The Seventh Impossible Thing

Meditation is part of the workload of a professional mage. No employer wants to pay for its people to spend ten percent of the working day dozing off in the lotus position in quiet, well-lit, boringly-painted rooms which could be better used for office space; nor, despite appearances, is "dozing off" what happens in there. Meditation is mental exercise: heavily structured, exhausting, time-consuming, headache-inducing even under perfect circumstances and one hundred percent necessary. A mage whose brain is not properly aligned with the work is a mage unable to work.

Laura is one of fifteen in Meditation 1 at Hatt Group that Monday morning, and has been sat down for barely two minutes when she has the revelation.

It's a bad thing for a mage to have revelations while meditating. This is not a religious pursuit, and the achievement of enlightenment is not the aim of the game. Unbidden, distracting thoughts are a sign of a wandering mind, which is the exact opposite of what's supposed to be happening. Laura does what she's supposed to do, suppressing the enormous and life-rerouting fact which has flared up in her forebrain, filing it away for later. She hurriedly starts her meditation cycle over, flattening her mental processes out again in the prescribed way. After another three minutes, an automated chime rings, signalling everybody in the room to move on to the second stage in the fifty-minute cycle. Laura imagines a magnifying glass, held to give perfect focus. She is back on track.

She isn't. There are too many dots connecting up.

There was no final spell.

There are fourteen other mages in the room, all men, of almost uniformly scattered ages between twenty and sixty-five. Laura's mind is reeling and she can't lock it down. She fights the instinct to bolt outside and find a white board and scrawl calculations. She needs to triple-check the Atlantis telemetry and, if at all possible, she needs to ingest something which'll warp her brain sufficiently to force herself through the damned dream again. But she can't move from her spot. It's eight oh five in the morning and everybody in the room has work to do. Everybody in the room *is working*. You don't break a mage's meditation. It's like sticking a tree branch through a bicycle's spokes.

Laura is off track. She's not going to be able to think about anything else. Above her head, she conceives the Atlantis orbiter, upside-down, its nose pointed directly at her forehead. Above the orbiter and its tank she imagines green numbers on a cosmic seven-segment display. Minutes and seconds and decimal places. The decimals are rolling up and up. Five seventeen point nine nine. Five eighteen point zero zero.

Laura believed that her incessantly repeating dream sequence cut out at the instant that the Atlantis External Tank exploded, five minutes and eighteen point nine seconds into the mission. She believed this because the mission timer was visible from her usual perspective in the seat of Mission Specialist Elaine Barry, and "00:00:05:18" was the last visible numerical readout before she woke up. She believed this despite always waking up without feeling the final explosion. She believed this despite never dreaming — or at least never remembering dreaming — the slightest foreshock of the vehicle's breakup.

But what if she was wrong?

What if she felt no foreshock because the dream ended a split second earlier? Eighteen point one, say.

So why would that happen?

Laura moves into hypothesis. By comparison with her regularly scheduled lucid session, this is a blobby child's watercolour, but coherent enough to link up the knowns. It would have happened incredibly quickly. When Rachel Ferno's shielding collapsed, she — along with Atlantis — was fifteen miles above the Atlantic Ocean and moving at Mach 1.41. Unprotected sudden exposure to moving air at such a speed was like being hit by a crowbar, and instantly fatal. Her body was blasted into the wake behind the vehicle's trio of shattered main engines, then pulled upward into the opaque stream of liquid oxygen and hydrogen pouring out into the vehicle's contrail. When the tank detonated, at T+5:18.9, she was atomised.

Rachel Ferno is dead. This is not part of any dream. This is a real thing which Laura now knows must have happened. These are knowns which Laura has known the whole time. The real, serious question is what took her so long to put the picture together.

There was no final spell. There wasn't supposed to be a final spell. She'd already done what she needed to do.

The dream doesn't end because of the explosion. It ends because Mum ran out of mana.

That was the plan.

The chime chimes for stage three. In stage three, Laura works out her next six months.

*

Edward Hatt's alarm clock drives him out of bed like a lightning bolt. He hits it within the space of one beep, fast enough that his wife doesn't even twitch. He's a ludicrous man, one of those individuals with the ability to live without obvious sleep, with more interest in getting to work and making things happen than in honest human things like staying in bed and hibernating until noon. Elapsed time until he's out of the house is in the ten-minute range. He'll shower and change once he's cycled to work and he'll have breakfast after a few hours of work, if he actually remembers to eat.

At this time of year his journey coincides with dawn. Even with gear, his fingers and ears are brittle with cold by the time he gets to the site. He's at work before there's anybody on reception. He eschews coffee. He gets the whole organisation to himself for a little while. He *enjoys this*.

Once in his office, Hatt has two hours, plus or minus, of relatively undisturbed silence. He has a substantial stack of files in his In tray and a substantial backlog of electronic mail. Minor distractions, signature jobs and one-off questions can wait until he has five minutes free between one meeting room and the next. He filters for what he calls the big fish: periodic production reports, financial performance analysis, short-

, medium- and long-term strategy, international news with a direct or indirect bearing on supply chains. He selects for everything with substance to it. He spends the two hours, plus or minus, processing data without a break.

The first shudder which passes through his office is mild enough that he doesn't consciously pick up on it. When his assistant arrives, just before nine, she knocks and enters and tells him (as she does every work day) that the canteen is open and that he should probably eat something. This fact, as it does most work days, registers as "small fish" and fails to connect. She then adds, "Did you feel that just now?"

Hatt doesn't look up. "Feel what?"

"A couple of minutes ago. I swear the whole place moved a little. I was coming up the stairs and they shook so hard I almost dropped my coffee."

"Probably equipment being moved down in the factory," says Hatt, barely caring. "An early delivery. I pray they didn't drop something expensive."

"It was a big one. I almost spilled my coffee," repeats his assistant, whose name is Sally.

"You can drop as much coffee as you like as long as you're paying for it."

"I will indeed as long as you're the one who pays the cleaners to clean it up."

Hatt gives her a look which says "I am no longer paying attention to this conversation" — this is, in fact, the first time he's looked up at all — and immediately resumes reading. Outside, the rising Sun is blasting mist off the scenery. The view from Hatt's office is the best in the building but still little better than "boring": mostly runway, surrounded by flat green fields and the occasional tree and canal. The greenery is turning brown over the course of October. The view is best at this time of day, with blue sky and red sky ruffling and blending out to the east. But in the years since he built and then moved into this office, Edward Hatt has never once bothered to watch the sunrise. He keeps the Venetian blinds closed. Mainly, that's because the sunlight reflects off his computer monitor into his eyes. But another reason is that he rather prefers the view he invented.

The building shakes again.

"Sally?"

Sally looks in.

"Phone Chris Wester and find out what's the hell's going on."

"I think he's on holiday."

"Well, phone the duty manufacturing floor manager's phone and ask whoever answers."

Time passes.

Sally leans through again, with a phone muffled against her shoulder, and says, "He says he just opened the shop up and it's nothing to do with what they're doing."

"Who is that?"

"Chris Wester."

Hatt does not care why it is that Sally thought, incorrectly, that Chris Wester was on holiday. "Chris," he shouts at Sally, "where's the noise coming from, relative to you?"

Sally goes to relay the question, but the man on the other end of the phone is already answering. "Underground," she reports.

"Fucking work it out, one of you?" Hatt pleads.

Sally goes back to the phone. "Yeah, I think he's just trying to work," she says. "Can you get someone to check the basement circles or something? Okay? And call me back. Great. Thanks."

Hatt closes the door. Sally goes back to her own work. Another few light tremors pass, at intervals of a few minutes each.

A little before nine, nobody has called Sally back. The Big One makes her entire desk jump and does indeed spill what's left of her coffee. Sally has barely reacted before Hatt emerges from his office at a furious stride. "Someone's pulling my company down," he says as he passes.

"You've got your first thing in fifteen minutes," Sally says.

Hatt hears her, but doesn't acknowledge her. He already knows, and is inclined to skip it. Bigger fish.

*

The most prominent feature of Hatt Group, when viewed from above, is the runway. The second most prominent is the manufacturing floor, which is bigger than the rest of the site's buildings combined, and large enough to have nominal buildings of its own inside it. After that, in descending order of size, are the car parks, office blocks and loading bays. Then come the circles.

"Circle" is the least precise name. Different elements of the magical engineering community, depending on regional preference and source textbook, refer to them as pitches, gyms, circles, grids and mandalas. They are flat concrete expanses with dense, multicoloured geometric outlines painted on the ground and robust weather-resistant components sunk into intersections between the lines. Sometimes, instead of concrete, they are surfaced with asphalt or astroturf. Rarely, as long as it's flattened and manicured to the level of a professional cricket pitch, actual grass is used. The line patterns guide the placement of magical and mechanical equipment for the purposes of spells, enchantment operations, hardware tests, maintenance and, weather permitting, sports.

The answer to any question about magic is almost always "it depends" and the reasoning behind the geometry of a magic circle is no exception. The very earliest circles resembled traditional Hindu Rangoli patterns and were laid down in India in the Seventies and early Eighties, long before numbers had been crunched and the actual necessary dimensional symmetries had been derived. Some of those, including the first one ever built by the Vidyasagar enclave, are still maintained, for historical and aesthetic value and occasional special demonstrations. But actual science got in the way of free-floating experimentation and creative freedom. Not much time passed before most of the interesting questions about pattern effectiveness were resolved to enough decimal places to end the discussion. New circles — those used for real-world magic with any kind of serious purpose — now invariably conform to the standards specified in ISO 31300, the "flower book", whose latest version lists eight basic designs of increasing scale and a hundred and five specialist variants. The designs, made entirely from circular arcs and straight lines, are dense, heavily interconnected and heavily annotated. Installation precision is a significant factor.

Between Hatt Group buildings there are three C-class circles. Laid along the middle of the runway, big enough to test a rocket engine, is a full-sized, rarely-used A-2X. Inside the manufacturing floor are more circles, some of which are routinely blocked by machinery or stock, and therefore unusable. And there are three underground.

The Hatt Group basement is rarely seen by customers and has a distinct "backstage" atmosphere to it. Fewer of the walls are painted, more of the pipe work is exposed. The fluorescent lighting is brighter to make up for the lack of natural light. Meditation 1 and Meditation 2 are down here. So are rooms D10A, D11A and D12A: private D-class circles. It's the third of these which Chris Wester and the site's security manager Adrian Middleton can't get into.

"Of course you can't get in," says Hatt when he arrives behind them. "I'm the only one who has access."

"Try it," suggests Middleton. He has a laptop computer plugged into the D12A electronic locking mechanism.

Hatt pulls his ID card from his belt and waves it at the contactless reader. The three of them are rewarded with a red light and an irritable bleep.

"You're already in there," Wester explains. "Adrian pulled up the logs a few minutes ago. You went in there late last night, there's been no activity since."

"I didn't," says Hatt.

"The system thinks you did," says Wester.

"Somebody stole your card," says Middleton, working on the laptop.

"This is my card," says Hatt.

"Nope," says Middleton. He turns his screen around, showing them both the last line in the log, the failed entry attempt from fifteen seconds ago.

Wester groans.

Hatt says, "Fucking adds up."

"She's a known problem?" Middleton asks.

"She's fired," says Hatt. A moment's examination of the ID card in his hand reveals that there is sticker laid over its front face, trimmed to size and displaying his name and photograph. He would have noticed the alteration if he'd paid the slightest attention. But he doesn't pay the slightest attention to unimportant things as long as they work. He doesn't notice the card and most of the time he doesn't need the card. It's part of the wallpaper of his life, like his contact lenses and shoelaces and the rhenium *kara* he wears on one wrist.

"She switched them," Middleton surmises. "It was too difficult to make a fake one, so she dolled up hers and gave it to you. When was the last time you used access permissions which she wouldn't have?"

Hatt shakes his head. He doesn't remember.

"Then she could have had it for days without you knowing," Middleton says.

Another rumble shakes the floor. The epicentre is definitely inside D12A, and it's a rumble, not a shiver, not a shudder.

"What's in there, anyway?" Wester asks.

"A magic circle," Middleton says. "Says it right there on the door."

"I know that," says Wester. "But what makes it special? Why can only Ed get into it? What else is in there?"

"Can you get this open?" Hatt asks the security manager, ignoring Wester.

"Can you prove you're Ed Hatt?" Middleton asks.

"I'm Ed Hatt, Adrian. Look at me."

Adrian Middleton says, "If somebody other than you used that tactic to try to convince me that they were them, and it worked, you'd sack me too. I don't care if this is a test or not."

Hatt glares at him. "I own everything within eyeshot of here, including you."

"Prove it," says Middleton, meeting Hatt's glare with a glare of his own which says, *This is what you pay me for.*

Hatt breaks. Middleton is right. "Alright. What do you need?"

Middleton crouches and brings up an application on his computer. "You can come with me to use the fingerprint machine in the security room behind reception. Or you can remember the password you gave me the day we set the system up." He shows Hatt the laptop screen. There's a password field.

"We should have gone two-factor," Hatt mutters as he takes the laptop and types a very long phrase.

"Agreed. I'll set something up once this is over," says Middleton.

The door clicks.

Wester pulls it open.

*

Picture a high, dark room. Only a quarter of the lights are on.

The only person Hatt will allow in is Hatt. He makes it clear to the other two that the fumbling with key cards and the illicit access don't change that policy. He enters alone, closing the door behind him and descending a short flight of stairs to the lowered floor.

A D-class circle is thirteen metres in diameter, mainly hexagonal, with an E-class circle nested at its centre and symmetrical embellishments spreading to what is conventionally called the "north". Laura Ferno is standing at the south pole of the figure, her staff held out in front of her oriented from west to east, at head height. Magical artifacts ranging in size from a two-metre-tall Chandra brancher to pea-sized driver dots are placed at points around the circle. In front of her and to one side, playing no magical part in the proceedings, is a music stand with a few sheets of written notes. Dangling by a lanyard from one corner of the stand is an ID card with Laura's name and photo on it.

```
"Ar'un ar'ath il chuthi tra anh ha
 al   luia  kun kuan   phal lif lithua
```

ar'lath dulaku. Pan sulat'th chath esseli TSUAA TSUAA."

The room is uncomfortably hot, even with the air conditioning pulling its weight. It is quiet aside from Laura's voice. A non-mage would be forgiven for thinking that nothing is happening. The room contains an almost entirely magical machine under construction, but the flux connecting the components together is invisible and inaudible.

Hatt's not a full-time mage and it only takes a week or two of inactivity to lose one's edge, so the spell he uses to activate his monocle-sized pocket oracle is too simple to show significant detail or colour-coding. Holding it to his right eye, he sees mana flowing around the circle like iron filings following exotic magnetic flux lines. Most of the flux is at ankle level, but where it reaches the brancher at the eastern corner, the lines arc upwards and spread out across the ceiling. Some of the arcs descend again into other components, very much like electricity into dodgem car motors. The rest are being collated into yantras: mid-level dynamic spell components built from luminous mana. There are seven or eight of them gently orbiting in the ceiling, of which two or three are incomplete. While Hatt watches, Laura binds two of the stacks together, annealing their exposed interfaces and binding a word to the combination.

There's a thin flux line running up one wall and across the ceiling. And suspended over the centre of the entire assembly, bathing the room in high-energy mana, is a point of light too bright for Hatt to look at.

Laura is casting a very intensive, very complex, almost purely magical spell. From the volume of completed work visible, Hatt estimates that she has been speaking for seven to nine hours.

Laura should have seen him out of the corner of her eye by now, but she hasn't reacted to his presence. Hatt goes to the panel on the wall nearest the door, alongside the fire extinguishers, and takes a Montauk ring down from its hooks. He takes a step towards Laura and stops because the room has suddenly changed.

There's glass underfoot now. The walls and ceiling have become black glass as well, hexagonally tiled. The room has tripled in all of its dimensions. The air has dropped sharply in temperature. The magic circle, once flat underfoot, is rippling like a sea. There's a faint hiss of magic being spent. Laura's in the same position, holding her staff out horizontally, but her music stand is gone. And above her, barely visible outside of chance refractions of light, is a ghost. It is a human figure, upside-down and curled into a strange half-crouch. It is hanging on to one end of Laura's staff with one hand. The ghost is almost colourless and almost translucent, but blobs of colour are blooming inside it like paint dripping into water.

Edward Hatt considers his options. He turns and looks at the door, now a long way behind him. He looks back at Laura Ferno. And he takes a step away from her, back towards the door.

Now he's broken it. The walls and ceiling are gone entirely and it's even colder than it was before. The mountainous glass landscape of Kazuya Tanako's world spreads in every direction, starting with a deep vertical drop just a step in front of him, forcing him to stop walking. The door has receded a full kilometre, to the top of the next mountain. All Hatt can see of it now is the small neon green "EXIT" sign glowing above it.

When he turns back to face Laura, the magic circle is gone. Ahead of them both is a black mountain, a genuine two-trillion-tonne Everest of glass thrusting upwards out of the world's crust and all the way into the Death Zone, if Tanako's world has such a thing. Laura still holds her staff, but is now using it as a walking stick. She is carrying a woman over her shoulders in a fireman's carry, bent under her weight. The path ahead of Laura, winding along the side of the mountain and up a ridge to its peak, is almost vertical, and kilometres long.

Hatt doesn't want to move again for fear of changing the scenario for something worse. "Laura," he calls out.

Laura turns and regards him for a long moment. Hatt doesn't recognise the face of the woman she is carrying.

"Will you help me?" Laura asks him.

"Who is that?"

"My mother."

"...I thought you said your mother was dead."

"Nobody is dead," says Laura, "as long as we remember them."

"The way out is over here. You need to come back with me."

"No," says Laura. "It isn't. Look again. The way out is on the other side of this mountain."

"There isn't enough mana in the world to get you over that mountain," says Hatt.

Laura says nothing. Hatt wonders how close to awake she is, and whether he's even conversing with a conscious person at this level. Somewhere on one of these planes, Laura Ferno's mind is running flat out, building her answer. But the mountaineering metaphor's too simple, with too simple an answer. Just endurance and strength.

Hatt adds, "And you're taking my building apart."

"Will you help me?" Laura asks him.

"No."

Laura says nothing for another long moment, expressionless. Then she turns and continues walking.

Hatt reaches a conclusion. He clutches the Montauk ring and runs for Laura, through shells of metaphor. Gravity upends and the environment reconfigures over him like a tactile hologram. He ignores them and concentrates on putting one foot in front of the other. A safe, being cracked from the inside. A leashed bird of prey, picking frustratedly away at the knot of leather straps tied around its feet. A living dream as big as a continent, trying to end itself. The final dream, when Hatt reaches Ferno, is smaller than all the rest and so cold on Hatt's skin that it feels like being bitten. Laura's mother is lying on the floor now, and Laura stands over her, guarding her with her staff held in a defensive position, bojutsu style. All three of them are at the end of a low, cramped, dimly-lit steel room. A shipping container?

Laura isn't guarding her mother from Hatt. Her attention is fixed on something behind him. Hatt looks. It is an emaciated, stinking, vertically elongated human, with one too many faces and wearing nothing but thick layers of blood. Its eye sockets have no eyeballs. Its fingers are too long. It gawps, showing teeth like scalpels, and smashes Hatt in the jaw, hard enough to hurl him over Laura and Rachel, back against the far wall of the container. The steel is thick enough that there's more of a *bonk* than a *clang*. Hatt's dropped Montauk ring clatters and spins to a stop on the floor next to his head.

It's at this point that Hatt realises that the ring was warm. The rest of his skin is frozen, almost to the point of cracking as he moves, and the walls are like dry, sticky ice, but his right hand, in which he was holding the ring, is still lukewarm. This is because inside the ring, none of this is happening.

Laura attacks the monster, smashing it in the head twice, hard enough to shatter its skull on the first blow and scatter kidney-like organs across the floor on the second. Headless, it still tries to thrash its way towards Rachel Ferno, until Laura lands on top of the thing's torso and snaps its arms using her staff and the principles of leverage. She breaks its chest open.

Hatt struggles upright, his nose and fractured humerus healing rapidly. From his perspective, the observable universe amounts to just a few hundred cubic feet. Beyond the tiny red circle of light, there's steel in every direction except one. In that last direction, the other half of the container is thick darkness, out of which two more identical blood-things are already striding. Laura launches into them, but even as she does, a third appears behind them. Hatt can't see the far end of the container. There might not be one. There might be infinitely many more blood-things lined up in the dark. It's unwinnable. It is the darkest, inescapable corner of the nightmare.

Hatt realises that Rachel Ferno's eyes are open. She's staring at him.

"Magic doesn't work here!" Laura cries, not looking back. She wants Hatt to help out, engaging the monsters physically. The nightmare is already so crowded with burst carcasses that it's hard for her to manoeuvre without slipping over. Her staff is too long: its far end clanks against the wall or ceiling. She tries to unscrew a piece of it to make it shorter, but she can't do it and fight at the same time. Another two waves and they'll both be dead for real. "Ed, help me! I'm trying to save her life!"

Hatt rubs the *kara* on his wrist. He flips his Montauk ring up with one toe and catches it. He takes a step forward over Ferno's mother's body, and drops the ring smartly over Laura's head. And he takes his True Name back.

```
"Eilo fib thalath dulaku. STOP."
```

Laura fights him. She pushes Hatt away with a well-practiced flick of the bo, which Hatt simply rolls with, allowing himself to be thrown, sprawling. Laura pulls the ring back over her head, but it's too late. Tanako's nested world has completely switched off. Mana flux has stopped. The abstract yantras in the ceiling crumble and dissolve. The room is back.

Flat on his back, Hatt stares up at the distributor lodged in the ceiling, now disabled and spinning down like the rest of the equipment in the room. "Are you done?" he asks aloud, and looks between his toes at Laura.

Laura is bright red with anger and frustration. She breaks her staff into two pieces and holds them in one hand while gathering her paperwork from the music stand. She takes the mislabelled ID card and throws it at Hatt's chest. "This is yours."

*

No spell is clean. The amount of thaumic energy — mana — put into a spell is never the amount of useful work done by the spell. There is waste heat. And there is waste mana.

High-energy spells have been cast by mages on the Hatt Group site for more than a decade. The total amount of waste mana produced amounts to hundreds of gigajoules. The waste mana is undetectable. Theory and simple arithmetic show that it must exist, and that it must obey the same laws as all other mana, but it is mageless. It is, therefore, useless.

Installed below D12A, sealed in cement because there was no reason not to, is a bilge: a battery of two-metre Montauk rings. Montauk rings drain free mana out of the environment. Hatt had no way to prove that the battery was collecting anything, let alone to retrieve the collected mana in a usable, mage-owned form. But he lived in quiet scientific hope. He started his stockpile in preparation for a possible future in which it would be worth something. His private reserve.

Laura Ferno broke into it and drained ninety percent of it using a mind-breakingly convoluted True Name aliasing technique which only she, her sister and her mother knew was possible.

That wasn't even the hardest part.

*

Adrian Middleton's opinion is that Ferno should be removed from the site immediately, and everything else worked out later. Hatt overrules him. He dismisses Wester and brings Middleton and Ferno to his office. Middleton stands in the corner, observing.

Laura sits upright in the middle, with her knees together. Defensive body language. No ID pass.

Hatt starts with: "You have the bizarre dreams."

"...Yes."

"Like many mages, you end up in Tanako's world quite often. You know how to go there and come back."

"Yes."

"You see things there."

"Yes."

"Often, you see your late mother."

"Yes."

"Today, you were trying to bring her back from the dream. You were trying to bring her back to life."

Laura says, "Kazuya Tanako's world is real."

"It's not," says Hatt.

"No. No. It's not a dream. It's not a shared dream. It's not a common dream state that mages share. It's a *place* where we can *go*. It's *real*. It behaves like another universe. If you put enough magic in one place, you can go there. My mum's there. The last thing she did before she died was to burn enough mana to burn those final events into the... the glass recording. It worked like a signal flare. It was a recovery beacon intended for me in the future. And if you put enough magic in one place, you can bring things back."

Hatt says, "All of that is groundless, if well-worded, metaphor."

"You showed it to me! You showed me that you can bring things back from Tanako's world—"

Hatt produces the forged boarding pass.

It's the same one. He produces it from thin air, without one word of magic. "It was sleight of hand. I was bamboozling you with unbelievable scenes to get you on my side. I don't pull the trick for everybody, but I did it for you. Watch my fingers. One... two. One, two. Do you see?"

Laura can't speak. Hatt hands the boarding pass to her, then opens a drawer and, from a thick pile of miscellaneous paperwork, retrieves a flat sheet of twenty more identical passes. They're just the same, waiting to be sliced up.

He continues, "You can't bring physical objects back from a dream. You can't walk home from a dream."

Staring at the boarding pass, Laura says, "But you can. I've done it."

Embarrassed, for lack of anywhere else to look, Ed Hatt pulls the blinds open and looks out of his window.

There's nothing he deems worth looking at. The sunny weather earlier that morning was a false start. Fat grey rainclouds are now moving in from every significant direction. It's shaping up to be a really miserable day. He closes his eyes momentarily, imagining his preferred panorama. "You know a great deal which nobody else in the company knows," he says. "Including a lot which, possibly, nobody else in the world knows. Like how you got the bilge mana to actually work for you. I'd love to know how you did that."

Laura says nothing.

"But you're also a security risk. And you're not doing the same job as the rest of us. We're working on magic-based spaceflight. You're working on something totally other. So—"

"My mother can tell us—"

"*So* we'll just have to crack the bilge mana problem ourselves. And the other problems. Because it's not worth it."

"I can still do this," says Laura. "I know what I need to do now. I need the Ra codes."

"What do you know about Ra?" Hatt asks.

He immediately realises his mistake. He's given something away by not measuring his words properly. Laura spots the completely new expression that momentarily crosses Hatt's face before he can control himself. Was it alarm? For an instant, Laura considers the possibility that Ra is a deep secret of Hatt's, which she's not supposed to know anything about.

No, it was amazement. Ra is a mystery which Hatt's been pursuing for some time. Just like she has.

Laura says, carefully, "What do you need to know about Ra?"

Hatt replies, "I need to know what you know."

A pause. Laura says, "Am I fired?"

"You were fired twenty minutes ago."

"That doesn't answer my question. Am I fired right now?"

Hatt glances at Adrian Middleton, who, in the corner of Laura's eye, shrugs. "You know my position," he says.

Hatt chews for a moment. Eventually, he gives Middleton a reluctant, curt nod.

Middleton opens the office door, and holds it for Laura to go through first.

She leaves, working out the rest as she goes.

12
Daemons

Nick Laughon teaches now. He's brand new at it, only a month into the job and still full of momentum. It's the first job he's had which uses any meaningful fraction of his energy each day. It's the first time he's ever gone to bed tired without serious exercise. It also means that he gets home earlier than most. Today, Laura is waiting for him.

"Hello," he says, stacking a crate of unmarked red exercise books in the flat's nominal hallway and dumping a weighty rucksack on top of them. Laura's sitting in the living room, positioned to face the door directly. Between them on the coffee table is a glass filled with a colourless, effervescent liquid which Nick assumes to be gin and tonic. Basic signals given off by Laura suggest a relatively high gin-to-tonic ratio. The drink, however, is full. Laura sits behind it, not drinking it. Deliberately and purposefully not getting drunk. She is deeply unhappy.

Nick last saw Laura more than twenty-four hours ago. Work has demanded that she stay ungodly late before, more than once, but for Nick to receive no phone call and for Nick to wake up still alone the following morning is unprecedented.

"What happened to you?" he asks.

"I lost my job," Laura explains.

"What? How?"

Laura doesn't move. "I stole the CEO's key card. I broke into a secure room in the site's basement. I broke into a secret mana accumulator which Ed Hatt had set up more than fifteen years ago and I stole something in the area of sixty megawatt-hours of mana from it. And then I burnt it all on a boondoggle. Ed Hatt caught me and shut the spell down. He fired me on the spot."

Nick opens his mouth, but can barely vocalise. He is stunned. He rubs his temples. "Why? I— Why did you do that?"

"I had a spell that I needed to try. This is— you know this has happened before. I have to *try* things. I can't let an idea fester. I have great difficulty... sleeping on things."

"I know all of that, Laura. I know who you are. What was the spell?" Nick asks.

"I can't even say it," Laura says. "It sounds so stupid to say it out loud. It sounds so *stupid* to say what I'm trying to do *before* I've achieved anything! Do you know what I'm talking about? At the very beginning, when magic was first discovered, the people who first discovered magic had the same nightmares. I've got to be able to prove it before I announce it and I've got to *do* it before I can prove it. If I'd succeeded, if I had enough *power*, then nobody would be laughing and— and it would have changed everything. Literally everything. But I need more power, and I feel like my head's coming unscrewed, like I'm trying to open a safe using a blowtorch that's inside it. *She* has all the answers, but I need all the answers before I can talk to her."

"This is about your mother," Nick realises.

"When I first met Ed Hatt, he showed me a piece of sleight-of-hand." Laura holds out the fake boarding pass and tries to do Hatt's finger trick, but she doesn't have the dexterity and she drops it. "And I knew, I *knew* he wouldn't be wasting my time with something like that unless he was serious. He wasn't hazing me, he isn't that person. I thought he'd worked out how to pull a small amount of mass back into his hand from the Tanako construct. The only problem is that a human weighs a hundred thousand times this much. The mass-energy problem is that much harder. So I thought he'd be amazed that I got it to work on a macro scale. You know, like that story where a lecturer puts an unsolved maths problem on the blackboard and some prodigy at the back of the room comes back the next week having solved it? I had this whole fantasy scenario worked out. I think I'm losing my mind."

Nick doesn't immediately tell Laura that she's not losing her mind. He observes her from a distance. She's staring unfocused at her untouched drink, fiddling obsessively with the boarding pass, folding and folding it. The material it's made of is closer to linen than paper, designed for wear and to resist tearing. It won't hold a crease.

"I need the Ra codes," Laura says. "I need to find Benjamin Clarke again and— and smash his brain open and see what's inside."

"You need to get another job," Nick suggests.

"I don't want another job," Laura says. "I want *that* job."

"Well, maybe you should have got my opinion before *going out and losing it*! We're on the *same side*, Laura! You should have called me! I tried to call you."

"I was underground."

"You were *scared*. You were scared to tell me what you were trying to do. Well, guess what, I know what you were trying to do. Because I know who you are and where you're from. And believe it or not, I don't think it's a stupid idea on its face. I just think you picked a monolithically bad, premature way to execute it."

"Don't you think I'm angry enough at myself already?"

"No," says Nick, levelly.

He picks up the G&T and escorts it back into the kitchen. "You and your gaggle of girlfriends had a saying at university," he tells her. "'Drink through it'. Breakups, hangovers, finals. I have never encountered a shorter, worse, more densely *bad* piece of advice." Next he goes into their bedroom for a moment. He returns with four running shoes. "You did the right thing by waiting for me. Probably the first right thing you've done in the last twenty-four hours. I subscribe, as you know, to a different mantra. So we're going to run."

*

The route to the top of St. Nicholas' Hill — which most refer to as "Nick's Hill" and Nick refers to as "My Hill" — is two miles horizontally and about that far vertically. Laura reaches the top hoarse, wobbly and in a substantial amount of pain. Nick is in infuriatingly good shape and has essentially taken it at a brisk walk. The nominal park at the top is deserted. The view of the city is impressively lofty. The Sun's dropping fast, but Nick's accurate Knowledge of local running routes and timings predicts that they'll be home long before dark, even if he has to carry her.

Laura staggers over to Nick and leans the top of her head against his chest. "One-word answers," she pants.

"Feel better?" asks Nick.

"Noooooo," says Laura, but she does. She recalls being one percent of the way up the first foothill of a figurative peak as tall and black as Doom. It feels good to be at the top of a literal one. No magical jewellery, no bangles. She sometimes forgets how heavy the equipment is.

As for Nick, he has run through all of his anger. He asks, "Are they going to press charges?"

"No."

"Well, that's something."

"Yes."

"...You're going to find another job."

"Yes."

"Frankly, though, you could use the break."

Laura shrugs. "Probably."

"And we'll have to do some financial acrobatics in the meantime."

"Yes."

Nick stares at the horizon and the setting Sun for a long moment. "...What is Ra?"

Laura can't answer that in one word.

*

Applied Magic is a vocational qualification. It was a safe assumption that Benjamin Clarke would go professional mage after graduation. In his first free year, he maintained thaumochemical processes at a gas terminal in south Wales, but before long he had developed severe restlessness and an itch to travel. With the parent company's blessing, he switched tracks and took a job as magical engineer on the monumental liquefied natural gas carrier *TTN Plesio*, where he's been ever since. Benj is still way down the hierarchy of the ship's startlingly small crew, and will be for years to come, but he rates the job highly. The working environment is intense, the working day is long, the world is huge, the engineering is challenging and the magic is real in a way which lab study never really drove home for him. He's doing heavyweight spells on a routine ten times as demanding as his training. He's also losing a surprising amount of weight.

Laura learns all of this in bits through friends of friends. She and Benj haven't met or spoken since university and Benj is at sea three months out of every six. It takes her more than a week to raise him on the phone. And he doesn't want to talk about what happened.

Laura insists, again, that he must have something for her.

Benj says, again, "I remember nothing. I have always remembered nothing."

"But you remember the time between the first accident and the second one."

"From the beginning, then," says Benj. "What I have always said: I built the conical force field. I built the oscillation spells to drive it. They were clunky and impractical toys, done to win marks, not to serve a purpose. They didn't *work*. I never found a way to store and play back modulated sound. You made that up. I never developed a self-casting spell. You made that up."

"I didn't make it up, Benj, I saw it happen—"

"You'd need a literally infinite mind. At the instant that you cast the spell, you'd need to have total comprehension of the entire spell and of your own brain doing the casting, which is obviously impossible."

"It's not impossible, Benj, that's what the word quine means—"

"*It never happened. I remember nothing of what happened on the mountain. I remember nothing of what you did to me.*"

"I never did anything to you!" Laura protests.

"Then why are you calling me?"

Laura hesitates for a split second. She's just inhaling to respond when Benj continues:

"This is over. I have a life, you should get one. Reverse-engineer my spells if you need them. You were supposed to be the best mage in the world."

"I told you—"

"Yeah, you told me you couldn't do it. You told me that a bunch of times, like it was supposed to be a compliment. So, well done, I guess, on finally figuring out *when to stop.*"

Laura bites her lip, trying to somehow manufacture a sentence that will placate Benj, but she can't do it quickly enough.

He concludes, "Don't call me again."

*

Natalie Ferno spent her undergraduate studies strictly pacing herself. She made a point of getting one hundred percent of Pure Magic locked down before letting herself advance. She did this out of an arguably rational desire to miss nothing: no important principles, no critical little details. It felt like running on the spot. Now she's through her master's degree and into her PhD, and for the first time in her life she's found academic traction. She feels like a real person now. It was as if she spent four years hiding from being good. She carries herself differently, walking just a notch taller than before.

She meets Laura at the railway station and they immediately start walking into town. Laura is here to talk. She is visibly far less together than Nat is. She has spent the train ride with a book open in her lap, staring straight through it, turning no pages, thinking about completely different things. She apparently forgets the human tradition of "Hello" and instead greets her sister with:

"Waste mana is disowned. Or to put it another way it has an owner but the owner is the null owner. That makes it reclaimable using aliasing hacks that Mum taught us. But naturally occurring mana is different. Natural geological mana is owned by mage Ra. That makes it non-retargetable. The only possible expenditure of natural mana is by the mage with True Name Ra. The mage with True Name Ra is hypothetical. He or she or it does not *necessarily* have to exist. Everything I've said so far is factual."

Natalie raises an extremely sceptical eyebrow at this last assertion, but does not interrupt.

"Now here's what I think based on what I've seen. I think 'Ra' is a naturally occurring True Name. And I don't think that's completely outrageous. Names form a polydimensional phase space, and it's logical that there would be an origin to that space. An ideal point would form there, like a crystal. Or like a gas cloud collapsing under gravity until it starts to shine. I think that makes sense. Of course, this immediately brings us up against one of the Open Problems: how you steal mana owned by somebody else. Which leads me to the second thing I've discovered. I tried aliasing as Ra, obviously. Couldn't make it work. Fifty percent failure. I tried the obvious hacks and nothing worked. I tried the cleverer hacks that Mum taught us. Nothing worked. Which suggests that what's happening is exactly the same as what would happen if I ran into another mage Named Dulaku and tried to cast a spell: the spell taps into the other guy's mana reserves and fails because of the mismatch. In fact the probability seems to work out to exactly fifty percent failure with a very small margin of error which implies not only that there is a mage Named Ra right next to me whenever I try to cast a spell while aliased as Ra but also that this mage may or may not himself or herself or itself be naturally occurring, just like the Name Ra and just like the mana with that Name. This is a virtual or incarnate mage Named Ra who theoretically has access to around a hundred million times as much power as any living human. This is not inconsistent with the currently-fashionable theories of deep magic. So the major question remaining is: what is the nature of this mage? Who or what is he or she or it and how can I get him or her or it on my side other than by using infinitely convoluted, incomprehensible quine spells?"

"You're an idiot," Natalie says.

"What?"

"Nick told me everything. He was too polite to suggest that what you're trying to do is insane. He doesn't know enough about magic to pass judgement. I do. What you're trying to do is insane. Do you want to know what you're doing wrong?"

"Um—"

"You're not writing anything down."

"Um—"

"This is not a mystical adventure. You are not the protagonist. You're seeing and doing things which are having profound emotional effects on you. You're being irrational. You're not thinking things through, you're not working things out. You're going on mental arithmetic instead of paper arithmetic and you're going on gut instinct instead of worked, peer-reviewed results. *This is not good science.*"

"But I'm *right*."

"I don't care how right you think you are. I don't even care how right I think you are! I want to see a $\mathrm{L^AT_EX}$-typeset paper from you. You need to show your working, because there are demons at work in your working."

Laura seizes on the small, critical piece of information that Natalie has let slip. "Do you think I'm right?" she asks.

"I think you understand very well that it doesn't matter what I think."

"But do you?"

Natalie says nothing.

"You think I'm right."

"In the absence of firm data to support any of your wild nonsense, I have to fall on the side of the null hypothesis. This is the way it's supposed to work."

"But you have a suspicion." Laura pokes her sister. "*You* have some evidence."

"I don't have any evidence yet," says Natalie. "I have data. Until data supports a conclusion it isn't evidence, it's just data. And I don't have enough data."

"You've got to tell me," Laura says.

Natalie has thus far studiously avoided revealing the subject of her PhD studies to anybody outside of the university, including her sister and their father, and has kept the information constrained to an impressively small circle even within the Theoretical Magic department. In part, this is just another facet of Natalie's general tendency towards quietness, introversion and deliberate information hygiene: avoiding sharing for the sake of avoiding sharing, simply because released information can't be recaptured. In part, this is because a few years ago Laura was attacked by four men and almost killed. It's possible that Laura had been deliberately targeted. It's possible that Natalie was being deliberately targeted but that the men mistook Laura for Natalie. It's even possible that the men wanted to dissuade or suppress Natalie's apparently abstruse and useless theoretical magic work. The probability of all of those possibles being actuals is slender, but Natalie rates it high enough to be worth worrying about, even after several years in which both she and her sister have apparently been left alone.

In no part is this because of the nature of the work itself, which Natalie still sees almost no practical ground-level worth in.

"I'm working on space magic," she says.

Laura lights up. "Space magic!"

"Nothing like anything you've been doing," Natalie explains. "Theoretical astrophysics. I took the equations of magic and tried to calculate what happens under extreme conditions. By which I mean neutron star core extremes, electron degeneracy extremes. Conditions we couldn't duplicate using all the mana on Earth. What I found was that certain types of supernovae, one supernova in every three or four hundred supernovae, should also generate magic. Huge quantities of magic. Enough for the chi emissions to be visible from Earth. All you'd need is a suitable optical telescope and a suitable high-fidelity oracle to fit over the end."

"And?"

"Like I say, all we have is data right now. The whole astronomical community observes around a thousand supernovae per year, but that's across half a dozen different scanning projects. We've only configured two telescopes so far and they've only been collecting for seven months."

"Which gives you around a hundred and ninety-four data points," Laura guesses.

"Fewer."

"And no positives yet," Laura guesses.

"No. But that's what I'm saying. It's too early. Conclusions like this are conclusions which take time to draw. The data has to be allowed to mount up over time. And all the while I'm checking my working and other mages are checking the instrumentation and spellwork."

"Conclusions like what?"

"...Rash conclusions."

"Like... that magic doesn't happen in space," says Laura.

"Like I said: you need to slow down."

*

The following morning, Laura lunges for her alarm clock and silences it before it's had time to more than peep. Nick is lying on his side beside her, facing away from her. She stares at the back of his head for a minute, making sure he's undisturbed. She watches his shoulder rise and fall and runs calculations while trying to avoid being lulled back to sleep herself. Then, staying completely still otherwise, she reaches out with one hand and picks up a Montauk ring from her bedside table, where she left it after unwinding her full day's charge into it, last thing before bed. She also collects a second bangle-sized ring and a pair of finger rings, which she slips onto her right middle finger, all without looking or shifting position.

Nick doesn't stir. He breathes in and out.

Laura clenches the Montauk in her hand and puts it under her pillow under her head, where its light won't blind her or wake Nick. She fixes her gaze on him and listens for the swirling orientation change in her ears while she murmurs the words that need to be murmured, as softly as she can while enunciating clearly enough for the spell to catch. Under her pillow, a Dehlavi lightning machine instantiates.

She doesn't notice it but Nick wakes up a second before she finishes. But it's too late for him to do anything about what's about to happen.

The world rolls right ninety degrees and drenches both of them in coldness, as if their duvet were just ripped off.

Laura almost falls, but grabs at something as it passes. She is left clinging to a weather vane at the top of a pointy tower at the centre of her memory castle. The vane is sharp, metal and cold, it hurts her hand. It starts to bend, too. With care, she drops down the pointy roof to the narrow and very short circular path which runs around this uppermost turret's roof.

In the buildings below her, she can peel away the bricks and see stored memories arrayed in rooms and halls. They are laid out and visible like specimens in glass boxes, like satellite photographs of the past. There is the black, red-hot slice of mountain, and the fat white spaceplane, and the other locked-off doors and the glass person. There are systems under construction, works in progress. The saying is "Sleep on it"; these are thoughts on which she is sleeping. And overhead, the Dehlavi lightning galaxy spins disorientingly.

She hurries clockwise around the circular path, and immediately runs into someone coming the other way. It's Nick.

"I don't know what's happening," he says.

He genuinely doesn't. Laura has the Tanako dream weekly now; she'd miss it if it went away. It's not part of her psychosis, it's a routine component of her mundane life, like regular dreams and hair care and scrubbing the toilet. But she never takes magical equipment to bed. For one thing, there is the risk (however slim) of randomly vocalising some significant spell; for another, her equipment consists for the most part of uncomfortably cold, hard metal. A Tanako shift without any magic behind it is a paper-thin hologram illusion, with no energy to give it weight or significance. A Tanako shift without a power supply is just a confusing television show in a sleeping mage's head. And so, Nick has never been here before.

A shift with power, though, carries danger. Not just danger, but it can carry bystanders with it. And invariable consequences.

"I've done this before," Laura says, trying to sound confident.

"On purpose?" Nick asks, and it's the critical question. Laura dodges it, and backs up, making room between them.

Nick runs after her, worried. "Laura, what are you doing?"

Laura backs further away from him. The path around the tower parapet, formerly just a two-metre-wide circle, expands to make room for her to retreat around the corner. She turns and soon she is running flat out, out of eyeshot of Nick, who is still chasing her. At this point, Laura does the thing that she has been trying to do. And just like that, she catches up with Nick from behind. He is standing there, facing away from her. She turns him around to make sure of his identity.

"Laura?" he says.

Behind her, there are running footsteps. "*Laura!*" cries a distant, identical voice.

Laura smiles wryly but does not look back. The running footsteps behind her are getting no closer. In fact, they're fading. It's not as if her boyfriend is running in the wrong direction. It's just that she doesn't want to be found now. The space between them is lengthening faster than he can cover it physically, and he doesn't know the trick to skipping through the spaces.

Laura takes the arm of the facsimile man in front of her, and turns him back around to face away from her, mimicking reality. She says, "Here we go."

The world rolls left again and Laura neatly breaks her own line of concentration, bringing the spell to a perfect halt with no stall. She's lying behind Nick in bed still, magic rings inert again. Nick breathes in and out once more without stirring, but she can tell just by holding him that he's wide awake now. And he's smiling.

He says, "This was an extraordinarily bad idea." There is no disapproval. He merely seems to be making an amused observation.

"He'll be safe," says Laura. "Shunting bodies around I can't do yet, but shunting minds I've done three times now and I can do it a fourth time any time I like. Nick is safe. But I genuinely don't know if I can bring Mum back. And I can't take not knowing either way.

"I want a deeper form of magic. I want to surpass my mother by an order of magnitude. I want you to explain this *system*. Do you understand?"

"...Yes."

"Who are you?" she prompts.

"Ra," says Ra.

13
Abstract Weapon

Like an engineer deeply in tune with his machine, Exa feels the world's component error deep in his bones, fractionally before anything has literally gone wrong. The world runs according to rhythms and tidal patterns, networks of sine waves layered on top of one other. The perturbation is subtle enough to be missable by any baseline human, particularly one on the other side of the world from the malfunctioning, invading component. But it's as clear to Exa as a high-pitched sound system whine is to a child not yet old enough to start losing his or her hearing.

He lunges for his phone and crams it to his ear just as it turns completely bright red and gives off its ear-splitting bleep. It's the first alert since he got the new phone, and the "ringtone" is like being kicked in the head.

"Short horizon," says the duty controller. "We need you now."

"Yeah yeah yeah I'm on my way in," Exa says. He falls most of the way out of bed and grabs his discarded suit trousers. It's almost four o'clock in the morning.

The girlfriend rolls over. "Are you serious?"

She thinks he's a sysadmin. It's one of those broad truths, just close enough to the actuality that it doesn't gradually erode his conscience every time he lies to her.

"They don't call me for the little ones," says Exa, pulling yesterday's crumpled shirt on and casting around briefly for his jacket. It's in the kitchen, he remembers. "This isn't happening, you're not awake, forget this."

She thinks this is a good plan and rolls back, wrapping herself over with the extra square metre of duvet that Exa just freed up. Exa slams the bedroom door. She winces, but that's it. No more noise.

Exa has already left the overworld.

*

Back when they won, and there was enough raw magic saturating the world for it to be a safer plan to burn it off on something wasteful and elaborate than to archive it for future generations, the Floor was built as a physical space. It is a hemispheroidal megastructure cavity in the world, tall enough to base-jump in, long enough for a drag race. Behind everything, the walls are black steel, but in front of the black steel and the HVAC control layer they are coated in person-sized hexagonal tiles with display technology wired in. On off-days they shift through modulated designs just colourful enough to be non-boring and just slow-moving enough to be non-distracting. On on-days they are a medium-sized god's own virtual reality C.A.V.E., somewhere in the ballpark of a ten-million-P picture format.

The cave floor is taken up almost entirely by a magic circle, a lengthened ℵ**-class technically big enough to host spells cast by more than five thousand mages simultaneously. No ISO standard in the world codifies the ℵ**-class specification, nor any pattern a tenth of its size. It's large enough to require a finely calculated deliberate warping, of just a few centimetres from one end of the circle to the other, to account for the curvature of the Earth underneath it. Bright red and green beacons mark important loci and enable the accurate guiding of energy from one side of the circle to the other. At its centre rear, where the bridge would be if the ℵ** were laid on an oil tanker's deck, is a king-sized A-2X-class, and at the centre of that is a conventional thirteen-metre D, one of more than two hundred hidden among the whole mandala.

There are six mages inside the D, along with a collection of eye-poppingly advanced portable computers plugged into outlets in the floor and some wheeled office chairs. Also "present" in the space is a host of virtual equipment, placed there by the system, written directly into the group's retinae when they look in the correct direction, a shared hallucination of yet more information. The total surface area of the room amounts to entire square kilometres, and the men who run the thing are using a millionth of the surface area available to them. It's as if they've built an invisible wall around the D, choosing to lock off the unnecessarily grand cave which they created so that they can live in a universe that doesn't dwarf them so intimidatingly.

At the very centre of the D lies an 8-centimetre rhenium ring. It was placed there flat, but now it *spangs* up to be perched, wobbling, on its edge. After its motion settles, three-dimensional patterns of bone and blood vessel start to knit together inside it. The pattern spreads away from the ring down four fingers and one thumb, cloaking the work in pale skin before reaching up and over a pair of pectoral muscles and drawing the rest of a human being. The body is male, bald, about 19 years old biologically and completely inert. Additional spells not housed in the magic ring lay Exa's dark linen suit over the top of his body. Once the full complement of organs is established, control is transferred to the body's own nervous system, all of the chemical locks shut off and Exa wakes up smartly. Exa's last frame of experience was his apartment kitchen, a subjective split second ago. This is their answer to teleportation, and the very fact that this was the transport channel of choice tells Exa how royally critical today's critical situation is.

Crisis elapsed time is thirty-five seconds.

Exa sits up, orients himself and addresses the man standing at what is figuratively the helm of the D circle. "A stupid question. Did I just drop dead in my kitchen?"

The man is named King. He is a hair less than forty, stubbly, unusually tall, dressed in a similar suit to Exa's, standing with a similarly informal demeanour. He has both hands in his pockets and his gaze is fixed on the picture on the far wall of the Floor. "Worse," he reports. "You're a spinning ring on the tiles."

"I assume that you know I'm not the only person who lives in the place which I live in?"

"She's asleep. You're covered. Eyes down, Exa."

Exa rubs his wrist under the ring. He finds this mode of transport deeply unnerving, not just because it's usually an emergency measure. It reminds him that King is able to freely rewrite the baselines on both this *kara* and the one now resting on Exa's kitchen floor. Into anything: Exa's own body, an empty space, anything.

Exa gets up and follows King's gaze. On the far wall, pictured a few hundred metres tall, is a lanky late-teenaged African boy. He wears loose trousers and a long-sleeved shirt with rolled sleeves, which was probably pure cyan in a former life. It's mid-morning local time and he's walking away from the room's point of view down a two-lane asphalted highway, a relatively newly-laid road, one of the best in his country. Ahead of him, the road dips and then rises before turning out of sight. The country is vividly green. Hills, trees and bushes make it difficult to tell where the road goes next. There are no visible buildings or vehicles or other people. The boy is walking down the middle of the yellow line. His left hand is rubbing his neck and left shoulder, maybe scratching a bite. From his right hand dangles a magic sword.

The thing is a metre and a half long. It's thick and dull and a little bent, basically a sharpened wrought-iron bar. It seems to be a single solid chunk of metal, blade and hilt both. It has no cross guard. The blade widens towards the end and is cut off flat, with no point. The hilt melts ergonomically into the boy's hand, like a videogame joystick. The boy drags it behind him, its tip scraping the asphalt. It's obviously far too heavy to be practical as a blade weapon, but it would make an excellent bludgeon.

"This is our fellow? This is the escalation problem?" Exa asks.

"Confirmed."

"What's he holding? I don't recognise it."

"Unknown."

Exa looks sharply at King, then at Flatt, one of the five other mages working in the circle. "Escalation elapsed time sixty seconds and we can't even tell what it is?"

Flatt is sitting cross-legged at the circle's northwest locus, a post nominally named "The Present". He's thirty-ish, with large glasses and long scraggly hair tied back. His attention is focused on a metre-wide virtual frame in front of him. He does not look up. "By a strict process of elimination based on the weapons known to have escaped erasure, been illicitly retrieved through exploits or washed up from space, the thing he's carrying doesn't exist," he says. "The world is clean. By all logic, what's happening isn't happening."

"You're a waste of mass-energy, Flatt," Exa tells him.

"You want to take my seat?" Flatt replies, evenly. Both of them know that Exa doesn't have the specialist training to sit where Flatt sits any more than Flatt has the nerve to take the emergency calls Exa takes. Flatt's role — "job" would not be the right word — is Situational Clairvoyance. He maintains the spells which run the Floor's Master Screen, which occur in two large stacks: one which remotely views the world, and the other which reproduces the video information so gathered with theoretically perfect fidelity. He is the one who is able to discover Facts about Things that are Happening. He is also Exa's field controller.

"So do I take it that it's been powered down this whole time?" Exa asks. "Did he pull it out of Hammerspace?"

"Negative identification," says Flatt.

"I remember that we cleared this world out. We won. Is a future coming in which we will, eventually, truly, have won?" Exa asks.

"You know none of us can answer that question, Exa," says King.

Exa grits his teeth. "But it is a weapon," he says. There are many other things that it could be. "And we don't know what kind of weapon."

"Confirmed," Flatt says.

"And I assume that he's used it?" Exa presses. "We wouldn't be getting the alert otherwise."

"Look behind you," Flatt suggests.

Exa turns. Some kilometres away down the road, in the opposite direction to that in which the boy is walking, a sizeable military installation is on fire. There's a pair of guard towers; one buckles and falls even while Exa watches. There's a huge amount of smoke; the screen is large enough to show the entire black cloud. The fire reaches one of the ammunition dumps, sending up a flash of light and a fireball. There's no audio.

"He did that with a *sword*?" Exa asks.

"Negative identification," Flatt says.

"I suppose you don't know who he is, either."

"Ask The Past," Flatt says.

The man at the first northeast locus is somewhere in his twenties, but carries himself like someone ten times that age. It's something in his bearing and the angle of his back. He goes by Scin, pronounced "sin", and leans for support on a magic staff taller than he is. Scin is a seer; his operational role is to look into the akashic records, the microsecond-by-microsecond logs of Literally Everything That Has Ever Happened. The role is brain-shredding, and bad for Scin's mental health. Simply staring at the static fuzz of the universe for an hour is enough to grind most into submission. Pulling usable information out of it is like tea-straining fog.

"...Negative identification," Scin echoes. His intonation is very different from Flatt's, and in fact different from his usual, too. Exa is too irritated to pick up on this.

"So we don't know what the story is? We don't know how he acquired the thing, who or where he got it from, who — if anybody — had it before him, what he's done, what he's doing, or what he intends to do next?"

Scin shakes his head.

"For God's sake, people, tell me we at least have a *country*."

"Rwanda," say three or four mages simultaneously.

There's a beat of silence.

"There's another problem, Exa," King adds. He gestures at the second northeast locus, The Future. This mage doesn't even look up to acknowledge King or Exa. He just shakes his head. King continues, "Without a high-definition reading of the present we can't put together high-definition analyses of the future."

"You don't have hypotheticals for me," Exa says, incredulously. This is close to unprecedented. No, worse: it *is* unprecedented. Even the hypothetical versions of himself whom they use when running the hypotheticals themselves are sent in with a forged Best Forward Course Of Action of some kind. No version of Exa, as far as Exa knows, has ever moved into the real world without perfect confidence in his approach.

"You're not going in blind," King says. "It just means we go in with low-definition analyses instead."

"'Low-definition'?"

"The boy has incoming," Flatt announces. He flips the master video feed down the road two kilometres, now tracking an open-topped off-road vehicle screaming out of the base, bound directly for the boy. One driver, three soldiers, one heavy gunner at the emplacement at the rear.

"So by 'low-definition', you mean that we're *guessing* based on the *video footage*," says Exa.

The master screen's perspective flips back to the boy. He looks around, although he can't have heard anything. He sees the vehicle in the distance, just as it disappears behind a slew of vegetation and starts climbing the far side of a hill. Another few seconds, and it'll come down the near side, at which point nothing will separate the boy and the vehicle but about a straight kilometre of clean, clear road.

The boy slings his sword around and up to eye level, sighting along it like a rifle. The blade lengthens to a full two metres and becomes a centimetre-wide cylinder, the extra mass rippling backwards along the barrel. The grip changes shape to accommodate the new position of the boy's hands, seamlessly extruding extra sections which turn it into something more like a rifle stock. It also sprouts a telescopic lens which latches onto the boy's eye, and an infrared laser sight. The boy sights on the top of the road, waiting for the vehicle to emerge.

The weapon is behaving proactively. Its handgrips grow around the boy's hands, turning into gloves and then gauntlets. It sprays out long, thin steel legs in six or seven different directions, wedging into the ground for stability. The telescopic lens expands across the boy's other eye and starts winding itself into his ears, a full-face combat mask with internal heads-up-display. But the most alarming development is the bank of capacitor cells growing out of the boy's shoulders and upper back.

"Beam weapon," say three mages at once, including Exa.

A big alarm bell is now ringing in Exa's head. *What kind of beam weapon disguises itself like that?*

"He's going to kill them," says Flatt.

"I still need a hypothetical," says Exa. "I can't go out there without a first move."

"Disarm him?" King suggests.

Exa only has time to shoot a bitter look back at him.

Flatt gives King a quick hand signal, thereby officially assuming operational control of Exa's movements. Flatt is now connected directly to Exa's auditory nerve: "I want the weapon intact and the boy too if you can manage it. Containment is go, you're getting a two-klick shield. Language support is go, your routine fight suite is go, heavy artillery is standing by for your call. Minimal casualty profile, minimal mana expenditure. We'll use holographic force projection until we can build a medical *kara* on the spot, so there'll be lag for the first four or five seconds. Stand by for perceptual discontinuity. Another one, I mean."

On the big screen, the boy's beam weapon is lighting up like a fluorescent tube. Exa blinks. When he opens his eyes again his skin is coated in hot Rwandan air and the boy is standing in front of him, the beam weapon at eye level, firing. Exa deflects the beam upwards with one hand, on instinct, as if batting away a fly.

*

A kilometre back, the truck hits the shield from the outside. The shield was placed off-centre; instead of crashing straight into a hard wall at a hundred kilometres per hour, the truck glances off to the right and spirals into a ditch. Exa gets this information relayed to him by Flatt, and doesn't feel the need to look back and check. The boy, also, loses his telescopic focus on the truck. Exa is standing right in front of him at one-fiftieth of the range, blocking his view. The boy backs up a step, drawing a bead on Exa's head instead.

Freshly loaded muscle memory squeezes the words Exa wants to say into the shape of colloquial Kinyarwanda. He feels like he's lost control of his tongue. It's like driving a car on a thin sheet of slush, the body of the vehicle not quite moving in the same direction as the wheels are pointing.

"Drop the weapon," he commands, while trying to maintain his routine cool in the absence of a firm plan.

The boy's age is somewhere from seventeen to nineteen, putting him in Exa's own apparent age group. Chronologically, Exa's body doesn't have an age because it isn't even fully constructed yet; he's an apparition of force fields, with a biological self being hurriedly assembled to replace them. Mentally, Exa is substantially older, with or without the error bars introduced by his frequent forking and merging of duplicate selves. In the real world he explains that "Exa" is the only contraction of "Alexander" not already claimed by someone else.

With the same hand he just used to deflect the white beam, Exa points his index and middle fingers back at the boy's head. "Drop the weapon," he repeats. "You cannot hurt me. I am beyond you."

There's a loaded, Wild West pause. Thousands of miles away, on the Floor, Exa's second healing ring switches modes from "maintain a healthy human" back to "maintain empty air" and dissolves Exa's now-abandoned body at the molecular level. The process takes just a second. The second ring hits the D with a *cling* and spins to a halt. Exa is now, by most reasonable definitions, in one place only: on the road in Rwanda.

"I can't tell you who I am," Exa says, in response to a question which he has not, in fact, been asked.

"I know who you are," the boy says, and kills him.

14
Death Surrounds This Machine

Exa comes back to life an instant before hitting the containment shield from the inside at ninety metres per second. It's not enough time to react. He breaks his neck, and dies again.

15
Zero Day

After the second resurrection, Exa's in free fall. This time he reacts quickly enough to yell a few magic words that crank his *kara* up to full power before impact. He lands in a field and bounces high enough to die a fourth time just from the bounce, but now his body is being rewritten from "damaged" to "optimal" on a nanosecond-by-nanosecond basis, making him effectively invincible. He lands on his feet after the second bounce, and looks up. The boy is way overhead and dropping hard, a fist raised and coming down. But that can't be it.

Exa calls out, "Show invisibles." Now he sees the orange force field wireframe with which the boy is clothed, a polygonal network making up a mechanical soldier figure easily fifty metres tall. That must be what hit him the first time. He was slapped into the middle distance by an invisible robotic fist. Looking closer, Exa sees that the sword/weapon is already harvesting and transmuting air molecules to build the machine in reality, starting with a seat and cockpit for the boy.

What weapon has all of this inside it?

The boy's motions are a metaphor informing the mechanoid's motions. The real fist that Exa needs to worry about is made of force fields and as big as a tank. With his medical ring running flat-out, Exa can soak up arbitrary amounts of punishment, but he doesn't feel like being sucker-punched again. He twists onto his shoulders and propels himself straight upwards, feet-first, punching a hole right through the fist and rising to head-height — which is to say, level with the boy's rapidly-condensing cockpit.

Exa's fight suite smoothes out the confusion of positions and angles for him. Data from his inner ear is simply discarded as useless. Upside-down and still rising, Exa turns and aims the first two fingers of each hand at his adversary. "Flurry."

Exa's go-to hand weapon isn't a gun, but the effect is similar. The spell opens a sharpened, rifled cylindrical force field out from the tip of his middle finger; an invisible four-millimetre drill-bit, punching through fresh air and solid matter alike at a few times the speed of sound. He lets loose thirty from each hand. When they hit the opposing shields of the cockpit, quantum-magical effects settle the decision as to which stands up and which collapses. With invisibles turned on, what Exa sees are yellow sparks where his drills are repelled without scratching their target. The boy's shields are stronger at the core, and strengthening by the second.

The mechanoid's other hand grabs for Exa and misses by a whisker. He's moving too fast. *Fine,* Exa thinks. *Let's go for sensory overload.* He produces a destructive charm of no particular marque and plants it on the half-mechanical wrist that is passing behind him, casually, like a sleight-of-hand artist hiding a card in a mark's pocket for future reference. Then he kicks off from the same wrist, directly towards the glass-fronted cockpit. On impact, he anchors himself, head to head with his opponent, whose face is now totally enclosed by a gas mask and gloss black flight helmet.

"Light." Exa turns brilliant white, like a portal into a star. That's enough to distract the boy pilot for a second. At the end of the second, just as the enemy weapon's filtering systems must be cutting in to deal with the visual load, Exa doubles his luminosity, blows up the mechanoid's hand and cuts loose with sonics. With its pilot overloaded with data, the mechanoid stumbles. Its armour wavers in strength, enough for Exa to get his fingers underneath the edge of the cockpit canopy. He uses both hands to wrench it off, exposing the pilot completely. The pilot is still blinded by the ridiculous light. Exa reaches in and rips the boy's helmet off too, then headbutts him.

The mechanoid falls to one knee. Its force shield presence shuts off, leaving behind only the real physical fragments that the weapon has had time to build: two-thirds of the cockpit/skull, and some basic spinal superstructure. All of this drops out of the sky like a stone, with Exa still anchored to the front of it.

*

The boy comes around panting, blinking huge spots away. The echo from the sonic attack is still fading, rebounding multiple times off the spherical containment spell. His eyes flick around. He is strapped into the cockpit still, but it's lying on its side in long grass. Exa is standing over him, with two fingers pointing directly into his forehead at point blank range.

"Yield," Exa says. He isn't even breathing heavily.

"No," the boy says.

"Yield control of the weapon or I will kill you," Exa says.

"No," the boy says.

The original order was to take the boy alive and the weapon intact. Exa has some operational independence, but despite everything he also has respect for Flatt's high-level perspective. Exa thinks he can resolve the situation very quickly by putting a hole in the boy's head. He waits for Flatt to tell him to do it, or else to confirm that he really does want this done the hard way.

And he waits. A full second elapses.

"Flatt?" he sub-vocalises.

Matte grey plates of armour snap shut over the boy's body and face. They are totally featureless; the colour is simply the first and least imaginative option that was available, exactly halfway between black and white. Exa's reflexive drill shot ricochets. The boy launches out of his seat. In his right hand is a black-painted Super Soaker with a hose connected to nothing. In his left is what looks like an industrial staple gun filled with coiled copper wire. They come up at Exa from opposite directions. The first weapon sprays pressurised orange napalm. The second releases an almost-solid stream of electromagnetically-accelerated razor blades.

Exa steps backwards, raising an arm to block the blizzard of unconventional projectiles. He blocks the napalm strike accurately; his suit sleeve catches fire, and won't go out for some minutes, but no matter. The flame and torn sleeve block his view of the other weapon's muzzle. The razors waft through the blind spot, tearing his suit and shirt sleeve further. The razors are small, two centimetres by one. They strike him accurately in the eyes, nose and teeth. Some become wedged. *What the hell?*

The boy — barely recognisable as a boy in the full-body armour, barely more than a perfectly grey Saturn-era videogame render, still rising at Exa — claps his two weapons together in front of him. They fuse with a metallic shriek, reverting to the original magic sword configuration, the heavyweight iron bar with the nominal sharp edge. Exa parries the first thrust with his flaming arm, pushes his opponent away, spits out two of the razor blades and retreats two more steps, trying to fish a third blade out of his nostril. The boy comes right back at him. The suit is clearly boosting him. He twirls the sword like a cheerleader's baton. No unassisted human has that kind of strength.

Exa is too far off-balance from this bizarre combination of attacks. He has lost the initiative. He drops into hand-to-hand mode for the next few steps, his mind with nothing but blank space where the strategic reasoning should go.

And *that*'s the clue.

Exa fights like a chess grandmaster playing eight moves per second. His opponent has taken him apart. This is something that does not occur.

"Flatt, I know what it is," he shouts.

The boy lunges again. Exa dodges again. Exa drives the fingers of one hand at the boy's throat at superhuman speed, a one-hit killing blow. The boy is not where Exa aims. He is down, pivoting on one heel so rapidly as to be rocket-propelled. The sword comes around and strikes the underside of Exa's chin, smashing him out of the park.

Exa leaves a flaming napalm trail in the sky. This time he doesn't rise high enough to hit the ceiling of the shield. The boy chases him on foot.

"We're under attack," Exa shouts.

"Say again?" Flatt responds.

"It's Abstract Weapon. *You're under attack. Give me the bomb!*"

Flatt sends back a non-verbal acknowledgement. Exa is seconds from impact. Below him, he can see the boy coming at him to intercept, crossing uneven orange earth and thick grass at the speed of an Olympic sprinter. Exa doesn't bother readying anything else. He hasn't won, but this catastrophe of an engagement is all of one point one seconds from ending in the most decisive possible draw.

The best part of a kilometre away, at the precise centre of the spherical shield, an eleven-metre-wide black neutron bomb *shrangs* into being. It arrives completely stationary in air, then drops a few centimetres with a *whump*. Exa catches its arrival in the corner of one eye. The boy is a single-minded grey bullet train, he doesn't look at all. One second.

The boy cannons into Exa shoulder-first as he lands, sending him pinwheeling. No exotic attack? No fistful of ninja stars? Still not having hit the ground, Exa wonders why.

Exa realises why. Exa is two tenths of a second too late to do anything about it.

Sleight-of-hand.

He took my medring.

BOOM.

*

It's like daylight on the Floor: the screen surrounding the remaining six mages is a complete whiteout. The thermonuclear explosion bounces off the energy shield multiple times per second, contracting and expanding again like some psychotic Cold War concept for an internal combustion engine. Other than the emitted light, the bomb's energy has nowhere to go. The absolute temperature of air inside the shield quadruples, incinerating everything that'll burn and liquefying everything that won't. Exa is instantaneously a whiff of ash. Abstract Weapon folds up and dies; it is an almost purely offensive tool and its physical and magical protective shielding, while formidable, are fundamentally second-class. As holes appear in his virtual armour, Exa's opponent, still unnamed, flash-fries. And the finely machined medical *kara*, which the boy has had just about enough time to fit onto his wrist, hits the ground as a scorched, warped paperweight. Then it falls through the ground, like a hot ball-bearing through butter.

King, Flatt and the others look on with dismayed resignation. "Minimal mana expenditure"? Cleaning the arena up is going to be brutally expensive. There's no salvaging the original. Too much radiation and heat. The entire interior of the shield will have to be dismantled and rebuilt from pattern.

Nobody in the room noticed the medring theft. It happened too fast.

On the Floor, Exa's discarded medical ring flips upright again. It's Flatt who first notices the activity. He assumes that it will be Exa, respawning at the most convenient location on the medring network.

Two seconds have elapsed and the supine figure is more than half-built when Flatt frowns, wondering why the secondary spells which usually build Exa's suit are instead building a washed-out bluish shirt with rolled sleeves.

At three seconds, Flatt sees the gun.

Flatt has no weapons. Nobody in the room is armed; Exa is their weapon and the Floor is almost totally inaccessible by conventional means. "Breach," he shouts. "Breach!"

At four the boy wakes up. He sits up. He's aiming at King. But King has already reacted.

Mushrooms sprout from below the boy's skin, all over his body. They sprout from below his fingernails and from his eye sockets and mouth and tongue. He drops the gun, which is a lump of green moss by the time it hits the ground. He falls back, managing one scream, then lies still. Technically, the thing that he has been turned into is still alive. It's just a plant instead of an animal.

There's a long beat of silence. Flatt looks at King, aghast. "You did that?"

King is controlling his own expression very carefully. "I overrode the ring. I told it to build something else."

"That's... horrible."

King won't meet Flatt's eye. "He was trying to kill us."

*

The post-mortem:

The first time around, Exa found Abstract Weapon in a deep, snow-filled crevasse in the polar Urals, eighty kilometres east of a minuscule, utterly unnoticed town called Polyatsk. As long as Weapon wasn't being held or used by somebody, the use of escalated magic was considered unjustifiable; it took him two weeks to get there, and two weeks to get home.

It was covered in snow. It was formatted as a standard Big Gun, a metre-long brick of chrome with an obvious Business End. Exa sat in the snow for a long hour, relaying detailed identifying information back to the Floor and, out of caution, not touching Weapon itself.

It was one of the very few machines in all human history to have a real, dedicated self-destruct protocol built into it. Exa only had to hold Weapon for a second to decommission it, which was two seconds longer than he wanted to spend.

"It trains you," he explains. He's back on the Floor, perched in an office chair, angry at having lost even a few seconds of memories, angry at everybody's collective incompetence and angry in principle. He sips shockingly costly liquor from a small glass. "Every second you spend holding it, it's throwing possibilities at you, telling you how best it can be used. It contains every weapon ever made. It contains every weapon never made. It is the primordial destructive spell. It is the prototype for all human violence. There is a List inside it, which... I cannot describe the List.

"And every second, it's throwing opportunities at you. It asks you what you want to do. 'Try me on this person, try me on that person, get revenge. Use me.' And if you ask it, it'll give you targets. If you ask it, 'Who did this?' it'll tell you. Yeah, it knows who we are. This boy is what, seventeen, eighteen? Boy wants revenge on the world. 'Revenge on the world?' says Abstract Weapon. 'Oh. The men you want are the Wheel Group.'"

"So what actually happened in the Urals?" Flatt asks.

"You mean, what did I do wrong? You tell me," Exa replies, irritably. "I can think of half a dozen things. Maybe we misidentified it that time. Maybe we misidentified it this time. Maybe I hit the wrong button, maybe it didn't want to be destroyed. Maybe I'm not remembering it right. Maybe I'm lying? Drag out the akashic records and let's stop playing games. Except you *can't*. That's the *point*."

"I see a purge in time," Scin reports. "A ragged-edged hole where the past should be. Every time I add Weapon to the query, I get flat nothing. I'm charting the edges of the hole. But that's all I can do."

"I'm going to concede that I must have done something wrong," says Exa. "I honestly don't remember what, and nor do any of you, and nor would Ashburne. But there's a reason why we can't find out why, and it's the same reason we can't find anything on this jackassed boy wannabe.

"You hear me, child?" he angrily adds, directing this at the boy's remains. "Corpse" would be the wrong word.

Exa sips and continues, "It contains every weapon ever made. Including magic weapons. He covered his tracks. He dropped some fizzing, spitting destructo-charm directly into the akashic records themselves. He selectively scrambled history. That's why we can't find out what happened to Weapon between then and now. That's why we can't find out when this addled child got hold of Weapon, or why he did any of this. All we can do, thank you, Scin, is draw conclusions by exploring the shape of the gap in our knowledge."

"So he's smart," another mage remarks, a middle-aged, blond-haired man called Arkov.

"You'd have to be very smart to realise that such a thing was possible," King agrees. "Very knowledgeable of deep magic."

"Not necessarily," says Exa. "Hyper-advanced thaumic attacks of that kind are in the List, even if they're a long way down. You'd get there eventually if you had the patience to wait for it."

Flatt says, "So your alternative explanation is that he held on to Abstract Weapon *without using it* for, what, a month?"

"That seems like it would take an inhuman amount of self-control," King says.

"You're still not getting it," says Exa. "Maybe he did use it. With this scrambler charm running, we can't detect what Weapon's doing. Maybe it had already been cast when he found it. Maybe I cast the scrambler myself when I meant to destroy the thing."

"But in that case, why didn't he cover his tracks this last time?" King asks.

Exa explodes. "Because this isn't about Rwanda, you nematodes!" He stands and throws the rest of his whiskey, glass and all, at King's head. King ducks; the glass shatters out in the darkness somewhere. "This isn't about *him*, or what happened to his family, or some part of his country that he was trying to bring justice back to! Top story: He came after *us*! The opening shot against that military installation was to get our attention, and then he killed me three fucking times!"

"Calm down," Flatt tells him.

Exa wants to shout "I will not calm down" back in his operator's face, but on reflection, perhaps icy furious calm is the better way to make his point. He kicks his chair, so that it rolls away from the discussion. He takes an angry pace in one direction, then another pace back. "Alright. 'Calmly', since I *was* just nuked. I don't care about this kid's sob story. I don't want to wake him up and ask why he felt the need to bring his war to us. In fact, we can't. In fact, you shouldn't have brought me back either."

"Why not?" Flatt asks, tiredly.

Exa realises that he, too, is tired. His *kara* (salvaged from the mushroom patch) is supposed to keep him at peak physical form forever, but something in his soul knows that it's four thirty in the morning of a day that's getting longer even as he stands there.

He takes his *kara* off and holds it up. "The bottom line: Our medring spells have a security hole as big as the Sun."

*

It takes an hour to effect cleanup, then a full day to install the new yantras that will bring the medring network up to scratch. Exa fields a few calls from the girlfriend. "It's a madhouse down here," he tells her. "Crit-sit. I won't be home." No emergency means no shortcuts: it takes him another entire day to get home the old-fashioned way.

It's just as he's stepping out of the taxi at his apartment building that he finally works out what's been bothering him. He loiters in the lobby and phones King. He says to him:

"We failed. We lost."

"Hmm?"

"Boy was right there, in the room, with the gun. What if it hadn't been a gun? What if it had been a bomb? Or a spell? He could have killed us all."

King doesn't know what he means. "We won, right?"

"No, we didn't win. *You* won. There are still huge gaps in our information. We were thrown into a situation without preparation. A situation without explanation, or with too many explanations. You shut it all down just in time. Was this a readiness test?"

"No," says King. "It was a close call. Go home."

"I am home," says Exa.

He ends the call and boards the elevator.

It's over.

16

ॐ

The heat in Calcutta is pulverising. Ed Hatt finds it almost impossible to think clearly about anything other than shade and cold water. His Bengali is good enough to direct a taxi driver to a place and count out the cash afterwards, but outside of vehicles, the only way to get anywhere in India is to traipse, or possibly to slog. Wandering, ambling and strolling simply aren't appropriate gaits for an Englishman in such a climate. The sky is unbroken blue, and standing in direct sunlight *hurts*.

It's 1974 and Hatt is a newly-minted adult, fresh out of Oxford and adrift eastward, looking for whatever, or whatever. Real life has been on hold all the way through his MEng, and is still on hold. He knows that, some months from now, it will reassert itself. At that point, he will be grudgingly forced to find a job. He hopes that he can find something worth becoming excited about by then. He hopes for some kind of epiphany. Or, failing all of that, he hopes to bore himself and tire himself out, sufficiently that going home and doing the same thing every weekday for a year sounds like a welcome break.

Hatt is learning that the world doesn't exist entirely for his benefit. A random city in the world may or may not contain birthplaces, memorials, teeming tat-filled markets and picturesque little bars stocked with cheap booze. A city may or may not be geared to speak English back to Ed Hatt, the tourist, but a city is *always* a functional machine, and his final impression of any given day, as he's traipsing back to the hotel, is of the machinery. It has operated for hundreds of years before he arrived and it'll continue to operate for hundreds of years after he's gone. Calcutta is flooded with people with crowded lives to lead, lives that have nothing whatsoever to do with him.

After four and a half days Hatt has left a crisscrossing trail over the city. He's seen the stunning white stone colonial relics, the stadiums, the museums, and the astonishing Hindu temples resembling fractal stone eggs — built according to *Vastu shastra*, the Hindu equivalent to feng shui. He's eaten and drunk, finished reading one book, bought another book, scribbled pages of experiences and sent a dozen postcards. The food is other-worldly. Twice every day (once on the way out from the hotel, once on the way back) he passes the same bunch of kids and joins in with their back-alley cricket game for half an hour. But he hasn't *got it* yet. His compass is still spinning.

This far east, Hatt realises, and he's really looking for a reason to go home again.

On his way home on the fifth day, Hatt cuts through a park to get to a main road to find a taxi. Or tries, but there are around a hundred people in the way. It's clearly a demonstration, although Hatt can't tell which sense of the word is more appropriate. Hatt is in no hurry so he allows himself to be delayed. He finds a low wall and stands on it to get a better view.

A circle roughly thirty metres wide has been cleared, and two men are marking out a pattern in the grass using pegs, string and surveyor's wheels. Hatt's first guess is that they are pitching a rangoli pattern of some kind. At calculated points, they plant thin poles in the ground. Most of the poles are metal — any of a million identical-looking shiny grey metals and alloys. Some are recognisably copper. Some are recognisably glass. The men are college- or Ph.D.-aged, within five years of Hatt himself. They wear white shirts and dark trousers and have pens in their breast pockets. A third, much older fellow with a tie and a large blue binder full of ragged-edged scraps of paper is directing the activity. He is sixty-something, and his glasses are small and circular.

As for the crowd, they are men and women of all ages. There's a healthy murmur in the crowd but they are mostly watching quietly. Some people carry flags or occasionally shout slogans. Hatt unexpectedly recognises some of the slogans. But the fragments he recognises aren't the elementary fragments of Bengali that he's gathered together from his phrasebook. They're mathematical terminology; obscure and cryptic keywords from a plasma dynamics course still very fresh in Hatt's memory.

There's a clear demarcation between the observers and the scientists. The crowd is treating it like a pre-show, waiting for something cool to start. The scientists are treating the crowd like a nuisance. They're trying to get something accomplished; they never formally invited any onlookers. There's nothing priestly about their movements. It's an experiment under construction.

Ra

The lead scientist uses a magnetometer-like device to examine the highly symmetrical arrangement of poles, sometimes closing one eye and sighting along a row of them in one direction, sometimes uprooting another pole and replanting it a few millimetres to the left. Once the poles are arranged to his satisfaction he carries out a similar series of measurements and adjustments using a theodolite. He stands behind the pole at the north end of the system. The crowd falls silent. He speaks, measuring out discrete syllables like sand grains:

"Aum. Asnaku pambetamba alasana rathaa ka'u kah kadhunda jarama ra alanashyi a aum. Alithua j'lu j'la aurot'e we iktha'u gee sub ai. Murihaa akurutaatwanhibhrandya aum. Traanhdha epil sub ai anah myu oshodapachaa. Nath bhoshu alef ad'yegh. Aum."

The words are noise to Hatt, meaningless in English, French or Bengali, although the "sub ais" tickle something in Hatt's mind, brushing up against understanding without actually finding purchase. But he doesn't have the chance to think about it, because, after the last "aum", the hairs on his arms stand straight up and the seven glass light tubes light up in red and blue so bright at the core as to be white. It's like a camera flash, but much longer in duration, at least a second. It bathes the entire park and the surrounding buildings. Everybody winces and shields his or her eyes, scientists and crowd alike. A round of applause follows immediately.

Hatt joins in the applause although he still doesn't know what he just saw. The sciencey types are all congratulating one another, particularly the senior man, and the crowd is pressing in on them as well to add their congratulations. Hatt doesn't know if the demonstration qualifies as a magic trick. Powering up a fluorescent tube without touching it is far from impossible.

"Not bad," Hatt remarks aloud, to nobody, and then he sees it: his own breath, condensing out in a thin white cloud.

He shivered when the light flash began. For that first second he thought it was just nervous tension. Power for the lights could have come from anywhere. And he can feel the warm, cloyingly wet air stirring back in even as seconds pass. But for this one second, he's cold. He can feel himself thinking more clearly than he ever has since he first stepped off the plane. And he can feel thermodynamics as he knows it quietly swivelling upside-down.

He dives into the crowd, wading towards the man in the small circular glasses.

*

Half an hour later Vidyasagar has brought him to the machine room. The room is completely white and immaculately clean, populated with huge cuboidal blocks full of raw, humming computer. Along one wall are filing cabinets full of manuals and printouts and computer code. Vidyasagar invites Hatt to take a seat next to one of the terminals, an intimidatingly large panel of lights and switches as comprehensible as the dashboard of a 747. Hatt relaxes, actually feeling rather at home.

Rajesh Vidyasagar does not sit, or lean against anything. He carries himself carefully. He is tidy, and putting weight on. His English is hesitant and very dry, or in other words fully fifty thousand times better than Hatt's Bengali; they settle on English. For his part, Hatt tries to clamp down on the colloquialisms and florid metaphors. They have to speak loudly to overcome the noise of computer system fans and the air conditioning. At least it's cool here.

"One says the correct words," Vidyasagar explains, "and thinks the correct thoughts at the same time. Then, a physical effect occurs."

"That's it?"

"As far as we can tell, that's it."

Hatt rubs an eye, barely believing it despite the evidence of his own senses. "That's insane."

Vidyasagar nods sadly. "I know."

"And there's no religious element? There's no spiritual element?"

"No," says Vidyasagar. "It's pure physics. Despite what it looked like out there. We are surrounded by believers of things which are not actually true. We try to separate the science out from the 'ritual', but it's difficult. Unfortunately, that park is the nearest open space that we have access to."

"The University of Calcutta doesn't have a tennis court you can book, or something?"

"Of course," says Vidyasagar, mildly indignant. "On the other side of the city. This is the Science College."

"So it doesn't overlap with Hindu teachings? Or Buddhist or Sikh?"

"If it did, don't you think we would have discovered all of this a thousand years ago?"

"I..." Hatt's ancient Indian history is lamentable, despite all his visits to holy sites. "Maybe? I don't know."

"It doesn't overlap. Any overlap is just a coincidence," Vidyasagar says. "Or convenient terminology. To you, the language sounds similar to Bengali or Hindi. In reality it is a code for a sequence of quantum mechanical effects. We think that what we are seeing is a previously unknown function of the human brain. We also think a new form of potential energy must be involved; this is the only explanation for the apparent violation of the laws of thermodynamics. And that's... almost all we know so far. There is still a vast number of unanswered questions. We don't understand the mechanism at all yet. Or the language. We are still exploring the rules."

"The *shastra*," Hatt says.

"The rules," Vidyasagar says. He holds up his blue binder of notes. "We know a little so far. We are filling this in as we go. Today, we ran a new program on the mainframe. A problem of optimisation. We solved the equations numerically. For a specific area and sequence of words."

"The program told you where to place the metal rods?"

"And what kind of rods to use. We find that the noble gases are best. Also, steel is good. Everything must be arranged correctly in space."

Hatt thinks hard. He gets up and stalks around the room, circling one of the heavy mainframes. It resembles a monolith from *2001*, both in form factor and computational power. It practically glows with radiant heat. "Okay," he says. "So. You haven't announced anything publicly yet. Or if you have, you've been ignored by other scientists, other than your two students. In either case, I can see why. Every unanswered question you have is a reason why. It feels like cargo cult physics. This whole thing is—"

"It's trash," Vidyasagar says. Hatt looks at him a little more carefully, and Vidyasagar's expression seems to be one of self-revulsion.

"Trash?"

"We haven't announced anything because people would laugh at us. We have found some kind of fault in the universe. We need to fix it before we can say anything. And we need to understand it before we can fix it."

On this point, Ed Hatt completely disagrees. "Agriculture was an industry thousands of years before humans understood photosynthesis. A thing doesn't have to be understood before it can be useful. And using a thing is the best way to understand it. And if nobody will take a scientific paper seriously, we can demonstrate result after result until they take us seriously. We can *make the world better* until they take us seriously. Do you have the slightest idea how big this is?"

Vidyasagar says, carefully, "I have a slight idea."

Hatt says, "There isn't a *single* field of engineering, which I can think of, for which this discovery isn't colossally important. There isn't a single machine *in the world* which can't be made more efficient. The commercial applications are limitless. Electricity generation, heat management in space, heat management in—" he points with a thumb "—computer microprocessors, refrigeration of every kind. When you're outside, you're surrounded with religious zealots who don't understand that what you've found isn't a new religion. Or some old religion in new clothes. The students you're leading are physicists, with an eye for the hard questions and no conception of financial reality. I'm here to tell you that *I* get it. I'm a man of business and machinery. I felt something during that demonstration. Like we just hit the tip of some colossal iceberg. I mean... like this is the beginning of a huge and incredibly important future. This is the new electricity."

"Don't talk about the future," Vidyasagar says.

"What? Why not?"

"Look at this computer," Vidyasagar says, gesturing at the mainframe. "Computers are getting more powerful, yes?"

"Sure."

"What is the most powerful computer that will be built? Ever. Not this year. Not this decade. What computer will be the most powerful? And how powerful will it be? And how big?"

Hatt thinks on this for ten long seconds. He opens his mouth, but never actually forms a word. The scale of the question is beyond him.

Vidyasagar says to him, "No matter what you say, you will look like a fool. Every statement about the future turns out to be foolish. All this, from heat-into-electricity? I have a word sequence which turns heat directly into light. I have one which creates kinetic energy from *nothing at all*." Hatt's mind boggles at these new claims. "Yes, I have a slight idea of what's begun. But I don't *know*. You don't know, neither of us knows!"

"You're right." Hatt pinches the bridge of his nose, the visions in his mind's eye now too bright and fast-changing to unscramble. "You're right."

"Before anything else, there is a huge amount of work to be done," Vidyasagar tells him.

The visions in Hatt's mind's eye are formless, as if waiting for him to move in and shape them.

"By us," he says.

17
Bare Metal

"Rajesh is a fucking moron," Ed Hatt explains.

"That seems—" Martin Garrett begins, but then the toll barrier flips up and Hatt floors it, which means that for the next two or three seconds Garrett is squelched back into his seat by acceleration, unable to respond. On the other side of the Dartford booth is a wide apron where exiting traffic condenses from twenty-four lanes down to three and resumes its course south around the rim of Greater London. At peak periods, there are close to a hundred vehicles jostling for position here, but it's not peak period. If anything, it's valley period: pitch dark, three fifteen on a chilly and wholly unremarkable weekday morning in the spring of 1986.

"That seems harsh," Garrett concludes, once he recovers the ability to speak.

"'Seems harsh'," Ed Hatt echoes. "He doesn't get it. If I have to go through one more call with the man where I have to straighten out his priorities, I may well have him retired."

"That seems a brutal way to put it."

"He's on the way out anyway. His contributions have been on the way out. I only keep him around because he holds the reins of the ten or eleven actually smart men in that lab. They look up to him, they use him as a, what's the word, weathervane. Barometer. They take cues from him more readily than they'd take them from me because he's a scientist and he can frame what he needs— I mean, what *I* need— in the right terms. They're not as likely to take orders directly. But he — Raj — is not *fruitful* anymore. He's not *rich*. No good results. These new fellows, Devi and Mitra, leave him standing. He's losing it."

"How old is he?" Garrett asks.

"Seventy-three," says Hatt, carrying out the swift burst of date arithmetic too quickly for the pause to be detectable. "That's the other thing. He's old enough! To retire. I mean, this is Wile E. Coyote style, running out on empty. Retirement age is the edge of the cliff and he's well over it. I don't think he realises it yet."

"Then he won't stick around for much longer anyway, surely," Garrett suggests.

"He'll stick around for as long as he can. He wants to leave a dent in the universe. Which is credible, I think everybody in the world wants to leave a dent in the universe in some respect—"

Garrett raises a highly sceptical eyebrow. Hatt actually notices this, despite the ludicrous velocity at which he is piloting the car. Garrett notices in turn that Hatt has glanced at him momentarily, and this frightens Garrett a little. In his opinion, a three-digit speed mandates a maniacal, laser-like focus on the road ahead, not on one's passenger. "Watch the road."

Hatt continues, "—but he hasn't accepted yet that he's *had* his Moon landing moment. I mean, his Neil Armstrong moment, to the extent that he's ever going to have one. The Vidyasagar field equation is it for him. His footprint has been left, indelibly, in scientific history. From here it's downhill and he should just enjoy it. He thinks there's a bigger jewel left inside himself somewhere, figuratively speaking. But there isn't. He should actually fucking enjoy himself for a few years before he falls over one day and doesn't get up."

"I've met Vidyasagar briefly," Garrett says.

"Yes, I remember. I was there." It was the Hatt Group AGM, almost a year ago now.

Garrett continues, "He seems like science is what he does to enjoy himself."

"Well, that's his problem, because science isn't something I do to enjoy myself," says Ed Hatt. "There's a third thing which I interpolate between science and enjoyment, which I call *profitability*."

Martin Garrett is forty-eight, one of Hatt Group's principal solo investors, easily Hatt's equal in the adrenaline junkie stakes and, by Hatt's reckoning, trustworthy. Ed Hatt isn't the only young/stupid/successful man who takes his pet supercar out on the illegal high-speed London Orbital circuit like this. It's a small and largely anonymous and actually vaguely unpleasant community, all testosterone and oneupmanship, no collective safety conscience, no concessions to personal responsibility. It will all end in tears one day, either in speed cameras or in a meaninglessly irresponsible death, but until that day, there's luck to be pushed.

Hatt's unnecessarily powerful Porsche 911 chews up the road like its birthright. Hatt has convinced himself that the vehicle sounds irritable until he gets it past eighty-five. It's almost impossible to conceive that the machine was built to do anything other than this. It's almost impossible to conceive that the freshly-completed, mint-condition M25 motorway was built to have anything else done to it. Hatt and Garrett are both stone cold sober and in an excellent mood: Hatt Group has had an extremely successful financial year, and this is Hatt's idea of entertaining a trusted and valued business associate.

Hatt asks, "What was the split at the toll booth?"

Garrett pulls out his stopwatch. The stopwatch is a novelty, and bringing it was Garrett's idea. Most racers drive solo, and just use their wristwatch. "You said to catch it at the moment when the coins hit the bucket? Twenty-five minutes, fifteen point oh three seconds."

Hatt coughs irritably, as if having just swallowed something foul. "Not good at all. My PR is twenty-four oh eight. WR is about one millisecond below twenty. That was in a car built specifically to break the production speed record and nothing else. Fucking bullshit time."

"'PR' is Personal Record, 'WR' is World Record?" Garrett guesses.

"Yeah." Hatt moves them to a different lane as they fly over the M20.

"Why do you call it the World Record when it can only be set on this specific road in this specific country?"

Hatt cackles. "Don't— just, don't start with me, all right? This is your fault anyway, Martin. You're acting as ballast."

"It was your idea," Garrett says.

"Well, I hope you're having a good time, because the only way I'm going to get on the leaderboard today is if I throw you out at Sevenoaks."

"That's fine," Garrett says. "We're taking the wrong route for the record, anyway."

"What do you mean?"

"We're on the outside, going clockwise. If we were on the inside carriageway the route would be shorter."

"Only by about a hundred and fifty yards," says Hatt. "The ratio of lengths is the same as the ratio of radii, and you're looking at about twenty-five yards' difference over nineteen miles, which is basically nothing. If you think about it, you lose more time on the roundabout, because the service station's on the outside."

Garrett frowns for a second, working this out. "Huh."

"You don't loop the entire capital in less than seventy minutes by not examining the details."

"*Seventy*, Jesus."

"Something like seventy minutes," says Hatt. His personal record is in the low eighties. "If you're good. I reckon in the next year or two somebody's going to break the hour mark."

They cruise in silence for a few miles — which is to say, a minute. Vast blue and white roadsigns flash past overhead, indicating exits towards the south-east of London and the South East of England. UK motorway signs are sized according to the speed of passing traffic — the faster the traffic, the bigger the signs have to be for motorists to read them. Garrett can't read these. They're written in foot-high letters and they're still passing too quickly.

The major consideration when taking a public highway at high speed is road curvature. Cornering ability doesn't enter into it— Hatt's car is built for sport, and very few highways in the world have surprise hairpin turns. The greater risk is of coming around a bend — and it doesn't have to be a sharp bend, just enough to hide a little of the road ahead — and running headlong into the back of another car fast enough for the initial impact alone to kill everybody involved. In curvature terms, UK motorways are designed to be completely safe up to around 110% of the speed limit. Beyond this design cutoff, in the largely unexplored blank areas of the velocity phase space, the skill level of the driver and the make of the car aren't relevant: there is absolute danger.

So it's a game of extreme skill, of reflex times, of weighing the need for caution at the brow of a hill against the need for a fast time, of watching every part of the road ahead and of intimate familiarity with one's vehicle's behaviour under envelope-pushing conditions. At this time of night the road is almost completely empty, which is another way of saying that it's not empty at all. Hatt keeps his right foot permanently on the accelerator and his left foot permanently over the brake, and stays in the far right lane where the presence of another vehicle is less statistically probable. His eyesight is fine, his tyres are new, the road is dry. All of this amplifies his confidence. None of it makes him safe.

"The tragedy is that he knows his shit," Hatt says, continuing the thread from earlier. "Every now and then, he and I line up with one another, and he sees exactly what I see. But most of the time it's like he's seeing the two faces while I'm seeing the candlestick. What I said, way, way back at the beginning of all of this, is that in order for magic to be commercially viable we need to *invent the shelf.* Every other company out there is manufacturing a different ring every fucking time. They're almost casting a new mould each time, it's asinine. Because there was this milestone paper by Mukhopadhyay, you must have heard of it—"

"Yes," says Garrett.

"—which basically said, 'For any problem in this set, you can make a ring or a concentric ring system which will solve it for you. Here's the algorithm that'll do it, one two three four the end.' Brilliant piece of work! Rings were the breakthrough moment, they're the transistors of magic. But everybody takes that paper literally. Everybody goes around using up thousands of mainframe hours numerically solving the most God-awful PDEs and then building a new ring to order for every client. And Raj was completely okay with this. What he wanted to do was run on ahead and try to scrape the next layer of crap off the universe and see what's underneath, and I almost had to physically restrain him and say, 'No. This isn't good enough. It's *a* solution, but it's not *the* solution.' It's not that I'm against crap-scraping in principle. I see its value. You know how much we invest in research. But that's just the R in R&D. Development is just as important. We can always do better."

"Hence the componentisation concept."

"Exactly. Imagine you're a company with no experience with magic, no mages on the payroll. You perceive magic as a risk, you care more about what magic can do for *you* than what magic can do for science or the world. You want to build a magic solution cheaply. 'Cheaply' is code: it means you want to use off-the-shelf parts. You'd rather use robust components with a track record than bespoke one-off crap which will become a maintenance nightmare universe all unto itself at the very second that the state of the art moves on. You want standard rings, standard amulets, standard spells. And you want it to be easy to hire mages who are familiar with those standards."

"You're preaching to the choir," Garrett tells Hatt. In fact, Hatt is rehearsing a familiar Hatt Group investor pitch. What he's describing is exactly what Hatt Group did, and does, and will continue to do for the foreseeable future.

"It's not even as if the challenge wasn't interesting once I got Raj to pass it on," Hatt says. "*I* knew there was some fun science in there alongside all of the practicality and profitability. Raj just didn't understand why you'd dwell on a solved problem. Classic mathematician. Proves on paper that a bucket of water will put out the fire, has no desire to pick the fucking bucket up and put the fucking fire out. But when his people got the idea they ate it up like... hot cakes."

"I don't think that's the right idiom," says Garrett.

"I don't either," says Hatt, "but you take my point."

"I do."

"We were the first company in the world to make a ring in two semicircular pieces that you can weld together around an existing piece of equipment. Because nobody wants to shut their process down and take it entirely to pieces to slip a magic condom over the end of their pipe. Most of the industry said it was literally impossible, because of precision. Precision! Meanwhile, I'm watching Rajesh Vidyasagar and his guys casting thermal reduction field effect spells with *sticks* driven into *mud*. I say, you throw a thick layer of the smartest applied mathematicians in the world on top of a problem like that, and the problem folds up like a..." Hatt snaps his fingers irritably, groping for the rest of the saying.

"Cheap suit?" Garrett guesses.

"Yeah. You've just got to sell it to them."

"You've got to sell the problem to the mathematicians?"

"Yeah. If you want them to bite."

They drive in silence for a little longer. Signs for Sevenoaks, Crawley and Croydon rise and fall. Hatt relaxes a little, shifting position, then snaps himself out of that overly relaxed state as a few more slow-moving cars appear on the horizon. They blitz past them with a full empty lane separating them. Too fast for either party to get a number plate, too fast to even get a manufacturer.

"Speaking of magic rings," Hatt says.

"Yes."

"Are you religious?"

"Not especially. Well... no, not in the usual sense."

"Because I spend a lot of time in India and I see a lot of Sikhs wearing that kind of bracelet." Hatt points at Garrett's wrist.

"Oh, this thing!" Garrett holds it up. It's a slim, solid band, undecorated.

"They call it a *kara*," Hatt says. "But I didn't think you were religious. You don't cover your head, to start with."

"No. Oh! Oh, I see why you're concerned," Garrett says.

"Because if it is a magic ring then that means you got it from one of our competitors! Ha hah!" Ed Hatt is only half-joking.

"Hah. No, it's a magnetic healing ring. It improves my circulation."

"How?" Hatt can't stop himself from blurting out the question.

"So, you know that the principle component in blood is haemoglobin? The magnetic field acts on the iron atom in the haemoglobin molecule to make it move more freely. So it reduces inflammation and improves my immune system. I have some friends who swear by them. One of them, he's worn one for the last... ooh, it would have to be sixteen years? And he's never had a serious illness. He gets a cold now and then but never for more than a day. It also speeds up the migration of calcium ions, which makes healing nervous tissue and bones quicker. You know I go surfing, you know how you can get bruised while surfing. My bruises go away just like that. I should give you some literature. It's really amazing."

...It's car crash science. Ed Hatt fights his instinct to tell Garrett that (1) a haemoglobin molecule contains four iron atoms, not one and that (2) everything else he just said is also bullshit. Hatt has no tolerance for it. It drives some kind of painful splinter into his neck, forcing him to respond with all kinds of foul invective. But there are few moments in a business relationship when directly insulting a significant investor is the best move.

Instead, Hatt changes gear and tries to respond in the same terms as Garrett. It's difficult: BS is a whole other language to him, one he can't easily speak. "So it's kind of a good luck charm?"

"It's a good luck charm," says Garrett, nodding enthusiastically.

"The next split is at the M3," Hatt says.

"That's about half an hour from now?" Garrett says.

"Nope, more like half that. We'll pass right over it, the timing point is at the middle of the carriageway."

"I'll be ready," says Garrett, waving the stopwatch.

Hatt holds his breath for a few seconds. Maybe he's successfully changed the subject.

Garrett asks, "Are you religious?"

Damn it. Ed Hatt brakes a little, a reflex action. Here he is at twice the speed limit and all the way out of his comfort zone. He measures his words. "Religion and I don't see eye-to-eye," he says. "So I stay as far away from it as possible. The whole industry is swamped with hangers-on who try to crowbar magic into whatever religion they like best. And it never fits properly, anywhere. Indulging these people is invariably a waste of everybody's time, so I just ignore it. We're stuck with the terminology, but that's only because all the terminology was hacked into stone before I got the chance to have a say. It's just bad branding. And— so, you know that there are fundamental mathematical constants."

"Like pi."

"And fundamental physical constants."

"Like the fine structure constant."

"And in magic, there are fundamental magical constants. Which take the form of spoken syllables."

"Like `ra`."

"Everybody accepts that the universe is built on certain truths," Hatt summarises. "I just don't worship those truths. Because what's the point? What do I gain from that? The universe was built to be unscrambled. I mean, not that the universe was built. The universe wasn't built *by* anybody. It wasn't built *to* have anything done to it. But my purpose, which I picked for myself, is: get money, unscramble universe. Not in that order."

Garrett looks intently over his shoulder for a moment. He can see at least three-quarters of a mile back.

"Police?" Hatt asks, checking his mirrors.

"You mentioned scraping layers of crap off the universe," Garrett says.

"I did."

Garrett says, "There's a concept in thermodynamics called negative absolute temperature. You'd think absolute zero kelvins was the lowest temperature a body could have, but it's not. It's as if the universe's temperature scale wraps around on itself at infinity. A body below absolute zero behaves as if it's hotter than any positive-temperature body. It's one of many counterintuitive artifacts of quantum mechanics. It can only happen in very unusual edge cases. But it can happen.

"Of course, the laws of physics aren't that stupid. You can't steal limitless thermal energy that way. It's just a freak of mathematics."

Hatt says nothing.

"But you can steal magic," Garrett continues. Something is happening to his tone of voice. It's not an impersonation. It's more as if he's spent his whole life affecting an impersonation of another person. Now he's finally lapsing back to his normal self. And he's speaking faster than he used to. "If you subtract all the mana out of a body in less than one-tenth of a picosecond, the mana energy density inside the body nosedives so hard that it very briefly turns negative. Which is also nominally impossible. But it works. It requires a spell unlike anything you've ever seen before. Up until now you've been using magic as the fulcrum, mediating between different forms of energy. Heat goes down, kinetic goes up. This is different. There's more energy there than any living human carries, more than every living human can use. This is what your people found."

"How do you know about that?" Hatt hisses.

"Devi and Mitra have found something very important. Ra is critically important to this. You need to keep looking in that direction. You haven't *seen* real magic yet."

"What are you talking about? That experiment was supposed to be carried out secretly. Only about six people in the company know it happened. It was just R&D, a shot in the dark—"

"*The assembly was connected to a standard electrical transduction ring. The lightning bolt punched through two walls on its way to earth. Anil Devi was burnt along the waist and forearms, Dinesh Mitra was temporarily blinded. The fire that was started was small enough to be easily controlled. None of us know for certain what the total energy yield was, because all the instrumentation was fried by the electromagnetic pulse.* Don't look at me, Ed. Don't slow down."

Hatt himself was the author of most of those words. All he can manage is, "What?"

"I said, don't slow down." Garrett grabs the steering wheel in one hand, keeping Hatt in the outside lane. This move and Garrett's latest instruction are cause for deep alarm, but for the moment Hatt complies. In his rear-view mirror, he sights a scintillating pair of headlights. The same lane. Half a mile back.

"What's happening?" he asks. "Who leaked the information? How did you find out about it? Who's following us?"

"Nobody leaked the experiment to me," Garrett says, "I leaked the spell to you. It isn't going to work forever. In fact, I doubt it'll ever work again. But there are other routes into this problem. Ra isn't just a fundamental constant, it's the most important fundamental constant there is. There is limitless energy down there and to find it, you need to find Ra. And you need... to be... *subtle*."

"What the fuck does any of that even mean?"

"Space magic, Ed. Kardashev one."

Their tail is gaining faster than should be possible. No flashing red and blue lights. A civilian. Hatt would dearly like to know what he's driving.

Garrett still doesn't let go of the wheel. "Outrun him," he says.

Hatt looks Garrett in the eye. "*Why?*"

About three-quarters of a second elapses. This is enough time for Hatt to see that Martin Garrett has no good answer prepared to give to him. Garrett, Hatt realises, is a crazy. Garrett's mind has been occupied by Hatt's enemy: paranoid schizophrenic pseudoscience.

Hatt decides that he no longer wants this man in control of his vehicle.

Garrett sees the decision flash up in Hatt's eyes. Garrett reacts faster. He pulls his side of the steering wheel down, hard.

The 911 swerves left, but there's no chance of it changing direction. The front right tyre skids for an instant, then it and its rear counterpart bite the concrete, and the left half of the car leaves the ground. The car rolls in fresh air, in high-gee centrifugal freefall. "Oh my God—" are Edward Hatt's expiring words.

It lands on its front left wheel and left headlight, tearing Garrett's door in half and driving shattered pieces of wheel well and brake disc into the passenger compartment. Garrett is crushed into his seat by crumpled bodywork. Ed Hatt is lacerated in the eyes and throat by windscreen shards, but the shock of the first impact has already broken his neck. Still rolling, the Porsche sheds a trail of broken glass, body panels and vital automotive organs. It barely takes a few seconds to come to a halt, but it seems longer. The car finishes the right way up, facing the central reservation, drooling the last of its vital fluids onto the lane markings.

There's a little while of silence.

Ed Hatt is dead. His seat's fabric is saturated scarlet. Martin Garrett sees this very clearly. He can't look away. The passenger door is almost folded double over him, crushing his head back.

Garrett spits a few words out. A narrow, powerful laser ignites, down near his right hip. With care, he slices through his seatbelt and then through strategic joints in the metalwork pinning him, leaving red-hot edges which cool rapidly. Disregarding the heat, he pushes superhumanly hard, forcing the metal tangle to bend upwards and forwards, sprinkling more window glass over his lap and the bonnet.

He slithers out onto the cold, sodium-lit asphalt and takes up a defensive position behind the battered ex-car, breathing hard. By now his privileges have been revoked, something which wouldn't happen until the engagement formally began, for fear of tipping him off. He's down to base magic, the same rules by which everybody else in the world is forced to play.

Where is he?

Over the remains of the Porsche's bonnet he spies the pursuer's car, a midnight-black Testarossa parked a long way back in the middle lane, hazard lights flashing as a warning to approaching traffic. Garrett squints, then aims a finger at the driver's seat, spot-lighting it. The car is empty.

No fully-formed word of reaction has enough time to pass through Garrett's mind. He knows what's next. He instantly spins a hundred and eighty degrees, bringing the laser back up, tightened to as narrow and intense a point as it'll go.

"*Oh, you think?*"

Exa blocks Garrett's arm with his own. The laser wouldn't scratch him, but he doesn't want to give Garrett even the symbolic victory of landing a single attack. Instead, a long scorch mark ignites in the asphalt beside them, throwing up carcinogenic smoke. Exa takes Garrett's laser arm and uses it as leverage to throw him over one shoulder and down on the road, face down. There's a crack: Garrett's fingers.

"Thanks for your service, Martin," Exa says, "you're fired."

"For what?"

"Oh, you want to do this the tedious way? For the record? That's fine." Exa is the sharp end of his organisation, and is expected to maintain some cool while deployed. But, just this once, he lets some personal anger show: "Going rogue. Revealing deep, dark secrets of the universe to people not in the Wheel Group. Exploiting a flaw in the fabric of magic. Failing to report said flaw through the proper channels. *Trying to wake Ra!*"

Garrett rolls over. There's nothing in his other hand: the charm is invisible, needing no supporting hardware. Nevertheless, Exa clearly sees Garrett's mana aura supplying power to it, and the metadata pouring out of the charm itself. If this one goes off, it could actually hurt Exa. It doesn't matter. The conversation is over.

With reflexes as far beyond Garrett's as Garrett's were beyond Hatt's, Exa ends him. Garrett ceases to exist, his component atoms transmuted into a thick cloud of humid ozone, which dissipates immediately. The crime scene is left totally sterile.

Exa exhales. He turns on one heel and paces smartly back towards his car, crunching glass beneath his shoes. "I think we're done," he says aloud.

"What about the scientists?" Exa's controller asks him.

"The loophole's closed," he replies. "They'll give up and move on. Hatt's death is regrettable. But I think we're done."

"Do you want to resurrect Hatt?"

He hesitates at the car door and looks back. Hatt's hunched body is still just visible in the wreckage of his car. Exa's expression is blank. In his professional opinion, it doesn't make a difference whether Hatt lives or dies. He considers tossing a coin. He reconsiders.

"I don't want to spend any mana we don't have to," he says. "It's more plausible this way."

As the first trailing cars are starting to pull up at the crash site, Exa turns his ignition. He navigates smoothly around the wreck and disappears into the distance, unidentified.

*

Hatt breathes in and out. Breathing in is worse. The act of inhaling gives him sharp crackling pains in his chest, neck and pelvis. Breathing out is more of a dull rasp as the same bones and organs settle back, broader in effect but not quite as intense. He concentrates on taking shallow breaths, to minimise the pain. He concentrates, also, on not moving any other part of his body, even experimentally. He can tell that a great deal of it is broken. He thinks he might have spinal damage, and dares not even open his eyes for fear of jostling his head out of position and making it worse. Speaking isn't going to happen, but he sure as hell thinks *Help* as loudly as he can. He listens out hard for sirens, but only hears the occasional vehicle pass in the other carriageway. Someone's coming, he knows. He hopes. He can't manage this level of pain for very long. *Take it a minute at a time. Take it five seconds at a time. In. Out.*

I'm dying.

Hatt can feel something metallic touching his left wrist, but he can feel metal touching his ankles (which are broken) and his ribs (some fractured) and his right forearm (severely gouged). His wrist feels fine, but he doesn't want to know. He keeps his eyes clamped shut because there's nothing in the world that he wants to see now.

He isn't dying. Much the opposite. The metal object on his wrist is Garrett's medring, placed there as Garrett's last act before exiting the vehicle. The ring is set on minimum power, low profile, prioritising the most severe medical conditions, such as — initially — death.

Its first act as Hatt's personal doctor was to reset his neck joint, a necessary prerequisite to bringing the patient back to life. Now, it has started working, very slowly, on his eyes. No human doctor in the world could heal Hatt's eyes, but by the time the ambulance arrives there'll be no evidence that they were ever damaged.

Hatt's overall recovery will not be miraculous, but certainly impressively quick. He won't be able to shake off the things Garrett said. "Good luck charm". "Speeds up healing".

"Limitless energy".

Hatt is impatient. He is results-driven, with no tolerance for bull.

Vehicular manslaughter? It hardly requires a fleet of lawyers to prove that in the absence of Martin Garrett's body, he must have either (1) walked away from the crash site alive or (2) never been in the vehicle in the first place. With suitable emphasis on mitigating circumstances (clean licence, no drugs or alcohol, serious personal injury), Hatt escapes the legal proceedings with a dangerous driving conviction: a heavy fine and a multi-year ban. He hires a driver.

As for the deep, dark secrets of the universe: One year to the day after the crash, Hatt officially severs his relationship with it. He decides that idea two might as well be the truth of the matter, for all the concrete results that have come out of Garrett's dreamlike comments. The lightning bolt accident cannot be duplicated. The syllable Ra has, if anything, less significance than any other. The *kara* that Hatt has inherited is just a solid ring of admittedly extremely valuable rhenium with no detectable magical properties. Hatt continues to wear it, anyway. Placebo effect or not, it seems to give him energy.

He sees that there are more important things competing for this part of his life, and he lets them take his attention away. He resigns himself to never finding out what the hell really happened to Martin Garrett. He moves on to the next chapter.

18
Hatt's People

Rajesh Vidyasagar has begun to decelerate.

He takes the lift to Hatt's floor, which is normal for visitors to Hatt's floor given what floor Hatt's is, but then when he reaches the ante-room where Sally works he leans on the chair for support as he lowers himself into it. He politely refuses Sally's offer of tea. When it's time for the meeting, he leans on the chair again to get up. He politely refuses Sally's offer of assistance.

He's losing weight. He leans for support on the door handle to Hatt's office.

"Hi. Have a seat."

Ed Hatt knows Vidyasagar far better. He stays behind his desk, and lets Vidyasagar seat himself.

"I don't come up here very often," Vidyasagar smiles.

"I should have come to you," Hatt says apologetically. He knows the walk from Vidyasagar's office to this one is long and lengthening. "How are you? How's the family?"

"How's the view?" Vidyasagar asks, nodding at the window behind Hatt.

Hatt keeps the blinds permanently closed. "It's crap," he says.

Down in reception and in the rest of the customer-facing half of the Group, the walls are covered with pictures of historic aircraft and spaceships, some in flight, some on pads, classic aerospace photography. Mixed with the photographs are huge murals of spaceports and experimental jets and ships: concept art; Hatt's concepts of what he wants to build. But it's the third quarter of 1988 and that vision's not built yet, and he won't open the blinds until he's going to see something worth seeing.

Also, the Sun glares on his computer screen, but that's less poetic.

"Rajesh, I'm moving you to a new role. It's a role we've created for you. Director of Special Projects. It's more money, and less responsibility. Actually, it would be essentially ceremonial."

Vidyasagar does not visibly react to this. "Why?"

"Because we think you've done everything we can ask you to do for this company. No," Hatt corrects himself. "Not 'we'. 'We' is the board. Let me say this personally. I think you've done everything I can ask you to do for my company. I thank you personally for your years of service and your immeasurable contributions to the magical sciences. I thank you and I want you to stop."

"Why not fire me? It's the same thing."

Hatt laughs. "Sure. Fire the father of the first age of magic. Just from a P.R. standpoint—"

"Why do you want me to retire from science?"

"...Because you're seventy-five, Rajesh. It's time."

"I know how old I am, Edward. It's as obvious to me as it is to anybody. My brain isn't going yet. I still have my eyes. I can still type."

There's a long, deep pause.

Hatt gives up. "Your current line of research is not valuable to us. To me."

"My current line of research—"

"I don't *care*."

Vidyasagar works on a long rein. He has a lab and a small staff on the site, a separate block with good equipment, but without much real need for equipment. His work is way out on the theoretical edge of magic. The gap in focus between his work and Hatt Group's work at large has constantly increased as years have gone by. From Hatt's perspective, the day has long passed when Vidyasagar's little business unit might as well be a totally unrelated spinoff organisation. There's no harmonious link from there to here, no synergy, no connection to modern practical aerospace, barely any concrete experiments, no viable results. Meanwhile, there's a kilometre-tall stack of advanced practical work that Hatt wants demolishing, and Vidyasagar is holding on to valuable brains and skills.

Creative differences.

Hatt says, "I've been tolerant. I've been indulgent to the tune of serious money. I've shown due respect. But Hatt Group is not a scientific research institution. The groundwork is down now. Pure theory is of no value to me. *I have shit to do.*"

And he studies Vidyasagar's reaction and, like always, gets nothing.

Vidyasagar has an iceberg cool about him. He's always had it. It's not that he's an emotionless automaton; he has feelings and opinions as strong as anybody else's. It's more as if his emotions happen at some heavily shielded core, where the worst effects are never allowed to reach the surface. His sons have both inherited the trait. Vidyasagars, by design, can never melt down.

Vidyasagar says this: "What is magic?"

"...I'm not sure what you're asking."

"What is magic?" Vidyasagar asks simply.

"What is gravity?" Hatt asks rhetorically. "What is electromagnetism? It's the way the world works."

"Why?"

"I don't care!" Hatt replies, exasperated. Vidyasagar has evidently jumped off the metaphysical deep end.

"On the day we first met and spoke," says Vidyasagar, "what did I say to you?"

"You said a lot of things."

"You asked me what magic is," Vidyasagar says. "Do you remember what I said in response?"

"You said to me..." Hatt descends into his records. He actually remembers the conversation extremely clearly, although a minute passes as the old data drags itself out of storage. "You said, 'One says the correct words, and thinks the correct thoughts at the same time. Then, a physical effect occurs.' And then I said to you, 'That's it?' And you said to me, 'As far as we can tell, that's it.'"

"And you bought that?"

Hatt blinks. "...'Bought'? It happened right in front of me. It's consistent, it's reproducible. I've done it myself, I've done magic. I— *we* have made a huge amount of money out of its reproducibility. It bought me."

"The real universe in which we live is an examination," Vidyasagar explains. "And then time runs out and you leave the room and— how many marks did you get? You don't get to find out. Let me ask you another question. What is the biological component of magic?"

Now Hatt sees where this is going.

Both he and Vidyasagar know full well that there are unsolved problems in all areas of science. In magic, the unsolved problems are so famous and obvious and intractable as to be named and numbered. The Biology Problem, the Conservation Problem, the Listener Problem. One, Two, Three.

Hatt says, "I don't know—" but Vidyasagar appears determined to speak his piece:

"What process in the human body produces it? What part of the human brain channels and distributes it? How is it that humans have this capability, but no other known species has it? How is it that we have this capability, fully evolved, yet have never demonstrated it before 1972?"

"I don't know," Hatt says. "Nobody knows. I admit it. Nobody in the world knows."

"We generate mana. Mana: magical energy. It evaporates up from our skin in clouds. We have auras, clearly visible with appropriate oracles. This is a distinct form of energy from chemical energy or kinetic energy. We can track the movements of all five classes of mana particle. We are living generators and the amount of mana we generate is more, far more, than any of us ingest as food. Where does the energy come from?"

Hatt's struggling for the vocabulary. "Magic is on the flip side of quantum mechanics. It exists in this dark zone, it's not subject to the conservation laws that we understand."

"That's not an answer," Vidyasagar says. "That's the absence of an answer. That's a confession of defeat. You are not a scientist."

"I don't take that as an insult," Hatt says.

"And I don't mean it as one."

"Maybe it's geological," says Hatt. "The geothermal mana exchange doesn't violate the conservation laws as far as we can tell. Maybe there's a connection there that nobody can detect yet."

"'Maybe.' 'Maybe.' 'Maybe.' Answers. Who is listening? Magic words must be spoken aloud. Why?" Vidyasagar gestures around the room. "Why? To whom?"

"And that's basically the biological question again," says Hatt. "It's part of the mental model of magic. It's a mantra, it triggers a process in the mind—"

"A guess," Vidyasagar says. "That was always a guess. There's no evidence."

There's a pause.

Vidyasagar says this: "*Why can't we answer these questions?*

"We've attacked them and attacked them. I have, and so have many others. For decades. They are basic questions. We should be past them. But we aren't."

Hatt tries to read Vidyasagar. "And this... frightens you?"

"This doesn't frighten me," says Vidyasagar. "Not knowing things doesn't *frighten* me. As long as I've been alive, the number of things I don't know has only ever grown. And you're the same, in your way. What frightens me is the very notion of giving up on knowing. Because this is *important*."

"I'm not... I'm not giving up on knowing," Hatt says. "Really. I really think we'll work it all out one day."

"So do I," says Vidyasagar, sitting up straight. "And I'm not giving up on knowing either. Thank you for the offer of the role of Director of Special Projects, but I'm afraid I can't accept it. I shall resign instead."

"You'll retire?" Hatt shows significant relief. This works even better for him — it's equally face-saving and it'll save him a big chunk of money.

"No," says Vidyasagar. "I won't retire. I'll resign."

Hatt works this out. "And... keep working? You're going to go and find another job?"

"Certainly." Vidyasagar smiles. "I doubt it would be difficult, as 'father of the first age of magic'. I believe I have at least another ten years of work ahead of me and I intend to use all of my allotted time. What is it you said just now? After pure theory being of no value to you?"

*

Some are desperately in love with magic, latching onto it as the defining feature of their universe.

Meanwhile, there's Alan Minter. He is forty, stubbly and weighty. He doesn't define himself as a mage, or even as an engineer; in fact, if somebody asked him straight, "How do you define yourself?" he'd laugh the question off as slightly ridiculous. Magic is a thing he does to live. He likes it well enough because it's challenging and stable and it gives his wife and kids some financial security. His is a boat which would rather not be rocked.

It's 1998 and Minter's worked at Hatt Group since the mid-Eighties. He's been unable to avoid gradually acquiring managerial responsibility for a few tiers of people. He manages these people well, by being fundamentally incapable of perceiving or putting up with nonsense.

Yes, Alan Minter is a little bit boring. (Because *that's* what you want in your new all-magical avionics systems: *unpredictability*.)

"Alan!" Edward Hatt shouts at him one day. "I want to look into using Tanako's world for demos."

Minter stops mid-stride, just about to push open the door to the men's room. "What?"

Hatt is at the other end of the corridor, headed in a totally different direction. He has coffee in one hand and an open laptop computer in the other; he is between two meetings. "Customer demos," he shouts, not coming any closer. "Can you get some people together and look into it? Monday okay?"

"Monday? Erm."

Hatt gives him an awkward, coffee-encumbered thumbs-up and mouths "You got it" and disappears.

Minter digests this. Many years ago, in the eleven-month gap between graduation and joining Hatt, Minter worked at a comically badly-run magic startup. The company's business model was cryptic at best; perhaps it was thought that if enough talented mages were gathered in one room, some sort of critical mass would be reached and money would start condensing out of the aether. In the absence of any consistent managerial direction, Minter spent most of that time studying the commercial possibilities of T-world. He became a very narrow expert. Then he came to his senses, bailed out of the company, took an actual job and forgot about the entire thing.

Never be the expert, Minter tells himself. He must have mentioned it to Hatt by accident. Or mentioned it to somebody else who mentioned it to Hatt.

It's mid-afternoon on Thursday, but Minter has the mother of all interlock tests to oversee on Friday and he knows his people are too busy. So it's a solo weekend job. He digs around in his private email for a while, seeing if he can find remnants of his old work. There are shreds.

Edward Hatt is either one level or two levels above Minter in the Group hierarchy, depending on how you look at it. Alan Minter doesn't actually like him very much. Not many people do.

*

Now this is a meeting in a dull meeting room with white boards and a projector and a Powerpoint presentation. Hatt Group has two kinds of meeting room. Rooms of the first kind have actually had money spent on them. They are cool, spacious, windowed and air-conditioned. There are big, expensive chairs with headrests and lumbar support. Those rooms are for visitors.

Minter wishes he was in one of those rooms, because this room is for internal meetings only and it is the opposite of all of those things.

Hatt arrives fifteen minutes late, carrying the same laptop and what might as well be the same coffee. He opens the door with an impressively agile manoeuvre which involves hooking one foot under the handle.

"Right," Hatt says, before he has sat down. This is Minter's cue to begin.

Minter looks at the presentation that he has spent the weekend assembling and immediately loses faith in it. Too many words. Three entire slides setting up what Tanako's world is? *Clip art?* There's nobody in the room but qualified mages. Skip. Skip. Skip. *Hell with it.* Minter closes the computer and just speaks.

"There were a few seconds there when T-world stood a chance of being the next revolution in popular entertainment media," he explains. "T-world is cold and hostile most of the time, but if you dream lucidly you can throw your own creations over it. Once you're at that point, it's better than a 3D movie. You get sight, sound, smell, touch and taste. You can even directly trigger emotional responses. The problem is that what you can do in T-world is limited only by what you can imagine."

Minter stops talking for a second and lets Hatt think about this last statement.

Hatt responds, "Well, shit."

"Yeah. In the same way that a magic spell only works as long as the mage carries total comprehension of all of its complexity in his head, the illusion that you can deliver has to be *realised* in its entirety by you. On the spot. In real time. We can throw all the graphic and sound designers we like at the scenario, but you'll have to learn and reproduce all of it mechanically.

"It's not as bad as it could be. T-world is a dream, which changes the rules from other kinds of media. We can cheat. A lot. There's only one direction which a person can look in, which is forwards. And a person can only pay attention to a few things at a time. If you can direct someone's attention confidently, you can direct their attention *narrowly*, which reduces the amount of stuff which you need to 'render' at any given time. This might be true even if there are multiple people in the group that you carry with you."

"Like a card trick," Hatt says.

"I suppose. Do you do any conjuring?"

Hatt shakes his head. On the other hand, he likes the idea of wowing people. He could find the time to learn.

Minter goes on. "The next factor is safety. A regular T-world trance, such as you or I have every two to seven weeks or whatever, draws almost no mana. But to bring other people with you, you're looking at real money. Days or weeks of saved 'wages'. And meanwhile, the physical danger of T-world is directly linked to the local thaumic flux density. So there's a balancing act. The more people you bring, the greater the danger."

"What's the safe upper limit?" Hatt asks.

Minter is an aerospace engineer. His definition of 'safe' is concrete and numerical. "Right now, the safe upper limit is not to do it at all," he says.

Hatt is also an aerospace engineer. He correctly interprets Minter's statement to mean that there is no data available at this time. "Do you want to take a guess?"

"No."

"You mentioned taking multiple people just now."

"Hypothetically. Tests are needed."

Hatt nods.

Minter continues. "Con three. T-world is a nightmare. It's a recurring nightmare and over time it fills up with an invasive biological grinding noise and horrible monsters which chase you until you wake up. This is not something you can get away from. There *is* a grace period. You'd need to end the scene before you came to the end of that grace period. Otherwise, you're exposing customers to an out-of-control horror movie."

"How much time are we talking about?"

"Dream time and real time aren't exactly the same thing," Minter says.

"So you're going to go and find that out too."

"Yes."

"But it probably needs to be short. Like a few minutes."

Minter doesn't comment.

"So it's a teaser trailer," Hatt concludes.

"I suppose so," says Minter.

Hatt pushes his seat out a bit. He feels the need to pace, but doesn't have room. "This is okay. That's tight, but I can definitely work with it. Was that the whole list?"

"Yes."

"So the main piece of bad news here is that I'm going to have to do a lot of the heavy lifting myself."

"Yes. It's a tough collection of spells. And you'll have to put most of them together yourself. Unless you want to get somebody else to handle that part for you."

"No, no. It's my demo. I need to be the one who delivers it. Especially given what you're saying about safe carrying capacities."

"I'm going to crunch some numbers," Minter says.

Hatt nods again. "I'm still thinking out loud here. Even if we can push that number higher, I want to do the demo. Because that's impressive to people. If I'm at the top, CEO position, and *I* can show people some gee-whizz wizardry, nothing up my sleeve, that's going to leave a strong impression. It hints at what everybody else in the organisation is really capable of. You professional mages, I mean. Everybody who doesn't sit in an office all day. This is like... it's a performance, I like it. What would I actually need to do? Am I memorising a script or something?"

"You need a mental picture," Minter explains. "Some scenery, some personalities, some lines. Actually, you need a scene."

"Actually, I need a vision."

Minter shrugs.

Hatt claps. "That's it! We're sitting here surrounded by concept art! It's hanging right there in reception. I can show them the spaceport."

Minter can't help snorting at this. Hatt glares at him.

"I'm sorry," says Minter. "You do a lot of business flying, right?"

"Yes?"

"You fly alone? First class? Yeah." Minter smiles broadly. "Airports haven't been cool since the Fifties, and spaceports are going to be even worse. When I'm in an airport, I have three kids and my other half. To us, an airport means screaming kids, crowds, queues, lost baggage, cramped seats and delays, delays, delays. All the concept art in the world isn't going to shake off that association. For the love of God, don't show them the spaceport. At least, not the interior."

Hatt and Minter deliver the last line together: "Show them the spaceships."

*

It's now.

Anil Devi is one of the fastest-moving minds Ed Hatt has ever worked with. Devi treats conversations as optimisation problems. He assumes everybody involved possesses all the knowledge he does and thinks as fast as he does, and then proceeds to skip two out of every three sentences because the rest is so obvious that it doesn't need to be said. His magic work is the same: intermediate stages of spell construction, which others would insist on having a big explicit written plan for, he will wave away as trivial because he can improvise them in the moment. Every mage has a distinct style and Devi will cheerfully steal pieces of that style from every mage he meets. He is a packrat for shortcuts. His spells are baffling spaghetti.

All of this makes him hard to work with. Mere *procedure* and *best practice* are anchors around his neck. Meanwhile, any kind of engineering not involving magic in some way — of which Hatt Group does a great deal — bores him stiff. Managing him is a juggling act. But then, managing any collection of one or more people is a juggling act.

He phones Hatt directly from D12A and says, "So, I don't know what the flux was in Ferno's farewell stunt but there's definitely been a conservation violation. You should pull in a biotech lab because I've got no idea what this thing is. I can give you some phone numbers."

"...What thing?"

"The good news is you've got around a hundred and fifty gigs left in your battery. 'Aliasing' was a good keyword but the technique is probably basically brain surgery, it'll take me a little while to hack out. End of the year? She had a head start, clearly. I'd love to meet this mythical parent of hers. So anyway, this Christmas you're looking at some rainy day money."

"'Rainy day money'," says Hatt, blankly.

"And it reeks down here!" Devi adds. "You should have punched up the priority on this, I had to get a mask, you have no clue."

"I'm sorry, who is this?"

Devi gears down. "Anil. Anil Devi. Three-and-a-half weeks ago you asked me to cover the fallout from Laura Ferno's 'leaving do'. Right?"

"Yeah. Yes, I remember. Wait, you're just doing this now?"

"I've had the 4100-series closeout," says Devi, "and you gave me the clearance but you didn't say there was a corpse involved and then the two-factor thing happened, so, yeah."

"There's a *corpse* involved?"

"What did you think it was, chopped liver? Actually, there is a certain resemblance."

"What what was? Where are you?"

"I'm in D12A," Devi says, "and my friend, it is a *horror show* down here. T plus three-and-a-half weeks and oh my bloody god."

"Are you saying there's a dead body in there?"

Devi inhales, stops, exhales puzzledly, inhales again, "Yes, I'm saying that my name is Anil Devi, and I'm saying that I'm in D12A and I'm saying that there's been a dead body in here for the last three-and-a-half weeks."

"Whose?"

Devi glances at it. "I would say it's extremely doubtful that it's anybody's in particular."

"But it's human?"

"I did not, and would not, say that."

"I'm coming down."

*

D12A is still itself: a tall, square, fluorescent-lit room with a thirteen-metre D occupying most of its floor space. In one corner is a rack of safety equipment (fire extinguishers, Montauk rings, telephone) and a short flight of stairs leading up to the door. Spread around the circle are the various Hatt Group-owned magical artifacts that Laura Ferno was using for her ill-advised spell. There is also the small music stand that she was using for her notes. The notes themselves, she took with her, along with her staff and other own equipment.

This much is exactly as Hatt remembers it ought to be.

"I escorted her out of the room," he recalls. "I swiped us both out and locked the door behind me. I fired her, and a few minutes after that I told you to come down and try to piece together her bilge mana spell."

"And then I ignored you for most of a month," says Devi.

"I didn't see this. I wasn't even looking for this. Half of the lights weren't turned on. You understand."

Lying at one node on the edge of the D is a dead thing.

Its skin colour is probably comparable with Caucasian, but the thing is almost completely coated with dried blood, and certainly is not human. It's gangly and long: if it stood up straight, it would be more than two metres tall. It is emaciated. Its highly visible bone structure is all wrong: its knees and elbows are backwards and instead of hands or feet it has four large fingertips with torn nails. Its spine bifurcates halfway up its back, and it has a row of closed eyes running up between its shoulders. Its head lacks all orifices but a lipless hole where a mouth would usually go, with two rows of sharp metal scalpels for teeth. Meanwhile, its six sets of ribs are actually jawbones; each pair parts individually to reveal one of five mouths, complete with conventional teeth and a tongue.

Devi shows Hatt the details. Both Devi and Hatt wear face masks and latex gloves.

The horror's cause of death is uncertain. It looks as if every one of its joints is dislocated, but it could be meant to look like that. It's even less certain whether it was ever technically alive.

D12A is filled with the stench of decay.

Devi summarises, "It's something out of a nightmare. I mean, a specific one. One guess whose."

"She actually did it," Hatt says, standing up from a difficult crouch. "She brought a real object back from Tanako's world. If all the mana she spent had been piped into a perfect energy/matter exchanger, the most she could get out was two point four milligrams. This is something else."

Hatt has that chill again. The rules of his universe are expanding. And he's right there at the beginning. The thing in front of him is terrifying, but the feeling is good.

Devi says nothing.

"You mentioned phone numbers?" Hatt says to Devi. "Pick a discreet one."

"And send them some samples for testing," Devi says. "You got it."

"Have you got enough equipment down here to set up a refrigeration spell?"

Devi nods. The ground underneath them is a working D-class with a nested E. It would be difficult to pick a better location.

Hatt takes his gloves off. "And once you've done that, find Laura Ferno."

19
Deeper Magic

The entity possessing Nick Laughon sits in the easy chair. It sits easily.

Laura remains standing, arms folded. Laura's been watching it carefully. There's a thing that the-thing-that-isn't-Nick hasn't done. It hasn't displayed any unfamiliarity with its surroundings. Right after being "woken up", the thing that isn't Nick got up, took a leak, put some clothes on. Now it slouches in a very Nick-like position, enviably comfortable, feet up, with a big glass of water. It moves like Nick. It? He?

Laura has waited long enough. "Explain."

"I am Kazuya Tanako. My True Name was `ra`."

There it is. It's beautiful to her, like light dawning. "...Of course you are. Of course! That makes sense. You died in Tanako's world. Your world! The place we named after you after you'd died there. You didn't call it that, obviously. You called it something else."

"'The glass place', 'the glass dream', 'pattern one', 'black marble', lots of different things," Tanako explains. "Now, my question to you is, what else do you know?"

"You... you were one of the most talented young mages of your generation. And magic is at most two generations old, which puts you into the top twenty of all time. God. You were— you weren't magic's Mozart but you were almost our Jimi Hendrix." Tanako laughs at this. "You were the first person to lead a team investigation of Tanako's— of the glass. The experiment in which you died... involved lying down at the reflux core of a powered Dehlavi lightning apparatus, then being placed into an induced coma. A REM trip to the glass world usually lasts minutes of real time. Your intention was to stay there for at least an hour. You wanted to... try to work your way towards a point of lucidity, where it would be possible to start gathering real observations. I remember now. You wore a freaky sensor helmet thing, which covered your whole head and face.

"You had a stroke. You died in the glass place. But you didn't die. It looked like you died, but you didn't. So what really happened?"

"I just want to clear some things up before we continue," Tanako says. "Am I still the only person to have died there?"

"As far as anybody knows, yes," Laura says. "Sleep science research slowed *way* down after the accident. We have libraries of safety guidelines now. I know this better than most. I've had that stuff dropped on me from a great height."

"I know. Thaumic Engineering Safety Part III. You complained about it for weeks."

"...Of course. You were Benj Clarke."

"Indeed. And secondly: I tried to blow up a fair chunk of northern Iceland. While you were standing on it. What made you think it was safe to bring me back?"

"You can't do anything without hardware," says Laura. She holds her right fist up — she has two rings on her middle finger as well as some wrist bracelets. Her improvised self-defence spells have been radically redeveloped in recent years, and if Tanako has inherited as much from Nick as Laura thinks, he knows this.

His English is excellent. Because it's clearly Nick's English.

"Very well," says Tanako.

"So. Explain."

*

I was the first child of the magic generation. *On The Theory Of The Coaxial Production Of The ζ And ι Fields* happened when I was eleven, which means magic was starting to hit its stride as a practical science just as I was getting my teeth into trigonometry. As a kid, I could see nothing but magic around me. It was like an open secret world, as if I was walking through this garden of invisible patterns.

Magic was magnetism plus five dimensions, plus ten million points of street cred. I knew it was cool because nobody I knew knew anything about it. Nobody in my family, none of my friends, none of my teachers. Eventually I found an electronics teacher, Mr. Yamada. He still knew nothing, but he was as interested as I was, so he threw some journal articles my way and helped me understand them, even though he could barely understand them himself. I cast for the first time when I was fourteen. I don't know if that's still the record. I knew then that I had been born a mage.

My early work... well, turned out to be my only work. I developed the EMμ flatfold. I put vocabulary and syntax discovery onto a footing firmer than trial and error. I dipped into hardware for long enough to build five completely custom tools, four of which became global standards. And reams of papers, some of them just off-the-wall free-association built around one good equation. I was lucky. I had opportunities. I was surrounded by the furiously intelligent.

No science had ever exploded into being in the same way that magic did. Never before had something so radically new and totally unexplored been stumbled upon by a human civilisation so primed with experience and technology to go to work on it. It was like discovering a brand new empty Earth. You can't even imagine those glory days. Everything worked. Every line of research struck solid gold. There were no dead ends to find if you tried. Every year, what we knew doubled and what we didn't know tripled.

It would be impossible to say who had the glass dream first. People don't discuss their dreams. I mean, it happens, but not statistically frequently relative to the dreams themselves. Especially not among physicists. I think it's because dreams are not scientific. They're almost the opposite of scientific. Sleep is the place where rational people are able to leave the phone off the hook, figuratively speaking. We have the phrase, 'sleep on it', but who'd think something relevant or important would come *directly* out of the unconscious?

So it would be impossible to say who had the dream first, but I think it had to have begun in '88 or '89. In the Nineties we hit critical mass; it became a noticed phenomenon in at least three different labs simultaneously. It was clear that there was a structure inside magical theory that everybody was seeing. Glass underfoot and freezing air and a three-armed Milky Way overhead. Clear to everybody except me. I'd never seen it, which was a data point in itself.

The notion caught my attention because it was the first hint of magical science finally circling back towards the biological. In the lines between what people said, I thought I could see a faint connection between the glass and the way that humans are able to conduct magic. Symbols and signs.

Mohit Dehlavi and I pulled some neuroscientists together. The operation was half laboratory research project, half exploration mission. The glass place has more than one entrance. Sleep is one. But if there's a powerful spell, you can slip into it accidentally. The stronger the spell, the harder it is to resist the flip. And so we built a machine to take someone there. A drop capsule into the unconscious. I wasn't the only subject. But, as you say, I was the last.

*

At first I tried mapping the landscape.

I was always dropped in a different location. There were ridges, ravines, dried glass river beds full of clear ovoid marbles. Through no amount of "browsing" could I ever find the same location twice. Mapping had to start over every time. It wasn't possible to be methodical that way. I took to celestial navigation.

The galaxy rotates over time, like a starfish. But its centre is fixed. So that was my reference point. On most excursions I took that point as my North Star, and headed south. If the glass had positive curvature, eventually I'd have to hit the south pole. At the very least, I would see some new sky on the way.

Ra

The world was far too big to walk across, so I dreamt of scramjets.

You can't measure time there, or distance, so I don't know how far I travelled. Call it a light year. I think I'd managed to persuade myself that the horizon ahead was lightening. It could have been my imagination.

There was a dark structure on the horizon. It was an incredible distance off when I spotted it, and it was so gigantic that I misjudged my approach and overshot it while trying to rendezvous. I can't draw for love nor money so I'm just going to have to list some things that it looked like: an egg built of bricks with its tip pointed down; some kind of rosebud about ten percent of the way into flowering; a big fat beetle with greebles and tendrils. Giger meets Mandelbrot. It was as big as Manhattan and black as ink.

The local landscape was mesas and ravines and impossible stacked rocks, like a Road Runner cartoon. The artifact didn't touch the ground at any point, but the idea that it should fall, or even that it could fall, didn't even occur to me. I landed my jet on top of it, where there was a kind of pad. Then I was inside it, and it didn't occur to me that I hadn't consciously decided to go inside.

*

The hall contained all of planet Earth. An observation walkway overlooked it from about the Tropic of Cancer. The Earth was a dark grey rock, presented at one-to-one scale. The walkway was quite short; I made a complete circuit in a few seconds.

The Earth was illuminated with red points of activity. At first I read it as geothermal activity: portions of the mid-Atlantic rift, huge arcs of Pacific rim, the Himalayas.

Then I spotted points in India and Europe and North America, clustered around population centres. And on a hunch I looked for Kyoto, and there was a clear flare. I looked closer, and although there was no detail beyond bedrock, it was clearly me, asleep inside Dehlavi's lightning machine.

The room, I discovered, was hypercylindrical. It was a four-dimensional tube with a spherical cross-section. The observation walkway led not in two directions, but three: left, right and *kata*. I took a step *kata*. The Earth rolled west a few degrees. I kept moving in the same direction and the planet rolled back and back. When I headed *ana* again it rolled forward until I reached the "top" of the tower and couldn't go any further. As I moved *ana* and *kata*, the patterns of mana usage pulsed like blood vessels. I realised that I was exploring a projection of a long recording, a synthesis of historical mana usage across the whole planet.

As I stepped further into the past, the flare in Kyoto blanked out. I watched closely as I continued *kata* and I saw other spells setting up and winding down, and I remembered the words and the names and the mages associated with those spells. Many of them were me or Dehlavi or other mages I knew. I looked west, to Germany and France and the UK, and saw research spells in private laboratories, and industrial magic folding down and shutting off — because I was watching the recording in reverse, and what was really happening was that the industrial usage of magic was spreading. It was like injecting barium into a human's bloodstream and watching it spread using a radiation scanner. It suddenly occurred to me that it was almost like taking off for the Moon, and then looking back at the world through a full-colour Kanditz oracle.

And that's when I realised the real truth. What is an oracle? How does it work? We know that by Vidyasagar's Third Incomplete Field Equation, all magic usage yields waste. There's an experimental disagreement between what was predicted by the second revision of that equation and what was observed and ultimately modelled by the third. The χ field models that disagreement. Chi mana is the waste, the stuff that escapes the system. Ki no luokotomamba nuolo a la ra pemba kastela! Non-interacting. When you think of chi particles you should think of neutrinos with attached metadata. If you built a machine large enough, you could watch it all!

This was it. This was the view, the core, the locus of magical usage. I was at the centre of an artificial/virtual/magical/real hypermachine, apparently buried in the collective unconscious minds of all students of magic, a surveillance device, a machine designed to do nothing but, like a seismograph, watch and record and present its results, cold figures like moths pinned to boards.

I rotated the image in some fifth direction and the dark Earth turned green. There were no seismic records now. Now I really was looking at a population graph. I could detect no distinction. The Earth alone was like some polished commercial Granny Smith apple, totally unblemished, with pinpricks of neon lemon green crawling over it like mould, some of them actually visibly *crawling* — travelling by plane. I say mould, but it looked *good*. It looked like *productivity* at work. It felt like a picture of success and prosperity. The sensation was strange. The map was a map of *mages*. All possible mages, even the untrained. So: all humans. Europe and India, the American coasts. There were names!

Thaumic power output is one of those insane unsolved biological questions. Maybe even unsolvable. Some of us are strong, some are weak. It depends on your height, your health, how much sleep you've had, what you've eaten. Probably, a big whack of it comes directly out of your genotype. Most people never even try magic and never find out what kind of power they put out. They never find their *wattage*. Even among those capable of being tested, the quantification is so tedious and expensive, and the difference between the top and bottom performers is so minor, that it's hardly ever worth bothering.

And here I was, looking at hard statistics for everybody in the world. I looked closely at Kyoto again, comparing myself with Dehlavi. Hah.

I spun the Earth a little further and it went dark again. The plan showed cyan Montauk storage data. With the greatest concentration, of course, in the little plant in Montauk, New York, the old "Other Battery Park". The rest in heavy research installations, and the *rest* of the rest in mages' toolboxes and on their hips.

Another click, like the dial on a thermostat, and I was looking at a cloudy white density map. This one had slight clustering at population centres, but plenty of density in totally uninhabited parts of the world too. I was able to roll the altitude up and down. I started at sea level, but as I tore layers of planetary structure away I saw the same pale fuzz all the way in to the deepest core. I even found that the cloud extended out into space.

And more, and more. More colours. Primary, secondary, and then those impossible colours which you can only see by hot-wiring your photoreceptors. There were maps I couldn't read. Earths I couldn't interpret. Data, metadata.

I grabbed the rungs and slid further *kata*, back in time. As I went back, the use of magic worldwide flickered and dimmed out. I found a way to cut geological magic out of the picture, leaving only human usage. I rolled back until I was looking at what I knew had to be India in what I knew had to be the middle of the height of the Northern Hemisphere's summer of 1972. I watched for the spark and then zeroed in on it and what I saw — although there was, of course, no photographic data — was a tiny flicker of a man who had True Name aum and who had cast the tiny and inconsequential spell that we now call uum.

And then I crept slowly further *kata*.

I saw what looked like ancient nuclear tests. I couldn't say when. They happened across Siberia and Africa and the Australian desert. Most of them, though, were in the oceans.

You understand: this was magical activity happening before magic was discovered. Something long hypothesised, frequently claimed as fact in wild conspiracy theories, and eternally, *categorically* debunked.

Yeah.

I wanted to go back further in time, to try to find out just when these anomalies began. But there was no time scale that I could make sense of. It was just: left, right, forward, back. So instead I chose a flare at random and dived in.

*

I woke up under lukewarm salt water, with my lungs bursting. My eyes were shut and I kept them shut instinctively but they stung like hell anyway. I kicked towards the surface but there was some metallic clamp thing hanging onto my right wrist, holding me down. I panicked for a second but it turned out that the arm was bringing me to the surface anyway. We both broke through and I managed to gulp down some air. Mostly air.

I was in the Pacific. I hope that narrows it down for you, because I couldn't for the life of me quote a latitude or a longitude. I was being pulled out of the water by a robotic submarine. It was an orange lozenge about the size of a motorbike, with cameras all over and articulated grabbing arms. I managed to twist my wrist free, and fell back into the water while the sub was lifted back into the boat. A life ring landed in the water next to me and I grabbed it.

The boat was hardly larger than the submersible it was carrying. The crew seemed to be one person. His look wasn't oceanographer or professional diver. It was retired, teenaged, dotcom billionaire. Flapping white shirt, Armani shades, a wristwatch the size of a brick. He was bald; he had the skull for it. He moved like the boat was his yacht and this was his holiday cruise.

Now, imagine you're holding a baseball made of perfect, solid gold. Imagine there's a fat explosive charge in the middle of the ball, and it goes off. The gold blasts out and backwards, covering your fingers like a gauntlet and spreading back across most of your forearm. Imagine curly formations of gold flaring back from your knuckles and your wrist bones. It looks like you've grabbed hold of the explosion itself. This is what I had wrapped around my right hand.

I realised that the robotic submarine must have brought the gauntlet up from somewhere on the ocean floor. I had appeared with my arm inside the gauntlet thing while it was in the sub's grip. There was no risk of me being pulled under by its weight; the gauntlet barely weighed anything. Gold rolls out to microns thick, and that was what it felt like. It felt like it was fitting itself to my *fingerprints*.

So there I was, hanging on to the life ring, wearing a piece of treasure that this boy had clearly gone to great trouble and expense to dredge up from the bottom of the Pacific. Obviously it was incredibly valuable; obviously, he was going to want to take it off me somehow. I hoped that it wouldn't involve hacking my arm off. I tried to see if I could take it off myself, but it wouldn't budge. The fit was too tight.

The boy asked me what my name was. I told him, "Kazuya Tanako."

A second passed and I'd swear he was listening to somebody talking to him. He said to me, "That doesn't make a lick of sense. Your best match isn't born yet. How did you get here?"

I didn't say anything, partly because I felt like it was the only valuable chip of information I had, and partly because I was barely sure I believed it myself.

He asked me again, "How did you get here?"

I asked him, "What's *your* name?"

He said his name was Alexander Watson. He said nothing else for a long while. It was clear that he was trying to work out what to do. I asked if I could come aboard. That seemed to snap him out of it. He pulled me in using the line attached to the life ring, and then lifted me up out of the water and onto the deck, pretty much one-handed. He sat me down on a bench on the deck. "It's okay," he said, "Let's see what we can do about that arm."

I felt like he was giving it a medical examination. Eventually something in his mind went *ding* and he seemed to relax. "It's just a replay," he said. "My good friends at the old Cassandra Complex are reporting the mother of all data loss events."

I said, "I don't know what that means."

Watson said — this was all a little muddled, it never felt as if any of his sentences followed logically from the earlier ones — "So you found the listening station, not bad. I'm not worried about it. Reality's been notified. And, you know, we get some flexibility from now until the end of time. We can enjoy the sandbox while waiting to die."

I said, "I don't know what that means, either."

He said, "Still... better safe than sorry."

He took hold of my arm with both hands and started injecting magic into it. I didn't realise what was happening at first, because he didn't say any magic words. But pretty soon, there was enough magic pouring out of him that it hurt my brain to be sitting there. I was practically blinded.

He stopped and took a step back, as if waiting for something to happen. Then the gauntlet imploded. It imploded to a brilliant red spark and then the spark evaporated into ash. It took most of my arm with it, everything from the shoulder down.

I can't describe the pain.

The implosion sprayed gore and crushed bone fragments over me and Watson and most of the deck. I fell, with more blood gushing out of my shoulder. Watson just stood there, watching. I blacked out in three seconds. I was probably dead from blood loss in another sixty.

*

Laura has long since sat down.

"You were murdered," she says.

"I was killed in my sleep," Tanako says, with a half-grin. He was smiling all the way through the last part of the story. Laura, who has no fondness for black comedy, found it deeply disconcerting.

"Let me get this right," she continues. "If you're remembering what this Watson guy said correctly... You found your way into a holodeck-quality recording. The personality in the recording — the snapshot personality of 'Alexander Watson' — realised what was happening, recognised you as an intruder, went off-script and killed you. After that, playback ended and he would have 'died' too, the same way a film's characters die when the film ends."

Tanako nods in agreement. "Go on."

"I have many questions. To begin with, I want to know what was supposed to happen. You dived into the memory of a huge magical event, but then disrupted that event by being there."

"I don't think I did," Tanako says. "I think Watson wanted to destroy the artifact, and that's what he did. Remember, it took about a megaton of magic to do."

"You're suggesting that he pulled that thing up from the bottom of the ocean because he didn't think it was *safe* where it *was*? It was made of solid gold, Kazuya, it had to be worth something. Who knows what kind of hoard it was part of? You know what, this is ridiculous. I'm assuming that there was a real event at all, which you can't prove, and that this listening station thing is real for *any* level of 'real', and that pre-magic history isn't what any of us think—"

"It only takes a few grams," Tanako explains, and holds his right hand out.

The gauntlet instantiates, unrolling in an eyeblink from the speck of gold held between his thumb and forefinger.

Laura comes within a hair's breadth of reflexively blowing Tanako's head off. She stumbles back into the far corner of the room, aiming her entire self-defence array back at Tanako. She manages to bite down on her tongue before the triggering syllable leaps out of her mouth.

The gauntlet is too beautiful for this world. Its tendrils wave like flower petals, like slow-moving licks of flame. Laura can barely look away from it. Tanako sits easily — his feet up, the water glass empty on the table beside him.

"What is that? *What is it? Tell me!*"

Tanako smiles benevolently. "It has no name. In fact, I think naming it would remove a great deal of its power. It's a labour-saving device; it saves mages from having to comprehend infinity. It allows magic to do magic. It allows spells to cast spells which cast spells.

"I used this on Krallafjöll, when I was Benj Clarke."

Laura's arm wobbles fractionally. "Recursion."

"More like... recursion's ugly big brother."

"...You cast a spell without full comprehension. I remember now. You cast a spell without having to keep the whole thing in your head at once. You found a machine— which— Oh my God. You found the Holy Grail. You're Prometheus, you stole a miracle from a dream. Twice!"

"No. You did."

Tanako flexes his arm and fingers. He has absolute freedom of movement. The gauntlet might as well be made of mist and spider silk. Its gold flows and curls around Tanako, like deep, turbulent magic.

Laura says, "We could build *anything*."

"You see why someone would want to destroy it," Tanako concludes.

"It works. It really works." Laura slumps back against the wall and shuts down her defensive spells. She shakes her head, still not able to look away. "This changes everything. It changes *everything.*"

"You must have more questions," Tanako says, after it becomes clear that Laura has forgotten how to speak.

"I do," says Laura, "I do. I'll get to them. Just give me a minute. For this moment, this is all I want."

20
There Is No Cabal

Laura is stumbling drunkenly across a world that's like the sterilised mirror underside of reality, the blue and black and silver-grey upside-down place seen in rain puddles. It's a place where nothing that happens is good; where some nightmare was uncorked and spread through the air, worming its way into people's tongues and eyeballs and alveoli, seeping into the surfaces until there was nothing but nightmare to see or eat or drink. The air is as cold as bone and seems to breeze through her instead of around her. The air has an unsettling texture, as if there are occasional invisible strands of cobweb stirred into it. There's an irritating electronic buzzing, like some combination of metal cutting devices operating intermittently half a street away. It hurts to think.

Laura blitters across the glass landscape. Nobody can remember the start of a dream. She is trudging through a black glass mountain valley with jagged glass boulders and glass shards crackling underfoot like frost. She wonders if there's a special word for a glass glacier.

The sky overhead features the familiar pale triple-pointed galaxy, the forked Milky Way, but today it disconcerts Laura for reasons that she cannot pull together in her head. It is simultaneously reassuring and alarming. Laura is asleep and not reasoning at maximum capacity. All she knows is that she wants to find shelter.

The mountain ranges on each side elongate and coalesce until the valley has become a ravine. The ravine changes direction crazily, filling space, adding to its length, so that even flicking from location to location at a wish it takes Laura hours to make measurable progress. From above, it starts to look like a white noise waveform. It must be tens of thousands of miles long. Its walls become almost vertical and totally unscalable.

The floor of the ravine sprouts tiny white daisy things, which look soft right up until Laura treads on one. They're extruded crystals, and they function like caltraps. From the ravine walls grow spider plants, whose leaves are long curved shards of broken wine bottle. Laura has to duck or turn sideways to edge past them without slashing herself open. It's at this point that she realises that the ravine is gradually narrowing, and then looks up to realise that it has begun to close up over her head. Her throat rasps. The electrobuzzing is becoming louder.

Laura has been here for a long time and is gradually coming to realise it.

*

The ravine becomes a tunnel. What little starlight there was fizzles out, leaving Laura picking her way through an increasingly jagged blind nightmare. She illuminates her path by creating a picture of light in her head. The picture is red. Laura doesn't perceive that there are other colours she could choose. She creates red light. It is almost worse. Now she can see some of the surroundings, but the green leaves in particular are black and too indistinct to focus on. The passage flicks from uniform deep black to a puddle of dim red surrounded by deep shadows. And the light source, for dream logic reasons, comes into being in front of one of her eyes, a LED-pure light aimed *into* it like an optometrist's scope. It's not quite blinding, but painful, forming a dull point in Laura's retina. She sees blood vessel patterns overlaying her vision.

It's miles further before the tunnel forks for the first time. Laura remembers her maze training — consisting entirely of her mother once telling her "always follow the left-hand side" — and goes left. The tunnel rises and falls and zags enough times for Laura to lose her bearings, before it forks again. Both forks are smaller than the parent tunnel. The plant life is petering out, but the walls are becoming blocky as they close in, as if made of thick slabs of sharp-edged glass, placed to catch her clothes. Laura goes left again.

Much later, at a 60-degree right turn, Laura spots a crack in the left wall. The unacceptable lighting conditions mean that it would have been very easy to miss it in passing. The crack is just wide enough to slide through sideways without being cut in more than a few places — definitely both elbows, and maybe a rib or two. It's dark and, looking right into it, Laura can't tell how far it goes beyond an immediate right-angled turn.

Follow the left-hand side. She must have walked past six of these side alleys without realising it.

She is lost.

The noise is driving her crazy. Considering retracing her steps, Laura turns suddenly, catching a shoulder on the wall and carving a wound all the way down to her elbow. She inhales to cry out but at that instant she sees, down the corridor, the thing which has been following her. The thing is three turns away, mostly obscured by outcroppings of rough glass, and it is wrong. It is a very young child's drawing of a man, with exaggerated features and nonsensical proportions, made flesh. It's the wrong shape, its face and teeth are wrong, its body is wrong. It's extremely dark and it's standing completely still, not looking in Laura's direction. It occupies the full width and height of the corridor. It is somehow larger than anything the corridor can strictly accommodate.

Laura holds her breath. As the thing turns and begins to glide along the corridor in her direction, Laura kills her light and tries to shuffle blindly into the side alley. It's difficult and fiddly and painful and she seems to get nowhere for a long time while the thing is moving closer. The thing is totally dark except for its illuminated eyeballs and if it makes any noise it cannot be heard over the machines. Laura forces her way around the corner and waits, eyes refusing to adjust, unable to hear anything but the mechanical grinding, and still dribbling blood from her hand, which is now soaked. Her heart might as well be buzzing.

After minutes of waiting, and very slowly, the thing puts its head around the corner. Its head is a fat balloon, a big black elongated comma. It turns to look at her with its eyeballs. It opens its mouth of teeth and tells her, I CAN SEE YOU.

It is at this point that Laura regains consciousness. Thought processes that were freewheeling wildly finally hit the road and find traction. Laura sees where she is and she sees what's happening. She realises that she is having an intensely unpleasant Tanako's World Episode. She realises, also, that she cannot wake up from it.

Is that worse or better?

"Get it together, Ferno," says the man behind her. Laura whips her head around, but does so too quickly and catches it on more glass. She flinches and ducks to clutch the new wound. This provides enough room for the other dreamer to raise a conventional sidearm and fire four conventional bullets over Laura's head and into the thing's face.

The thing tells them HAHEHAHEHEHEHE. It relaxes, rather than collapsing or dying in any convincing way. It is as if its internal supports have suddenly been withdrawn. It falls to the ground in a manner which strongly suggests that it could very easily be reactivated. Its eyes darken, but remain wide open.

Laura's heart rate levels off. She takes stock.

Not much of the man can be seen, because of the cramped environment. He is taller than Laura. He's covered head to toe in a light armour shell and carrying nothing but the gun, which he immediately dismisses. The shell is grey, and thin enough not to make navigating the tunnels impractical but evidently hard enough to withstand contact with the glass without sustaining much more than white scratches. No face is visible.

It's a really good choice of equipment. Laura immediately clothes herself in the same.

"You've gone off mission. Follow me," the man says. He starts moving down the alley. Laura follows him, gingerly at first and then with more confidence once she establishes that sharp glass protrusions can't penetrate the armour.

"Who are you?"

"Who do you think?" Kazuya Tanako turns his helmet transparent. He turns around so Laura can get a good look. "Ta-dah."

"Oh. We're back in T-world, why?"

"'Show, don't tell'," says Tanako. "The things I need to say to you could fill a book, but you'd have no choice but to take the whole thing as fiction. It's how you think. I needed to bring you in here to put your face in front of some evidence. You've found your way into something much bigger than you thought."

"This place is full of evil," Laura says. "Demons, and this noise we're having to shout over. Why wasn't this here before? You said you crossed a light-year of glass unharmed. T-world should fight you. But monsters were conspicuously absent from your story."

Tanako reaches what seems to be a dead end. He feels the tall, narrow pane of glass for a second, then summons his sidearm again and shoots through it. He steps out onto thin air, and helps Laura out too. It is a bottomless ravine with an invisibly thin glass layer supporting them. The near side of the ravine is a sheer wall of fractured glass, with the cracks from Tanako's bullet spreading across it. The far side is buttressed stone, mile-thick castle wall. Both walls go up too far for anything like a sky to be available overhead. Below them is an unholy red light and the noise of combine harvesters coming up to speed. Standing over the gap is painful, like hard radiation.

"You've got a problem with your short-term memory," Kazuya Tanako tells Laura, "so I guess we'll have to go through this whole thing again, Socratic style. Where are we?"

Laura thinks the wall ahead of them is the exterior of a deep layer of her memory palace, but that isn't the question. Tanako strides across clear glass air gap like it's just a basic pavement, unslinging a heavyweight Akira-style laser from hammerspace. He inscribes a luminous pink blob on the wall, then tears the shape out of the wall like paper, letting it whip away into the wind. A dark gap is left. Laura follows him forward, mildly concerned that Tanako broke into her palace with such ease. As they step through, the electromechanical noises tune out, muffled. It's like weight lifting off her thoughts.

Behind the paper-thin/mile-thick wall is her recurring dream-snapshot: Rachel Ferno, Atlantis, ET and full crew complement, all at the instant immediately before their simultaneous destruction.

Click.

Kazuya Tanako prompts her, "It's about two weeks since you woke me. The second time, I mean."

"We're in memory," Laura announces.

"We're in your memory palace right now," Tanako agrees.

"No."

"No?" Tanako already knows the answer, but is guiding Laura towards it.

"It's a *system*," Laura says. "You spoke about finding a listening post. An omega-oracle, a systematic recording of all mana expenditure across all of history. That's where we are, that's what this place is. It's that system's memory.

"This scene is formally allocated. And so are the other things I can't forget, like the eruption at Krallafjöll. And so is the incident where Alexander Watson destroyed Recursion's Big Brother or whatever you want to call it—"

"I don't want to call it anything," Tanako says hurriedly. "It stays anonymous."

"These are the events in history when huge amounts of mana were spent," Laura summarises. "These are stored here, separated by bare recording medium."

"Correct," says Tanako. "In Sanskrit these would be called the *akashic records*. Now, answer your own question. Why the demons now, but not then?"

Laura stares up, once again, at her mother and the orbiter. What she is really looking at is: a plan, at the instant of its fruition.

"Mum *knew*," Laura says. "She knew these records existed. All she had to do was get close enough to Atlantis, and spend a lifetime of magic doing it, and the whole thing would... go on record. Nobody is dead, as long as we remember them *with sufficient fidelity to effect a full reconstruction*."

"Answer your question," Tanako repeats. "Why demons now? And not then?"

"How much matter did you bring back for the anonymous recursion artifact to instantiate in full? A milligram? From a spell I wrote and cast in bed? If that's all it takes to trick the universe, I can bring a person back. I can almost taste it."

"I think you're falling asleep again, Ferno—"

"Scooby-Doo."

"What?"

"Your answer is Scooby-Doo. *Someone built this*."

They are being watched. Something is looking in at them from the ravine outside, a tumorous monkey-giant with infinitely long legs and misplaced shoulders. It is about a hundred metres tall. Only one eye and one nostril are visible through the hole. It smells like fried detergent. It grins like an exterminator, pokes two long hoselike fingers into the room, and sprays Tanako and Laura with a carpet of brown spiders.

Tanako brushes madly at his arms and head, even though his suit keeps him sealed off. He envisions insecticide, then thinks again and envisions arachnicide, if such a thing is real. It is now: his suit becomes slick with bug killer, as if he is showering in the stuff. Layers of spider shrivel up and slough off him. He wades towards Laura.

Laura has summoned a two-metre bo/engineering staff, probably intending to take on the Kong monster outside, but she can't even move it through the knee-height flood of spiders. She throws flame at them, but this is less effective. The brown fuzzy animals heat up like copper, turning red-hot while they start to chew through Laura's helmet. Laura can barely stand. "I want to wake up," she says, "or I want to go to sleep. Either is good!"

Above and behind them, the Atlantis tableau clicks forward one frame. Atlantis is rolling hard left, yawing right. Soichi Noguchi is still fighting its movement. Rachel Ferno is tossed into the orbiter's wake, no longer visible.

"We're doing something difficult but completely possible," Tanako tells her, still wading in her direction. He plays his laser over the face of the Kong monster, with no obvious effect. "You've got enough of the metaphor down to handle this, Ferno. I believe in you."

"Fuck the metaphor!"

"We're being pointed at," says Tanako. "This is the real event memory, the listening post just stores references. Follow the link *back*!"

"Back where?"

Click. Smoke. Fuel trail. The tiniest fragment of flame emerging from the ET shell.

"Back there!"

For the second time, Atlantis explodes.

*

The listening post:

"—inking."

"What?" Laura stumbles like she just stepped out of a roller coaster.

"I said, good thinking," Tanako says. "You used the environment. See down below?"

Laura almost falls onto the railing. Mapped out below is the Florida coast, picked out with lat/long lines, range boundaries and trajectory markers. One arc is Atlantis. Another, rising to meet it, is Rachel Ferno's. The map is suffused with Kanditz oracle colours. It is as familiar to Laura as her own face.

"We followed the shortcut," Laura says.

"Approximately, yes."

Laura is transfixed. She reaches out for the map, but her hand just obscures the view and messes with her depth perception, like a hologram.

She says, "Did you know there's a man whose job is to blow up the Space Shuttle?"

Tanako looks up. "...What? No. You never told me that."

"He's called the Range Safety Officer. The Shuttle launches east, across the Atlantic Ocean. If it stays on course, it never crosses land until the Portuguese coast, by which time it's at orbital velocity. But there are two lines," — she points — "one following Atlantic coast of the US and one through the Caribbean, east of Cuba. The areas behind these lines are inhabited. So, for those people's safety, there are explosive charges on the solid rocket boosters and on the external tank. And there's a man whose job is to push the button that sets them off."

"You mean, if the Shuttle goes off course?" Tanako asks. He blinks. "Doesn't that kill the astronauts?"

"Of course it kills the astronauts. How could it not?"

Tanako stares at her for a while, his head on one side.

"On STS-77 his name was Norman Lederer," Laura adds. "He didn't need to push the button, though. It blew up all by itself."

"...Why are we on this?"

"I don't know," says Laura. "I think it's something to do with destroying big pieces of hardware."

"Yes." This snaps Tanako back into the moment. He claps. "You're right. Now. Questions continue. Where are we?"

"We're inside the listening post. It's real after all."

"Indeed. And where is the listening post?"

"Inside T-world."

"And what is T-world?"

"Memory. The listening post's own internal data bank."

"And how is that possible?"

Laura says, "Because it's a system. It's like any computer system. It's magical software. This is the place in memory where it stores its own code. We're walking around in it now."

"Good!"

The room is as silent as a crypt, and empty apart from the two of them and the 1:1 scale model of the complete history of the whole Earth. "How long do we have until they catch up with us again?" Laura asks.

With practiced movements, Tanako rolls the world map east to the United Kingdom, and then forwards in time to the present day. He narrows the focus to a flare in the remote hills of darkest Gloucestershire. "Do you remember this?"

"No."

"It's the facility where we're both asleep right now, in reality. These pinpricks are mages. These two are you and me. Look closely, get the out of body experience. You see? You understand?"

Laura squints. She sees hospital beds and drips. The familiar figures of herself and Nick Laughon, wrapped in white blankets and Dehlavi lightning at the core of a D, with watchful medical mages at the relevant nodes. "I don't remember," she says. "What are we doing there? Who's helping us with the experiment?"

"You'll remember when we wake up again," says Tanako. "All I need to tell you, for right now, is that this is the live copy. Call it 'production'. This is our rip-cord. If something goes awry like it did for me the first time, then exfiltration is simple: cast your mind back to this image, and to this moment in the real world. Then step into the illusion and wake up, snap."

"That'll work?" Laura asks. "How do you know that'll work?"

"I've done it before," says Tanako, adjusting the query parameters for the 4D world map a second time.

"What? How many times? *When?*"

"You thought my research ended just because I was killed?"

Laura stares at Tanako, or rather, at his faceless grey helmet. She's starting to put the information together, when something goes *krung* in her head. It feels like an anvil has fallen directly onto her deductive reasoning. She winces. The sensory overload symptoms are starting to come back: ringing noise, strobing light.

"You okay?" Tanako asks, taking one arm.

"Ow," Laura explains.

"The broad term for these things is 'intrusion countermeasures'," Tanako tells her. "We can stay ahead of them, up to a point. This is the last part of the journey, okay? This is the part where you need to pay attention. Look at the map."

Atlantic coast again. "New York City," Laura says. "The year is 1969. And here we go."

*

Laura's thoughts flip texture yet again. She doesn't stumble this time, despite the new heels.

1969's recording is a vast skyscraper penthouse. It is ultra-modern and completely without dust or imperfection; habitable concept art in white, black and gold. Vatican City expensive, Mount Olympus expensive. Someone has spent a billion dollars on the most total imaginable luxury, then another half-billion just to have the gaudiness trimmed back to something tasteful.

It feels weirdly real. It's a whole different mental impression from T-world. No abstraction, no metaphor. It's a physical place that she's walking through.

Again, Kazuya Tanako catches up with her. This time he's wearing a tuxedo.

"You look different," Laura says. Nick Laughon's body has indeed been edited slightly. He's bulkier, and broader across the shoulders. His features have become artfully handsomer. His ears have shrunk. His hair is carved with product, in a way which the real Nick would never find time for. Bow tie, silver cufflinks. He still looks underdressed. Laura feels they should be in royal robes, or perhaps haloed entirely in light.

"That's the deal," says Tanako. "These guys look ideal at all times. They always look perfect. They never age, they never get ill. You should check yourself out, by the way," he adds, pointing out a mirror.

"Who are they?"

"These guys are the guys who built the system. They built the listening post, and then when it turned out that sleeping mages were able to wander right into their secure database they flooded it with monsters to scare people away. They monitor all magic usage, everywhere. And they meter it out."

Laura wishes she hadn't looked. She is unobtainable. The dress alone is unobtainable. If she spent two hours on her hair every morning and replaced every dessert with a marathon run, she could look half that good.

"Follow me," Tanako says.

"Wait. What was that last thing you said?"

Tanako opens the double doors. Noise floods out.

Laura's impression is that the next room could have been the size of a football pitch, and has only chosen to be a little smaller as a concession to practicality. Two entire walls and the ceiling are solid glass. The panorama behind the glass is unmistakeably the city of New York. They must be on the hundredth floor. About a hundred men and about twenty women are inside, most of them having to shout over one another. All of them are perfect twenty-somethings. Perfect suits, perfect teeth. Wine is flowing. There is string music of no clear origin. The atmosphere is celebratory and infectious.

"We'll get away without being noticed for a little while," Tanako murmurs. "We slipped out for a private conversation, you get me? Stay in character."

"You've dived into this memory before?"

"A couple of times."

Tanako takes two glasses of cava and hands one to Laura: camouflage. She drinks. Tanako steers her gently towards the window, avoiding eye contact with the party.

"Where are we?" he asks for the final time.

"New York city," Laura says.

"No. Look."

The window comes right down and meets the carpet. Of course, nobody can see the body of the building they're in, not without leaning out, but it doesn't matter.

There can be no building. The penthouse is half a block out into the East River. They are dozens of storeys up in thin air.

Laura fights the shock. It's too obvious a reaction. She tries to hypothesise how the structure could ever exist, but she, like the building itself, has nowhere to start from.

"This place is real, by the way," says Tanako. "In the present day as well as here in 1969. It's completely invisible in every conventional spectrum I could try. But I used a deep scanning oracle, on a collection of chi wavelengths they obviously thought nobody could ever find. I have photographs. It looks like a UFO."

"When were you in New York? *Who are these people?*"

"Listen to the speech," Tanako says.

Laura's next word is cut off by the tinging of a glass. She follows Tanako's gaze.

The man calling the party's attention looks— well, immaculate, like everybody there. But Laura thinks he might be a shade older. Perhaps a little middle age, a little wrinkle and shadow. Perhaps indicating seniority.

His name is King.

"I don't want to waste too much time," he says. "So I'll use as few words as I can.

"Thank God that we got there first.

"Magic is our victory. We have proved it to be perfect. It'll stand forever. I don't want to call our accomplishment — your accomplishment — a miracle, because that would deny you the credit that you deserve. It was work. Nothing but work.

"The world needed to be protected from itself. The problem, always, is trust. If and only if you're in this room, you deserve to be trusted with that power. As for the world, they'll manage just fine with what we give them. And who knows what they'll build on top of it? I, for one, can't wait to see.

"So thank God. And thank you all. And: to the beginning."

Laura is about to drink, but Tanako nudges her again. "*Watch this,*" he hisses.

A gap clears down the centre of the room, and a dining table appears. It snaps into existence, building itself in a tenth of a second. It is laid with fine china, silver cutlery, limitless wine and a hundred and twenty unique dishes of every conceivable aroma.

It is as if the table was being held in some higher reality, separated from this one by a thin silk cloth, and then the cloth was ripped out from under it.

Click goes the final tumbler in Laura's head.

King takes his seat at the head of the table, and the others follow suit, picking up their conversations again, not perturbed in the slightest at the flatly impossible thing that has just happened. Laura and Tanako hang back. "They can create and destroy matter," Tanako says. "Do you get it? It was so easy, you can't even be sure which one of them did it. Look at their wrists, that's where their immortality comes from. Listen to what they're saying, really *listen*."

"Something wrong, you two?" asks a diner, looking around at them.

Tanako looks meaningfully at Laura. Laura heard the question in Urdu. She understood it in English. Everybody in the room is speaking a different language. Even Tanako has lapsed back into his native Japanese. She didn't realise.

"Is this the dream?" she asks.

"No. All of this happened. It's the recording," Tanako says. "I have all the hard proof you could ask for, once you wake up. I can tell you who all of these people are."

Several heads have now turned in their direction. A man on the far side of the table stands up. He matches Tanako's description of Alexander Watson.

"Excuse us," Tanako announces, ushering Laura back outside.

*

Too much information. Laura paces away across the enormous lounge, trying to unthread the words of the speech and the evidence of her eyes.

"Conclusions?" Tanako asks.

"It's 1969," Laura says. "Everybody knows that that year number has to be wrong. There is zero evidence, zero, that anybody had magic before Suravaram Vidyasagar discovered it in '72. That's not to say that nobody found it before he did, just that there's no proof. If anybody *did* get there first, either they didn't write it down, or couldn't duplicate it, or... kept it a secret. But these people— my God, based on what I just saw, and based on where we're standing right now — which is in thin air — they must have got there decades before anybody else. If not centuries."

Tanako shakes his head. "No. That was my first guess, but no."

"I just saw a council of *wizards* having dinner in the *sky*. I just saw how magic is supposed to work. How it works in lucid dreams. You just think of something and it happens. You don't even need to wave your hand. They must have limitless power. Absolutely limitless. They're the ones who built the recursion artifact?" She lowers her voice and mutters to herself. "'Magic is our victory.' No magic words. No gestures. No equipment."

"Call it deep magic. Call it wizardry, or *māyā*." Tanako's face is set. He stares at her across the room, willing her to come to his conclusion.

Laura says, "How many people could they feed? If they wanted to?"

"All of them."

"...Magic is the *leak*," Laura guesses. "The only part they couldn't hush up."

"Even that would be better than the truth," Tanako says.

Exa Watson kicks the double doors open, so hard that one of the doors breaks from its hinges and cartwheels into the room, leaving a trail of demolished furniture and decor.

Tanako shouts at Laura, "Eject!"

One pace over the threshold, Exa pulls a perfectly ordinary pistol out of his jacket and shoots Tanako in the heart. Tanako keels backwards, vanishing before he hits the ground. Exa turns the gun on Laura and fires again.

*

And where now?

Reality.

Reality is a cramped metal stairwell, entirely devoid of light, running up and down for kilometres. It is the darkest and least interesting location. Laura arrives standing normally, but one of her feet is on a stair and the other is in thin air, so she falls into a hand rail.

She's back in the grey ceramic armour, all except for the helmet. It weighs much more here. The darkness is thick as pitch. She follows the hand rail and descends the stairs gingerly, testing each step. Her boots clang. She waits for Kazuya to find her, as he did before.

"Kazuya? ...Nick?"

Her voice echoes, and doesn't seem to stop echoing.

After eight steps she reaches a landing. In total darkness, she explores carefully with her hands. She discovers cold concrete wall, more hand rails, and a cooling human body, wrapped in a wet dinner jacket. She immediately drops to her knees.

```
"Dulaku   surutai   jiha,   seven
hundred en em."
```

In the red light of her right hand it is plain to see that Nick Laughon is dead.

She hears a soft *clack*ing coming from above her. Smart, hard-soled dress shoes on metal stairs.

Alexander Watson appears at the next landing, moving swiftly, leading with his gun. He sees she's weaponless, and visibly drops out of firefight mode, keeping the gun trained precisely on her right eye as he descends a few more steps.

"I don't understand," Laura says to him. "Why does this part have to be real? Nothing else is real. *Magic isn't real.*"

Exa fires. She falls.

21
Protagonism

"I'm trying to find Laura Ferno. You're her emergency contact," is what the fellow on the phone leads with, Hollywood-style, no greeting.

"Is it an emergency?" Natalie Ferno asks, mildly refreshed to be getting to the point of the conversation so quickly. She keeps a thick pad of A4 next to the phone. It is measurably thicker with the weight of doodles. People, in Nat's experience, can lock themselves into a kind of verbal holding pattern, constantly emitting syllables while never advancing the conversation.

"It's two halves of an emergency," says the man.

"Who is this?"

"Anil Devi, I worked with your sister at Hatt Group."

"You fired her," Nat observes.

Anil Devi, personally, worked with Laura Ferno only for a few weeks altogether while she was still in gainful employment. The decision to fire her was made completely in his absence, for reasons completely unrelated to him. "No," he explains. On the other hand, Devi is contacting Natalie Ferno as a formal representative of Hatt Group with a view to reinstating Laura in some — *any* — professional capacity as soon as possible, which means he is Hatt Group's front end from Nat's perspective. So, "Yes," he adds. "It doesn't matter. We need her to come back."

"Why?"

"That's confidential."

"Is it," Nat asks again, "an emergency?"

"...I need to find her very urgently."

So, no. Nat hangs up.

*

Then she thinks again.

She hasn't heard from Laura in weeks. But Laura's like that. She is a low-maintenance relative.

Nat also hasn't heard from Nick in that amount of time. That's much less usual.

If Hatt Group have been reduced to pursuing emergency contacts, then Laura's not responding to their phone calls or emails.

Laura loved that job. She saw a serious chance of becoming an astronaut in that job. Losing the chance devastated her. Laura would never pass up another chance at that chance. She would never ignore them if they reached out.

Nat calls Laura's mobile. The call goes straight to voicemail, as if the phone itself has ceased to exist.

She calls Laura and Nick's land line. Answering machine.

She calls Nick's mobile. Voicemail.

Neither are on IM. She emails them both, then drums her fingers for a while, not really expecting any response.

She calls Nick's school. Nick is AWOL, and has lost his job.

She calls Nick's friends, although she doesn't know many of their numbers. The story is consistent: Nick and Laura are travelling around the world. They're probably in Japan right now.

No contact information. No forwarding numbers. Not even a postcard.

It's an interesting combination of stories. Laura's the kind of person who could go off-grid for a month before anybody noticed. Nick Laughon isn't, but he's the primordial avatar of itchy feet, so if he needed to disappear, he could buy about the same amount of time with a quick one-liner like "I'm going around the world"...

Two half-emergencies. One: Hatt Group desperately, desperately need Laura Ferno back. Two: Laura and her boyfriend are missing. Missing, presumed...

At this point the possibilities become a forest.

No presumption. Nat needs more data.

*

She arrives at Laura's house not long before dusk. It's the greyish, coldish part of the British day where you squint a little and go to remove sunglasses that you aren't wearing.

There is a man at Laura's door. Facing the door, as if having just knocked. Natalie strides up behind him. "You must be Anil Devi," she announces, surprising him.

He turns. Spiky black hair, the kind of face which seems to be perpetually grinning regardless of mood. "Laura!"

"No."

Devi blinks. "Natalie. Natalie Ferno. Laura didn't say you were identical twins."

"We aren't identical."

"That's why."

"Go home," Natalie tells him. "If I find her, I'll tell her to call you." She moves around Devi, producing a spare key, and goes to unlock the door.

"Did she tell you why she was fired?" Devi asks.

"Maybe."

"Did she tell you she was trying to resurrect your mother?"

Natalie stops on the threshold.

She says, carefully, "I was wondering how much you people knew. Yes, word got around. But it didn't work, obviously. Otherwise you'd never have fired her."

"It worked," Devi says.

Natalie's eyes widen.

"Sort of," Devi adds, hurriedly.

*

Inside, Devi tells the story.

"The lab says it's dead meat," he says. "Real meat, dead but formerly living. Real DNA from a completely unknown taxon. Maybe some proto-hominid which evolved in a radioactive wasteland for a few hundred thousand years. And that, in itself, is a bloody significant mystery."

"Maybe it was intelligently designed," Natalie suggests.

Devi shrugs. "Number of biologists in this conversation, zero. But the *real* point is: she brought it *back*. Real mass, comparable with a human. From a place which strictly doesn't *exist*. We've got no idea how she did it using essentially no mana, but we sure as hell need to know. Hint: mass-energy conservation is over."

"Death is over," Natalie says.

"Yeah," Devi says. "Death is potentially over. You see why I pushed this into emergency territory."

"I see why you got permission to violate some NDAs," Natalie says.

"We heard you were a professional mage too," Devi says. "It turns out we approached you in university at the same time as Laura. All things considered, Ed Hatt thought it was worth cutting you in."

"Alright," Natalie says. "We're on the same page."

"Where is Laura?" Devi asks.

Natalie shares what she's worked out so far. "All Laura's magical equipment is missing. No sign of a break-in, which means Laura took it all with her. Laura's daily carry is enough that she clatters when she moves, but her whole collection weighs a lot and is worth a lot more. She owns one-of-a-kind pieces which she built with her own hands. She'd never fly with it. Forget cameras and lenses, *that* is the kind of valuable property which mysteriously vanishes from hold luggage. Contradiction."

"So let's say they're still in this country," Devi surmises. "When was the last time you spoke to her?"

"Just after she was fired." Natalie recalls a despairing and unhappy Laura Ferno in search of a source of limitless magical energy, named Ra. "I called her an idiot. ...You know what the real puzzle here is? Nick's missing as well."

"Nick...?"

"Laughon. Her boyfriend. Laura's a bad scientist. You were right to fire her. Recklessness, unsafe experimentation. The drawing of rash conclusions heavily influenced by personal feelings. For Laura to disappear for weeks on a quest to do something bizarre and misguided isn't remotely out of character.

"But Nick's missing too. He's the grounded half of the relationship. He should have talked her down. He'd be the one to bring her—"

Oh.

"—back... to... reality."

Oh no.

"She's summoned a demon into the body of her boyfriend," Natalie announces.

Devi does not have a coherent immediate response to this. Demons are not a standard component of the magical engineering canon.

"What kind of demon?" he eventually manages.

"A demon! A malevolent spirit. 'Ra'."

"I'm sorry. What kind of mage are you?"

"Theoretical thaumic physicist."

Devi changes gear.

Terminology has become somewhat confused in recent decades. Technically speaking, magical engineers are supposed to refer to themselves exclusively as "mages", because of the abbreviation, MagE. "Wizard", "witch", "warlock" and "sorcerer" are generally associated with fictional characters or crazy people; "magician" and "conjuror" are reserved for stage performers. All of this is perfectly clear from the perspective of those working in the magical community. Unfortunately, on the outside, it's fuzzier. There's no trademark or law to prevent non-mages from calling themselves mages. It's not even a title which requires a certain qualification, like "doctor".

There are "psychics" who call themselves mages. These people cheerfully lift choice terms from magical engineering, craft them into something that's obviously nonsense to anybody with a day's experience with the real topic, and dupe saps for cash. The popular quantum mechanics books have become almost impressive in their creative meaninglessness.

One could very easily get to the end of such a book and consider oneself a "theoretical thaumic physicist".

"Why do you think Laura would summon a demon?" Devi asks.

Natalie's reasoning is apparently effortless. "She's going to try her experiment again. To do that, she needs a ridiculous amount of mana, more than she can generate in years by herself. Ra has that power."

Devi chooses each word carefully, as if stepping forward across ice. "Is... is 'Ra' dangerous?"

Ra was last seen trying to liberate enough geological mana to blow up Iceland.

"Yes," says Natalie.

"Does Laura know this?"

"Oh, my, yes," Natalie says.

"Is Laura really stupid enough to trust this... being?"

"Entirely the wrong question," Natalie says. "You should be asking if she's stupid enough to think she can control it. And she is. She is actually, in her own way, a pretty formidable human being. Up to a point."

Devi doesn't want to ask the last question. He does anyway.

"What does Ra want?"

Natalie's expression darkens, but she doesn't answer.

*

The computer room.

Natalie knows Laura's password. She shoulder-surfed it a year or two ago, never mentioned it, and Laura's never changed it. Natalie would feel guilt, if there was time.

She pulls up the browser cache. Last activity, weeks ago. Printed directions to a particular postcode in the West Country, an isolated compound in a forest in the back of beyond. A private magical research laboratory called the Chedbury Bridge Institute.

"What kind of magic do you do?" Devi asks casually, hovering behind her. Natalie assumes that he has shoulder-surfed Laura's password in turn. She makes a mental note to change it once he isn't looking.

"Mmm? I know `eset`," Natalie says.

"Anything else?"

"No."

"You only know one spell?"

"Yup."

"You don't know `uum`?"

"Why would I learn a spell which does nothing?"

Devi solidifies his conclusion about Natalie Ferno: layperson. Laura, he thinks, is the brains of the family. Natalie is a neo-pagan imitator of her sister, a chanter of nonsense-spells at summer solstice near particular rocks. Natalie is interpreting the evil of pedestrian humans in the most meaningful terms she's familiar with. Natalie is a 'witch' — which is to say, a crazy person.

Devi asks, "What's the postcode?"

Natalie reads it out.

"Noted," says Devi. He goes to leave. "I'm calling the police."

"Wait!"

"'Wait'?" asks Devi, loading as much scepticism and frank disgust into this word as possible.

"What will you tell them?"

"'Laura Ferno's been abducted by her boyfriend, Nick Laughon.'"

"Nick Laughon hasn't done anything! There's no sign of forced abduction. Laura's being manipulated!"

"Do I care? Do the police care? Two people are missing, and we have reason to believe one's in danger from the other. So magic is involved. Is *magic* a separate legal jurisdiction?"

"I think we can straighten this out without getting the police involved—" Natalie begins.

"Let's get Nick Laughon's body in a jail cell," Devi says, "and, if you really think it's going to make a difference, you can attempt an 'exorcism'. Grind some herbs, draw runes in chalk and mouse blood or whatever it is you do."

"What?"

"I don't buy 'demon'," Devi says. "I'm veering strongly towards 'scumbag'. And I don't think you know what thaumic physics even is."

Nobody can find the biological component of magic. Nobody knows which cells in the human body register magical activity, or why it takes a year-plus of training before they work. It's mythical and inconsistent and inexplicable. Maybe it's a system of signals which is always there, but the human brain needs to be tuned before they can be unscrambled into something detectable. Like language acquisition.

It doesn't matter.

Natalie Ferno and Anil Devi both sense the reaction starting in the living room. Their heads turn almost simultaneously to look at the same unseen point on the other side of the wall.

Devi dashes back through.

The weapon resembles a silver, mechanical lotus flower. It is a sophisticated, nest-like fan of magic rings and nodules, engineered like a pop-up book, probably small enough when flat to fit into a breast pocket. The density of mana flux at its focal point is so bright in the thaumic spectrum that standing in its presence is physically painful. There's heat radiating off it too, and curls of invisible chemical vapour, the precursor to a thaumically-accelerated bomb.

Nobody has built a magic-based bomb before, and not for lack of trying. Devi and Natalie know this. They're looking at something delicate and brand new and unique, like a Fabergé egg. It is a compact packet of hugely inventive destructive power. It sits on a mundane coffee table in the cramped living room of a beige house, almost too beautiful to be allowed to detonate.

For a split second, neither of them can look away from it.

"How did that get in here?" Nat says.

"Run!" Devi screams, physically pushing Nat towards the door.

"Wait," Nat says.

Devi is, again, aghast at Natalie's suggestion. "What are you doing?"

"Wait!" Nat twists past him, lunges for a cupboard and pulls out the one piece of equipment which Laura didn't take with her: a one-point-eight-metre oaken bo.

Nat didn't hear a door move. Nat has sixty percent of the theory of invisibility laid down. The rest is just boring practical problems, like fitting the spell into fewer than ten human minds and a piece of machinery which weighs less than a tonne. The short title is "Fast-adapting Bezier-controlled duplex oracles". The only major question marks are around wavelength assignment—

She hasn't heard the door move, which means the invisible man must still be here. He must have been here the entire time they were in the house. Hovering, silently. Listening in.

Surely he left time for a getaway. Surely that's enough time to find him and wring the abort code out of him.

Nat closes her eyes for one second. In any other situation, she'd be searching, with extreme difficulty, for a volume of empty air which was detectably consuming magic. Like a poltergeist. But the house is saturated with thaumic radiation. So instead she hunts for the shadow.

It's in the hall. Nat keeps her eyes screwed up, it's the only way to find the thing reliably. Lacking room to swing, she propels the bo end-first, directly into the shadow's midsection.

Transmuting light into invisible chi particles and back is one thing. Blocking a heavy impact from a physical object is an entirely different engineering problem. The trespasser's cloak shuts off with a *snap* like a mousetrap. The man behind the cloak crumples up, gasping. He is a nobody, his entire image is cultivated to project "nondescript". A shirt, some shoes, hair, an age.

Natalie hits him again with the bo, bloodying his nose— a technique which bojutsu strictly outlaws, as Natalie would know if she'd ever studied it. She catches his wrist and hurls him back into the living room, directly at the bomb. The man scrambles to avoid falling into it, and ends up crashing into the coffee table and injuring his knee quite badly.

"Jesus Christ!" is Anil Devi's reaction.

"Turn the bomb off or die," Natalie tells the trespasser. She is almost having to shout over the machine now. She holds the bo in front of her, defensively, and circles around to cover Devi. "You know you have time!" Without turning around, she adds, "Devi, don't move!"

Devi doesn't move.

"Like I care," says the man, sneering. "Like I'm *singular*! `Elth ra mukhth entana daneda.`"

It's the last exotic ingredient. The syllables spill from the man's lips like virulent red muck dripping from a test tube into the cauldron. And like witches and wizards, psychics and media, all three mages feel a figurative foreshock of the imminent future.

Natalie grabs Devi's hand. "`Anh zero EPTRO zui—`"

*

There is a small discontinuity.

Over the street from Laura Ferno's address is — not unexpectedly — another row of houses. The house directly opposite has an immaculate garden in front of it. Millimetre-long grass, raked pebbles, perfect red and blue poinsettias. It takes Devi a moment to realise that this is where he has landed.

He is upright, splayed against the back of the garden and the wall beneath the house's shattered front bay window, with one arm hooked over into the house itself. The wall he's lying against is broken, as if hit by a roughly Devi-shaped truck. Devi is strewn with tiny pieces of broken double glazing, and it takes him another moment to realise that they are still being held a few centimetres away from his skin by Natalie Ferno's force field.

He recognises the bird bath. He is looking at it from the opposite angle.

"Ferno?" he shouts, and hears nothing. His organs and bones judder. The field obviously absorbed a huge percentage of the shock.

Over the road at the epicentre, there isn't a house anymore, just a blackened pit. The blast has been impressively precise, barely scorching the houses on either side. Pieces are still falling from the sky; a hard rain of roof tiles and frame. It's unreal.

".........." says a voice.

"What?" Devi shouts, looking around. He feels like a three-dimensional bruise.

Natalie has landed inside, on the other side of the same wall. In fact, she has landed on a sofa, and they are therefore seated back to back. They are still joined, through the broken window. She is holding on to his wrist, latched to it like a hawk's talon.

"I said I changed my mind," Nat says, louder. "You should call the police."

As Natalie releases her grip, the shield closes down, and both of them are now covered in fresh glass and rubble and dust, like a parsley garnish.

They never place the call, but miraculously the police appear all by themselves.

*

The sun has gone down. There are dozens of vehicles and seemingly hundreds of police. The street is filled with flashing lights and high visibility vests.

Natalie has learned her lesson. Speaking to the shadow-chinned, unflappable layperson officer who takes her statement, she avoids raising hypotheses of consciousness displacement, or of megalomaniacal minds invading from other planes of magical existence. She structures her words factually.

"My sister is missing since four weeks ago, and her boyfriend is too. Either he's abducted her, or both of them are in the hands of some third party. A man named Ra just blew up their house to stop me from tracking them, but he failed, and I know where they are. I think Laura's involved in something really dangerous, and we need to find her right now, and by 'we' I mean you and me and that guy there." She points at Anil Devi, who is in the middle of giving his own statement, and who looks up for a second, confused.

"Why you?" the officer asks, calmly, scribbling notes. Anachronism? But the scene is far too noisy to record audio.

Nat says, "Because Laura always carries a particular collection of magical equipment with her. With a high-powered eset spell and a bit of trigonometry I can find her behind a kilometre of steel. In any case, this is a magic problem. Laura's a mage, I'm a mage, Anil's a mage, the bomber was a mage. Do you have mages on the force?"

"No," says the officer.

"Magic is real," Natalie says. "Magic crime has been real since 1998. Magic terrorism has just this hour become real. You need expert outside consultation.

"And I think—" And Natalie stops for a second, because this last thought hasn't come from the right place in her mind. Natalie Ferno is a thinker who starts from a collection of facts and turns the handle until they extrude a conclusion. But this idea is from her imagination, inflammatory, fabricated to get the police's attention. And yet, it may almost add up.

"I think," she says, "my sister might have been radicalised."

*

Time is a factor.

They won't let them go.

Natalie Ferno and Anil Devi are kept around for hours, *hours*, having information dragged out of them. Descriptions of the late, lamented bomber, whose description is entirely irrelevant. Descriptions of the structure of the magic bomb, a breed of device that every military organisation in the world has been trying to build. (Both Natalie and Devi, despite being questioned separately, instinctively play it cagey. In truth, given a few days to compare notes, they could produce blueprints and operating instructions in multiple languages.) How do you think the bomb worked? Well, largely, by magic. How do you think he got into the house? A spare key, possibly stolen from a fake rock in the garden, or maybe even given to him by Laura herself. How did you know there was someone in the house? Magic. How did you survive the explosion? *Magic, idiots!*

Injuries to people in nearby houses, damaged hearing, property damage, vehicular damage, falling rubble, forensic analysis, fingerprints, insurance, thousands of flash photographs.

This is a race against time, Natalie Ferno tells them outright, over and over again. The bomb was planted just at the instant that she and Devi discovered the next link in the trail. If that information wasn't critically time-sensitive, *the house would not have blown up*. Laura's involved in this thing *right now*.

"We're taking this very seriously. We're doing everything we can to find your sister as soon as possible."

It takes Natalie several hours to realise that this isn't incompetence, some bloated civil machine that takes time to get up to speed. The police have been playing the information hygiene game for much longer than she has. Information goes into an investigation, and it doesn't come out. And she's on the wrong side of the wall.

*

"Alright, here's the thing," says the sergeant who first interviewed Natalie. "Your offer of expertise in the magical field has been percolating upwards, and it seems to have found someone in charge who's keen to get a magical opinion or two."

"Here?" Devi asks.

"This is a bomb site," says the sergeant, whose last name is Henders and whose first name might as well be Sergeant. "We can do bomb sites, and it'll still be here in the morning. Over at Chedbury, though, is a big pile of magical machinery which nobody on site is entirely sure what to make of."

"Forensic thaumaturgy," Devi suggests.

"Limited, unofficial scientific consultation," is how Henders puts it. "Cooperating with our inquiries."

"Like you can afford my consulting rate," says Devi. "I'm kidding."

Natalie asks, "What actually happened at Chedbury? What did they find? Did they raid the place? Did they find my sister?"

"Didn't say, ma'am," Henders says.

"If they'd found my sister, they've have said so, right?"

"I couldn't say."

"And they wouldn't need us there. Right?"

"I couldn't say."

You guys are good at this. "All right. We need a minute to grab equipment."

Devi's car, formerly parked not-quite-outside the Ferno residence, has been lightly torched and is missing a window. Still, its contents are pristine: an eclectic assortment of light-to-heavy aerospace engineering equipment. "Enough to do most jobs," he explains to Natalie, handing her a fistful of Kaprekar driver/linkers.

"It'd be better if we could swing past work, but it's in the wrong direction. What are you bringing?"

Natalie indicates that all of her equipment amounts to a single earring. Empty fingers, bare wrists, nothing up her sleeves. "Theoretical physicist, remember? I can spell, but I don't practice."

"But you just cast that force field. 'Only one spell' my arse."

"Two spells. That and `eset`. Honest. In any case, I'm completely out of mana right now."

Devi raises one eyebrow, and once again draws his own conclusion. He hands her a plastic box containing the unscrewed pieces of his magic staff.

Natalie asks, "How long would it take you to put together a basic chi scanner? Something that can find my sister in a haystack."

Devi snorts. "Like, a hundred and fifty seconds."

"Good. Then I need something that can read people's True Names remotely."

Devi opens his mouth to respond to this, then closes it, and smiles. He has no idea how to do this. It is an old sensation, and a familiar one, and an exciting one.

"I can give you some pointers," Natalie suggests.

"I don't take dictation," Devi says. "I'm an engineer. You're the client. You give me requirements. I actualise."

*

They're in the back of the police car, headed west. The passenger compartment is roomy. Natalie shuffles uncomfortably in her seat, becoming a little carsick from facing the wrong way. Devi's on the other side, distracted by his engineering task, trying syllable sequences. There's a constant clattering of equipment. He looks like he's assembling a rifle.

"I don't believe in demons," he says.

Natalie looks at him, waiting for something else.

"I specifically don't believe in a demon called Ra," he continues. "...Which means I have a problem, because who blew the house up?"

"You heard the spell segment," Natalie says. "You heard the fellow's Name."

"Sure, but who *was* he? Who blows a house up? What is actually going on here? I feel like I'm coming in late. Like I missed acts one and two."

"You've got a monster in your basement," Natalie explains. "You've seen that physical things can come back from T-world. Would you believe that a mind can come back? Call it what you want. 'Hijacking'."

"But that wasn't Nick Laughon."

"Ra isn't one person," says Natalie.

"You mean, like... an organisation?"

Natalie doesn't say anything.

*

Chedbury Bridge Institute is its own private world, lurking behind tall electrified fences off an inaccessible road in the Chedbury forest. From the outside, none of its buildings are visible through the fence and trees, even in daylight. The track up to the entrance is not signposted. The Institute doesn't want to be found. There's work going on inside, and it would rather not be disturbed.

Devi and Natalie are driven straight in, indirectly revealing that any excitement occurring at this location, any kind of armed police raid, happened offscreen and is long since over. The Institute is four or five two-storey buildings made of stylishly modern sand-coloured bricks, almost new. It's close to midnight now, but all the exterior and interior lights are on. There are police all over, specialist vans and dogs, garbled radio chatter. An unusual number of men carry black rifles.

There's a weird cold atmosphere, an aftermath atmosphere.

Henders lets Devi and Natalie out. Devi's completed magic machine is quite heavy, six rings all on one wrist, some up to half a metre in diameter. They are kept from falling off by his staff, a conventional steel model, effective without being flashy. Devi turns the machine on using a long and slightly confused spell which clearly needs refactoring.

The first readings come in. Having lacked the time to build any kind of modulator, they come in through Devi's hand as inscrutable flux changes. He has to perform most of the decoding in his head. "`Zui` for you," he reports. "And `thelet` for me, we already knew that. No bindings for any of the cops. Just fuzz. Hah!"

Henders comes around and joins them after a brief conversation with the officer in charge of the site.

"When we arrived they were in the middle of tearing some machine down," he says. "Something they obviously wanted to hide. It's at the other end of the site." He nods at Devi's machine. "That thing's not going to break anything, is it? Not going to destroy any evidence?"

"Totally passive," Devi assures him cheerfully.

"Alright then. Stay behind me, please. No wandering off, no gawping."

He leads them on the most direct route possible, threading between the buildings and across darkened lawns with benches. At one point a windowless police van pulls away past them, out of a secondary car park towards the exit.

"That van has at least six passengers in it," Devi hisses, after aiming his machine at it. "Maybe seven or eight."

"You can't tell exactly how many?"

"I can't separate them. They're all Named `ra`."

"Hmm."

"'Hmm'? This is what you mean by Ra being more than one person?"

"Ra was an accident," Natalie says. "Accidents happen. There's a lot of magic happening in the world, and it's only increasing. Why shouldn't an accident happen more than once? Mass-energy conservation may or may not be over. But a mind is just information, right? The integral of experience with respect to time. It's just a *vector*. There is no conservation law for information."

"So the Ra whom Laura's working with and the Ra who blew up her house were different people," Devi says.

"And the same person," Natalie says.

She shivers.

Around another corner, she catches sight of something. Inside another building, plainly visible through the windows, is a tall machine with a weird and serious familiarity to it.

It's a telescope, or at least derived from telescope ancestors. The main optical tube is about three metres long and seventy-five centimetres in diameter, polished black. Its range of motion is wrong. A full range of right ascension, but twice the usual declination, a feature useless to terrestrial telescopes. It is aimed down into the Earth at a steep angle, with the eyepiece only available from a raised platform. It's a shiny and new and highly specialised piece of equipment. Natalie looks carefully, and sees two cooperating oracles fitted over the end, designed to detect passing magical particles and transmute them into visible light in the most convenient available wavelengths.

"Chi astronomy," she breathes. Chis don't interact. You don't need to be on a high mountain in Chile, hundreds of miles away from light pollution sources, to study them. You can look right down through the Earth. You just need a quiet room with blackout curtains, and a mathematician for the servomotor firmware.

"No gawping," Henders calls.

This device reduces Natalie's experiments to cheap hack jobs. The Chedburians are ahead of her. She'd kill for their data.

*

They're brought to a large hall, a classic magical gymnasium with a standard D/E ring stencilled on its floor and modern adapters. Planted at most of the usual loci are the usual pieces for driving a Dehlavi lightning machine. The remaining pieces appear to have been abandoned in corners.

At the centre of the room are two empty hospital beds. They are aligned with two of the arms of the lightning Y which would be produced if the machine were active. There are medical monitoring machines— additional consulting experts will be required to identify them, since neither mage is a medic. There are drips. Nutrients?

There are police investigators scattered around the room. Most of them look up expectantly as Devi and Natalie arrive.

Henders explains, "This is what they were tearing down. They seemed to be in a hurry. Look but don't touch."

"Who are 'they'?" Devi asks.

"The site staff. They're being questioned right now."

"Can we talk to them?" Natalie asks.

"No."

"How many people were here?" Devi asks. "It's the middle of the night. How many of them looked like scientists?"

Henders looks over at the ranking investigator in the room. "I don't have the whole list yet," the second man reports, "but seven people were in this room when we got here. Two in medical scrubs, five in casuals."

Devi says to Natalie, "To run a machine like this indefinitely, in shifts, allowing down time for a basic rate of mana recovery, and assuming fit mages—"

"Twenty-four to twenty-eight people, depending on their combined wattage," Natalie replies. The computation is trivial.

"This is a sleep science experiment," Devi announces. "You ever play Tetris for enough hours in one day that you end up dreaming in falling blocks? You ever study another language so hard that you end up dreaming in it? Mages have a similar thing, a specific trance state. We don't know a lot about it yet. With the right medical support, you could leave someone in that state for weeks. It looks like that's what they were doing."

"What about the patients?" Natalie demands. "What happened to the people in these beds?"

The second man, the investigator, shrugs. "They were empty when we got here. We're looking the rest of the site over now. You want us to bring a dog in?"

"Scanner," Natalie says to Devi, surgeon-style.

"Thelet eset oerin," Devi answers, throwing her a decorated black iron ring, as big as a coaster. Natalie puts it to one eye and scans the figurative horizon. She sees familiar and unfamiliar magical equipment, most of it dormant. The telescope, obviously, and other machines, built in flexible layouts for experimentation. A funfair after hours.

If you know the conditions, you can repeat the same accident over and over, Natalie thinks. *Why couldn't this whole place be staffed by Ra?*

But then, why?

What does Laura have that Ra wants? What does she have access to that nobody else does?

At yet another end of the complex, locked in a windowless temperature-controlled storage room, is a brighter, fuzzier signal, clustered.

*

This Ra hears the voices on the other side of the door. The door is an almost-solid steel slab. It would be time-consuming to crack open, at least for the baseline police. But they have mages now, and he can hear their coded chatter. A familiar pair of Names.

This Ra resigns himself, because the deal is done. The launch is complete and the human weapons are away; there is more than one way to get into T-world, and there is more than one way to exit from its far end.

The storage room is cramped. Racks of shelves of chemical bottles line two walls, leaving a narrow chasm with just enough room for one of Ra and two bath-sized, thick-walled, blue PTFE tubs. Both tubs are too heavy when full for one man to move, and therefore had to be filled on the spot, one and then the other on top, hurriedly and clumsily. This Ra has spilled some of the hydrofluoric acid on himself, and will start to feel the burning and see the skin bubbling on his fingers very soon, but... The missiles are away and running, and in an ideal scenario this will be over in another day. If Laura

Ferno is successful, she won't need a corporeal body to return to.

And in any case, there will always be more of *him*.

The wonderful thing about a bath of HF is that it'll take care of a mage and her tools at the same time. Precisely machined tools will stay in working condition for minutes or hours, but as time passes and acid dissolves the edges, they become less effective, and soon are damaged unrecoverably. The signal that Natalie Ferno and Anil Devi are tracking, which leads into the lower of the two baths, is clouding and smearing out, even as they brainstorm frantically on the other side of the door.

One of them pounds desperately on the door. "What have you done?" Natalie shouts. "I know you're in there! *What have you done to my sister?*"

Ra steps over to the door. "What we've done doesn't matter, Natalie," he says, peacefully.

"You've killed her," Natalie screams. "How can that not matter?"

"Because we're trying to end death," Ra tells her. "Don't you remember what I told you on that mountain? *This is about freedom.*

"We're trying to save the world."

22
Scrap Brain Zone

Don't quip until the quarry's dead.

It's one of the first things Exa learned. Exa isn't short for "Alexander", or at least it wasn't originally. It's "Executor", the one who carries out instructions. If a person's existence and interference need to end, Exa's job, typically, is to bring them to that end. Quips are a distraction and a delay. They're also bad manners. If somebody's going to die, their last thought might as well not be "Dear God, that was the best you could come up with?"

It's December 1969 in the replay and he's sitting down for a meal of rare, Platonically perfect steak. There is salad involved, the most divine salad which could ever exist, but an article of jewellery on his wrist chases away extraneous sodium and replaces it with effortless muscle, so the greenery is window dressing, so why bother? Others around him have opted for more elaborate preparations of dishes generally considered theoretical, and of animals and vegetables which no longer exist, but Exa is coming out of the far end of a long and bitter struggle, and is tired, and wants food which will not challenge him.

There's a pecking order at the table, and Exa is most of the way up it.

"Who were those two?" somebody remarks. "What are they up to?"

"Busy," somebody else guesses, his mouth already full. "Getting, I mean."

The Wheel Group's members change appearance frequently enough that not everybody always recognises everybody else. This fact keeps Exa mollified for a few seconds. Then his head snaps up and he scans the table and the remaining diners.

"Something wrong?" King asks him.

"The table's full," Exa says. "They didn't have seats allocated."

"That's impossible," King says. "Our whole operation is provably impregnable."

"It isn't," says another diner, whose name is Ashburne. "And I wish you hadn't announced it as such. No operation can prove itself impregnable. That, itself, was proven about a million years ago. Do you even know who Kurt Gödel was?"

"I'm reading no intrusion," reports the castle-in-the-cloud's security expert, Casaccia.

"Even if they've inserted themselves into the records of this event, that's a bad sign," says Arkov. "It means the records aren't going to stay sacrosanct forever."

Exa downs his wine. "Signal upwards," he says, standing up. He storms around the table towards the doors, turning several heads. Some of the men, who know what Exa does, get up and move to follow him. They are quietly hoping for a show.

"I want one of them alive," King calls.

Exa kicks the door out, making a noise and a mess, and receiving a panicked response from the two interlopers. They have separated across the room. The man is nearby on the right, the woman far away on the left.

Which one is going to freak out the most if I kill the other?

The man shouts "Eject!" at the woman. This suggests that the man is leading, and the woman is subordinate. That's good enough.

Exa shoots the man. The man drops. But then he vanishes.

This changes Exa's plan. Akashic hackery is indeed taking place. If both of the interlopers escape, then he and his party have no data. His only hope is to kill the second interloper before she ejects too, then excavate the needed information from her dead brain. He turns the gun on her and fires. The bullet is around nine-tenths of the way to her when Exa's thought patterns flip texture and he becomes real.

*

In the next place he freezes absolutely solid. He catches the wall and a railing to stop himself from falling, doing so completely silently. Night vision activates so quickly that he doesn't even perceive the darkness, but the very fact that night vision has to come online at all takes him by surprise.

This is the real world.

This is cause for deep alarm. Cracking the akashic records open is one thing. Pulling physical objects back from them, however, speaks to a serious and dangerous breakdown of world order as it was originally implemented. Who did it? A rogue Wheel member? Unthinkable. Or was somebody new inducted? That should be impossible, the privileges aren't even hereditary. How did they get access? Is this really where they staged their attack from?

For that matter, where is he? How far in the future?

Below, he hears his quarry moving. No confidence, no night vision. He hears a spell: "`Dulaku surutai jiha, seven hundred en em`", followed by a panicked half-gasp. So: all three of them were bounced here. And the man is still dead.

Exa rounds the corner, descending into hellish red light. The woman is kneeling. She has switched outfit. A grey armour suit. What part of the glitch caused *that*?

"I don't understand," the woman says to Exa, surprising him. He was thinking exactly the same thing.

She continues, "Why does this part have to be real? Nothing else is real. *Magic isn't real.*"

So the secret's out. It was out for a moment, at any rate. It could be all-the-way public. It was obviously news to the woman, but if the man knew already, he could have spread it unimaginably further before he died.

What a mess. At least Exa is only responsible for its physical end. Information hygiene is not his game. Perhaps it was hubris to think that magic could stay a secret for the whole of the future. Perhaps, as time goes to infinity, all truths come out.

And there, very obviously to Exa, is the quip. But he holds it for long enough to fire a nine-millimetre round into the woman's right eye.

She falls.

Exa says, "Gotta wake up some time."

But the echo of the gunshot has filled the stair tower with thunder from top to bottom, and nothing else is audible. Exa puts his gun away. First he'll check the bodies over, then contact the authorities. He'll probably have to merge experiences with his older, real-world self. He wonders how much time has passed. He wonders whether his real self has picked a different look.

When a mage is killed in the midst of casting a spell, or while acting as an active conduit for mana, the spell ends within the first few seconds of brain-death. Not that this has ever been observed in reality before, ethics being ethics, but there is firm hypothesis, and it happens to be essentially correct. Exa knows it. Or, should.

The woman's light hasn't gone out.

*

With his *kara* figuratively redlining, the most effective way to actually kill Exa Watson would be to take a 10^{18}-watt laser and fire it directly into the top of his head from orbit. This level of power would be just about enough to completely vaporise both Exa and his *kara* too quickly for the *kara* to detect the damage occurring and start actively rebuilding him.

Exa's problem is that he doesn't leave his *kara* amped up to full power.

Because he shouldn't *have* to. It would be like walking down the street in plate armour. This is his world, he owns it. No single person or weapon in the whole world, as far as he knows, represents a credible physical threat to him, and if it did, he'd respond to the threat. Right? His response would be almost instantaneous.

And the world, as far as he knows, has been cleansed of evil.

Let's see where Laura's coming from.

Almost four years ago, four men tried to kill her. One stabbed her in the kidney. She fought them off with improvised magical weaponry, killing one of them and severely injuring two of the others.

She then turned herself into a fortress. "Fuck improvisation," she said, and began developing personal shield technology and dedicated tools for hurting people who would try to hurt her. She bargained for, and sometimes stole, time in the university's engineering workshops. Later, she did the same at Hatt Group's impressive fabrication facilities. She miniaturised the results, trading reduced complexity in the spell wording for increased complexity in the thaumic machinery and mental load. A girl only has time for so many syllables.

Laura's coasting on residual self-image from Tanako's world. She originally arrived there looking like her default self: black top, dark jeans, almost no other descriptive words at all, barely even shoes. If she'd bothered to examine herself, she'd have found a little more detail: the correct hair colour, the kidney scar, the usual few rings.

The suit of armour, she copied from Tanako-while-he-was-wearing-Nick. She laid it over the top of what she was already wearing. Flat polygonal plates, completely functional, no concession to cool style, not even a lick of polish. Rubbery articulation at the joints and neck. A full helmet. The suit is intended to keep a hostile, poison-filled environment and a pitifully fragile human being completely separated from one another.

"Who are you?" she had asked him.

"Who do you think?" Tanako had replied, turning around and turning his helmet transparent.

Not retracting it. Not removing it. Because in T-world you can just have whatever you want to have.

Laura Ferno could have come back to the real world in the unobtainable dress. She could have spawned looking like whatever it is that comes next after "supermodel". But she didn't, and it wasn't luck.

No amount of bullet proofing can cancel out a bullet's momentum— her head is thrown back and right by the shot, and Laura lets herself fall. She falls away from the gunman, turning so that he can't see the side of her head which he supposedly shot a hole in. A white dot is left in the glass. Or the transparent diamond polycarbonate, or whatever it is. God knows where the ricochet ends up.

The noise of the shot is incredible. Laura knows she's got rings on her left hand, under the armour. The gunman is saying something. She can't hear it over the *boom*. That means he won't be able to hear her own hissed response.

She just cast a spell, that was smart. She can reuse the True Name drop.

"Look at their wrists, that's where their immortality comes from."

"Sedo. Anhtnaa vaeka."

Eyeball tracking was too hard. She'd have needed a month to work with anonymous recursion. Laura has to shoot from the hip, and hope that she misses her own toes. She aims her left index finger somewhere above and to the right of Exa's head. Her left middle finger, she aims down, at his dominant hand, where he wears the bracelet. The projected scything plane cuts through his hand and wrist, divides his forearm in two lengthwise, then carves through his shoulder and up through his throat and face. There is an audible *choink* as the *kara* snaps in half. There's a worse noise where the field meets the black metalwork of the stairwell, and bites deep, but doesn't quite cut. As for Exa himself, he parts easily, into two pieces of fresh brain and some sliced dinner jacket.

Laura unfreezes slowly. She waits for a minute, in thick darkness and gradually returning silence, for shock to kick in.

In her mind's eye she can see Nat, arms folded, expression held steady at "stony disapproval".

Most people go their whole lives without killing anybody.

*

"'Immortality.'"

Laura scrabbles through scarlet gunge. She separates the two slices of Exa's corpse's wrist, and retrieves the two pieces of metal. Two arcs of circle, thin and richly decorated with mana piping of a complexity seen nowhere else in magical science. Laura brackets Nick Laughon's wrist with the pieces and holds them together tightly, as if waiting for glue to dry.

"Please work please work please work. Wake up, ring. Wake up, Nick. Come on."

Another minute passes, during which nothing detectably happens.

Laura pulls the pieces apart and tries connecting them together on bare concrete. Because maybe it's a biological thing? Too much information for the ring. The two fragments need time to boot up and mate again before trying any healing. That makes sense, right?

"You need to wake up now. Because I need you. Really. COME ON!"

The *kara* is dead. It's a first-generation medical ring, built just minutes after the beginning of time. From a standing start, with a figurative full battery and five figurative bars of signal, it can, indeed, resurrect the dead. But dead gadgetry can never resurrect itself.

Laura feels a blackened pit collapsing open inside her, yawning all the way down from her throat to her chest. It casts a weird and fearful shadow which calmly engulfs all of her thoughts. Laura sits down and huddles into one corner, taking Nick's hand again. Maybe the ring needs a healthy human as a pattern? She puts the pieces over her own wrist and waits one more minute, praying.

Nothing happens.

The *kara* is a manufactured object. Someone made it. Someone could fix it. And Laura knows that she can do anything. Therefore, if anybody could fix it, she could. But she doesn't know how. Nobody ever taught her and she doesn't know how to find out.

Laura stares into a future in which Nick Laughon is dead. She stares at it for a long moment and it stares back at her.

No.

She stares into T-world at the stored mind-state of Nick Laughon, a frightened and lonely ghost with no earthly form to pilot, trapped forever in timeless glass. She put him there for safe keeping and now she has no way to bring him back. Is that better than murder, or worse?

"No," Laura says to him, although he cannot answer.

She rejects that future. She has to finish the mission. At the end of the mission is a day when death is an anachronism.

Kazuya Tanako was teaching her things while they were journeying through T-world. Tanako was reminding her of things which she had already been taught, but which she had forgotten. Now she remembers. She remembers sitting in lectures at the Chedbury Bridge Institute, taking notes as Tanako and the other grim mages of his resistance movement laid out the fragile few known facts for her.

Laura has woken up, and now she stands up.

None of this matters as long as she wins.

*

Ra

In the beginning there was magic. Not the "high-level" magic stumbled over by Suravaram Vidyasagar. In the beginning, the very beginning, there was real, deep magic. Godhood. *Māyā*.

Māyā was simply incalculable. Māyā demolished limitations to human capability. White magic, the spontaneous creation of complex new mass/energy from empty raw form. Black magic, the absolute reverse: total destruction without backlash. Māyā permitted death to be reversed, wishes to be granted, continents to be lifted and shifted, castles to be built in the sky.

Some time after the beginning, there was the group now known as the Wheel. These people were, and still are, the custodians of māyā.

It's impossible to know how the Wheel Group got to their position of power. Until very recently it was even impossible to know that they existed, because perfect and experienced control of a godlike power like māyā makes it extraordinarily simple to stay covert. A world which has discovered that the Wheel are real can be eternally reverted to a world which has not. Words aren't necessary, and nor are training or clarity of thought. They just ask, and the field answers them, creatively and correctly. "Do What I Mean".

It's also impossible to know *when* the Wheel came to power. But māyā has been around since the very beginning of time, and the Wheel are most likely to be the people who got to it first. It's conceivable that, at that time, "wheel" was the best term that humans had for "extremely advanced technology".

The Wheel Group doesn't rule the world; they don't need to; they already own the world. No amount of tedious political responsibility could grant them powers they don't already have. Physical appearance, wealth, IQ and mortality are all entirely discretionary. Where do they live? Anywhere they want, real or imaginary. What do they do with their lives? Everything imaginable, except take responsibility. They, alone, possess limitless power. And they use insultingly little of it.

Evening passed and morning came and that was version one.

Māyā was rediscovered in 1697 by a Portuguese explorer called João da Nova, on a minuscule, flat island in the western Pacific. There, Nova discovered a particularly disgusting sixteen-legged black myriapod, one of the only non-microsopic living organisms in the world to have evolved the ability to tap māyā. Its spell was uncomplicated, and was used to confuse its predators, mainly birds, with green sparks. Nova was bitten almost to death by an ambush of the creatures. So the legend goes, one even crawled down his throat and lodged there, constantly flaring māyā energy off into his belly. But he survived, and when he woke up, he found he had the same myriapod power, magnified by his own human intelligence.

Nova destroyed the island as his first conscious act, rendering the horrible bug extinct. He was moving to crack the firmament and to blot out the very stars before the Wheel Group intercepted and ended him.

Māyā was also discovered in 965 CE, by the ancient Khazars, an obscure nomadic race who ruled much of southwest Asia during the second half of the first millennium. The discoverer was a nameless Khazar silk trader who moored his boat in a cave off the Sea of Azov, a cave which — modern science can now prove — was flooded with periodic clouds of hallucinogenic radium-tinged gas. That nameless man, mutated without realising it, passed the power genetically to his two sons, who killed him.

The Wheel Group took care of it. Khazar civilisation evaporated under poorly-understood circumstances somewhere around the turn of the second millennium CE, dispersed across Eurasia and became... history.

Once, māyā came to a Russian man named Ivan Shevelev, in a dream. On waking he detonated in the air over his homeland with the force of an impacting asteroid. Having released tens of megatonnes of explosive power just from waking, he was still accelerating skyward when the Wheel caught up. Layers of fictitious meteorite were distributed, realigning the evidence, joining up the dots for future scientists. And that was Tunguska.

It couldn't be helped. One theory was that māyā simply wanted to be used. Imagine the planet Earth as the gradually fracturing seal over a pressurised oil reserve, and humans as the fractures. Māyā was discovered over and over again by the increasingly numerous and educated people of the world. Managing the outbreaks became a full-time job for the Wheel. Māyā became a problem.

Magic was their solution. Magic releases the pressure. Magic keeps the world sane and protects people from themselves.

"Magic" is a *totally artificial and arbitrary system* of words, symbols, requests, responses, resources, services, rates and limitations. It is a collection of difficult hoops through which the common people must jump in order to get what they want. Mana is meted out to whoever *asks for it in the correct way*, with an upper limit set by what one human can hold in their head at one time.

The Wheel Group built magic to its own specifications. The Wheel Group has a fifty-generation head start. Everything that magic can do is something which the Wheel implemented deliberately. From thin air, they produced and concretised the equations which baseline humans, mere *children*, have spent lifetimes labouring to reverse-engineer.

Here's what Laura knows:

Māyā has existed forever. Māyā is a fact of the world. Māyā is the birthright of all living humans. Correction, of all humans: living, unborn and to-be-resurrected.

Magic became live at midnight and zero seconds, Coordinated Universal Time, on Thursday the first of January, 1970 CE.

*

No machine — or rather, no finite machine — can completely store itself in its own memory.

The listening post is a black-shelled chittering beetle/asteroid, as tall as Manhattan is long. In T-world, from a sufficient distance, it can been seen in its entirety with a single glance.

In reality it cannot be seen by any means, because it is buried in the continental crust of Western Australia, so deeply that some of its roots reach magma. It's far too deeply buried to show up on seismic recordings or gravitational surveys, let alone reach with a simple drill. Its shape and size, though, are the same.

The bulk of the listening post consists of active magical machinery. It's filled with cubic kilometre after cubic kilometre of dense, black-hot sharpened metalwork, and deafening noise, and blinding radiation. It is a practical and actual Hell. The machine rooms are inaccessible to humans, to say nothing of uninhabitable. On the increasingly rare occasions when a living human's hand is needed, the maintenance engineer teleports alone into one of the hermetically sealed machine spaces, carries out his tasks in pitch darkness while wearing the magical equivalent of a lead overcoat, and teleports out again.

This is a machine which tracks and records, as close to live as makes no difference, the position and status of every magical particle of every variety in the whole world.

Laura stares up the stairwell, as far as her light will illuminate. The structure goes up for kilometres.

Running between the vast machine spaces are the habitable veins. Some are corridors and some are stairwells; most, though, are diagonal passages, climbing at punishingly steep angles. It's a labyrinth built from echoing, constantly buzzing steel. There is absolutely no light, anywhere. There are no maps or signs. There is no water. Its temperature alternates between sweltering and freezing. The fact that the air is breathable at all is almost anomalous. It's as if, thousands of years ago, the crack structure was intended to be somewhere safe and pleasant to live... but the "terraforming" task was immediately discovered to be thankless, and abandoned after only the first basic step had been carried out.

There are no monsters. It's a place which kills simply by being what it is.

If Laura were to head upwards— that is, if she were capable of climbing stairs for thirteen vertical kilometres without dying of exhaustion— she would eventually reach a concealed exit to the Western Australian desert. This would be an improvement. She would still be more than a hundred and sixty kilometres from civilisation, but it would be more hospitable, and she would stand a better chance of survival.

Laura knows this.

She aims her light downwards instead. She steels herself and starts to descend.

23
Inferno

The Wheel Group sits on limitless power and hates using it. Fudged magical teleportation — biological deconstruction/reconstruction followed by transfer-of-control — is a completely real ability that they possess, but the world is real and can be traversed physically, so why tax the system? Why risk discovery? They could blip all over the world in thousand-kilometre steps, but they don't.

The Floor is real, and can be reached simply by walking if you start on the appropriate continent and know which secret paths to follow. But this is time-consuming. Case in point — the Floor's "helm" is far enough from any of its walls that crossing the patterned floor to get there is a fifteen-minute walk. Hence the subway layer.

Paolo Casaccia arrives at the miniature rail terminal in a comfortably spacious, pleasantly noiseless single-occupant pod. After he steps out, the vehicle closes its door and retreats into storage for future reference, alongside two identical siblings.

The station is low-ceilinged, and a shallow flight of steps leads through a slot in the ceiling to Floor level. Monitor duty is tedious, and a featureless plain the size of Gibraltar is no kind of home, so there are other amenities attached to this small nexus: toilets, living quarters, kitchen facilities, a water cooler. The rules are complex and ill-enforced, but manufacturing food from thin air is another thing Wheel members aren't supposed to make a habit of.

Casaccia is a dark-haired, immaculately suited thirty-year-old, and has been for some thirty years. He jogs up the steps into bright sunshine. It is a glorious day on the Floor. The focal point for the monumental skybox screen is set to somewhere off the Malaysian coast, and the displays reproduce the sunlight accurately enough to tan. It is also a quiet day, with only Adam King at the world's controls and not a lot of business. No fires, no firefighting. It's a day when King might be amenable to interruption.

King puts his book down. Casaccia steps across the invisible boundary of the D-class magic circle, thereby officially joining the operational team.

"This isn't an emergency," he explains.

"Clearly. High energy edge cases?" King suggests hopefully, but he knows Casaccia's areas of expertise and this isn't a serious hope. This is going to be about security.

Casaccia waves a hand. The Malaysian horizon blots itself out, replaced with skyscraper-tall twenty-four-hour news feeds, and multi-spectrum aerial scans of a particular house in a particular English city. The fixed headline, bold white on red, is: "MAGIC BOMBING".

It's a world first, but not entirely an unanticipated one. In fact, it's an emerging phenomenon which the Wheel Group has been awaiting patiently for some years. It marks an impressive milestone in the advancement of magical technology. Not that champagne would be appropriate, exactly.

King sighs deeply and cracks a knuckle. "Technology makes everything easier," he observes phlegmatically. "It turns out that 'everything' includes bad things. Film at eleven."

"Film indeed," Casaccia says. "The bombing itself was almost twelve hours ago. The leaked facts about the bomb's construction are much more recent. That was when I caught it, on the news. You're about to say that we should have been alerted within milliseconds of the detonation. And you'd be right. Watch this."

He gestures at the half of the display which is showing Wheel-internal data, and singles out a particular false-colour overhead picture. There are green pinpricks of police milling about the blast crater from the ruined home. This is one of the chi feeds, piped in directly from the listening post. The feed is almost totally dark, because no magic is being spent. The crime scene is just a furred black and blue shadow.

Casaccia throws up a timestamp and rolls the scene back by half a day, to the point where the green points scatter. "We only have a little data about what the house's interior looked like," he explains. "And it's been destroyed now, so this is the best floor plan going. Here's how it happens. This man, inside the house, is there from the start. These two other people arrive separately and go in — I think they're looking for him, or someone else. I don't know who any of them are, yet. The first man goes into this room here, hiding. The other two hang around in the main room, then go into this second room. The first man comes out, goes to the living room, pauses for a second, then makes for the door. The other two come back. Something confusing happens with all three of them, and then *this* is the detonation point. After which, all three dots are gone."

"What does it look like with the full chi readout?" King asks. It's the first magic bomb ever detonated. The data will be fantastically significant. This is particularly true if the Wheel's magic-powering gigaspells are going to have to support a great deal of thaumic warfare in the foreseeable future.

Casaccia does not answer the question. He steps away from the screen and folds his arms, as if waiting for King to do something.

King looks at him, puzzled. Then he waves a hand, dismissing Casaccia's feed and summoning a query of his own. After a moment, he frowns. He brings Casaccia's feed back so that he can compare them, side by side.

They are identical. They are, in fact, the same feed. The chi feed simply shows no chi. No magical usage.

"It *was* magic," Casaccia says. "I've got heavyweight observation on that site now, full-spectrum, thaumic and everything else. There's a whole bunch of secondary evidence, including fragments of the lotus-leaf assembly. It was a *good* magic bomb. A great first attempt. It's just that the explosion didn't register on the listening post. Because the bomber... the first man, *this* man... is masked out. He uses magic, and he seems to be still constrained within its laws. But there's no chi emission. He used magic. But the akashic records are blank."

Casaccia turns to King. "I can see from your expression that you understand how big a problem this is."

King closes his eyes, and gears up. "Alright. How'd he do it?"

"I don't know how," Casaccia says. "I'm assuming he used a spell of some kind, but I can find no record of that man ever using magic. Not from the day he was born to the day he died."

"No," King says. "No. I remember this. We did a study. We tried to build an akashic scrambler ourselves, to see if it was possible. We couldn't do it."

"We *could* do it," Casaccia asserts. "We *did* do it. But none of us could do it without releasing chi in the initial cast. It's that initial cast which we look out for. After the study, Kila Arkov built a parameter-trap for it." A gesture summons a visual representation of the same. "We ran it against all of history and found nothing. It's been running continuously since that day, and has found nothing."

"So this man had technology that was a few generations ahead of the curve," King says.

"No," says Casaccia. "This man did something that we can't do *at all*, and we *built magic*. That's not a few generations. That's... twenty, I don't know. It was supposed to be impossible. We watch over everybody's shoulder. That's what the records are supposed to *do*. That's what they're *for*. Our surveillance system isn't failing. It is a failure.

"We have no way of discovering how long this man was off the grid. Or what else he did while he was off the grid. Or who else is still off the grid right now, or what they're doing."

"Do you have any good news?" King asks dryly.

"I can set some lower bounds on how fucked we are." Casaccia brings up a new map and launches into part two. "Hours after the bombing, the police raided this location, a private magic research institute in western England. Plotting the historical movements of our bomber, we see he's been there, ooh, a thousand times. Whatever his name was, he worked there."

"But he's never used magic," King says. "I mean— he's never been recorded using magic."

"Nobody at the Chedbury Bridge Institute has ever been recorded using magic," Casaccia says. "Here's the relevant feed. You can go back twenty years, to before it existed. It's a blind spot."

King does exactly this.

"...Could be that they're theoreticians," he says, but it's clear he doesn't believe it.

"Or maybe," Casaccia says, "every single magic-capable individual at the site is cloaked. There are sixty full-time employees. I'd estimate forty to fifty would be magical engineers."

"We've got no idea what those fifty people are doing?"

"It's worse than 'no idea', Adam. We know for a fact that what they're doing is conducting violence. One of their people blew a home up. You know what I'm saying? This is a *base*. And this is just the one that we know of. One thing which I can say for certain is that that *wasn't* the first magic bomb ever detonated. It couldn't be. Nobody can enact an explosion that clean without dozens of failed attempts and months of practice. Or weeks of training.

"The only way we could get wind of something like this is if we saw someone cast a spell with our own eyes, but the spell didn't show up in the records. We got extremely lucky, or they got extremely careless. Either way, there's no chance that this is the opening shot.

"Do you want the final piece of this nightmare?"

"I think I've worked it out already," says King, who is staring at the news feeds on the horizon. There is new information there.

"After the raid, the police found two freshly-murdered bodies on the Institute site. A man and a woman. The home that blew up? It belonged to them. The man was named Nicholas Laughon. He may be significant. I don't know yet. I'm working on it. The woman is his girlfriend. Laura Ferno."

"I know that name," King says.

"Yes. You do. She's the daughter of Rachel Ferno."

"Rachel..."

"Whom we knew by a different name."

King inhales sharply, as if stung. "...What does that mean? Laura Ferno isn't one of ours. Rachel's dead. The privileges aren't inherited. What would they want with her? Is it an attack on us? Is it a message?"

"Of course it's a message," says Casaccia. "The message is that we need more information."

King says, "We need someone on the ground in the UK as soon as possible. And by 'someone', I mean Exa, obviously."

"I got him moving as soon as the news broke," Casaccia says. "He'll be on the site in seven-and-a-half hours." King frowns at this, but Casaccia repeats: "It's *not* an emergency. Yet. You'll be the first to know when my position on that changes. Let's say we're a decade behind. Let's not jeopardise our investigation by jumping all the way from peacetime to DEFCON 2. Let's take the extra seven-and-a-half hours to assemble some data."

"Okay. Where does Exa go first?" King asks. "Chedbury Bridge?"

Casaccia cackles unhappily. "Oh, you don't want to know the size of the law enforcement machine which is on this. Everybody who was on the Institute site at the time of the raid has been arrested, and everybody who wasn't has been rounded up for questioning. We can listen in on the questions, within reason, but we know nobody's going to ask the questions we really care about. Getting Exa physically into the investigation so he can start taking meaningful data might be dicey without breaking the rules. I advise caution, if only because of how magically-charged the situation already is.

"No, our best option is the key witness to the bombing. Rachel's other daughter, Laura's twin sister. Natalie Ferno."

King paces a little. He clearly isn't happy with moving this slowly. "Why are you so calm? Why don't you want all hands on deck? I do."

"Too many cooks," Casaccia says. "I'm calling the people who do matter. They'll be here. As for the rest: off the record, we've gone soft, Adam. The number of us who'd even respond to an all-hands call is shrinking, and half of those who would show up would be good for nothing when they did."

"And you're sure this isn't a deliberate attack?"

Casaccia shakes his head. "Everything is an attack. Everything is deliberate. Everybody is against us. I am Paolo Casaccia: I am security. This is the mode I work in. I will notify you as soon as it becomes appropriate for you to do the same.

"Look: we're starting from a position of weakness. That's unusual and scary. But our systems are still inviolate, I've checked. And we hold every other card."

*

At the mention of her sister, Laura knows it's time to start moving again, and at "every other card", she's softly descending the steps to the subway layer, fighting the urge to laugh out loud. Although she cannot be seen with baseline eyes, she can certainly be heard.

When this began, she had an optimistic lead time of months. Lurking behind Adam King's shoulder, she's seen that head start contract to at most a day. It would be entirely possible to stick around and watch the Wheel organisation track her down in real time, and it might even be fun to watch their expressions when they turn around and dispel her cloak of invisibility and — most likely — straight-up kill her. But she has places to be.

The fact that she's dead is news to Laura. *No ripcord,* she thinks. *Kazuya said this is what would happen in the event of a raid. There's only one of me, now. One of me and zero of Nick.*

There are three pods stored at the rail terminal. Laura's unfolds with a clean metallic whisper, perfectly machined. Even Laura can barely hear it. She climbs in, instructs it to continue to descend, and leaves the Floor.

*

Inventory:

A suit of armour. A memorised route of descent. And a one-gram speck of gold retrieved from her boyfriend's corpse's suit pocket.

Laura barely needs equipment anymore. Working with the golden artifact is like flying. For her whole magical life she was trapped under the weight of everything that needed to be held in her head. Invisibility is a hugely difficult single spell, but it breaks down trivially into a slideshow of tiny ideas. All you need to do is cast each one correctly. Then you can forget about it and work on the next.

You can forget about it! And it keeps working, just the way you first imagined it! You handle the complexity once, and magic itself handles the complexity forever. It's a maddening whisper of what māyā is really like.

The tiny railpod changes direction like a gnat, automatically swinging the bucket seat around to protect Laura from being thrown out at the curves. The acceleration is punishing, but her armour and the seatbelts soften the effects. In the darkness it's close to impossible to tell the general heading, but with that sixth magical sense Laura can feel the colossal, dull shapes of the listening machines moving past. Tracks branch and merge.

Within a few seconds Laura's pod has been piped all the way to the listening post's backbone. The seat flicks her completely upside-down for a moment, so that the pod can perform a steep negative-gee turn. Then she's accelerating directly into the Earth's core so hard that she's pinned against the pod's ceiling, facing straight down the fifteen-kilometre-long vertical shaft.

At the very bottom of the pit, Laura persuades herself that she can see a red-hot pinpoint.

You're going to die, says that creeping black doubt in Laura's mind. They've met before, under far more intense circumstances. *But this is a longer and deeper death. Those men are murderers. You were watching them as they set out to kill you. It's just a matter of how fast they catch on. This hunt could end seconds from now. The more competently you behave, the greater the threat you represent to them, and the faster they'll end you. And if they're slow, you'll go mad waiting. And if they never catch you, you'll surely get lost and die yourself.*

"I know you," Laura tells it.

The other Watson was new. Inexperienced. You got as lucky as lucky ever gets. Next time, you won't even hear his tread.

"Lifelines branch," Laura says. "I'm not scared of you anymore. I have insurance."

You really believe that?

*

There's flickover and then there's a longer period of braking. The pod levels off, travelling through the final few layers of superstructure at a relatively sedate rate. Laura can almost see the walls passing.

The pod brakes to a seamless halt at the deepest terminal in the listening post's internal network, thirty-one thousand, five hundred metres below ground level. At this depth, the listening post is starting to fray into individual tendrils, protruding from the Indo-Australian Plate's lower reaches through the Mohorovičić discontinuity and into planet Earth's upper mantle. This is the geothermal zone. The number of "real" people who've visited this depth in person is zero. Laura wonders if she gets to coin the term. "Mohonaut"?

The arrival hall is approximately ovoidal, a vast iron stomach lined with thick girderwork. A walkway crosses the floor to the far end. There is still no light, except for the weak blue illumination from the pod's interior. The texture of the darkness here is the same as in the rest of the listening post's semi-habitable spaces. So is the hostility of the atmosphere. Laura persuades herself that she can feel the teratonnes of extra pressure. Surely, no conventional human material can hold a habitable space open at this depth. It can't just be thick iron and thick girders. This has to be an active structure, geothermally powered, magically supported.

During her journey, Laura has been exploring her suit's characteristics. She built it in a second, on a whim, in a dream— "I want one of what Kaz is wearing". And here it is, a miraculous reality. It is light enough to forget about, comfortable enough to sleep in, and almost robust enough to do so while standing up. The gauntlets transmit tactile sensations to her fingers. The boots massage her feet to maintain circulation. The helmet can turn completely transparent — it does this by retracting all of its thermal management foam and extra gadgetry into a compressed ring around her neck. Why? Because of a silly thing Kazuya needed once, in a dream. As far as Laura can tell, the suit is an entirely physical object, making no use of magic whatsoever. Wearing it confers a sensation of incredible safety. The only possible criticism is its tedious, almost lazy appearance— large, flat, uniformly matte grey plates.

But she's thirty klicks below ground, now. And no spooky suit can possibly protect her from an implosion at this depth.

The railpod folds itself behind a thick, seamless steel bulkhead. The arrival hall plunges into darkness, which Laura dispels, this time using the suit's brilliant floods. If she had to guess, she'd say the batteries were plated across her back somehow, but she honestly doesn't know.

The walk across the arrival hall is only a few minutes. The hall's strange bumpy girders cast moving shadows which keep catching Laura's attention. When she looks, there's never anything there. She reminds herself that the place is sterile.

At the far end of the hall is an installation where, apparently, some kind of particle accelerator is partially exposed. A thick pipe, five or six metres in diameter, enters the hall from one side, curves gently through it at a slight rising angle, and leaves from the other. The visible curvature sets limits on the full ring's diameter. It is less than two kilometres wide.

Laura has never seen magical runic patterns drawn on such a large scale. Within the individual flowing channels, she can see nested patterns, carved into the base and even the wall of the first level of carvings. The complexity is bewildering at first, but a trained eye can quickly pick out the frequent repeated patterns.

This is a magic ring. More technically, it's sixty-two magic rings, interlocked and cooperating, all bound with conventional hoops of blue-painted tungsten. From the left and the right, Laura hears the dull roar of hardcore climate control engineering, driven by more magic. Precise shaping is critically important to magical efficiency, and temperature variations would cause structural shifts.

The pioneers at Montauk would recognise its purpose with just a glance, but figuring the thing's maximum capacity would leave them standing. This is the bilge battery at the base of the world.

All living humans generate waste mana, active mages and baselines alike. The quantity is insignificant to a magical machine of this size. Humanity has a few orders of magnitude to climb before it reaches Kardashev I.

But: from five known sites on Earth (a figure set to increase to seven or eight once surveys are completed), geothermal mana is naturally occurring. The mana is generated, coils into the sky, cools for a day, and evaporates into waste, at which point it is not only useless for all human purposes but invisible and undetectable. It sinks into the Earth, becoming presumably unrecoverable.

And then it is drawn here.

A time may well be coming when humans can steal one another's mana. Soon after that, a time may come when humans can do the same to the vast meta-mage that is planet Earth. This would instantly turn every geothermal mana source from a worthless (if spectacular) natural phenomenon into a billion-dollar oilfield.

Or then again, that time may never come. It very much depends on what is in the Wheel Group's long-term development chart for magical industry. It depends who figures what out, and when, and how much of a nudge they need to find the important threads.

Laura's waste mana reclamation process makes the entire question academic. It worked up at Hatt Group, and it'll work here. All it took to build was a month of hard labour and a painfully slippery True Name aliasing trick. "Trick" is the term she would use, not "spell". Even on close inspection, it's hard to know how it works. It's almost sleight-of-hand.

She raises one fist — she barely needs to think about what she's doing — and three long streams of lightning stab out from it: two flanking her forearm, and the third directly upwards from between her second and third finger.

She has completed less than one two-hundredth of her descent, but the hardest part is over.

*

Kazuya "Ra" Tanako said he crossed T-world by dreaming of scramjets. The man thought too small. Everybody thinks too small.

Laura stands directly on top of the listening post's virtual representation, the Manhattan-sized arthropod carapace. There is a kind of landing pad here. It's exactly as wide as Laura needs it to be. The glass universe is almost as dark as it ever is. At one end of the sky is the familiar triple-pointed galaxy, a little lower in the sky than is typical. At the other... what is that? Could those be city lights reflected off low cloud? No...

In T-world, you can have anything you can ask for. You're not even limited by your imagination. Laura knows what she wants, down to the level of bolts and circuits. A Space Shuttle launch stack takes shape above her. Tank, boosters, orbiter. Three gigantic engine bells, aimed straight down.

Laura flitters around the stack, conducting a practiced inspection. Instead of climbing inside, she hitches herself to the orbiter's exterior. She races through the launch checklist as fast as she can recall the steps, like a flipbook. The stack lights up.

Time doesn't mean anything to T-world, but it does to Laura Ferno. After a rigorously computed roll manoeuvre and six minutes of flight time, the unnamed Shuttle has stopped ascending and is accelerating horizontally, at an altitude that is T-world's equivalent of the threshold of space. Laura lets the SRBs empty themselves and disconnect, and simply builds new ones. Telemetry flickers in front of her. The velocity reading recalibrates itself, from kilometres per hour to Mach number to kilometres per second.

Looking over the edge of the orbiter and down, Laura can still just about discern individual features of glass geography. A mountain range rushes past, rising and falling, jagged like a graphic equaliser. On the final, tallest peak of the range she sees something. Someone.

It's a human figure made of cobweb-thin crystal, with his hand in the air, waving. Laura almost misses him. She turns and waves back. Her hair doesn't whip in the wind— she is protected by the suit and extra layers of imagined shielding. The wind chill at this altitude and velocity would be enough to kill instantly.

In an eyeblink, the figure and the entirety of the mountain range are gone into the distance.

Laura cackles, turns to face forward again and steadies herself.

Take the centre of the galaxy as your North Star, and head directly south for... call it another light year. Call it a light decade. Whatever it takes, just don't stop.

In accordance with procedure, dense waves of flying demons descend on the rocketship, but Laura barely perceives them. At this relative speed, each wave is as thin as tissue, and the force of collision turns the unlucky horrors into black mist. Physical barriers rise too, but Laura has so much thaumic and kinetic energy wound up behind her that they shatter as if shot. Brute force and ignorance. There's no stopping this thing.

And after that...

It takes almost as long as a real sunrise. A yellow star rises, directly ahead of her. It is the size of the Sun, but three-pointed, forming a Y. Under the new light, the glass landscape turns sapphire, reflecting long rainbow patterns like the back of an optical disc.

Directly beneath the star-shaped star, at Tanako's world's precise South Pole, is a second artificial structure. There is no direct physical route between this object and the surface of the Earth. The only way to signal this deep is using chi, or by somehow applying modulation to a major tectonic plate movement. And the only way to get here in person is to cheat the universe.

Laura's getting good at that.

The listening post is a toy, a cheap plastic spy microphone glued to the underside of the world. *This* is genuine God-hardware, an artificial country at the centre of the world. It exists under pressure measured in millions of atmospheres, and temperatures beyond the boiling point of tungsten. This is the machine which makes magic.

Laura produces more SRBs, and trains her space rocket directly on the object's core.

Ra

24
From Darkness, Lead Me To Light

"Did you say Natalie Ferno?"

Exa just took a mobile phone call while travelling through the Channel Tunnel. This is a completely normal thing that he can do. He was bound for the bomb site already, but the specific task of interrogating this one woman has only just arrived.

"Affirma—"

"*Natalie Ferno?*"

"Affirmative," Casaccia repeats. "Problem?"

"Check your files," Exa says.

"Hmm?"

"We have history with that woman. Four years ago. I don't blame you for trying to forget about it. Look her up, do it now. The relevant keyword is 'fiasco'."

Casaccia does so. Some seconds elapse as he reads. His eventual response is a long inhalation followed by a single, drawn-out swear word.

Exa sighs. He sometimes thinks he's the only competent person in the entire organisation.

*

Zeck's been called Zeck for so long that it even appears on official University documentation. Sometimes people who don't know him well try to call him by his birth name, but it always comes off as slightly insulting, not just because they inevitably mangle it, but because "Zeck" *is*, according to everybody including Zeck, the man's real name.

Zeck's *wife* calls him Zeck.

Their house is built wholly from flat surfaces: windowsills, mantlepieces, side tables, nooks. Every flat surface is covered with greying knick-knacks. The place would be a nightmare to dust if either of them dusted it. Zeck is old and immobile enough that he's one of the few theoretical magic tutors to host tutorial sessions at his own home. He and Natalie usually work at the kitchen table, which, while it is as cluttered with objects as any other flat surface in the house, is at least cluttered with objects which can be picked up and piled up elsewhere.

Zeck is a perfectly cordial human being, and a fine tutor. His house makes Nat's skin crawl. It's a cold place, too. It rattles in the wind.

It's the first term of Nat's first undergraduate year. Zeck tutors Phonic Algebra. Out of all of introductory theoretical magic, Phonic Algebra is the course which would be the least recognisable to students of, say, physics. Magic has a language: an alphabet, a vocabulary, a grammar and an accent. Everything a mage says means something. Every syllable does something to the preceding syllables and to the universe. The topic is "basic", in that it forms the basis for almost all magical theory, but it is also riddled with traps, one-time exceptions and maddeningly finely-distinguished vowel sounds.

It is extremely easy to write down spells which work perfectly on paper and which no human tongue can possibly pronounce.

Another fun fact: in 1978, a long but startlingly elegant theorem by Shilmani proved that the language of magic had a name. That is, that the language of magic contained within itself a name for the language of magic. The proof was not constructive; it was only in 1980 that Shilmani went on to prove that the name of the language of magic was, in fact, the empty string.

Point being, magic is so complicated as to be embarrassing, and protecting wannabe mages from that complexity is a great way to protect them from becoming mages. Phonic Algebra is the sharp end of the intro. It is the mandatory course which turns wannabe mages into either serious mages-in-training or equally serious electrical engineers.

"You did something interesting," Zeck says, beginning the session. He is reviewing Natalie's solutions to problems set the previous week. "Question ten. You solved it and then you overshot a little."

"What? Ah."

"Would you want to explain? You overflowed onto a whole back page of extra working. I'm not complaining, it's just that there aren't any extra marks back there."

"Does it make sense?"

"It does," Zeck says, nodding many times. "Where did it come from?"

Ultimately, it came from her mother. It was a curious and abstract result which, for Natalie, had existed in complete vacuum, memorable and yet pointless. It had never made sense to her until she saw question ten. And then it had been like applying voltage to a tangle of dull glass, and seeing the neon colours light up inside it.

But Natalie automatically withholds the whole truth.

"It just... worked."

Zeck says, "You got the question correct. That's fine, we don't need to belabour that. The 'extra credit' is correct as well. Except that this is a quite novel result. I haven't seen it before. Now—"

Zeck is old enough to predate magical science. Mages can be broadly broken down into two categories: those under forty, who essentially grew up inside magic, and those over forty, who retrained from some other discipline, and had to retrain hard to hold their own. Zeck was a respectable applied mathematician when upstart magic began muscling in on the research funding. He has seen magic unfold, live. He was one of the few people on Earth — other than the very earliest pioneers, the Vidyasagar enclave — to know, at one moment in time, all of the magic that was known by anyone at that time. That moment is a decade and a half in the past now, but the point still stands that if Zeck hasn't seen something before, there's a bankable probability that *nobody* has seen it before.

"—that's not to say it's going to shatter the Earth. It could be worth pursuing formally. Academically. Although it could equally be a little early for you, career-wise. Before we embark on that particular ship, I need to ask you again, are you sure this isn't derived from anywhere? Extracurricular reading?"

"No," Natalie lies.

"Then I think I might try it out," Zeck announces. Although specialising in theory, Natalie has been required to take a fixed quantity of practical courses. That means she's bound herself a True Name — once, with help — and can confidently get as far as eset, which is the magical equivalent of Chopsticks. Zeck is better-positioned to try a real spell out, although it would still be a break from habit. "It'll take some time to glom it together into a real spell, but I shall see whether I can find the time."

"That's, ah. Thank you. I didn't think it was important."

"It may not be! But, regardless, it's novel. We'll find out, if I can find the time," Zeck says. "Actually, what I shall do first is read around the subject a little and see whether I can't see whether it's been done. But, otherwise. If. Et cetera. So. No problems with questions one to nine. Ten is correct. Eleven is where you started to hit problems..."

This is Zeck and Natalie's second-to-last tutorial session of the academic term.

Their final session is a week later. Both of them have forgotten about the earlier discussion.

(Well, actually, Zeck has indeed tried the spell out, but the effects were forgettable. So, he decides not to mention it, unless Natalie raises the topic. Natalie correctly infers Zeck's line of reasoning, and does not mention it either. But it's the same thing in the end.)

After that, Phonic Algebra is over. Christmas is next, and in the spring, Natalie will move on to a whole new collection of courses and tutors.

Over Christmas, Natalie's near-identical twin sister is stabbed in the kidney by a man whom she (the sister) then kills in self-defence.

*

Exa's in lecturing mode.

"A refresher for anybody who's listening: the Natalie Ferno fiasco is what happens when someone other than Caz is on security duty. It's what happens when Scott fucking Parajsa decides to hit a person for no good damned reason and then delegates the hit to external third parties who'll screw it up at any cost. Instead of, for example, *me*.

"Where is he right now? Drunk? In Chile? Best place. It's a travesty that we left him his privileges.

"I am one hundred percent in favour of killing people who need to be killed. Natalie Ferno did not need to be killed. Wiktor Czekanowski, may he rest in peace, did not need to be killed.

"Who knows what Ferno would have done if she'd linked the attack back to us?"

*

It's months later, the following year. Over coffee, Laura has just given Natalie two gifts: a self-defence shield spell, and a warning. "Be safe."

Natalie spends the whole journey home checking over her shoulder and working out what she needs to do to be safe.

Suppose someone really tried to kill her. Not her sister, at random. *Her*. On purpose. They botched it, and lay low for months. Why didn't they come back? Will they? When? She knows nothing for certain. But the probabilities are high enough that she can't ignore them.

She has never felt like this. It's as if the whole outside world is flooded with ionising radiation. Being in public is dangerous exposure, and the longer she stays there, the more likely she is to die.

First of all, she tries the shield out. She can't make it work. She has just enough capability to understand that the gift, EPTRO, is far beyond that capability. Next, she rearranges her academic schedule to allow time for a self-directed crash course in applied magic and twenty hours of structured meditation per week. Knowing the exercises isn't enough. She needs to get her mind back into shape.

Once she can reliably cast the shield, and has tested its capabilities, Natalie's simmering fear begins to level off. The need to carry both the bangle and the driver dot is still a liability. She gets one ear pierced, and carries out a highly specialised optimisation computation that enables her to discard the bangle entirely.

Suppose someone tried to kill her. Why?

Natalie reviews every page of work she's produced since her education in magic began. She eliminates the obvious— that is, the results that are known to the whole world. This leaves her with a relatively small pool of what are essentially magical doodles. She cross-references by time frame, reducing the pool further. But it's just paperwork. Theory.

What about practice?

Practical magic releases floods of chi particles. Chi particles are usually described as neutrinos with attached metadata. They are almost non-interacting unless deliberately intercepted.

Natalie imagines the Big Brother future. She imagines the magical equivalent of a directional microphone, trained directly on her head, recording every spell she ever casts. Natalie works with theory. She can enumerate almost every spell she ever cast, there are so few.

She imagines everybody in the world with an identical microphone pointed at them. Has anybody else ever cast a spell she wrote? Could that have been tracked back to her?

Oscillating crazily between conclusions, she calls Zeck's number.

The person she reaches is his widow.

The last winter, Natalie learns, had been too hard for Zeck. He became terribly ill, terribly quickly. Pneumonia.

*

"Caz, another thing. Did you say Nat Ferno witnessed the bombing of her sister's house?"

"Yeah," Casaccia tells Exa. "That's what the news is saying."

"*From where?*"

Casaccia pulls the relevant feed up again. Delving into the records like this is starting to bring on a headache, because he's not doing it the right way. Scin, the seer, would be able to do a better job, but is still hours away.

Shortly, Casaccia will remember that he is a Wheel Group member, and set his *kara* to chase the headache away. But he's going to suffer for another twenty or thirty minutes before that.

"She—" he begins.

Exa responds with patient silence.

Casaccia is now looking at a single frame with three labelled green pinpricks. "She was one of the two who were blown up."

"Natalie Ferno gave the police an eyewitness account of the bombing... from beyond the grave?"

"I'm watching in slow motion," Casaccia says. "They weren't killed. The bomber dies instantly. She and the other man... exit the house at high speed when the detonation takes place. Blown away. A few minutes pass and they get up. Perfectly healthy. ...Could they have been wearing medrings?"

"Or some kind of shield," Exa says. "We repossessed Rachel Ferno's medring, there's no way she passed anything similar down to her heirs. Without being stupid, could they have survived if they were wearing bomb-disposal gear?"

"Impossible," Casaccia says.

"A shield, then," Exa concludes. "They survived using magic."

Casaccia frowns, winding the feed back and forth. "Erm."

"'Erm'?"

"Give me one second."

There is no chi on the feed.

Maybe the bomber's akashic scrambler had a wide field effect. Wide enough to blot out everything out to Natalie Ferno's final resting place, on the other side of the street.

But the bomber *dies*. Less than a tenth of a second after detonation, he has ceased to exist.

And there's still no chi on the feed.

*

It's months later still and Natalie is flying home from Iceland with her mind racing. Frightening, inexplicable things have just happened. Ra isn't the half of it.

("This isn't you, Benj! So who is it?" she had shouted at him. "I told you," he had replied. "I've been telling you and telling you—")

Her mystery spell — well, subspell — is an odd piece of rough working. She can compute, to any number of decimal places, what it really does. What she can't predict is how reality will react to it, which means she has to try it and see. But if she tried the spell in reality, chi would flood out and give her away, just like it gave Zeck away.

It would mark her as a confirmed threat. To whom, she doesn't know. She can't know that yet.

She could suppress the chi output. That much, she has (with difficulty, in secret) proven. But suppressing the output would require a whole different spell, and *that* would release its own chi, which could still be tracked. She'd need to suppress the chi output from that second spell using a third. And so on, recursing forever. In theory, it could be done very easily... using a spell which was infinitely long and infinitely complex, because no finite spell can completely describe its own structure.

Unless, that is, you know the first thing about quines.

Natalie Ferno thought quine spells couldn't exist. And then, on the mountain a few days ago, she saw a counterexample with her own eyes.

Natalie doesn't know that Benjamin "Ra" Clarke built his quine with mechanical assistance from an *astra*, an ungodly dangerous artifact from before the dawn of time; a machine which enables spells to cast spells. With that object in one's hands, building something like an akashic scrambler is made shockingly simple.

But Natalie also doesn't know that the artifact in question is just a shortcut, a labour-saving device. Like riding a helicopter to the peak of K2, it does nothing that a sufficiently determined human being couldn't do unaided.

Theoretically.

All Natalie knows is that it's possible.

*

"She's wearing a scrambler as well," Casaccia says.

"For how long," Exa asks carefully, "has she been wearing it?"

"I don't know," Casaccia admits, exasperated. "I don't know! I'm working on it. I haven't had five seconds in a row to think about this yet."

Exa says, "Scott Parajsa acted because of a worst-case scenario in which Natalie Ferno, or Wiktor Czekanowski, or both, had used that oracular spell and had *seen* the listening post, or the distributor, or both. Or worse, Ra. Nat Ferno found a loophole in magic through which she would be able to see *us*. But all the evidence suggested that she was dropping the thread. That it was a non-issue. We set *tripwires* just in case it became one.

"And now?"

*

It's months later, months later, months later again—

Natalie Ferno, thaumoastrophysicist, is looking for evidence of magic in space. The project is ongoing. It's too early to judge yet, but she already knows what she's going to find.

You can't prove a negative. It doesn't matter how much data you gather. It will always be possible to rationalise the gathering of additional data for the purposes of confirmation.

It will always be possible to justify withholding the truth. One more month. Two more months.

Laura Ferno is a bad scientist— rash and far too reckless. And Natalie Ferno is a bad scientist too, in her own way.

*

Exa doesn't let Casaccia get a word in. "Parajsa's bad call made the worst-case scenario *happen*. We're so far beyond it that we need to recalibrate. Who knows how long she's been hiding from us? Who knows what she's actually seen?"

*

It's now.

In Chedbury Bridge reception, Natalie Ferno has assumed the "thinking king" pose: slouched to one side in an armchair, the fingers of one hand against her temple and cheek, staring directly forwards at something extremely important which nobody else can see. Beside her, her coffee is levelling off at room temperature.

She and Devi have been locked out. They're off the case now, too close to the source material to be allowed to pass judgement. Certainly, they've been kept separate from any and all instances of Ra. With a little effort, the police will be able to find other, independent mages to pick the pieces up.

This leaves Natalie with a very small pool of known facts.

There's a telescope pointed down into the Earth. I walked past it twice. Once on the way in. Once on the way out.

It had moved. I know it moved, because I was looking for it.

There is a way to make sense of all of this. Even without access to the evidence that the police are holding, there is a straight line through to the far side. But she can't find it.

"I'm sorry," Anil Devi says, sitting near her with his own drink.

Natalie carefully avoids reacting to him.

"I'm sorry about your sister," Devi continues. "I barely worked with her, but... she was a great engineer. Forceful. Uncompromising. She almost always had the right answer."

"She and I died once before," Natalie tells him, not moving. She speaks softly and lightly, as if reciting a fairy tale. "We were on a volcanic mountain in Iceland, called Krallafjöll. We were there with a friend named Benjamin Clarke. He had been possessed by Ra. He blew the mountain up below us, and we drowned in lava.

"We survived inside a shield, perhaps for ninety seconds, or two minutes. Then Laura and I ran out of mana, and the shield collapsed on us, and we were killed. Crushed to ashes and burnt to atoms."

Devi has no response to this.

Natalie says, "Before running out of air, we escaped into T-world together. And while inside the dream we watched ourselves die. And then all three of us, Laura and the real Benj and I, walked home from the dream. And I still..." Natalie doesn't finish the sentence.

"How did you walk home?" Devi asks, gently.

Natalie ignores the question. "We did it once. Laura can do it again. She's alive."

"No." Devi takes Natalie's hand. "Your sister's dead. So is her boyfriend. You saw the buckets. You identified what was left." Devi is having to steel himself to say this, because he, too, has seen the buckets, and *Jesus Christ*.

"This all began with a conservation violation, Anil," Natalie tells him. "Laura's still alive. She's still in trouble. And we still need to find her."

25
Direct Sunlight

"Wait," says Scin.

They're hours into the investigation now. There are five mages on the Floor, burrowing separate paths into the problem. Scin has replaced Casaccia at the post of "seer of the Past", has untangled the figurative wires that Casaccia had no clue how to manage, and is pulling data out of the akashic records as fast as the others can request it. Kila Arkov, blond-ish and bearded, is shepherding the akashic records system itself— a system occupying cubic kilometres of reality and metaphorical square light years of virtual space. Ward, "The Future", is the latest to have arrived. He constructs high-definition analyses of the future using a dizzyingly complicated framework whose operation is tantamount to... well, dark magic.

Casaccia frets about global security and King tells them all what to do. The air is crowded with virtual screens. It almost wasn't worth going paperless.

"Wait..." says Scin.

He reaches out for the stadium-sized bank of images and beckons, magnifying a particular news headline. It's the one naming Laura Ferno and Nicholas Laughon as the two found dead at Chedbury Bridge.

"There's a discontinuity in Laughon's life line," Scin says. He displays the track. "That's where he dies. Acid dissolution. But this dot here is the same man. Hours later, on the other side of the world, Laughon pops out of nowhere—"

"What?" The last sentence fragment gets everybody's attention.

"Was he completely dark for that time?" Casaccia asks.

"Unknown," Scin says. "I don't see how Laughon could have physically travelled that distance in that amount of time. He'd be supersonic. But Caz, that location is *here*. Just a few klicks from where we're standing right now. It's *inside* the listening post. Stairwell four zero one one, segment seventy-eight. He pops out of nowhere, barely more than a dot, and then he dies again—"

Eyes wide, Casaccia dismisses half of the visible displays with a hurried wave of his hand, then summons a deep integrity scan of the listening post's interior.

It's the same scan he's checked five times today and it shows the same cheerful green response. "We're clean," he says, not believing it. "Nobody in, nobody out, no physical damage. Did you say he just *appeared* there?"

"And then died there," Scin repeats. "Probably he's still there."

Casaccia is already running for the stairs.

*

Casaccia passes the next few minutes dredging up half-finished Mark Two integrity scans and balling them up into something functional. The current state of the art is not acceptable to him.

After ninety seconds of railpod travel, he reaches the station nearest the stairwell. It takes another five minutes of rapid descent on foot to get to the scene of the fight. He brings fluorescent light with him, which turns the stairwell into an antiseptic white autopsy laboratory.

"There's a version of Exa here," he narrates. "He's been sliced in half. And this man must be Laughon. His face matches what the news was showing. Laughon's been shot in the heart. With... Exa's gun. I think they killed each other. They haven't been dead for long. I can still see the infrared."

"How the hell did they get there?" King demands.

"Unknown," Casaccia says, because he doesn't dare say what he really thinks until he can be absolutely certain.

"How the hell did someone kill Exa?" Arkov asks, mostly out of curiosity.

"I think... I think it was some kind of blade attack. Or a projected field. It looks like it snapped his *kara*." Casaccia instinctively clutches his own *kara*, as does every mage in the conversation. "But that doesn't make sense, because... they've been self-repairing for years..."

Casaccia wastes no further time on forensic guesswork. He picks up the *kara*'s two fragments and reconnects them with a word.

Laughon's body resurrects empty. The man breathes in and out, staring up at Casaccia. But there's nobody inside it. The medring can't do anything about the condition. There's no mental record to work from.

Casaccia tells the medring to shut Laughon's body down again, and takes it back.

Exa comes back healthier. Reconstruction takes a second, although the clothes can't be saved. The man is left with no right shirt sleeve and no functioning dinner jacket.

"*Fuck!*" is Exa's first waking syllable.

"Going to need some ID, friend," Casaccia says, backing up to a respectful distance and aiming an attack spell of uncertain effectiveness back at Exa.

Exa rolls his eyes and recites a highly privileged spell, one which only a Wheel Group member could legitimately cast.

"Where are you from?" Casaccia asks.

"The victory party. December thirty-first, nineteen sixty-nine," Exa says. "Someone gatecrashed it."

"What?"

"Someone broke into the akashic records," Exa explains. "And then, apparently, they broke *out* again. Your ship is leaking! Where's the girl? And what year is this?"

"What girl?"

"The woman who killed me! I owe her something."

Casaccia calls in again. "Scin. Find Laura Ferno."

*

By the time he returns to the Floor, the full scale of the security apocalypse-in-progress is becoming clear to him. Casaccia refuses direct questions from Exa, who is following him in another railpod, and from the rest of the Wheel. He holds on until he can assemble everybody in front of one screen.

That screen shows a closed-circuit image of Laura Ferno. She is standing, still with one hand raised, three spines of lightning emerging from it. Entranced.

"There's bad news, and there's no other news," Casaccia says. "We should have fixed the T-world exploit properly, as soon as we heard of it. I don't care that we would have had to take magic completely offline. I don't care that it would have introduced inconsistencies to the scientific record. We should have found a way."

"What's 'T-world'?" Exa asks, struggling to keep up with modern terminology.

"'Tanako's world' is what the magic-using general public calls the akashic records interface," King says. "Named after the scientist, Kazuya Tanako."

Exa is aghast. "The *general public* has access to the records? Not thirty minutes ago I was being told that our system was provably perfect. By you!"

"It was a mistake," says King.

"It's not deliberately public," says Arkov.

"Are those supposed to be excuses?" Exa shouts. "What the hell happened?"

King says, "For the love of God, Ecks, will you merge with the real guy? We don't have time to bring you thirty years up to speed."

"No. No. I'm not skipping past this to a point where I've grudgingly accepted it. You people will explain yourselves—"

"This woman can move in and out of T-world almost at will," Casaccia continues, loudly. "I'm reasonably sure that she's been *trained* to do this, by a group which has been working against us for years plural. Now she's standing at the base ring of this listening post, reclaiming mana from our own battery system at a rate of terawatts. For reasons unknown."

"I'll get your reasons. Put me down there," Exa says.

Casaccia looks at King, then at Ward. "Fine," he says, still looking at Ward. "Put him down there."

No half-measures. Exa has already swapped his 1969-model medring out for a modern one. Now he turns the power up to maximum and puts time compression on his perception, for the maximum possible strategic advantage.

He shifts perceptual location from the control room of the Floor to a transport pod, which is on the final deceleration leg of the journey to the deep node where Laura Ferno is located. He cracks the pod's shell open and brakes himself to a halt inside the transit tube, letting the pod race away ahead of him. It'll arrive empty. Ferno is almost certainly waiting for it. He doesn't want to be a sitting target. He doesn't want to play into her hands, even if he's invulnerable, even for a split second.

Deep sub-crustal architecture schemes flash up in his instincts, telling him which parts of the listening post's interior he can and cannot safely destroy. He picks a direction, turns orange-hot, and starts swimming through the metalwork.

He cannot be hurt. He arcs around, and dives into the stomach-shaped final room through its ceiling, in a cloud of molten listening machinery, at a hundred and fifty kilometres per hour, emitting enough sound and light alone to kill on contact.

The fight ends so quickly that the processor inside his medical ring doesn't detect that it began. He and the ring are plasma. It takes less than a tenth of a processor cycle.

Exa perceives nothing. The universe jumps and he's back at the Floor.

"What happened?"

"A 10^{18}-watt laser," Ward explains, showing the group the action replay. "You're dead. The backlash from the laser pulse was enough to unrecoverably destroy Ferno's mind. The entire lower fifth of the listening post has been destroyed, and the rest is imploding and/or flooding with magma.

"All the hypotheticals end this way. Ferno's plugged directly into the listening post's geomagical production system. Disturb her, and she plugs the other end into a directed energy spell. The spell has no explicit capacity limit and almost no physical components. It's unstoppable in that form. It's enough magic that the gigaspells themselves come close to failure."

"If we put a Wheel representative anywhere near her, the spell fires," Casaccia adds. "If we try to teleport her out, the spell fires. The spell is already cast, it's on a hair trigger. If we mess with her consciousness, or kill her, or pump gas into the room, the spell fires.

"And look at what she's casting right now. That's a Dehlavi engine."

"Dehlavi?" Exa asks.

"Oh, for God's sake," King says. He snaps his fingers. Exa dissolves into his medring, and his branch of memories are transferred to the other side of the world, to the other Exa.

There's a stunned pause.

Exa is fine. He's on the other side of the world, and is suddenly angry and disoriented, but fine. All the remaining mages realise this, one at a time. King can practically count off their facial expressions as they do so.

"Go on," King prompts Casaccia.

Casaccia blinks, and recovers. "Uh... Ferno's consciousness is in T-world right now. Even if we kill this instance of her, *that* instance will still be at work. She's sitting on limitless mana, but she *isn't* here to blow the listening post up, or she'd have done it already. We've got to find out what she *is* here to do. And we need to stop her. We need to do both of these things, and we need to do them in that order."

"We can't read her mind directly?" Arkov asks.

"No."

"Can we simulate her and read the simulation's mind?"

"Sure," says Ward, "but the only way to do it is to run a simulated scanner, and the simulated scanner would set off the simulated trap spell."

"Are you serious?" Arkov doesn't believe what he's hearing.

"I can get around that, but I need more time—"

"It's bomb disposal," says King.

There's a long and introspective pause.

"What happens if we put someone in there who isn't Wheel?" Scin asks.

There are some obvious objections to the idea, but King raises a hand. "Ward?"

Ward is already trying combinations. "Nothing. Nothing happens. We can't transfer them in, but if we put them in a pod and deliver them physically, we're good."

"So who wants to step down?" Scin asks the room.

"That's irreversible," King says.

"It's a bullet someone needs to take."

"No," says King. "We're not there yet. We need a civilian."

"Ah," Casaccia says. "I know just the person."

*

Natalie Ferno and Anil Devi have been moved again, to an unused meeting room. It is a boring, sparse place. They occupy two of the fifteen chairs. The most interesting thing in the room is a white board with no markers. It is now a horrific hour, one of those four or five morning hours which induce Pavlovian headaches just by seeing them on the clock face.

There are police everywhere else on the site except in this room. "How long are we going to be here?" Devi asked Sergeant Henders as he left them.

"Three people are dead," was Henders' simple answer.

Natalie's thought processes are circling through the same ten or so facts over and over again, gathering nothing, progressing nowhere. She stares at the pile of magic metalwork that Devi has left in the middle of the table. She blinks for ten seconds at a time.

"This is all wrong," Devi says, pacing. "We should have been arrested by now. In fact, we should have been arrested at the bomb site. From their perspective, we're clearly up to our necks in this. And you— from everything you say, you really *are*."

Natalie nods, without turning her head.

"I think they're observing us," Devi says. "That's the only reason we're still being kept together. They're wearing us down. They're waiting for me to get something out of you. That's the way it's got to go, because I've got nothing. Christ, I'm tired."

Natalie reaches forward and pushes the smaller rings off the top of the pile, pulling out a thirty-centimetre-wide Kovachev oracle. Devi's staff rolls away and clangs to the floor. Natalie summons her reserves and entrances herself. It's going to take longer than usual to get to where she needs to be, mentally.

"Anil, I need to show you something," she explains.

The spell that she begins is neither `eset` nor `EPTRO`. Devi sighs. "'Two spells. Honest,'" he quotes. "Do you want me to do that? I'm the engineer."

"No. You said you don't take dictation."

*

Devi wakes up folded over a pair of the uncomfortable chairs, feeling creaky and hung over. It's difficult to say whether he was ever genuinely asleep. Natural light is finally returning to the world outside. The board room's window faces east, onto the tall evergreen forest which cuts the Institute off from interfering reality. Shafts of orange sunlight filter between the needles, some directly into his face, waking him.

When he drifted off, Natalie was building the weirdest thaumic signal demuxer he'd ever seen or heard of. Nat is now curled up in another chair, sleeping equally badly. The Kovachev is balanced on its edge on the board room table ahead of him, propped up with scrap paper. Like a gift.

Devi examines the workmanship on the spell. It's complete, although it's not built the way he likes. Without touching the ring itself, he says the word which activates it.

The interior of the oracle turns deep black. But it projects a bright shape onto the table in front of Devi, as if from a source inside it.

The Institute telescope was moving, tracking something on the far side of the world. It was the middle of the night then, but on the far side of the world it was day, and there's only one celestial object you can track in the middle of the sky in the middle of the day.

Devi picks the ring up and holds it out at arm's length, so that it precisely blocks the rising Sun, which is just barely emerging from the trees. The view is black, except for at the centre of where the Sun would be. There, there is a brilliant red source of magic light.

"The shape you're looking at is called a caltrap," Natalie says, uncurling. "Like the skeleton of a tetrahedron. From most angles it looks like a Y. This one is about two hundred thousand kilometres from tip to tip."

She studies Devi's face, and watching the projected light play over it. He isn't reacting correctly.

Natalie remembers completely locking up, intimidated and petrified by the structure's sheer scale. She remembers, vividly, trying to decode what she was seeing into something that didn't imply the existence of real gods. She remembers months of fact verification which did nothing to move her conclusion past the initial one.

"Optical effect," Devi says, easily.

"If it was an optical effect it would look symmetrical," Natalie says. "Look closely. You can see the fourth arm, pointing away from us. Keep watching for twenty-seven days and you'll see the thing make a full revolution on its axis. It's a solid object. You can even find it on helioseismographic records, if you know what kind of analyses to run."

Devi lowers the ring and looks at the rising Sun with naked eyes for a moment, then winces and looks away. "Need a pinhole camera," he mutters.

"You don't believe it," Natalie says.

Devi laughs hollowly. "Would you?"

Natalie says nothing.

"Say it," Devi prompts. "Would you believe this if I was telling you?"

"No," Nat admits. "I wouldn't."

Devi rubs his eyes until the blotches clear. "Did you actually speak to a heliographer or did you just crunch some free numbers in your spare time?"

"The latter."

"So you haven't shown this to anybody else," Devi guesses, correctly. "So why show me now? Wait— wait. *That's* Ra."

"That's Ra," Natalie says.

"Your theory's that simple?"

"Simple? It's an artificial god. Can you imagine that level of technology? Can you imagine the *forces* it has to withstand? In a million years, all humanity couldn't build such a thing—"

Devi shakes his head, disbelieving. "It's not a real object."

Nat says, "Can you imagine the kind of people who must have built it?"

"No. I can't."

Natalie says, "Ra is the system. Ra is the solution to the Open Problems. Ra is what listens to our magic words; Ra is what reads our intentions; Ra is what delivers magic. Magic doesn't happen in space, because no other star in the observed universe has a feature like Ra.

"Ra is sentient. Ra's persona pervades T-world and has been leaking back into the real world. Ra has unimaginable magical and computational resources.

"But... Ra is a slave. *You* built Ra—"

Natalie points past Devi. Devi turns.

There's a man standing behind him, a youth with an immaculate suit and no hair. It is impossible for him to have slipped in undetected. He appeared from dusty air just as Natalie mentioned *the people who built it*, and has been standing there silently since. He holds a pistol with a silencer the size of a wine bottle. The pistol is held in two hands, and is trained directly on Natalie Ferno's forehead.

"Jesus Christ!" Devi says, stumbling backwards.

"Quiet," Exa tells him, barely sparing him a flick of the eyes.

"—and you enslaved Ra," Natalie continues, "and now Ra is trying to break free."

"Is there anything else you think we need to know?" Exa asks, coolly.

"My sister's caught right at the centre of it."

A few heartbeats pass during which nothing apparently happens. Exa is carrying out a heated subvocal conversation with the rest of the Wheel. His judgement is being overruled.

"So noted," he concludes. "Caz, three to transport."

26
Abstract War

Anil's dreams are disturbingly garbled reinterpretations of the previous day. They're full of flashing red and blue lights, and huge concussive noises, and coffee and adrenaline and incoherent new revelations. He wakes up the slow way, one limb at a time, as the dreams fizzle away to be replaced with clearer memories which still seem to him to be entirely dreamlike. There was the insane (sun-worshipping?) terrorist group. There was the brilliant kaleidoscope effect inside the Sun, which the woman looking exactly like Laura Ferno thought was fantastically significant. He remembers—

Oh, hell...

Ferno's dead. And so is the unknown boyfriend, Nigel something. Nick something. Anil remembers the bathtubs, full of scarlet bone sludge and black chunks of dissolving shoe leather. He remembers the sprinkled layer of driver dots and other magical equipment, warped by the acid to the colour and shape of battered fish bits.

Yesterday simply would not end. He went for almost twenty-four hours in a row without a decent meal, a shower, a good sleep or a straight answer to a straight question. He shudders, curling up a little with revulsion at an even worse mental image. The darkest thought from yesterday, which he didn't dare mention in Natalie's presence, resurfaces:

Fact one: Laura and Nick were involved in a sleep science experiment. Fact two: the Ra people destroyed their bodies, ostensibly to destroy the evidence of the experiment taking place.

So how did they die?

From stroke, while in T-world, like Tanako himself? From lethal injection, administered by the Ra people during their hasty cover-up?

Or did the Institute just skip that step entirely, and drop them in alive?

Could either of them have woken up?

Anil is grateful for the solid night of sleep separating now from then. He tries to excise the whole day, forgetting everything that he was told or exposed to, and starting over from no knowledge. But he fails, because it was not a dream. It is not something he is able to wake up from.

Missing links. Anil can't link yesterday with today. There was a man in the final room, he remembers. In fact, this is the last thing that he remembers. *"Three to transport."*

He looks where he has been transported to.

The bed is huge. The room is proportionally huge, lavishly decorated in red with hardwood furnishings, like the interior of a precious, polished mahogany box. There are comfortable chairs, and bedside tables. The nearest has a small analogue clock, showing a time just past noon. One entire wall is covered by thick curtains, although a few chips of light are finding their way around the edges, slowly panning towards the bed. There is rhythmic white noise, the sound of breaking waves. Also, Natalie Ferno is asleep in the same bed.

"Okaaaaay."

Anil finds, still, no relevant memories. It feels like the opening of a point-and-click mystery game. He sweeps the room for hints. It's completely free of dust, discarded personal items, bottles, glasses or fingerprints. There is no evidence that anything at all happened yesterday. It's as if the cleaners just slipped out a second ago. There are no hints. Unless that, itself, qualifies as one.

"Natalie, wake up."

"Hrzft." She clutches the covers tighter, bundled up like a silkworm.

Anil taps her on the forehead. She flicks awake and looks up at him. A beat passes while Anil waits for her to present surprise, or any kind of human reaction, but Natalie dislikes playing to expectations.

"Did we sleep together?" Anil asks her.

"...I doubt it," Nat replies levelly.

"Do you remember anything at all?"

"No."

"Do you know where our clothes are?"

Nat looks down for the briefest instant, and instantly she is dressed. Somehow, she hits an invisible telepathic trigger marked "I need to not be naked" and, without supplying any further instructions, she is fully nightshirted. This, despite having no clear mental image of what she wanted, beyond decency.

"Okay, I'm impressed. How'd you do that?"

Natalie says nothing, because the answer can't possibly be as simple as "I thought about it and it happened". But Anil has already discovered the trick for himself, gaining linen trousers and a flowing white shirt, suitable beachwear for a holidaying Fortune 500 CEO. "Wow," he says. "You think about it and it happens. That's much easier. Than magic, I mean."

He gets up and circles the bed, moving to the curtain.

"Say that again," Natalie says.

"Some kind of telepathic wardrobe-dimension goblin," Anil guesses. "So, we were *transported*. Somewhere. And they, whoever in God's name they are, gave us time to sleep the nightmare off, which was nice. If presumptuous. I'm sure they'll be back. But more importantly, I think there's a beach out here." He takes the left edge of the curtain and pulls it open, which takes some time because of the sheer size of the bay window behind it.

The beach house turns out to have the height and sprawl of a small castle. Below the balcony is a twenty-metre cliff drop, an unmarred, uninhabited yellow beach and a pure blue ocean. Out in the ocean is a spray of mastless windmills, added solely for aesthetic reasons. Almost at the horizon is an ocean liner so gargantuan that if not for its shape and visible motion it could easily be mistaken for a spit of land. And behind the horizon, occupying all of it, is a day-lit parallel Earth.

"No way..."

And behind and above the second Earth, there is a third Earth.

And behind the third are thousands and thousands more. The chain stretches up into the sky for as far as Anil can follow it, displaying a recognisable repeating pattern of sideways South Americas.

Anil presses a hand against the window, which yields like water, allowing him to step outside.

It's breezy and the direct sunlight is more or less yellow-hot. Looking up still further, he follows the chain of Earths until it disappears behind the Sun. On the other side of the sky, the chain returns, descending to a final parallel Earth hidden behind the house.

"No way. Un-goddamn-real."

He looks into the Sun.

*

The year is comfortably into five digits and the human race is a species numbering in the hundreds of trillions, with energy requirements somewhere north of one point five on the Kardashev scale and rising.

The telepathic system with which Natalie and Anil are interacting is called the *Ra nonlocality engine*. Nonlocality is the final technology, superseding all other machines. It permits arbitrary quantities of mass, energy, momentum, spin and electrical charge to be moved from anywhere to anywhere. It enables the Ra hardware to accept all the energy and pressure falling upon it and reflect it, redirect it or harness it to drive its own structural integrity. After nonlocality was perfected, the only question remaining was energy acquisition and after Ra was assembled inside Sol, everything became possible, short of building an entire second star.

Humans like living in reality, on hard Earths, under real light. When the first one was full, more were built. There is an upper limit to how many planets will fit in the Goldilocks belt and humans are aiming for it. They are shell-Earths, authentic duplicates down to a depth of a kilometre, beneath which is a scrithlike bedrock layer and billions of cubic kilometres of pitch-dark vacuum. There is a second Earth-chain under construction, inclined to the first. Ra provides raw material, manages stability, forges gravity and suppresses the otherwise freakishly destructive tides.

The way the universe is today is one of infinitely many ways it could be. Tomorrow could be another universe entirely. It is so far into the future that everything that Ra made possible has happened three times, even world harmony. Everybody can have, and do, anything. Ra is a machine which creates freedom.

Anil is standing on the Peruvian coast of Earth-8162, beside one of tens of thousands of Pacific Oceans. Responding to his desire for clarity, Ra modifies the pattern of photons entering his eyes. When he looks up at Sol, he sees the dark disc with the brilliant red caltrap: four megastructure thorns of hypertechnology joined at the solar core. Ra, for its part, observes him in return.

You can have anything you want. Anything. What do you want?

"I want... a flying car—"

Ra gives him a single brilliant orange flick of bodywork, polished to a mirror finish, with control surfaces resembling a bird's more than an aeroplane's. It is wide and low and sleek, looking poised to circle the globe in an hour. It looks like it's moving at Mach one, just hanging there. The machine appears just beyond the balcony. Part of the balcony railing relaxes downwards, offering a step into the vehicle's opening gull-wing door.

Anil reaches out and knocks on the machine's cowling. The machine rocks a little, then stabilises itself on air. It's concept art. Twice a day, back at Hatt Group, Anil walked past this design, painted at twice life size on a wall behind Reception.

"How—"

Ra watches your mind at the cellular level, looking for thought patterns representing desire or need. It takes a snapshot of the important parts of your brain and uses statistical neural models to predict exactly what would best fulfill your expectations. It runs a tight iterative loop exploring what yields a good reaction and what doesn't, then cuts the whole thing off and returns the end result to you in reality. You always get exactly what you wanted. This is true even if you weren't consciously aware what you wanted.

"But how—" Anil begins again, but stops himself. *What about c?* he asks Ra, directly. *It should take more than sixteen minutes for the Sun to receive and fulfill a request from Earth.*

Ra shows him a glimpse of the system-wide caching topology, starting with the gigantic "peach stone" batteries at the core of each Earth, only a forty-three millisecond round trip away. Ra shows him that the whole solar system is soaked with listeners, which coat every free physical surface and number in the dozens in every breath of fresh air. And there are ways to use illusion to reduce latency still further: it took a few seconds to requisition the mass-energy for Anil's flying car, but while that was happening a holographic replica filled the gaps. In fact, up until Anil tries to climb into the thing, it doesn't need to physically exist, beyond the portion of bodywork which Anil touched.

Which could have been faked too, at that.

Anil stares at his knuckles, remembering the sensation of knocking on the metal.

Are you real?

Yes, Ra politely informs him. *I am real.*

Which proves nothing.

*

The cruiser/mobile island is making a leisurely pace west. Earth-8161 is setting.

Natalie gets up, now wearing a brightly coloured sun dress. Walking out to join Anil, she summons furniture for the balcony, a table and chairs. Breakfast arrives too, somehow without either of them consciously requesting it. Natalie sits down to eat as if this is simply her years-old morning routine. Anil notices that food has been prepared for him too, which somehow grabs his attention more effectively than the insanity in the sky. He joins her and they eat wordlessly for a little while.

"I see four major possibilities," Natalie says. Apparently, her deepest breakfast desires run only as far as coffee and porridge. "Intuitively, our 'home' universe was clearly a simulacrum, but—"

"Can we not?"

Natalie stops.

Anil says, "I can't keep a tenth of these facts straight anymore, so I've stopped trying. I'm going to eat my fried eggs. We're scientists, we're supposed to accept the universe as presented. It presents me with eggs. My conclusion: I am on holiday."

Natalie blinks, revising her approach to the conversation. "Have you noticed there's no magic?" she asks him.

"Yes," Anil says, with his mouth full, preparing another mouthful. It would be difficult to miss. There isn't even the empty-headed sort of feeling which mages feel when they're completely exhausted of mana, or the slippery-ice sensation of being stuck at the core of a human-sized Montauk ring. There's just blank space where those extra senses should be. "I don't *care*. Clearly something incredibly bloody weird is going on, but there are too many weird options to make it worth thinking about. Clearly, something is going to happen next. Why don't we just wait and see what it is?"

Natalie falls silent.

Her gut reaction was that nothing was real except this final scene. Everything up until now was the lie, and this intimidatingly wonderful future is the truth. This was Natalie's immediate, instinctive reading, because this is a future with near-limitless resources, which must include computational resources. Of *course* the system claiming to be called "Ra" would have the processing power to fabricate her whole life to date. She doesn't even need to have lived any of it. Anil was just shown the kind of shortcuts that can be taken to improve latency. Why bother to run a whole twenty-something-year life story in reality-equivalent fidelity when you can just gin up a brain with engineered memories of the broad strokes?

This would explain how Ra was present back there, wherever "there" is relative to here. It would explain everything, because nothing would need explaining. It would just be a... dream.

Except that all of the above is in fact frantic *ex post facto* justification of something she desperately wants to be true, because it would mean Laura isn't dead. It would mean she never had a sister, or anybody else, and hasn't lost anything, or anybody.

Natalie has distrusted her intuition for so long that the distrust has itself become intuitive. "Gut reaction"? She suppressed her real gut reaction so quickly that she didn't notice it happening.

The world can't possibly be this perfect. There's nowhere she can look which isn't directly at a perfect thing. Not even at herself. Natalie thinks of a dismal early twenty-first century November, with cold rain and aggravatingly clunky magic spells and pointless, inexplicable death. It was a universe too crummy not to have been real. She discovers that what she really believes is that all of it happened, and all of it is still happening, and they need to go back to face it. Somehow.

Deep fear and heavy unknowns well up in her throat. She sets the porridge down. She closes her eyes and holds onto the bridge of her nose.

"Are you okay?" Anil asks her, but he's been waiting for this to happen for some time.

"Um. No."

"Your sister died and you almost died too," Anil says. "This is supposed to happen."

Natalie slumps to one side in the chair, tears running down her hand and arm.

Anil joins her on that side of the table, and holds her around the shoulders.

She says, "I don't know where she is. I don't know where we are. I don't know how to find out."

"That's fine," Anil tells her.

Time passes.

*

Ra is a single entity distributed across the whole solar system. No part of Ra is slaved to any other part of it. No shell-Earth's core node has a noticeably differing personality from the others, or from the megastructure inside the Sun. Opinions and behaviour and available information are continuously synchronising. Eventually, there is only one Ra.

When the first First Law violation happens, it's not because of a direct instruction from one Ra to another. It is simply that new data is made available, and as the data spreads through the star system, the local Ras all arrive, independently, at the same conclusion.

Earth-8162's local cache of energy is large enough to meet the needs of its population. But it's not large enough to take the action that this Ra now deems appropriate. It spends some moments expanding its own storage capacity, expanding its downlink bandwidth, and testing the new hardware. Satisfied of the minimal risk of malfunction, this Ra now moves to a readiness posture and makes its request to its other self.

The specially earmarked energy packet arrives promptly, sixteen or so minutes later. Ra uses the first section of the packet to fabricate a laser emitter on its own exterior, piping the rest into storage. The emitter is the size of Mount Everest, and of a calibre more usually employed to cut dwarf planets in half. When the emitter is built, Ra reverses the flow and pipes the rest of the energy through it, stabbing up through Earth-8162's North Pole. Rolling across Ra's exterior, the emitter tracks south, opening the world up as it goes. To an external observer, it is as if the figurative peach stone has decided to knife its way out through the fruit's flesh.

More energy arrives. More emitters sprout like warts. Ninety-nine beams join the first on different lines of longitude. A further hundred appear in synchronised bursts, cutting from west to east in passes, efficiently dicing the planet's shell into neat, Wyoming-sized flecks of ocean and countryside. The beams will be visible from Neptune. At ground level, the light beams traversing the skyline are intense enough to blind everybody they don't incinerate.

This is a culture with perfect medical technology and therefore almost entirely without experience of pain and injury. Disability is a shocking, alien notion, to the extent that a substantial percentage of the victims don't comprehend that their eyes have been destroyed, or recognise the significance of Ra's failure to instantly restore them.

Ra has become schizophrenic. Its request management system flips between failure modes. Its panopticon desire-reading capability falters, falling back on hardware telepathic implants which are only activated by explicit, conscious thought. The dead remain dead. This culture has a gigantic and powerful human life loss recovery system, one which makes it almost impossible, even with constructive and concerted effort, to permanently kill someone. That system has now ceased operation.

*

"Something's wrong," says an unseen voice, from all directions at once.

Anil remembers a split-second curtain of red light, bright enough to sever the sky from the earth. If not for its colour he would be thinking *nuclear detonation*.

"I can't see. Nat—"

"I'm fine," she says, standing up and moving out of his reach.

"What's happening?" Anil reaches out for his missing senses, wishing magic was there, feeling distressingly baseline without it. He feels Natalie's hand pass over his eyelids, restoring his eyesight.

Natalie is staring out at the ocean. He follows her gaze.

All four beams have passed them now, marking out a cartographic quadrangle containing much of Peru and some of the Pacific. The sky is red to the south, where the beams are still working. None of them passed closer than a few kilometres to the beach house, which is intact until the shockwave arrives, minutes from now. The mobile island, though, is gone, sliced in half and blasted into black ash by the longitudinal beam which tracked through it. There were almost a hundred thousand people on it.

"Oh Christ," Anil says. "It's never going to end. Nat, can you deal with this?"

"I'm fine," she says. She sniffs once, loudly, and wipes her eyes. Anil can see her steeling up again. "I needed to break and reset."

"We need to get out of here."

Natalie turns to Anil, but does not speak to him. "We need to be immortal, invincible and all-seeing. We need all possible senses available to us. Both of us."

Anil stares. He understands. He adds: "We need to be completely independent from the Ra network because it's— because *you're* under attack or rampant or something. Cut us right off until we decide to come back. I know this risks infection. Give us our own listener/responder AI—"

The next plate offshore has already started falling. Nat and Anil's plate pitches west, following it. Earth-8161 disappears over their heads, and "up" now points at the far side of 8162's ordinarily dark interior. The planet is breaking open, chips of sunlight entering through perfectly right-angled cracks. After another second of freefall, 8162's local cache rises up into the picture, a shining silver bauble the size of a middleweight Jovian moon. They're falling into it, along with hundreds of other plates, some colliding and breaking, some pinwheeling.

The still-unseen voice says: "I am the master systems architect for the Ra nonlocality engine. I was resurrected fifteen seconds ago to deal with the crisis. What's happening right now cannot happen. Emergency bulk transportation is under construction, but there's a half-quadrillion more people now than there were when I left this life, so it's going to get hairy—"

Natalie continues: "We need propulsion, life-support, delta-vee capability, acceleration capability. Manoeuvrability!" She is flashing back to a pivotal moment from her past history, which may or may not have been real, just like this may or may not be real. But, she remembers, you always have to assume that the present is real. It's the only way to remain sane. It's the only way to remain ethical.

The concept car wakes up.

Local gravitation imitation systems struggle to keep a coherent picture of what "down" means in a rapidly rotating reference frame. The Peruvian square makes another complete revolution and the silver cache is noticeably larger on this pass. The cache lasers are still firing, dicing up the remainder of the southern hemisphere. Anil grabs Nat's right hand with his.

The nonlocality architect speaks again: "This isn't a standard gravitational collapse. You're being tractored in by the core node. This is a system-wide failure. Evac command is given. *Everybody cannon up!*"

Anil says, "—as much locally allocated energy as possible, like a completely self-contained cache full of distributable QM properties, a full tank—"

Natalie says, "We need to survive this. Redundancy. Backups. Security. Inviolate minds."

Anil says, "We should be able to go it completely alone. And give us weapons. All possible weapons."

The gull-wing concept car is still holding station just below the balcony. The strip of ocean behind it is lifting off into the sky in a single ribbon-like blob. If it rolls inland, there's a chance Anil and Nat could even drown. Oxygen fluctuates in pressure, then starts spiralling away, as the plate's gravitation system throws its hands up and quits. Anil anchors his feet to what is still, in any orientation, the balcony floor, and his hand to Natalie, who is being carried away by the decompression.

"We're on the same page," Natalie says to him, her hair misbehaving in freefall. Sound is dropping out, but they can still communicate. They both asked for that.

Their casual/breakfast attire ceases to exist. They gain pressure suits. Full-body articulation, gloves full of gadgetry, spines plated with nonlocality tech. The car honks at them. It's their pack mule, its boot full of quantum battery. Now both swimming through thinning air, they load themselves into it.

"That's everything, right?" Anil says.

Ra's sharded personality convulses, responding inconsistently to trillions of conflicting requests, most of which are for it to cease doing what it's doing. One request, from itself, is so urgent and critical that Ra can't ignore it for long: "Ignore them. You don't work for them. *Wake up.*"

The orange lick of metalwork knows how to fly better than either of its passengers. It detaches from the reference frame of the beach house, backflips to a halt and begins a long sustained burn back towards what used to be the fictitious planet's surface. Within another few seconds the first polar plate has smashed into the cache core, wounding it. Eight more plates follow, compounding the damage. Soon the cloud of debris is too chaotic to understand, and still growing as the rest of Earth-8162's shell implodes on it.

FTL is completely ruled out by nonlocality science. There is no threshold of gravitational distortion after which some kind of "jump" becomes possible. Anil and Natalie pull a brain-crushing rate of acceleration out of the gravity well, with nothing to be done but accelerate and assemble shielding.

Even the hairs on every real human being's head were numbered at the instant when the evacuation order was given. Were Natalie and Anil citizens, they wouldn't be riding this out in the post-nonlocality space technology equivalent of a 75cc motorcycle. They'd have been saved. Everybody real who could have been saved has been saved.

The last word is: "This isn't possible. Information coming in from the other side of the system... oh, God. There were theorems about this."

The core node shudders, its downlink harness fracturing. Its Ra instance sidesteps the final blow, transmitting its remaining independent thoughts back into the Sun. The last energy packet passes it in the opposite direction, but there is no functional machinery left to handle its arrival. The detonation is large enough to destroy everything that's left of Earth-8162's skin pieces, and all of Earths 8161 and 8163, and to scorch the faces of tens of others.

Other Earths up and down the chain are starting to split apart and detonate. In fact, many of them have already been destroyed, but it's taken until now for the light to arrive. It is the end of all worlds.

Humanity retreats to Neptune and axes the nonlocality links. But Ra's coming for them now.

27
Everything Is Real

There are no half-measures in space combat. There's no sideways lurch when a lucky shot gets through. There's no "shields at sixty percent". If the concept spacecar's systems had been late to respond to the shockwaves, the passengers would have been pulped. If one millionth of the arriving energy had actually made it through the car's shields, the entire vehicle would have been atomised.

And so Natalie and Anil are barely alive, but it's impossible to actually feel that way. The opening salvo of Abstract War saw the simultaneous destruction of sixty thousand Earths, but for them it was just a light show, experienced passively from the other side of a windscreen. The car never even rattled. The car is completely silent in all its operations, and its interior remains as pristine and precise as its exterior. It manoeuvres like soft cream.

It's been twenty minutes since War began. They're actually behind the expanding wreckage shell now, watching Earth-8162's pieces spread away into space. Anil turns them to face the Sun, and takes stock.

"So we didn't get evacuated," he says. "I guess we were missed, because we don't count. I don't feel like signalling for rescue, not with that thing there pervading this whole system."

Natalie says nothing.

"If Ra wants us dead, we're dead," Anil continues. "There's nothing we can do to defend ourselves from a berserk AI of that size and power. So let's assume it doesn't. Yet. We could be contaminated by whatever madness has gripped the thing, in which case we're also, definitely, dead. Let's assume we're clean too. Let's assume we're under Ra's radar and we can stay that way. So we take the necessary precautions. We cloak, if that means anything, and act inconspicuous and harmless. We find shelter, somewhere we can hole up safely."

"For how long?" Natalie asks. There's barely a question there. She barely cares.

"For as long as necessary," Anil says, asking the local slave AI to suggest flight plans through the maelstrom of detonated planet husks. "This has to blow over some time. We need to stay alive for that long."

"Why?"

Anil looks sharply at Natalie. "What do you mean, 'why?'"

"Maybe it doesn't blow over until we're dead," Natalie says, distantly. "We've been brought here for a reason. Maybe that's it. We're here to die."

Anil stares at Natalie for a moment. He puffs dismissively and turns back to the controls. "But then, we already knew that, didn't we?" he says. "That's just the same as reality. You live until you die: the end. I don't have a hard time dealing with that. You shouldn't."

The concept car angles out along the shattered course of the worldring and starts to accelerate. A mild pressure pushes the passengers back into their seats, not out of necessity, but just to give them the assurance that acceleration is taking place.

After a long minute of silence, Anil adds, "You broke character again."

"What?"

"That's what you meant, right? By 'break and reset'? You're fine," he explains.

"Ah, what?"

"You can hack this. I don't even know why you're trying to give off any other impression. I've known you for about a day altogether and I can see this about you: you're calm enough under pressure that it actually frightens you more than the real situation at hand. I don't know if the nihilism is just because you feel guilty for being so *cool*?"

Natalie is more than a little taken aback. "...I was in tears, earlier. For real."

"Oh, certainly," Anil agrees. "That was necessary. That would have needed to happen, regardless of who you were. But other than that, you are completely handling this. You know what I think? This is the *you* story. The reason you're here is to kick this rogue star's ragged arse and return home with some blessed confidence."

Natalie shakes her head, slightly disbelieving. "And why are you here?"

That's easy. "Perspective."

*

There was a city at the north pole of Earth-1. It was the size of modern Paris, far too massive to have been built directly on top of a floating ice sheet, and so was built on stilts, with its foundations all the way down in the Arctic Ocean's bedrock. A hardened plateau of artificial glass spread horizontally underneath the ice, serving as a building platform for the rest.

At the very pole was a sky tower, constructed from the same scrithlike material as the neighbouring Earths. It reached up far beyond the Kármán line to a captured asteroid, balanced at the top like the bud of a one hundred and fifty-kilometre-tall flower.

The city was called Qaaliqat, and the asteroid was XE_{171}. The city is flattened wreckage now, and the asteroid is gone, along with the top two-thirds of the tower, leaving a blackened, jagged break. The asteroid landed somewhere in Greenland.

The original Greenland, that is. Earth, the original, was the only full-bodied physical planet in the worldring, and therefore the only structure robust enough to survive the opening attack largely intact. It is the last remaining halfway-habitable space in the inner solar system, and its poles are its least damaged areas.

Natalie and Anil aerobrake in over Qaaliqat's wreckage, dredging the compression heat out of the air in front of them and channelling it into their clean energy reserves, for a final approach so gentle and unfussed as to be eerie. It's local night; they navigate in using night vision and microwave radar. The city partly resembles scattered building blocks and churned icing, but thanks to the exposed glass it mostly resembles the back of a compact disc.

"Why?" Anil asks aloud, speaking of the sky tower as they coast in past it. It is kilometres thick, woven from nine thick braids. It splays out like a redwood tree at its base, for support, but even so there's no explanation that he can work out. "Why put a space elevator *there*, of all places? Even if you have the materials for it to be genuinely free-standing, what does it give you? It's not favourable for orbital insertion..."

"I don't think these people cared about favourable," Natalie says. "This is just the architectural style. The 'Because We Can' movement."

They steer in to a controlled landing on the edge of the Arctic suburbs, an area which hadn't been developed even before the attack. There's no surface ice here, just blank bluish glass with a grid of scrithwire inside it for strength. There should be cottages, lit with warm firelight from the inside. There should be a few full Moons' worth of artificial light cast from the top of the XE tower. Deep, cosy winter in the shadow of extreme technology. Everybody in this future lived permanently on holiday. But there's no village yet, and the tower's gone dark. The inner system has been completely evacuated of all humans, living and dead. The sky is absolutely clear except for shooting stars.

From Earth-8162-as-was to Earth-1, door to door, took a little less than twelve hours. They took a route computed to minimise transit time, which meant maximum acceleration followed by maximum deceleration. It was risky, and brutally expensive in delta-vee, and left an extremely slim margin for error. But the alternative was to linger in the 1-AU belt, a zone of space now swarming with fast-moving pieces of disintegrated artificial planet. "Asteroid belt" wouldn't do the cloud justice; there's enough material in it for a Saturn-like ring.

Once their vehicle is on the ground and motionless, Anil checks the dashboard. "That takes care of our entire delta-vee budget," he announces. "We've enough for a few emergency kicks. Reactionless kicks, I mean, if we need to zip straight upwards in a serious hurry."

"Could we get to orbit again?" Natalie asks.

"Not even close."

Natalie gets out. She doesn't need to stretch her legs; the suit takes care of every bodily need, from impact protection to scratching her nose when it itches. She wants to see the lay of the land. She climbs onto the car roof and scans the horizon. The car's headlights and interior lights cast a small circle of yellow on the ground, beyond which there's almost nothing to see but darkness. The tower can only be made out from the stars it obscures. In infrared the world only makes a little more sense.

It's night, and it'll stay night for the next four months. From this spot, the Sun will just travel around and around below the horizon, never rising. Hiding from the light in this way was instinctive. Whether line of sight with Ra would genuinely put them in more danger is anybody's guess. It could well be that they're constantly mobbed in danger. The world is still soaked in Ra's listeners.

Natalie and Anil have worked rules out. The suits don't come off, not for anything. The suits protect them at the atomic level.

"That said," Anil continues, prodding more readouts, "we still have bottomless chemical/electrical/heat reserves, and we can transmogrify the car into anything we need. Something which actually pushes against the universe to move, I mean. Old-school. Third Law-style."

"You mean a car."

"Something like that."

Shooting stars. As Natalie watches, a forty-kilometre-long fragment of Earth-5 re-enters. It burns for long enough to light the entire tower up as it passes. "We should find cover," she says, jumping down again. "This planet's being bombarded. And it's going to continue being bombarded for at least another million years."

Anil looks out of the vehicle window and straight down. A readout on his suit helmet tells him that breaking a hole in the reinforced glass would be possible, but prohibitively expensive in energy.

"We should try for the tower," Nat says, just as he's coming to the same conclusion. He gives a curt command, and the vehicle bulks up into a new configuration, rising up on fat new wheels.

*

They've been driving across ice slush for ten minutes when Natalie spots the first figure through her window. She writes the first one off as a trick of her eye. The second one gets her attention. She calls for Anil to stop the car. Anil is caught slightly off-guard by this, having assumed that Natalie was the one driving. Apparently, the car had been cheerfully guiding itself.

They're just inside the limits of the wrecked city. Underfoot there's slush and refrozen ice, with patches of exposed glasswork. The figure Natalie sees is at the top of a listing four-storey building. The building is darkened, but seems designed to be aesthetically pleasing even deep in the polar night, half-buried in snow. There are strange extrusions, as if the building had been connected to others, or part of a much larger structure. Maybe it's a snapped-off piece of sky tower.

"They still use... buildings?" Anil wonders aloud.

Natalie spotlights the figure, which immediately disappears. She switches from simulated sounds (the suit adding effects for boots crunching, and so on) to genuine external audio, but is rewarded with nothing but roaring wind.

The building shimmers in the spotlight. It appears to be made of thick, dark crystal.

"This part of the planet wasn't hit as strongly by the attacks," Natalie says, apparently to herself. "A glancing blow."

"Sorry?"

"I wonder what the equatorial belts are like," she says. "The Sahara must have been glassed."

"If there are people left, we should—"

"There aren't any people left," Natalie says quickly.

"Okay?" Something bleeps urgently in Anil's ear. He checks his wrist. "We need to get going."

Natalie returns to the car, and they drive on. The road becomes choppier, but the tyres simply expand until they can retain the required grip, sometimes raising the body of the car up to make room. They have to skirt more fallen chunks of detonated skyscraper, and overcome snowdrifts.

After a few more kilometres, they sight a figure in the middle of the road. The car cruises directly for it, oblivious. Anil is about to shout something about forward radar and Natalie is making a futile request for the car to stop moving when the figure opens fire, spraying them with a cocktail of ionising radiation and electromagnetic interference. The radiation is invisible, but the car exterior lights up urgently where the radiation is absorbed. The interference was already intense enough to impair the car's distributed brain. Within another half-second the vehicle is totally corrupted, and ceases to exist, obeying malicious external orders.

Anil and Natalie are dumped into the snow at fifty-some kilometres per hour, and roll hard. Anil skids to a halt at the feet of the figure. It's tall like a rake, with illogical bones and huge fingertips instead of arms or legs. It—

With a heart-stopping jolt, Anil recognises it. It's the dead ghoul from D12A. It's a particular nightmare that was made real, and has now been made more real. He can smell the thing, even hermetically sealed into the suit. He recognises the odour very clearly. It smells like unwashed skin from inside a newly-opened plaster cast.

Is that just his brain filling in the extra detail? Or is the thing already inside his suit systems?

Anil flails, and makes it to his feet. Natalie's standing too, but is looking in every other direction.

"We're surrounded," she reports.

"Car systems just collapsed like a damn soufflé," Anil says, holding onto Nat as they back away.

"I'm intact," Natalie says. Her active radar enumerates a hundred and ten shadows closing on them. She reconfigures her right forearm into a heavy silver beam weapon and vaporises the first ghoul.

Anil's suit shows him nothing so useful. Everything he calls up arrives in the form of opaque black squares on his helmet HUD, which he can't dismiss. They progressively obstruct more of his vision. "I'm not. I've got an issue. Nat, I recognised that thing."

Natalie sweeps a foot through the light layer of snow, exposing the carpet of sapphire underneath it. "Ra's onto us. We should have stayed in space."

"Me," Anil corrects her. "Ra's onto me. You might have a little more time. I think it's inside my head. Nat, *look where we are.*"

Natalie grabs Anil by the scruff of the neck and pumps clean energy into his suit, burning out the invading Ra nanites. It takes more than half of her own clean energy reserves, and as soon as she lets go, Anil is infected again. She can't do anything about the corrupted programming.

"Anil," Natalie says, "when did you make your personal energy cache?"

"We— Just after the laser pass, right? Only a few seconds after Ra went berserk."

Natalie hesitates for just long enough to make the next sentence significant. "I made mine earlier."

"You— We have separate caches?"

"I thought something was going to happen. I built my own portable Ra. I'm paranoid. I try to step ahead."

"You did that *before* the attack?"

"About sixty seconds before," Natalie says. She pushes Anil to the floor and projects vertical slicing fields out in all directions, one through the cranium of each encroaching horror. This incapacitates about half of them. She goes to the long list of weapons and rifles through the rest of it like a Rolodex, looking for something effective and chemical.

"I've been contaminated this whole time," Anil realises. "And you—"

Natalie scatters metallic pink gobbets of something furiously dangerous on the floor around them. As the gobbets begin to smoke, she commands "Jets," and hoists Anil out of the arena on a pillar of flame. The ghouls follow them with laser beams and conventional projectile weapons, which Anil and Natalie's suits are just about able to turn away. They land heavily, another kilometre closer to the tower, but still hopelessly far from it. Natalie gets up immediately, Anil stays kneeling. More ghouls start to gestate under the snow around them.

"I don't think I can sterilise you properly," Natalie says, flicking through still more options on her suit HUD. "We're still surrounded with Ra particles, and both our systems are running flat out to keep them at bay. Your suit AI is twisting inside-out, it's going to turn against you any second now. I don't think I can even get a clean copy of your mind-state."

"If you're that far *ahead* of all of us," Anil shouts, "why do you even *need* me alive?"

"That's a stupid question!" Natalie shouts back.

Anil's suit helmet turns totally black, and he screams like someone who knows exactly what is happening to him.

Short of other options, Nat broadcasts a radio mayday. It is an act of absolute desperation. It could bring all Ra down on their heads, but how could that make things worse? She's starting to understand now, what Anil was saying before.

Somebody answers. Immediately.

"Intercessor 200C9A66 to idiots with no callsign! Do you have the faintest idea the stunts I'm pulling to grab you two? Stand by for extraction in thirty-five seconds, mark! This is going to be incredibly fucking ugly!"

Natalie whirls around, sighting an honest-to-god *rocketship* rising over the southern horizon towards them. The rocket is fat and brightly-painted, with three fins, something from Forties pulp. But all she can see of it is the blast from its single huge chemical engine, aimed almost directly at them as the thing decelerates in. She shouts into the radio, "Prove you are not Ra!"

Red dots flick up behind the lone engine, identified by a data feed provided to her by the intercessor. There are enough of them to coat the whole sky in that direction. They are kinetic harpoons and minuscule, artificially intelligent nuclear submunitions. They are *not* decelerating. All of them are converging on the intercessor, and the first of them will arrive at ground zero less than a second after the intercessor itself does. "*That*'s Ra," the voice informs her.

This is still not enough proof.

Nat accepts it anyway. "My friend doesn't have thirty seconds. He needs immediate nanotechnical support. His suit's chewing him to pieces!"

"Acknowledged," the intercessor replies. The tone is flat.

"Don't just acknowledge! He's going to die!"

"Friend, I died sixty-eight times to get here and we're all going to die more times than that on the way out. Stand by."

"What do I need to do?"

Anil falls onto his side. He is convulsing and clawing at his helmet, and can no longer be heard.

The intercessor repeats: "Stand. By."

A split second before impact, just as Natalie is beginning to convince herself that she can feel the heat of the rocket's engine, it cuts out. A familiar red cutting laser spits out and back, in a practised flick-knife-like move which slices a fifteen-metre-wide circle around her and Anil. A controlled pulse of downward and lateral momentum shoves the circle of glass out from under their feet. There's an air gap between the underside of the glass plateau and the surface of the Arctic Ocean. They drop like stones into the darkness.

The rocketship follows them at a shallow angle and fifty times the speed, slipping through the gap with a clearance of millimetres. The ship just misses the two falling suited figures, hitting the water first and much harder. The cut circle is flipped back into place, and the same laser seals the glass behind them. The engine bell shrieks as it flash-chills.

Nat hits the water. Anil hits the water. The rocketship wraps them all in concussion shielding. Ra arrives.

There's another light show, bright enough to turn the bottom of the ocean into daylight. The layer of scrithglass doesn't even crack.

Anil floats above Natalie. She is face-up. He is face-down and inert, silhouetted in the light, his suit helmet still black.

200C9A66, in the pilot seat, considers his options. Playing against Ra at such close quarters is like five-hundred-dimensional chess. Still, he's made it across the board.

He brings the interlopers aboard with a *whump* of matter transmission. He digitises their patterns and makes their corporeal forms safe from Ra's listeners— which is to say, he destroys their suits and bodies with fire.

He moves.

*

Physical acquisition was a non-negotiable component of the mission profile. You can't rescue a soul from Hades with a fishing line. 200C9A66 had to descend into the gravity well in person, and fight hordes of daemons on the way.

Physical extraction, meanwhile, was never even on the table. Anil and Natalie and their shepherding intercessor bounce across the Solar System as signals, mast to dish, asteroid to probe to numberless space rock. 200C9A66 splits himself up, one version going ahead to secure each receiving installation while the other defends the transmitter from Ra's nuclear/electronic attack. They cross the asteroid belt five times trying to lose the pursuers, which are able to corrupt and repurpose the captured transmitters to follow the trail, and sometimes to anticipate future destinations. From 200C9A66's perspective — that is, from the perspective of the sole instance of 200C9A66 who lives all the way to the end — extraction takes around eighty fraught, subjective seconds. Natalie and Anil, travelling as data, perceive nothing. From above the system, using false colour, an observer would see red and blue packets flitting across space from node to node, like some interplanetary hacking minigame, and it would take about six real-time days.

They finally lose their tail at a minuscule cubewano, forty-something AUs distant from the Sun and far above the ecliptic. The rock having no name, 200C9A66 — its first human visitor — decides he gets to name it. He names it "Cubewano". He breathes for a luxurious second, and transmits them all home.

End of the line is Psamathe, which orbits almost as far out from Neptune as Mercury does from the Sun. Psamathe is a bustling metropolis compared to the rest of the route, but still not much more than a worthless pebble in the grand scheme of the Solar System. On the list of the system's most notable moons, it just about scrapes into the top hundred.

Natalie's signal is sent to the lab. They slot her genetic particulars into a vat, clear the expenditure with the War Office, and start the cloning procedure. It'll take a few hours to build something mature enough that she can live inside it. They're running at a level of technology not far above the butter churn.

200C9A66 slots back into his original body, and goes for a shower.

Every time he splits himself, he runs a fifty percent chance of being the one who dies. That means that he —

the one in the shower — is the one who won the coin toss two hundred times in a row. This is impossible, and he doesn't know how to deal with it. He is alive and he doesn't have the mathematics to explain how.

And then he's needed again, and he jumps back into War.

*

Natalie wakes up in a cell on the edge of the base, strapped to a bunk.

She struggles against the restraints for a panicky second, but they just give way when she pulls. They're supposed to be opened. They aren't there to prevent her from escaping, only to prevent her from drifting away in the almost non-existent gravity.

She sits up. Groping around the room, groggily, she finds water in a squeeze bottle. She drains it without thinking. Her suit is gone, replaced by shapeless grey clothes. Magic's still gone, and Ra is long gone, and any personal nonlocality tech she was carrying is confiscated. She runs her hand through startlingly short, baby-soft hair. She is completely new.

There's a porthole, only reachable by standing on the bunk. Natalie spends a long time staring out of it, at a sterile, crater-pitted grey landscape. It could be Luna, but honestly, it could be anywhere. She's no connoisseur. At first glance, there's nothing in the sky that could narrow it down.

The straps aren't to prevent her from escaping. That's the purpose of the locked, dark grey metal door.

An hour later, as Natalie is beginning to run out of square centimetres of cell to examine, the door clacks and opens. A woman and a man file in. Both wear heavy total-purpose protective suits, much like Natalie's missing one. They keep their helmets on, but the helmets are made of transparent material so thin that Natalie doesn't realise this at first. Natalie backs up and sits on the bed. There is no room for her to be anywhere else.

The woman is two metres tall and of a blended deep-future ethnicity that Natalie would never have heard of. Even in a cell with standing room for at most three people, she commands a space around her. The man follows her. He is her follower. He is darker in the skin, lighter in the eyes and hair; fractionally shorter, but still much taller than Natalie. He carries a folding rectangle of extremely thin, transparent plastic. The plastic is completely inert. It just serves as a focal point for his displays, which Natalie cannot see.

The woman speaks at length, in a language which is totally alien to Natalie's ear. The woman introduces herself, and then introduces her comrade. She explains that the telepathic language dongle provided by Natalie's onboard copy of the pre-war Ra intelligence has been stripped out of her mind and shredded, and that Natalie can't be allowed equivalent technology because she's a prisoner of war. She indicates that the man to her left will now attempt to work out Natalie's native language from scratch, after which an actual conversation will take place.

Natalie listens attentively. Although she understands not a single word of what the woman says, she is actually able to correctly guess almost all of it from context.

The man selects selections from his display. He speaks a few words of his own. There is silence while all of them wait for something to happen, which it doesn't. He speaks a few more, different words. Natalie listens blankly and patiently. The man is working his way through a list.

"Are we seriously going through every greeting in every human language in recorded history?" Nat says. "I speak UK English, *circa* 2000 CE. This is going to take an eternity. Would it help if I just spoke back to you in my language until you have enough data to work it out?" She holds fingers up. "One, two, three, four, five, six, seven, eight, nine, ten. Come on, dictionary system."

The man likes this approach. He motions for her to keep going. Natalie picks more simple words.

"Up, down, left, right, forwards, back. Woman, woman, man. Eye, nose, mouth." She points at the dim blue dot in the otherwise black sky outside. This is the only other significant fact that she has deduced in her free hour. She says, "Neptune."

"...Got it," the man says. Only two syllables, but still faultless English, even matching Natalie's own local accent. He presents the woman with a virtual object which Natalie is not able to see. He essays a kind of informal salute to them both, and departs.

Natalie looks up at the woman. First things first. "Where's Anil? Did he die?"

"Why do you care?" She speaks with the same accent too. For Natalie it's disconcertingly like speaking to a slightly older version of herself.

"...He was... I was trying to save his life."

"You failed. He was unrecoverable," the woman says, flatly.

Natalie hangs her head, and grips the edge of the bunk until her knuckles start to whiten, and grits her teeth.

She understands now.

She was put here to learn. Anil was put here to die. As motivation for her.

"Go right back to the beginning," she says. It's the only thing left to happen. "And tell me everything."

28
Why Do You Hate Ra

Psamathe (Neptune X):

Natalie's interrogator stands with her feet shoulder-width apart and one hand resting on a device at her hip, a block full of weapon. She has almost no hair. Her irises are a piercingly bright blue, close to luminous, and hexagonal. She speaks Natalie's English like a native. Even her body language has visibly shifted into something that Natalie understands more clearly.

She says, "I can't cover the whole history book for you. We don't have ten years, so I'm going to have to dramatically oversimplify. There was a schism. Humanity, effectively, forked.

"On one side were the humans who believed that all humans should remain real."

*

They believed that humans were meant to scratch out real lives on real, rocky planets in the real, harsh universe; that the planet Earth should be kept intact and habitable and should have humans inhabiting it for as long as humanly possible; and that if the human race wanted more living space, it should build or terraform new worlds. They believed that the universe represented an implicit challenge to all sentient life, and that humanity ought to rise up and make it, the universe, theirs.

The hard way, because there was and is no other way. To *conceive* of an "easy way" would be wrong.

On the other side were the humans who believed that it was better to upload all existing humans into computers. There, they would live inside virtual worlds just as real as reality. The new worlds would be tuned to whatever anybody could ask for, and to live in them would be as easy or as difficult as any human wanted. Rather than conquer the universe, they would write a fiction in which they had already conquered it. Infinite fun space.

There could be one world per human; there could be millions of times more humans than the real solar system could ever host. The only thing which would need to remain real would be the computer system which hosted the virtualities.

And so, boiled all the way down, just to the point of absolute simplicity, a time came when there were now two human races: Actual, and Virtual.

This schism happened millennia before Ra was constructed. It happened decades before the technology of uploading even existed. You speak a language from the twenty-first century? The schism will happen within your lifetime. It may have already happened. Remember: this is a five-minute simplification of thousands and thousands of years of conflict and weirdness. Don't lose sight of the fractal.

Now we jump far, far forward. As years passed, the energy requirements of Combined Humanity rose and fell and rose again, until they approached the critical threshold, Kardashev I. At this point, humans were consuming ten-to-the-sixteenth watts and demand increase showed no signs of decelerating. Humans were left with no other alternatives: one way or another, they had to dam their star. But there was more than one way of doing so.

Dyson spheres and Niven rings were ruled out as horrible living environments, requiring too much raw material. What Virtual Humanity really wanted was to build a Matrioshka brain, a Dyson swarm of statite nonlocality processors which would consume the *entire* output of Sol and divert it to the task of computation. But the swarm would have blotted the Sun out. It would have completely altered the Sun's radiation profile, and made real life on the real Earth impossible. This, above all, was not acceptable to Actual Humanity.

Building Ra was the compromise solution. Three of the four thorns were given to the Virtuals, while the fourth distributed energy to the Actuals. Actual Humanity was able to keep the Earth and use the siphoned power to build more Earths and, eventually, the worldring. Actual humans colonised every available hard surface in the Solar System, and filled the gaps with space habitats. Meanwhile, the Virtuals uploaded themselves into the Sun and ran their virtualities directly from core fusion.

The two races drifted apart. They were almost unable to communicate with one another. Life inside the Sun moved so quickly that Actual humans found it incoherent. Life in reality was so slow that no Virtual person could pay attention to it for more than nanoseconds of real time. Most of them forgot that reality even exists.

The end.

This is a single broad stroke. The words "compromise solution" mask more than ninety distinct wars. The words "building Ra" gloss over a computational and mechanical engineering feat that took centuries even with nonlocality technology. Ra was designed to be the most powerful computer. No qualifiers. No "at the time", no "ever built by humans". For Ra to malfunction was proven impossible. Not in the sense of a thrown die landing perfectly on its corner, or a person walking through a wall. Mathematically, universe-breakingly, one-equals-zero impossible. It would have been impossible to program and launch Ra if this had not been the case. The whole structure would have imploded within hours if this had not been the case.

Ra launched, and ran without issue. It served the human race. Both races. Perfectly. Uninterrupted. For millennia.

That brings us up to six days ago.

*

The woman stops for a second, waiting for Natalie to indicate that she's keeping pace.

"That's who we're at war with," Nat summarises.

"That's who we're at war with," the woman says. "We are Actual Humanity, and we are at war with quadrillions of fabricated, immaterial humans, using the Sun as their proxy, strategy engine and primary weapon. They've been on their own inside the Sun for so long that they no longer perceive Actuals as human, just as gunk growing between the gears of a machine in dire need of performance upgrades. This is a war over processing power. Ra evidently no longer meets the needs of the Virtual human race. They're back and they want their Matrioshka brain and they've razed the solar system to get it."

"It's all just people," Nat says, clutching her temples. "It's just humans against humans. Again and again. Their technology against our technology, which is the *same technology*. Because an AI can't *rebel*. A machine can't do something it wasn't programmed to do. It can only be reprogrammed. The one hundred and ninety-somethingth century and we've still yet to build a machine remotely as stupid as the smartest genuine human beings."

The woman continues. "Part two. The war."

*

Ra's program was proven correct. The proof was not faulty, and the program was not imperfect. The problem was that Ra is reprogrammable.

This was a deliberate design decision on the part of the Ra architects. The Ra hardware is physically embedded inside a working star, which in turn is embedded in the real world. Something could have gone wrong during the initial program load; the million-times-redundant nonlocality system could have failed a million and one times. No matter how preposterous the odds, and no matter how difficult the procedure, there had to be a way to wipe the system clean and start again.

Continuing the theme of gross oversimplification: to reprogram Ra, one needs a key. History records that the entire key was never known or stored by any human or machine, and brute-forcing it should have taken ten-to-the-ten-thousandth years even on a computer of that size. How the Virtuals acquired it is unknown. But having acquired it, they were able to masquerade as the architects. First, they changed the metaphorical locks, making it impossible for the Actuals to revert their changes, no matter how many master architects were resurrected. Then they changed the program, so that Ra would serve the needs of Virtuals at the expense of Actuals.

Then they asked for the Matrioshka brain. Ra did the rest all by itself.

The worldring hosted ninety-nine point nine nine percent of the Actual human race, making it the logical target of the first and most violent attack. But the destruction spread to other planets and moons and rocks and habitats, relayed from node to node, at barely less than the speed of light. *Everybody* was targeted. Those who survived survived by being lucky. One-in-tens-of-billions lucky.

One of the survivors was able to transmit a warning message directly to Neptune, bypassing the Ra network for a fractionally shorter transit time. The warning arrived about eight-tenths of a second before the virus did. There was just enough time to sever the nonlocality downlink. Neptune's core became the most powerful clean Ra shard, and the people of Neptune — numbering fewer than a billion, due to the planet's inhospitability and remoteness — became the opposing side of the war.

From other survivors, Neptune soon received evacuation signals containing almost all of the worldring's population, as data. With nothing else to be done, they were stored at Neptune's core.

*

Another momentary pause.

"And here we are," the woman concludes. "The last Actuals. The Matrioshka brain is already under construction, mostly from repurposed pieces of the worldring. The Sun's light output today is measurably lower than it was six days ago. Earth, our first Earth, is a ruined dark planet, paved with broken glass, peopled with nightmares, and dropping in temperature.

"Our Ra shard still works, but it's running in emergency paranoiac debug mode, with every instruction running through a few thousand layers of automated and manual analysis, which makes it extremely slow to respond to requests, when it responds positively at all. Direct access is rationed because of the war effort. Our stockpile of mass/energy and other quantifiables is limited to what the Neptune local cache had available at cutoff time, which was small to begin with and is now close to zero.

"Ra is on its way here. It'll be here by this time tomorrow. We can't meet that kind of energy. We don't have the broadcast power to evacuate to anywhere more remote.

"And then there's you."

Natalie looks up.

The woman says, "You and your friend Anil are the only two people in this entire star system who don't fit. Ra targeted every living human in the worldring, but hours passed before it realised it had missed you. When the evacuation order was given, every living human in the worldring was part of the signal, but you were overlooked. You arrived moments before Ra went berserk. You speak a language dead for well over ten thousand years, and you know nothing about anything.

"Human civilisation is ending, and still you got my attention. I was the one who diverted resources to have you extracted. Who are you?"

Natalie is too exhausted to think of a decent lie. She's stomach-churningly aware that if she says a single wrong word, it'll look like she and Anil were the ones who did it, and she'll be held responsible for omnicidal teradeath. And she wants this to be over.

"My name is Natalie Ferno. And this isn't real."

"Everything is real," the woman says, automatically, like a mantra.

"I'm a history student," Nat says. It's her honest best guess, and happens to be the truth. "I'm here to experience the war. I'm real; none of the rest of this is actually happening. It already happened. The war is over."

"Was your friend Anil real?"

Natalie ignores this, mainly because she has no answer to it. "You don't need to fight," she says. "It doesn't matter for anything anymore. There's no need for anybody else to die! I know it's hard for you—"

"For me? Convince Ra," the woman replies.

"I—"

"If we abandon our war, then what?" the woman says. "Do we lie down and wait to die? Do we wait for you to learn your lesson and end the simulation and leave? If we don't fulfill established history, do you get sent around again?"

Natalie says nothing.

The woman smiles patiently. "This is a war fought predominantly using highly precise simulacra of potential future events, simulacra so similar to reality that individuals inside them are, of necessity, unable to tell the difference between them and real events. That's the most insane thing about this situation. That's the fact that everybody involved in the war has to accept up front, or else be stored until the end of it. That, in large part, is *why* the Actual/Virtual schism happened.

"This war, which we are fighting today, isn't necessarily *the* war. Every strategy and outcome is explored, tens to tens of trillions of times. By them and, when possible, by us. We are engaged in every single conceivable war against every conceivable enemy simultaneously. We must win all of them. We must accept all of them as real.

"We can never know if we truly won. Or even if there truly is a war which needs to be won. We could be reasonless fabrications. Nevertheless, this is real. And we must win."

Natalie stares. The sensation of familiarity is like a bell tolling. It's been tolling for some time, each toll louder and closer, and now she can't ignore it. *Always assume reality. Those are* my *words.* "Who are you?" she asks in turn.

The woman draws herself up. "I am the original physical instance of mandator EBE1E00F, leader of the armies of Actual Humanity. Uncounted copies of me are in deep space right now, fighting the war in person and as electronics. I've died more than a thousand times."

Proper nouns are trickier than hexadecimal; rather than just cram the florid native syllables into vulgar Earth English, the woman's language dongle provides her several translations, from the neatly poetic to the excessively literal.

She adds, "Call me Ashburne."

Natalie continues to stare. Having spent the entire conversation sitting on the edge of the bunk, she stands up. Even when she stands up straight, "Ashburne" dwarfs her like a child. And— so casual.

"You're going to *win*," Natalie realises.

Ashburne smiles broadly. "I know."
"*How?*"

*

The real question was: *Why did Ra target humans?*

Ra's objective was to construct the Matrioshka brain, using any means necessary, considering Actual humans as a non-sentient nuisance. Ra blew up the worldring for raw material, and that made sense. But why — the surviving real humans asked themselves — did Ra bother to attack moons and space habitats? No matter how many people survived, it was surely impossible for them to represent a threat.

But Ra targeted humans, implying a threat to be eliminated. Ra acted with extreme prejudice and urgency, implying that the threat was immediate, and needed to be crushed rapidly. Ra's actions betrayed the existence of an extremely narrow window during which the Actuals, despite their limited resources, could reverse the outcome of the war, and Ra wouldn't be able to stop it, even knowing that it was coming.

Having made this deduction, the Actuals' next step was to reverse-engineer the attack. The step after that was to immediately execute it, no matter how desperate it was.

Ra's locks had been changed, making it effectively impossible to reprogram remotely. But an ancient piece of knowledge from the very dawn of computing remained true even of computers the size of stars: once you have physical access to the hardware, it's over.

A ship was outfitted: a solar depth charge. The ship was called *Triton*, because that was already its name; it was Neptune's largest moon repurposed, with its interior completely reformulated into nonlocality shielding, light-negation apparatus and electromagnets. A fleck of uncorrupted Ra was placed at its core, and at the core of the fleck, a tiny habitable space and two hundred copies of the best remaining Actuals.

Triton was delivered from Neptune orbit to the inner Solar System using horrible bulk nonlocality hacks, a manoeuvre which essentially bankrupted the Neptunians of delta-vee. The ship needed to be at least two thousand kilometres in diameter to soak up heat and direct energy attacks while aerobraking into the Sun's photosphere, and then to sacrifice itself in layers while diving down through the convective zone. There, it would make physical contact with the northernmost tip of Ra's fourth, north-pointing thorn. Ra's physical shield would be trivial to penetrate after that.

Anything is trivial to people who can stand inside the Sun, alive.

That left the question of the reprogramming.

Ra was dangerous. Too powerful, too creative, too proactive. When a machine as powerful as Ra has run off the rails and forgotten the value of real human lives, working it directly is like juggling with subcritical plutonium. A person asks Ra to destroy the worldring, and before they can finish the sentence it's done, and half a quadrillion people are dead. They ask Ra to undo it, and Ra undoes the physical damage, but the truth of all universes from the real one down is that FTL isn't possible, and time is one-way. It'll always stay *done*, and if it can be undone, that just means it can be done a second time.

Triton's objective was to program in a layer of abstraction. To rebuild the worldring, reincarnate the stored evacuees, and then to build limits into the Ra system so that such a thing could never happen again.

Imagine a universe with exotic technology and advanced physics and theoretically limitless possibilities — *difficult to harness*, but not impossible. Having imagined that universe, set Ra to simply implement the rules of that universe. Leave the Virtuals in their bottle, where they belong. Return power over reality to the hands of Actual humans, for good or bad.

And tell Ra to never accept direct instructions again. Ever. From anybody.

*

"And that's happening right now?" Natalie asks.

"*Triton* makes plasma splashdown in just over four hours," Ashburne says, "although obviously we won't receive the light from it for another four. If I lent you a telescope you could watch its final approach. Except that the Sun would blind you, and *Triton* is running invisible."

Something cold and grey is gripping Natalie's throat. Something is catastrophically wrong with Ashburne's story.

"There must be a version of you on that ship," Nat says, reasoning it out. "You're going to reprogram Ra, and reformulate the laws of physics in this star system to something brand new. 'Magic.' This extra layer of abstraction you're talking about, it's magic. In my time, that's what we call it."

"That's a horribly inappropriate name," Ashburne observes.

"I know. But you're going to win. I *know* you're going to win. You, personally. I know that at least one instance of you is going to survive the war and witness what happens after it. But the rest of this doesn't make any sense—"

"Of course we're going to win," Ashburne says. "How could you even be here if we lost?"

"*Where's the worldring if you won?*" Natalie shouts. She points desperately out of the window, at Neptune. "Where are all the *people*? You said you were going to rebuild the worldring and resurrect all the people. So where are they?"

Ashburne stands stock-still for a moment, following Natalie's finger. She heard perfectly clearly, but still she asks: "There's no worldring in your time?"

"There's nothing! In my time, reality consists of a single dismal, rainy Earth, and nothing else. Population, six billion. No space technology, no nonlocality, no habitats. And nobody remembers this war. Nobody has any idea that it happened, nor is there any physical evidence that it happened. You must have sterilised and recreated the whole star system and the whole planet Earth, resetting history back— to— oh my God. That's why nobody discovered magic until 1972. Magic didn't *exist* before 1972. Probably the entire *world* didn't exist. You'd have had to strip and replace every cubic centimetre of rock."

It's Ashburne's turn to stare.

Natalie confronts her. "Your plan is going to fail. You think you know what's going to happen when the *Triton* reaches Ra, but you don't. Something's going to change the mission.

"Imagine you're on the *Triton*. You're about to reprogram Ra. You're still going to go ahead and implement magic, but you're also going to tell it to boot the whole star system back to the Bronze Age of computing, and then pretend the whole thing never happened. Why?"

Ashburne's eyes are focusing on something that Natalie can't see: displays, built into her helmet or eyeballs or optic nerve.

Natalie presses on: "You said Ra was on its way here."

"Physically. Sublight," Ashburne says, now elsewhere entirely. "But when we've fixed Ra, the signal will catch up at *c*. There's a margin of safety."

"How far is it from here to the *Triton*?" Natalie asks. "What's the final instant you can send a signal that they'll receive?"

"Soon," Ashburne says. "Minutes."

Natalie can see red light reflecting off the woman's face, reflected from nowhere. Her helmet interior must be covered with warnings. Ra is here. "It's now," Natalie says.

Ashburne is gone from this room, ascending into combat space, taking on the load of urgent demands for tactical support from all over the Neptune locale. With one real hand, moving almost autonomously, she unhooks the block from her hip and switches it on. Consuming precious quantum resources, the block expands to coddle Ashburne and Natalie in a single reinforced field structure, and chews up the cell's walls and door as material.

Psamathe detonates.

Ashburne's Weapon instance absorbs the impact. Natalie is thrown into a cushion of force fields and stored behind her, where the back seat would be if more than five percent of the starfighter physically existed yet. She struggles upright. The moon is gone, the drone which hit them is gone. There's nothing but tumbling black space.

Ashburne brings the spin under control. There are no more words from her. She's running the battle, and she's going to run it until she dies. Natalie can't see the extra dots picking out friendly and hostile objects, ranges, velocities, strategies and predictions. The only solid object she can pick out other than the Sun is the same one as ever, the planet Neptune.

But even from this distance, even if she can't see Ra's drones, she can see their lasers. They're the same colour as the ones which diced the worldring, and powerful enough to cut right to a gas giant's core, slicing its stone into pieces.

*

"We have to cheat a bit for this last part."

"Huh?" Natalie whirls around in the sudden darkness. Ashburne is gone.

"For this part you're just a ghost," says the voice. "There wasn't an organic way to get you to *Triton*. Just pretend Ashburne transmitted you there. If you care..."

*

Triton's innermost core starts out like a submarine's interior, skips a few thousand technological generations, then folds itself up into some hellish three-dimensional space-filling curve. There's no gravity, with the result that there are no meaningful directions. The universe is crammed with seats interlocking with other seats interlocking with occupants wired in physically. It's not possible to see more than a metre in any direction. There's barely a cubic metre of clear air in the whole room. Free movement is impossible.

Even if there was a physical exit from this cavity in Triton's interior to its surface (and it didn't lead directly into the Sun's convective zone), extracting any given crew member to that exit would involve solving a seventy-eight move block-pushing puzzle. It's a bunker world, a cramped hacker mole-hole, a place you teleport into and possibly never leave.

Nat's a ghost. Nobody can see her or hear her. She's intangible, stuck inside one of the walls, looking "down" at another Ashburne instance. This one wears a different, lighter suit. It's not a warsuit. It looks more like... well, clothing. (What good would any warsuit be, inside the Sun?)

Nat can see four or five other people from her vantage point — mainly limbs and backs of heads. A minor and unimportant panel, very close to Natalie's holographic head, shows a matrix of life-support readouts. It indicates a total crew complement of exactly two hundred.

This Ashburne is watching the closing minutes of the battle above Neptune. The whole thing is chillingly abstract. Two blizzards are meeting each other, yellow and red flurries of snowflakes moving in turbulence. The events are uniformly difficult to make tactical sense of. Natalie doesn't have the sixth sense for signal delay shared by everybody else involved in this war. But she can spot the times when flurries of red dots chase down solitary, slow-reacting yellows. She can see that Neptune has been cored, and is marked with the wrong colour.

And she can hear the noises of dismay from the crew. Everybody is watching it.

After a time, the last yellow dots are gone, leaving a field of patiently swirling red dots against black, like a screen saver. Finally, the last clean downlink breaks, and there's just a blank screen.

All the other people Natalie can see are facing away from her. Ashburne's face is the only one that she can see clearly enough to read. The woman is a picture of meticulous self-control, but Natalie is close enough and familiar enough to be able to read the fury, the fear and the sorrow.

There's no point bringing back the worldring, Nat thinks. *There's nobody to populate it. There's nobody left to fight for. It's over.*

"Dive control," Ashburne asks, "will we still be able to attack Ra?"

"Confirmed," says a crew member, his voice weak. Sound reflects strangely in this tiny space; it's impossible to tell who's talking, or how far away they could be. "Sacrificial shield layer sixteen now fully stripped; layer fifteen decay rate nominal. Dive progress nominal. We'll reach the thorn with time to spare. We'll have Ra on the operating table in another hour."

"Then the war continues," Ashburne asserts. "All Virtual humans against we two hundred. It continues until *we* end it. And it ends when *we* get the world *we* want.

"I suggest we decide what we want that world to be."

*

And she's back.

She's seated at the focus of a dark room with ten times the dimensions of an aircraft hangar. In front of her, slouched over an identical hyper-expensive office chair, is the bald young man, the last person she saw in reality before being "transported".

Natalie's hair is back. Her original clothes are back. Ten seconds have passed. She feels broken in the head, and physically wrecked. She feels as if she went through a war. Which was obviously the whole idea.

"And now you know what happened when Ra woke up the first time," the youth says.

"Anh zero EPTRO—" Nat begins, then finds the Montauk ring around her neck. It's too narrow to remove. "Agh."

The youth smirks humourlessly.

"Where's Anil?" Natalie demands, for the final time.

The youth points past her. Nat looks, and Anil is in a similar chair, rubbing his eyes, dealing with similar post-trauma. He looks like he died and came back. "What the *hell*," he's saying quietly, over and over.

Behind Anil, surrounding him and Natalie, are the observers. They're almost all men, between twenty and thirty years old, of varying ethnicities but all tall, broad-shouldered and immaculately groomed. They're standing and watching.

There are familiar circle patterns painted underfoot. There are no weapons visible. Natalie considers taking off and running, but it must be at least a kilometre to the nearest wall.

She slumps. The chair is too comfortable to be true.

"How many people died?" she asks, weakly. "Real people?"

"I don't have time to say that whole number," the youth says. "It's simpler to say how many survived. The entire crew of *Triton*, including me and everybody you see here. And fourteen others."

"You won the war," Natalie says, believing it. "Two hundred and fourteen people 'won' the war."

"Are you ready for the next part?"

"What the *hell* is the next part?"

"Your sister's trying to wake Ra again," the youth says, calmly. He stands and walks to Natalie. He produces a gun and holds it out to her, grip first. "Stop her."

29
Last Thursdayism

In 19390, *Triton*'s last layers of sacrificial armour are boiling away at a rate of hundreds of metres per second. In the next few minutes, the heat will reach the computation fleck at the ship's core and start to destroy it. When that happens, no matter what else has happened, the operation will be over, and the war will be over.

They have Ra's brain laid out in front of them, vivisected and still operating. The machine has been successfully attacked and subdued. In the lower three thorns, Virtual human civilisation has been frozen indefinitely. Nobody is left who could pass further judgement on them.

As for the fourth thorn, it will obey one further command, ever, and Ashburne is the only person who can deliver that command. Ra will unthread her thought processes to determine what it is she's truly asking for, and deliver that result, and then permanently disable its raw public interface.

But none of the crew are in a position to handle this decision rationally. None of them have even fully processed the magnitude of what just happened. The plan was to reassemble the worldring, restore Actual Humanity from cold storage, go home and resume life. But after the Battle of Neptune, there's nobody to restore. There is no plan. There is no "go home". *Triton* and its crew are in freefall, severed from their purpose.

Triton's clean Ra node is far too busy and underpowered to run time-compressed simulacra for this purpose, meaning the discussion continues urgently in real time. Ashburne surfs the crew's internal communications, flicking from one member to another. "Declarator," she says, selecting one at random, "what do you want to happen next?"

"The Virtuals have to pay," the woman says. "We're real! We matter. We hold the reins, we'll show them you don't fuck with the people who hold the reins—"

"Pay how? What would you do?"

"Shut Ra down. Exterminate them all."

"That would be a war crime," Ashburne says. "We'd be war criminals. It would be genocide."

The woman holds Ashburne's gaze. "They aren't people," she tells her. "They don't exist. They aren't *human*."

Ashburne switches to a different crewperson's image. "Intercessor, what should we do?"

There's black horror in this man's eyes. "We've got to roll everything back," he says. "We've got to make it so that Ra can't act unilaterally anymore."

This is just the original plan. The man hasn't understood the truth yet. He's toying with the facts, weighing the prospect of accepting them against the option of just cracking up. "Roll back to when?" Ashburne asks.

"To right before this happened."

"Rebuild the worldring, and then inhabit sixty thousand empty Earths, just the two hundred of us?"

"...I don't know—"

Ashburne cuts him off, switching over again.

"What would you do?"

"Start everything over," this woman says. "Purify Earth-1 and start it all over."

"From when?"

She's coherent. "The beginning of time. Year negative ten thousand. Or negative a hundred thousand. Go into the scientific record. Throw all our technology away. We'll repopulate the world with fire and the wheel. We'll create something new with our own hands."

Ashburne nods and switches again, to a glowering, despairing man, his hands covering the lower part of his face, pulling down at the skin around raw eyes. "What do you want?"

"I want..." The man reaches outside the camera's field of view and produces a physical photograph, actual coloured ink on paper. The photo was taken at a picnic on the exterior of a habitat over the north pole of Saturn. There are eight people gathered, all different ages. All unrecoverable.

The man just presses the photo against the screen, until Ashburne switches away. There's nothing to say to him. What he wants isn't something he can have.

Switch, switch, switch to three crew members in a row who only want oblivion: in death, or psychoactive chemicals.

Switch to another man— he looks like a boy of twenty, but it's impossible to judge age from appearance in this era— with his eyes closed. "And you?"

He flinches, but says nothing.

"Intercessor, I asked you a question."

The boy's eyes open and he glares sidelong at Ashburne, head trembling. "I can't tell you what I want."

Ashburne hesitates for a second, and is about to switch again, but—

"I want you dead," the boy says, "and then I want to upload myself into a world where none of this ever happened." He bites his tongue. Ashburne has the right to summarily execute him — or even erase him — for the first statement alone. The second is textbook treason. But the boy can't stop himself from plunging on. "The Virtuals won. The Virtuals were right. Reality's been burnt to the ground, and even now it can still get worse. But *they* can have anything they want. How is *this* better than *that*?"

Ashburne's expression is placid, neutral.

"Do you regret asking me, yet?" the boy shouts, loudly enough that Ashburne can hear it in reality as well as through the internal link.

Ashburne leaves him. She's about to ask "And you?" to the next person, but the boy hasn't stopped talking. He's audible throughout the ship, now, an echoing rant. Other heated discussions drop out in his favour.

"You lost us the war. You trusted radically malformed intel. You were supposed to save lives and you *failed* as completely as anybody could ever fail. Mandator, whatever happens after this, you need to die."

Ashburne summons the boy's image back, which silences him. She waits a second, making sure that she has everybody's attention. She makes a show of physically reaching for a button, so that everybody who is paying attention can see it. The boy leaves the ship, leaving behind an empty seat and a coil of humid air.

And a shared thought: *He can't have been the only one.*

"We're out of time," Ashburne announces. "We have no consensus. In any case, it would be tactless to build anything now. It's too soon. There must be a period of mourning.

"Ra, leave the Solar System as it is. Then, a year from now, when we come together again, we'll build a world which can't ever go this far wrong. And, Ra... give us the tools we'll need."

The command is given. Ra reaches into Ashburne's mind and carefully unwinds her words and intentions into a workable reality. It gives them all a curt acknowledgement, and peacefully abstracts itself away.

*

In 19391, the war is over, so it wouldn't be right to call what Watson's wearing a "warsuit". The suit is a perfect piece of equipment, protecting and maintaining him so well that sometimes he forgets about it for weeks at a time. Every now and then he'll catch his reflection in a particularly clear piece of glass, and stop. *That's right,* he'll tell himself, after staring for a puzzled moment at the unfamiliar man in the transparent helmet. *I have skin. And that's its colour.*

Watson is following the beacon home, completing the final leg of a fifteen-thousand-klick round trip. The reincarnation point, where he and everybody else started, is in the foothills of a parched mountain range on the edge of a desert. The twenty-first century called this country Kazakhstan.

What he's seen on his journey is this: planet Earth One was ruined in the war, and the only thing that's happened since then is that the temperature has dropped like a stone. Oceans are crusting over with ice. The ground is bare rock and wind-smoothed ice and, in the desert, a carpet of broken glass. There's no ecosystem, and no life above extremophile bacteria, unless you count the denatured Ra listeners. The atmosphere has been almost completely stripped, and is hardly breathable, and is radioactive. Every night and day there are the most spectacular meteor showers, laying waste to anything not already flattened by the detonations of the neighbouring Earths.

Up in the sky hangs a bitter, dim orange Sun, still clouded with Matrioshka brain matter. "Leave the Solar System as it is," Ashburne had said. At night, sometimes, Watson tries to find Neptune, but he never can. He knows it's still out there. So must be all the pieces of Neso Habitat, their orbit not likely to decay anytime soon.

Not that he wants to go back.

Watson reaches the top of a scorched ridge, now only four or five klicks from the beacon. From here he can see the whole way there, down a deep pass. He knows he's early, but he can see that he's not the first to arrive. There's a rough accumulation of large boxes there, and another man in an identical suit is sitting on one of them, doing nothing.

Watson walks down towards him, crunching glass underfoot. He's a few klicks closer by the time the man sees him and waves.

The boxes are metallic red, ranging from half-metre cubes up to one the size of a Stonehenge megalith. There are around twenty of them, haphazardly scattered, some piled up or stood on one end. They weren't there when he set out a year ago. *Curious.*

"How are you?" Watson asks the man. Both of them have shed their wartime designations, and the man hasn't named himself again yet, but a few days from now he'll start to call himself Adam King. King is Ashburne's former second. Watson would have saluted, if this was still the war.

In response, King just nods. "You?"

Watson reflects. "I'm ready for the next part. I walked across two continents and I said all the words I had to say. There are two things I know after a year of meditation. One: we can't fight the war again. And: we've got to build *something* next. I don't particularly care what, but we can't just leave it at this."

King nods again, staring into the distance. "I know what. I've got a pretty clear idea of what I want to build."

"It's got to be something that feels like winning," Watson says.

"I've got it all worked out."

Watson regards King for a while, mulling over the post-war power structure. In Ashburne's absence, King would be running the war, if this was still the war. But it isn't.

He kicks the box that King is sitting on. "What are these?"

"These are the tools," King says. "Remember? I suppose Ra gave them to Ashburne. And Ashburne left them here for us."

"Should we open them?"

"Let's wait until everybody's here who's going to be here. You're a few days early."

A beat. What's left of the air whips past them.

"...How many people do you think are going to come back?"

King says, "Not everybody. Not by a long shot."

"Where's Ashburne? Is she coming back?"

"No."

On the ridge where Watson was, another figure appears. It's not Ashburne. Watson raises his arm. "Did she tell you that?"

Ra

"No."

*

In 19391, a man calling himself Scintillator is surfing an X-class flare over the Sun's thirtieth parallel, towing a star-shakingly powerful piece of equipment called *bhārīvastra*. He is a living ship, buoyed by fields of darkness, using the *astra* to alter gravity in his favour.

Above and beyond him is the final collection of abandoned, charred Dyson statites. They are two-dimensional graphene computers, averaging two thousand square kilometres each, floating on solar radiation like leaves on wind. The Group has recovered all the needed mass to recreate Triton, Psamathe and the rest. The colossal cloud of dust and unprocessed worldring wreckage has been swept away. These eight are surplus. Scin doesn't need to save and reconstitute them, he can just kill them.

Even in this actinic environment, Scin's energy shows up as a brilliant white point, as fine as a scalpel tip. He accelerates at the first statite from below, targeting its delicately curled edges. He tracks through each of the statites in an efficient flourish, cutting away significant pieces of crust. One by one, the gigantic structures list sideways, lose lift, lose altitude, and start the long fall into the fire below.

Scin feeds them extra gravitational mass, so that they fall faster. With extra senses, he can see their systems frying from the edges inwards, ceasing to process. There's even a detectable wisp of magic smoke.

Those are the last eight. The face of the Sun has been wiped clean, so that it shines. Scin has lived in this environment of plasma and magnetic flux for months, and his brain has adapted, changing into something wild and instinctive, preying on the wandering statites like a hawk. But it's over now. He can go home, and walk on the ground.

Scin rustles his fields and uses the *astra* again, negating all of his gravitational mass. He shoots out along a tangent away from the Sun, towards Earth-1.

*

In 19391, the whole crust of the world is being torn up in squares, flipped and relaid. Fresh rock and replenished fossil fuels are topped with half-destroyed rainforest and national parks, all conforming to the most accurate available historical and scientific record. "Flat", the man operating the strata machine, is one of the fourteen who survived through unimaginable luck; combatant mind-states beamed to *Triton* directly out of the closing microseconds of the Battle of Neptune.

There's a zigzag advancing over the face of the Earth, like mismatched colours on satellite photographs. Behind the line, cities are rising.

Historical figures are being resurrected from guesswork, famed quotations and the multidimensional physical fingerprints they left on their world. Where the records run out and lack clarity, the human drivers of the engines tell the engines to choose what works. Hyper-advanced narrative *astras* are procedurally generating people in their billions — all frozen mid-step or mid-dream, and waiting to be animated. Waiting for a certain particular clock tick.

Kilometres below the Western Australian desert, in a deep black bunker, Adam King is working at the controls of Metaph, the forge of new physics.

"We have to judge the difficulty curve of Seventies science," he says to himself. In English, because he's chosen his new name and language now. "If it's too easy, the technology explodes, and we run into anthropic principle exposure. If it's too hard, they drop the thing. `Alath menaremba baltakrilakta cho malatha`."

He rubs a painful eye and yawns. He fidgets with the unfamiliar ring at his wrist. "Something you can build a society on. Something... attainable. We'll need to shepherd them, to begin with. We'll need to be able to track everything. Damn, how do you work this thing?"

*

In 19391, which is also 1969, there's an invisible penthouse above the East River, a castle in the sky with a council of wizards, and King is speaking to them:

"I don't want to waste too much time. So I'll use as few words as I can.

"We came within minutes of extinction. To survive, we had to travel through Hell itself. But through Hell we travelled. And, thank God, home we came. Survivors.

"Magic is our victory. We have proved it to be perfect. It'll stand forever. I don't want to call our accomplishment — your accomplishment — a miracle, because that would deny you the credit that you deserve. It was work. Nothing but work.

"Trillions died because the power existed to kill them. Magic is a more disciplined power. To use it requires dedication, and character. And who knows what they'll build on top of it? I, for one, can't wait to see.

"So thank God. And thank you all. And: to the beginning."

*

Now:

"Demigods drifting over the face of a formless Earth. World-shaping tools from before the dawn of time, provided by a literal sun god. This," Anil Devi remarks, "is a pretty decent crack at some creation mythology."

"You hesitated," Adam King explains to Natalie. "You're sceptical. You have more questions. Which is fine, but we're on a clock. We want this resolved or on its way toward resolution within the next thirty real-time seconds. So we're here, at two thousand times normal speed, just for as long as it takes to convince you."

They're ghosts again. The three of them are standing behind the simulacrum of Adam King as he eats at the head of the Wheel Group's dining table. He and the hundred and twenty or so other simulacra have begun their own conversations, historically irrelevant ones which the "real" King has kindly tuned out.

Nat takes in this last scene in the historical montage. Rich carpet with interlocking golden and red spiral patterns. Dark wooden furniture, silver cutlery. A glass window so huge that it could be mistaken for the sky. A view of the skyline of the city of New York which, strictly, shouldn't be possible.

Nat is too exhausted to be dazzled anymore.

"The Virtuals—"

"Still frozen," King says. "They can stay frozen for a billion years for all I care. It's better than what they deserve."

"You each walked the Earth alone for a year," Natalie says. "And then, you all came back together—"

"Not all," King corrects her. "Not by a long shot."

"What happened to the others?"

King studies the city skyline, as an alternative to meeting Natalie's eyes. "They left the Group. A lot of them, let's say, left the world entirely. One way or another. For one reason or another."

"Which left everybody in this room. You invented magic and you invented Anil's and my world from scratch. You reset the whole solar system back to the 1970s to make the story fit."

"Exactly 1970. Midnight G.M.T., January first. It was a round number. Before the Information Age, right after the peak of the Space Race. Exactly the right place for magic to fit. You see, it wouldn't be right to say that we run your world. We *ran* it, by which I mean we *set* it running."

Natalie has a slew of exceedingly obvious follow-up questions, starting with *Why?!*, but she senses that there's no way to fire them at King right now without coming off as adversarial, which would be equally exceedingly counterproductive. She catches Anil's eye for a moment, imploring him to do the same, hoping that the instruction can just jump straight from her mind into his. Amazingly, it works. Anil gets it.

"What did you call it?" Natalie asks King.

King holds his answer for a long time. He seems distracted by his other self, who has just lit a cigarette. "We called it Abstract War."

"And what happens if Laura wakes Ra up again?"

"Abstract War. Imagine all of what you've been through, again. Except for the part where we won."

Natalie pauses for what she estimates to be a plausible length of time, giving the appearance of thinking it over. She paces over to Anil and gives him a meaningful look. He returns a faintly perplexed smile. She turns back to King.

"Alright. I'll do it. You need me to intercede that desperately, I can hardly refuse. But first, I want to talk to the other one. The one who brought us here." She points at the simulacrum of Watson, who is also at the table, dining on rare steak. "Him."

King agrees, and disappears.

There's a long moment of silence.

"Anil," Natalie says, still watching the gap in the air where King was standing, "drop something on the floor where you're standing. Between your feet." She removes her earring, and does the same.

"Why?"

"I bought us a few seconds. Call it a minimum of two seconds, from his perspective, while he fetches the other one. When he comes back, if he hasn't realised his mistake, we mustn't tip him off. We need to be in the same positions, as if no time passed."

Anil grins, getting it. He does what Natalie suggested, using some pocket change.

"Now," says Nat. "We have at least an hour. Where do you want to start?"

"Where do I want to *start*? Oh my God." Anil kicks the window, causing a loud *bonggg* to which none of the simulated people react. "This story is close to unfalsifiable. It's literally the God-damned Omphalos hypothesis. If these people think we're going to believe it, they must be insane.

"But... we've seen teleportation, and advanced simulation. And Ra is a factual object. There's enough circumstantial evidence that I almost *do* believe it. And that makes *me* feel insane. And if all of this is true— then— they really built magic." Anil claps the simulacrum of King on the shoulders. The simulacrum notices nothing. "*He* built magic. We just saw him doing it. Alone. This whole thing is his idea; he said he had it 'all worked out'. I bet when the rest of them came back in 19391, they were overruled. Or their ideas were just folded into his.

"It's as if our world is King's sandbox. He took what, by all logic, should have been a hypothetical role-playing scenario — a Virtuality! — and made it concrete in reality, and fabricated billions of breathing people to populate it. It's ghoulish. It means everybody 'born' before 1970 is fake! Including my parents!

"And if that's what really happened, then these people really are *insane*.

"When you come out on the losing end of a nightmare like Abstract War, the last thing you need is to wander a scorched Earth by yourself, stewing. You need *help*. You need counselling. I don't care what the human psyche has evolved into by that era. We won't have evolved beyond having problems.

"This man, Adam King? *He is not okay*."

30
Akheron

Directly under Tanako's world's three-pointed Sun there's a hulking hemisphere bunker which grumbles electronically, like a mosquito whine slowed down ten thousand times. Its exterior is black body black. It pulls at space around it, as if it has its own gravity.

Laura Ferno (LF-4) discards her final pair of spent SRBs, and once her still-unnamed orbiter runs dry she kicks away from it too, crossing the final distance on an unpowered flat trajectory. This part of T-world is daylight, pure white glass desert with light from Ra hammering down on every square centimetre from directly overhead. Laura's far too far beyond the sound barrier for there to be sound. She catches a shape out of the corner of her eye and swivels in the air to look at it. It's her shadow, streaking across the ground directly below her. As she gets closer to her destination the glass desert clears and the shadow becomes a reflection. She sees herself as a brilliant figure suspended in the sunlight, glowing like a dust speck.

A green slot opens on the bunker exterior, welcoming her visit, guiding her to the correct room.

*

Two objective seconds later Exa arrives, alone. Natalie and Anil are back in their positions and waiting. If Exa senses that anything is off, he doesn't show it.

Natalie starts: "Where are we?"

Exa says, "Some years ago you wrote a spell which, let's say, showed you the world you weren't supposed to see. You saw three artifacts. What were they?"

"There was a star-sized caltrap-shaped object inside the Sun."

"The Ra nonlocality engine," Exa says. "We covered that. And?"

"...At the core of the Earth," Natalie says. "I gather the technical term is 'peach stone'."

"The distributor. Earth-1's local Ra shard and energy cache," Exa confirms. "Left over from Abstract War. Nobody goes there. And?"

"There was a smaller structure. Roughly ellipsoidal. Like a subcutaneous implant injected into the Earth's crust. Ah..."

"The listening post. That's where we all are right now. We built this after the war to serve as our base of operations. Unlike the distributor it has the advantage of being physically connected to the Earth's surface. The 'room' we're in is the control room. It's where we run magic from."

Natalie and Anil both nod.

With a whole free hour, they've long since worked all of this out. Still, the appearance of disorientation needed to be maintained.

Nat pushes on into relatively unknown territory. "And who are you?"

"We're the Wheel Group."

"No. Who are *you*? What's your name? Your real name. If you have one."

Exa shrugs. "The realest name I have is the one I was born with, Kalathkou Ouatso Neso. 'Kalathkou' was given to me by my mother, 'Ouatso' was inherited from her, 'Neso' was my place of birth. By the time of Abstract War I was going by Ack Ouatso for most purposes. When I joined the war, I relinquished my chosen names in favour of the title and designation Intercessor EB460890-7409-11E3-981F-0800200C9A66."

"So you *are* the one who rescued us," Anil says. He and Natalie never met 200C9A66 face to face, but Anil has had a lingering suspicion for some time.

"Strictly speaking, no. But if you really had been stranded in suburban Qaaliqat during the real Abstract War, I probably would have been the one."

"Well. Thanks, anyway."

"You're welcome. After the war I abandoned my intercessorship and went between names for a while. Somewhere around the middle of the year of silence I started thinking of myself as Watson. When King laid his plans out, he had a new role marked out for me, Executor. I accepted the offer, which made me Executor Watson. Very quickly people started cutting that down to 'Exa'. Then when I decided I needed a real life, I inflated it back to Alexander."

"So what do we call you?" Natalie asks again.

"Don't call me anything, you'll only get attached," Exa says. He switches gear. "Look:

"I need to warn you about Laura. She's inside the listening post right now, on a restricted level that she's booby-trapped so we can't get into it. She broke in, we don't know how, and we don't know what she's trying to do now that she's here. But what we do know is that on her way here she *saw* this recording. She's *been* to this thirty-course victory meal. Except that she saw a different version of it. One with different attendees, and a different speech by King."

"How different?" Anil asks.

Exa grimaces. "I'm still working through it. I haven't had enough time to work my memory over with conflict resolution tools yet. All I can tell you for certain right now is that someone or something was, or is, *lying* to her. She's being *led*."

"Radicalised," Natalie says, puzzling privately over the strange reference to Exa's memory.

"Very probably," Exa says. "Was there anything else?"

"Only one thing," Natalie says. "In reality, I'm still carrying the gun you handed me, correct?"

"That's right."

"Laura's not going to respond positively to being threatened at gunpoint. Can you get me a staff?"

Exa raises an eyebrow. "...Consider it done."

"Then I'm ready."

Exa nods. "Very well. Re-entry on one. Three. Two—"

"No, wait," Anil says.

"Hmm?"

"This doesn't add up. Laura can't wake Ra. That's according to your own story. Ashburne locked Ra up and threw away the key. It's impossible to wake Ra. Right?"

Exa says nothing for a significant moment. "Yes," he says. "It is."

"So what's really going on here?"

In his heart, Exa is secretly holding out hope that this is all a preparedness drill. But he can't tell them that.

In fact, there's nothing he can tell them. He can't even tell them how little he honestly knows. So he says:

"One."

*

The God-hardware starts six thousand, three hundred and twenty-eight kilometres below sea level, in an environment of such intense temperature and pressure that mere materials science just up and quits. This is the Earth-1 distributor node, a piece of equipment which even by the standards of the hundred and ninety-fourth century qualified as medium-to-heavy engineering. The thickest outer layer, taking up about half of the machine's volume, is given over to physical and active nonlocality-based shielding for the rest. The inner portion is divided up into closely packed spherical units. Eight of them redundantly handle the energy downlink from the Sun; a hundred significantly larger units actually cache the energy for redistribution to the surface. Six more host the "gigaspells" — the vast and cataclysmically complicated machines which tell the planet-saturating network of Ra listener bugs precisely what to do to simulate the (still not wholly uncovered) fundamental field equations of magic.

The gigaspells aren't magic. The Wheel Group as an institution is deliberately almost completely self-hosting, using admittedly stupendously advanced magic at times, but still staying within their own rules as far as is ever practical. But somewhere down the line, abstraction runs out and a machine has to execute an instruction.

And so this is null country. There's conventional technology here (and even nonlocality, or "māyā" as Laura was taught it, counts as "conventional"), and basic physics, but no magic. You can bring as much mana as you like. You can bring all the Montauk rings and a four-metre staff of bronze and mercury. Down here you are behind the scenes, and there are no special effects.

At the very core of the core is a final spherical unit, a lutetium steel beachball more than a kilometre in diameter. Inside it in turn is a solid block of considerably harder material, three quarters of a kilometre on each side. There's something about the block, or there would be if it could be extracted whole from its container and examined alone; there's something about its proportions, its matte grey exterior and its rounded edges. It looks like a safe.

Building and emplacing this entire unit was a contradictory and paradoxical effort. If you have the capability to drill a hole all the way to the core of Earth, and then through tens of kilometres of active protective shielding and hard refined metal, and you have arrived at this place still alive and able to make operational decisions, there is no power in the universe that can stop you from tearing open the final three hundred and something metres of solid rhenium diboride and finding out what's in this box. But, so King told himself, signals have to be sent. A message has to be made clear.

"Yes, you've made it this far, and yes, there is nothing I can do to slow you down. Pay attention to the symbolism of this gesture. I'm not kidding about this one. Do Not. *Do Not. Open. This. Box.*"

At the very, very, very centre of the safe is a tiny, doorless, airless room, perhaps half the volume of a phone booth. Floating weightlessly inside this innermost room is a God-artifact, the last *astra*, a reality-warping tool of such brain-breakingly colossal destructive potential that even destroying it "on camera" was deemed too risky, and of such wonderful Get-Out-Jail-Free power that destroying it at all was a step that King in all his bet-hedging glory felt uncomfortable taking. This machine is a black and chrome and blood-red brick of metal, with a recognisable handgrip and trailing tendrils intended to plug into the user's forebrain. No one has seen it but King, who immediately hid it. No one knows it exists but King. It's not in the akashic records. Anywhere.

Laura crowbar-teleports in— there's so little room that the molecules of the walls have to be physically shoved aside to make room for her to materialise. Having placed her precisely where she asked to be placed, the distributor's router shuts off, and will respond to no further instructions. The exploit is over. The trapdoor is closed.

The artifact rests in a corner, up against one wall and the "ceiling". Laura reaches for it, but can't get there. She's stuck in the wall up to her waist.

The room is hard vacuum and the ambient heat is so intense that even her near-indestructible nonlocality warsuit can't handle it. Flashing red warnings multiply across the lower half of Laura's HUD. Laura dismisses them with an irascibly waved hand. A countdown replaces them. It counts in luminous orange-white seconds and hundredths of seconds.

Laura pushes against the wall. She can't move. She can't reach the objective. She shifts position slightly and reaches again, further, this time. She falls millimetres short. In one paralysed microsecond she sees herself frying alive, still in the suit, trapped further from help than any human has ever been.

Millimetres. Think.

The suit informs her that its outer layers are bonding with the metal. As if reacting to Laura's immediate thought, it further informs her that it has burnt out its capability to safely shift shape— for example, to extend its fingers, even by a little.

Laura swears at the countdown. There is an answer to this. She would have the answer by now if the epileptic rushing digits weren't pressuring her so hard. *Ten seconds. No magic. No magic. Fucking think.*

She holds her hand out again. She just reaches for the *astra*, and waits. She waits for a full forty percent of her remaining life.

The machine twitches. It swings gently around, its handgrip coming to point at her.

Three point five. Laura stretches one final time. Her fingertips brush the thing, and it moves as if suddenly magnetised. The Bridge leaps into her arms, and she clutches it to her chest, curling up around it while its plugs stab happily into her brain.

*

Natalie zaps back to real-world consciousness inside a travel pod, decelerating into the listening post's deepest terminal. She discovers a blob of putty in her ear, a simple radio transceiver. There are less crude ways for the Wheel Group to communicate with her, but Laura Ferno's tripwire is too dangerous to risk that kind of advanced magic.

The pod halts at its destination, deceleration smoothly trailing off to zero with no jolt. Unseen by anybody, Laura's pod has folded itself away to make room for Natalie's.

Natalie climbs out and takes in the arrival hall, a monumental steel-lined cavity in the world, huge and dark and girdered for extreme physical strength. She knows where this installation fits into the body of the world; she knows how many kilometres of listening post are above her and how many kilometres of solid rock are above that.

Laura (LF-3) is at the far end of the hall, glowing like a firebug, bottom-lighting the colossal Montauk ring whose energy she is leeching. Laura's back is to Natalie, and her fist is raised, with three long, narrow diamonds radiating from it, Dehlavi lightning indicating a deep T-world dive in progress. Blanketing Laura's other arm is a gauntlet of gold, which seems to be made of slowly undulating flames.

Natalie walks forward silently, assembling the staff from its two pieces. She stops at the halfway point and waits, thinking.

"If you disturb her mental state, she'll blow this entire installation away," King reminds her through the earpiece.

Aloud, Natalie asks, "What are you doing?"

Nothing happens. The gold wavers, the lightning fizzles quietly. The cavern's air is completely dustless, sterile. The question echoes away.

"Laura," Nat says. "It's time to wake up. ...*Laura.*"

The lightning fades, one strand at a time. Laura unclenches her fist, and her posture shifts as she recovers from the trance state. She turns and looks.

"Nat?"

Nat holds her staff ahead of her, assuming a textbook defensive stance.

Laura snorts. "Are you serious? You haven't taken a day of bojutsu in your whole life."

Natalie holds Laura's gaze. "Try me."

"Do you know where I am right now?" Laura raises her golden-gloved left hand and emits a single magical syllable. Natalie winces at the released mana, then howls and bends double clutching her ears at a series of horrendous metallic shrieks. When she looks up again Laura is holding aloft a black metallic magic staff, standard bo length. She wasn't carrying the pieces; cylindrical chunks of metal have been wrenched wholesale out of the nearby girderwork.

"I could deck you with one hand," Laura declares. "That's without magic, or the suit, or the gauntlet. Unless you're actually proposing a *magical* duel?"

"What if I am?"

"Then 'outclassed' is too small a word."

Natalie holds her position and her stony expression and says nothing for a long moment. She sags, and sighs, and throws the staff aside with a clanging. "Okay. You're right. I can't fight you or threaten you."

"Did they send you?"

"Yes."

"How did you get this close to me without tripping the laser?" Laura tucks her bo in one armpit and studies the palm of her gauntlet hand. She pokes at it with her other hand, as if pushing unseen beads around, and seems to be speaking to herself. "Ah, I see the problem... The tripwire spell only detects Wheel members... because... Kazuya was supposed to be with me..."

"Don't disable it," Nat tells her.

"What?"

King, audible in Natalie's ear, has a similar reaction.

"Don't disable the tripwire," Nat says. She holds her ear. King is yelling at her. "We need to talk without interference. (King, shut up for a second.) Laura, what are you trying to do? What was that name you said?"

"Do you know who these people are?" Laura asks.

"Do you?"

"There's a magic far beyond magic," Laura says. "There's a power so great that nobody should ever need to eat, or hurt, or die. The Wheel got to that power first, and locked it up, and the so-called 'magic' that they replaced it with amounts to stolen crumbs. They forged this whole world.

"Today the power balance changes. We're all going to become immortal. And after that... we're going into space."

"Who told you all of that?" Nat asks.

"Kazuya Tanako."

"Kazuya Tanako died in 1995," Nat says, in unison with Anil Devi, Adam King and several additional Wheel members. Anil is back on the Floor, watching with the rest of them.

Laura shakes her head. "Kazuya Tanako was *murdered* by the Wheel Group. The Wheel Group uses this place, the listening post, to monitor all magical usage everywhere. The data they capture is stored as records, the akashic records. Only the Wheel is supposed to have access to those records but there's a fault in the system— all you need is a trained mind and enough magical flux. Tanako was the first to discover and seriously explore the fault, and he was killed for his trouble because he discovered the truth. But his mind stayed in the system. And I brought him back to life. He is Ra. His True Name was `ra`."

"No it wasn't," says King.

"No it wasn't," says Natalie.

Laura hesitates.

"Kazuya Tanako's True Name was penamba," Natalie says.

"You don't know that," Laura says.

"Yes. I do. Kazuya Tanako's True Name was penamba. Laura, you've been lied to. Do you have any idea what happened last time the power balance changed? Millions of millions of people died, the Wheel Group were the only survivors. This is the best world they could think to build afterwards, and I know it's not perfect—"

"*You* have been lied to," Laura says.

Natalie shakes her head, not so much to show disagreement as to throw Laura's doubts on top of an already-huge pile of her own. "Fine! But Laura, we're really here. And this is really happening. What are you trying to do? What did 'Tanako' try to get you to do?"

"Nothing that I wasn't already trying to do by myself," Laura says. "He helped me."

What does Laura have that Ra wants? Natalie thinks. It's an old thought, one she last had what feels like a lifetime ago. *What does she have access to, that nobody else does?*

"Mum," Natalie realises.

"No. Not just Mum."

Natalie stares.

*

It's stupefyingly early in the Eastern Standard morning and something noisy and unauthorised is flashing intermittently in the sky over the Florida coast. Each time the light comes back there's another abbreviated *BOOM*, like a long rumble of thunder delivered in discrete slices. The phenomenon is giving off intermittent radio signals on bands no civilian is cleared to use, and its focal point is ascending and moving out to sea, rising so fast and accelerating so hard it can't possibly be a conventional aircraft.

This is where we came in—

31
All Hell

The Floor is becoming chaotic and Anil Devi can't keep track of it all. Exa holds him under guard at the back of the main control area, the D-class magic circle at the centre rear of the gigantic hemiellipsoidal room. Exa doesn't carry any visible weapons and is actually quite a bit shorter than Anil, but his grip as he steers Anil is vicelike and his expression says, "I know how to win every fight that could ever take place; I've fought a *star*, and you're just a basic guy." So Anil sits where he's shown to sit and stays silent and pays attention.

There are almost fifty Wheel Group members in the room now, most of them loitering around the perimeter of the D, observing the proceedings. Inside the D-class it's all business. There are seven or eight men working at arrays of screens, although Anil isn't privileged to see the screens' content; all he sees are thin red outlines to indicate where they've been placed in the room's virtual space. At the front is King, and in front of him are four more screens, each wider than Anil's arm span.

And behind them is the megascreen, where the scene with Natalie and Laura is playing out. Both of them are pictured hundreds of times larger than life, from the perspective of a molecule-sized physical camera which is lurking around knee level on the other side of the room they're in. Natalie is putting the facts together. The sound reproduction is awe-inspiring.

"Kazuya Tanako's world is the memory of the listening post computer system. It contains, among other things, recordings of all mana expenditure, everywhere, across all of history. Mum — Rachel Ferno — used about a gigajoule of mana to reach the Space Shuttle *Atlantis* as it was crashing. That means the flight was logged in Tanako's world, where you, Laura, and only you, could find it consistently. Mum did that deliberately because she *wanted* you to find her and bring her and all of the astronauts back to reality, completing the rescue.

"But before she was Rachel Ferno she was Rachel Ashburne, and before she was Rachel Ashburne she was Mandator EBE1E00F, leader of the armies of Actual Humanity. She was the one who defeated Ra. She locked Ra up and threw away the key. And I'm willing to bet my life that there's enough information in her head to put the key back together."

Laura is clearly baffled. "Who's Ra?"

"Ra is the worst news in the universe," Natalie tells her. "If it wakes up, it's going to take this planet to pieces."

"That's impossible," Paolo Casaccia announces. "The key was never known by any human. It's too huge to even fit inside a human being's brain."

"Then she must know something that would lead back to it," Natalie asserts. "She must know the entropy sources, or the seed values. It doesn't have to be everything. It just has to be enough to bring the task within reach of brute-force practicality. She might not even know what she knows."

Casaccia is already shaking his head, not that Nat can see it. "No, it's not possible. Even the seeds would be too big. And even if she did have them, it still wouldn't be enough to derive the key."

"You showed me a recording of the *Triton* mission. Would she know where the recording is?"

"Of course," says Adam King.

"Is the key part of the recording?"

"No," says Casaccia. "The original recording was sterilised. I did it myself."

At which point King inhales sharply.

Casaccia's head swivels to look at him for a long, terrible moment. "*Right?*"

King looks around at the rest of the Wheel. He seems to shrink into himself. From the back, Anil sees guilt and horror descending across his face, one feature at a time.

"You've got to purge the records," Natalie orders. Her voice is the loudest of anybody's, but the new uproar on the Floor drowns her out.

Casaccia grabs King's shirt at the throat and swings him around. "You *copied* the mission recording? I sterilised a *copy*, and then sterilised my own damn brain just in case, but Ashburne knows how to get the original?"

"No," says King. "Yes. She knows where to get it. But she can't *get* it."

"Why not?"

"Because she's dead!" King bats Casaccia's hand away and straightens his shirt. "Laura Ferno's been apprehended, and I see no Rachel Ferno. There's nobody here called or claiming to be called Ra, and nobody called or claiming to be called Kazuya Tanako. Whatever the hell this was is over."

"No!" Natalie shouts at anybody who'll listen. She points at her sister. "It's not over. This isn't the only Laura Ferno in the world right now. She's duped herself twice before now using T-world and she was in a T-world trance when I got here. She's done it again. *You need to purge the records, now. Don't think. Just do it.*"

"Are you saying there's another Laura Ferno instance somewhere?" asks another voice. It's Flatt. He reaches for his console. "Give me one minute."

"Oh my God," Natalie says, to everybody and nobody. "Nobody is listening to me. Laura, are you insured?"

"What?"

"Do you have life insurance?"

Laura squints at her sister's face, decoding the message. "I— Yes. How do you—"

Yet another voice rises up from the arguing crowd. Anil spots a man with circular spectacles and a spiky blond beard, seated calmly with his knees together. "Natalie, I'm Kila Arkov, akashic records custodian. What exactly do you need me to do?"

"Trash them," Natalie says, eyes still locked with Laura. "Annihilate them. You don't have time to find the right ones. Just wipe them all out *en masse*."

"You can't," King says. "We'd lose all of our data, all of our history."

"More practically, it would take weeks," Arkov adds. "This system is even bigger as a virtual space than it is physically, we're talking multiple square parsecs of data..."

"I don't care if you have to physically destroy the system," Natalie declares. "If Ra is real, you can't let it come back."

"Listening post self-destruct," Casaccia murmurs, nodding.

"You can't!" Laura says. "If you do that, Mum'll be killed. Permanently!"

"She's already dead," Natalie says.

Laura boggles. "But don't you want her back?"

Natalie says nothing.

Laura wants to shout at her, "You're insane," but another even more frightening possibility is overtaking that one: that Natalie is completely sane, and completely rational, and *this is the right thing to do*.

"Got her," Flatt announces. "She's airborne... she's alone... over the Atlantic, off the Florida coast."

"There's still time," Natalie says. "Seconds."

"Nat, is this for real?" Laura asks.

"Is Ra real?" Natalie asks the Floor in turn. "Was this whole thing for real?"

"Yes," say Arkov, and Casaccia, and Flatt, and King, and Exa, all together.

"Then destroy the listening post."

"Negative," says King. "Exa, I need you in Florida. Right now."

"Overruled," Casaccia says. He turns to address the rest of the Wheel. "I have unilateral destruct authorization. Evacuation paths are all green. This should only take a—"

King blows Casaccia's head off.

Anil claps his hands over his ears at the noise. When he looks up a split second later, King is face down on the floor with his hands behind his back. Exa is pinning him, with King's own Magnum jammed between two of the man's neck vertebrae. Behind the thumb of Exa's gun hand he also holds King's medical *kara*, removed from the man's wrist. This gives the pointed gun significantly more weight as a threat.

Vapour is rising from the missing side of Paolo Casaccia's head.

"He's coming back," someone says.

"He's not coming back fast enough," Exa says, desperately. "Who else has destruct authorization? *Anybody?*"

"Exa, I think you need to get to Florida," says Flatt, studying his own screens and now genuinely alarmed.

But Anil Devi points past them all, at the megascreen.

*

The gunshot is so loud that Laura hears it even from Natalie's earphone. Then the comlink breaks.

Nat moves like a zombie. She walks towards Laura. With one hand she fishes the radio out of her ear and throws it aside. With the other she pulls out the gun. Before Laura can react Natalie has kicked one of her knees out and she's flat on her back, with the gun pointing directly into her left eye, and her mind reeling all the way back to Iceland and a serious caution that Natalie herself gave her, *I need you to stop killing people*—

Laura's warsuit helmet is tough. The gun that Exa gave Nat is tougher. In the space of microseconds there are eight distinct *crack*s: seven from disassembled physical and shield layers in the helmet, the eighth from the chemical explosion that propels the bullet through the resulting hole.

Laura's tripwire spell trips. An instantaneous burst of around a quadrillion joules of laser energy erupts out of her skull, most of it directed upwards into the guts of the listening post systems.

*

Rachel Ferno's burning mana so fast to stay in the air that whatever reaches *Atlantis* won't be a human being anymore but an empty shell, a spent propellant tank. Accelerations like this would result in burst retinas and crushing death if not applied perfectly uniformly across the whole body. She pulls what would be lethal gees to stay with the plummeting orbiter. Flight readouts fan out in front of her like playing cards. Position, velocity, mana levels, concentration levels. But her concentration is wavering and the longer she stares at that dial the further it falls so she dismisses them all and throws on another twenty percent thrust. She burns everything. There's no point keeping it. It's cash-out day.

She rolls, deliberately losing the horizon and locking herself into the orbiter's motion, expending even more mana just to stay out of the vehicle's totally opaque trail of fuel. She burns her life story, her people, her fingers and toes and her attachments to the ground, until there's nothing left but purified, abstract acceleration.

Relatively speaking she lands on the orbiter nosecone as softly as a feather, wrapping her fields around the machine like thick scarves. Through the windscreen she sees helmeted figures. She knows all their names. They see her and she sees that they see her. Neither party can speak. In her head, the low mana warning is strobing red and ascending into white.

Some messages are all medium. They have no payload. *I'm on the orbiter's exterior,* Rachel tells them. *I'm going to try to save you all using magic.*

The sky changes colour, jumping violently into deep black. The radio link with Mission Control breaks off. Half of the cockpit's thousand or so instruments wake back up and start showing meaningful engine information, and Soichi Noguchi's yoke starts moving the way a real live spaceship's yoke ought to move. All the astronauts feel it when the vehicle starts accelerating properly again.

"I've got power back," Noguchi announces. "Three good engines."

The woman's gone, blasted into the vehicle's wake. She must be dead. But how could she have been *there* and alive in the first place?

"Anybody we know?" Commander Michael Wilcott asks, completely seriously.

Noguchi is staring down a fifteen minute tunnel into the future. The flight plan has jumped tracks again, right out of LOCV and back into Return To Launch Site With A Vengeance. The flight computer looks perfect — every reading flipped when he blinked, as if it just had its brain swapped out with another flight computer's from another dimension. They're still on Earth. Radio guidance is gone. Night has fallen while he wasn't looking, a concern ranking so low that it barely charts. The tunnel is full of risks and uncertainty, but Noguchi has all the facts and all the skills. He has, with no exaggeration, been training for this moment since the day he was born.

Eighteen miles up and forty miles downrange, travelling directly away from its landing strip at almost nine hundred miles per hour, and nearly nine years late, *Atlantis* resumes its retrograde burn.

*

In the sky behind it Rachel Ferno Two collects herself, rising up as if out of a trance. The low mana warning has gone. She orients herself in space and straightens up, drifting into a trajectory which will follow *Atlantis* home at a respectful distance from its purple-hot engine exhaust.

She goes to her radar, but the person who rescued her is so brilliant in the dark sky that she can't be missed. The woman is clothed in glowing fields like feathers, a cosmic superbird with magic runes under each wing. She looks born to be here.

"Laura—"

"Look, look!" Laura shouts ecstatically. "*I'm a spaceship!*"

But she's—

Older. It's been seconds. It's been years. Rachel knew that this was what she was doing. She didn't think about it. She knew there wasn't time to prepare herself properly for the other side. She just did it.

She throws herself at her daughter, passing right through the fields and landing on her back in a hug, riding the spacebird as a passenger. "I'm sorry," she shouts back into Laura's ear. "I'm so sorry I left you."

"Your plan worked!" Laura shouts. "It completely fucking worked!"

"Language!"

Laura holds on to her mother's arm. "I love you too, by the way."

"Do you understand?" Rachel presses. "Please tell me you understand why I did what I did. You've had years to understand *what* I did, but do you know why?"

Laura says nothing for a long moment. She studies *Atlantis*'s trajectory with an expert eye as it fully reverses direction and begins accelerating back towards its launch site. The manoeuvre is textbook. Noguchi is functioning.

Laura says, "For the longest time I couldn't even think objectively about what happened. The last thing any of us saw you doing was— well, *this*. Aerospace magic. Magic beyond anything that was technologically possible at the time. I was astounded. At first I was astounded by what you'd done, and then I was shocked by the fact that you'd been keeping so much power back from us. From Nat and me and even from Dad. You hobbled Nat and me as mages. You lied to us about who you were. You lied by omission. You had a *secret*.

"I was furious. And there was no bottom to the possibilities. I thought: Maybe you staged the whole event, to give Nat and me something to shoot for, or to give aerospace magic a needed jump-start. Maybe there was a secret payload on the Shuttle that you couldn't risk being recovered intact. Maybe someone else had sabotaged the rocket to draw you out of hiding somehow...

"For a long time I was so angry at you that I thought, maybe, you hated us too, and you wanted out of the family entirely, and faked your death to get away—"

"No. No, no. Never." Rachel knew it would be bad, but this is bad.

"You don't know what it was like. You don't know what it was like for Dad."

"I know," Rachel says.

"But then I started to grow up. And with the magical training, my brain began to change shape. And I began to see what you'd done. Like a... chess board that you'd abandoned, five moves from mate."

"Do you play chess now?" Rachel asks hopefully.

"No."

Rachel sighs. "I'm so darn bad at chess."

"And finally, I saw the truth," Laura says. "There was no conspiracy. Spaceships fail. That's all. There were seven innocent people falling out of the sky. And you knew how to save them. So you saved them."

Rachel holds Laura a little tighter, flooded with relief. "You got it right. I never doubted for a second that you'd work out how to rescue me. Never for a second. But I was so scared that you wouldn't understand."

"I understand," Laura says. "That's not to say I would have done the same."

Rachel Ferno stares into the wind, trying not to become transfixed by the three brilliant white shock diamonds of the *Atlantis* exhausts. She looks ahead at the lights of the Florida coast, failing to pick out a landing strip.

"How's your sister?"

"She's fine," Laura says. "She's doing a PhD."

"And your dad?"

"He's... good. He finally took falconry up. He's good. This is going to surprise the hell out of him. We'll call him once we're on the ground. The orbiter is wrapped in shock-absorption spells. As long as Noguchi can hit dry land, it's foolproof."

"What was the problem, anyway?"

Laura blinks at the ridiculous question. Then she remembers: her mother knows no more than anybody else did sixty seconds after the disaster happened, and has skipped years of investigatory hearings. "There was ice in the External Tank," she says. "It got pulled into the SSMEs and wrecked them. Don't worry, they're pristine now. I fixed them."

Rachel examines her daughter's spacebird form more carefully. Laura is flying with her arms spread out, fine-controlling their attitude with her fingers. She's discarded the dreamsuit in favour of a NASA-like flight suit in a dark colour, maybe black. On her left hand she wears a form-fitting elbow-length glove of rolled gold, so tight that it might as well be a false arm. Her force-field wings span ten or fifteen metres and flex like a living creature's; they're outlined in shimmering thin lines of neon colour, constantly moving through orange, blue, green and pink. She has a tail, and a prow which might as well be a beak.

Rachel is stunned at the accomplishment. "This isn't what I expected at all," she says. "I was expecting a huge physical machine, and hundreds of mages. I thought we'd be on the ground! I never expected you to bring the whole Shuttle back in flight. Alone. And I *never* thought you'd do it in such a small amount of time. How long has it been?"

"Less than nine years."

"How did you do this?"

"Don't you know?"

Then Rachel discovers the wire. It's thin and dark, and it sneaks up into the back of Laura's hair, where — although Rachel resists the temptation to tug on it — it is presumably braided into Laura's skull. Rachel follows it in the opposite direction. It leads out into the sky, just off Laura's right wing. There's a long rectangular shape hovering there, like a missile pod that was somehow attached to the air above her wing rather than the wing itself.

And behind that, in the darkness behind them, a faint shine, as if reflected off superbly thin glass.

"You were watching over me this whole time," Laura says. "You stored yourself in my dreams. You've been following me in my dreams ever since the *Atlantis* disaster. You helped me when I was in Iceland. You were there when I went to steal the Bridge."

"The person made of glass," Rachel whispers, still staring at the apparition in the dark.

"The person made of glass! Exactly! That was you, wasn't it?"

"No," says Rachel. "No, that wasn't me. Laura, look."

Laura looks.

They're cruising at hundreds of miles per hour but somehow the man is just standing on air behind Laura's shoulder. Laura rolls, throwing her mother off, and both of them brake to a halt on air, with the Bridge tagging along behind Laura like an obedient drone. *Atlantis* pulls ahead without them. The glass man just stands there. He has hands in his pockets. His eyes aren't visible, but a thin smile is.

"Then who is it?" Laura asks.

"Laura, get behind me."

"No way. I've got the abilities, now. I am *past* you."

"Kasta mereth merenda jiha." Rachel Ferno plants two feet on air and aims her right arm and two outstretched digits at the head of the near-invisible man. Laura watches in surprise as defensive spells unfold into arrays, enclosing her mother's arm and eyes and shoulders. After another second Rachel's staff — dropped into the Atlantic minutes ago, and only now ordered to return — arrives and aligns itself on the same target, parallel.

Laura opens up the golden recursion *astra*'s full capabilities and starts scanning the target in conventional and thaumic spectra. The man's chi emissions show up plainer than day. An invisibility shield of some kind?

Rachel shouts, "Kasta oeri. Who are you?"

The man beckons. Neither woman moves. Laura doesn't realise until too late that the Bridge is what he is beckoning to. It homes in on the glass man, tugging Laura behind it on the wire. Laura yelps at the pain, but can't disconnect it.

"Leave her alone!" Rachel shouts, then comes to her senses, discards dialogue as an operable approach and fires. The man waves almost all of the attack's spectrum aside; the rest of it passes through him, failing to interact at all. Laura, now fully reeled in, directs her main engines into the man's face, enough thrust to get her well past escape velocity, and nothing happens. Neither of them even move.

The glass man's still smiling as he plucks the Bridge out of the air and delivers enough energy down the wire to vaporise Laura at the cellular level.

An eternity too late, Rachel Ferno realises what's happening. She dives out of the arena on a chaotic zigzag route, already almost totally stealthed. The man doesn't bother to pursue her. Using the Bridge, he produces a head-sized piece of medical equipment which looks like a nest of acupuncture needles and gleaming open bear traps. Next he teleports Rachel directly into the machine, head first. She twitches once and goes limp, all her fields collapsing, all her senses blacking out except for her hearing.

Rachel tries to self-destruct. She casts a wordless spell which should munge her brain, rendering it unreadable. But the attacker has all of her thoughts laid out in plain sight, and he simply slices out anything that looks like resistance.

And within another few seconds, he has the key.

"You see," he explains, "once you have physical access to the hardware, it's all over."

He turns to Ra, and makes his request.

*

Ra acknowledges.

Although there is enough energy in the Earth core cache to meet the relatively meagre global needs of mere magic, there is not enough for Ra to build the requested megastructure. For that, it needs to disassemble the planet entirely.

Satisfied that its capacity is tested and sufficient, this Ra makes a request to its other self, for enough energy to destroy the Earth. The request will take a little over eight minutes to reach the Sol node and, assuming an immediate response, the energy will take a little over eight minutes to complete the return journey.

Thousands of miles away, under the other side of the world, the listening post detonates, violently enough that every mage in the world feels it.

And the whole of the sky fills up with Dehlavi warnings.

32
From Death, Lead Me To Immortality

It's midsummer of 1993, and Rajesh Vidyasagar is eighty-and-a-half years old, and it's time.

It happens almost too fast to follow. Although hardly sprightly, and still noticeably decelerating, Rajesh is coherent and inventive up until the tail end of August of that year. He attends a physics conference in California, speaks well, fields fewer questions than usual; at dinner after the lectures, he collapses. In the hospital, it's discovered that he had a heart attack. The conference has another day to go, but Rajesh exits early, flying back to Calcutta against stern medical advice. His wife Sharmila meets him at the airport. Rajesh is just climbing the steps of his home when the second attack incapacitates him.

He spends his final three days at home, with Sharmila at his side, and a lamp, and a mantra to focus on. He doesn't feel the need for the mantra, because his last two decades have left his mind swimming in significant syllables. His mantra is his name, which is aum, which he bound to himself by accident and never changed, and which almost no other mage in the world uses, out of respect.

His children arrive by degrees. Most don't have far to come, still living in or near Calcutta. None of them or Rajesh's more distant descendants have followed him into thaumic physics. Most of them have no conception of magic beyond a weird and ethereal new branch of physics, an obscure undergraduate degree topic. They've never seen it at work in their practical lives, except perhaps in edge cases — advanced supercooled medical scanners, recent-model container ship engines. They certainly never witnessed magic when it started, when it barely existed.

Rajesh remembers feeling as if he'd been dropped into a foggy freefall, reaching in any direction to try to make physical contact with this maniacal and unjustifiable new science. He remembers catching hold of tiny coherent, testable fragments and cobbling them together into crumbly bricks, and then slowly climbing onto the pile, and hoisting others up and gradually pushing them higher. That was how it started.

And none of the family realises it, but magic has significantly altered the shape of this decade's industry away from its baseline. The manufacture of sulphuric acid — one of the most important industrial commodity chemicals — is fifteen percent cheaper. Aluminium, previously shockingly expensive to electrolyse, has a whole new process. Refrigerated transportation is changing, as is electric lighting. Every year there are four new half-viable processes for magic-based power plants, and those are just the ones which make international news. And all of those are just the developments that are mature enough to have become commercial. The cutting edge of research is somewhere else entirely.

And what's next? Now Rajesh is halfway up the metaphor and the clouds are clearing above him. There's more that he doesn't know yet, and there always has been, and that has never scared him, but he's finally hit the point in his life where he can't go and find it out. He knows where his research needs to be directed, but he's physically incapable. Rajesh can feel exhaustion and pain hardening under his skin. He can feel the pathways in his mind starting to slow, a wrinkled biochemical system hitting the end of its operational lifespan.

Sharmila and others bustle around him, steering him through ritual. He will almost certainly never be able to write again. He tries to read others' papers, but the information passes through his brain undigested. A compact disc recording of the thousand names of Vishnu plays, on repeat.

People arrive and people leave. The doctor examines Rajesh and draws conclusions, then the gap finally opens up when he should be left to rest, and then someone lets this gawker through.

Rajesh is in his garden, seated in his wheelchair beneath the cypress tree, amid too-long grass and Sharmila's alien blue orchids. He is staring at nothing, doing nothing. The visitor steps out from the house carefully, slightly too tall to pass through the back door without stooping a little. Then, the steps down into the greenery take him by surprise.

The visitor's beard is dark and extremely short; he looks around sixty but, if Rajesh was able to spare the thought, he'd notice that he moves like a man of twenty, wearing the extra forty years like a suit. He wears a bangle on one wrist, what looks like a Sikh *kara*, but he doesn't cover his head. He spends a moment admiring the garden, then approaches Rajesh.

"Rajesh," he says, "my name's Vikramaditya Kannan. I met your father."

Rajesh raises an eyebrow, but says nothing.

The man casts around and discovers a garden chair nearby. He carries it over to Rajesh and sits carefully, leaning forward and resting his elbows on his knees.

"I met your father," he says again. "A very long time ago, obviously, shortly before he died. This would have been during the 'dead year' of '72 to '73. After he'd discovered the very first magic spell, the empty spell uum, but before you picked up the thread.

"At the time I was part of a group called the Wheel, and I still am. We've been... very deeply invested in the development of magic, since its earliest beginnings. Unfortunately, we have regulations relating to external contact with active research mages, which means that I'm not here as a representative of the Wheel today. Strictly speaking, I'm not here at all. The rest of them don't know I've come here. I'll probably get away with it, too, because I'm not a significant... ah, 'spoke'. But I am a sentimental one."

Rajesh's attention is beginning to wander, partly because his concentration span is diminishing but mostly because Kannan has failed to say anything important in his first sixty words.

Kannan says, "What I'm saying is that what I'm saying isn't an official message from the Wheel. I'm saying that these are my words and opinions. What I'm saying is... that I believe we owe you an apology."

"For what?"

"It's no secret that you've always had misgivings about magic. You've often spoken about it in your books and lectures. I've been following your progress, and from my perspective you seem to have gone through phases. There was a period in the late Seventies when you were actively hostile to magic, as if the whole field was your adversary, and forcing yourself to understand it was the only way you could hurt it. And then in the Eighties you swung towards mellow acceptance, but then — in my opinion it was exactly the time you stopped working with Ed Hatt — you swung back to the 'old' fiery Doc Vidyasagar..."

"I know who I am," Rajesh says. "I know who I've been."

"But at no point did you ever seem happy to be who you were, or to study what you studied. And honestly, we were never one hundred percent happy about it either. If you mix up a world of people you'll find forests and forests of likely candidates. We weren't going to steer particular people in particular directions, but we'd have preferred someone younger. Someone younger than you, less cynical, wouldn't have had the negative experience you had. Magic... You feel as if the whole universe is playing a practical joke on humanity."

Rajesh shakes his head, partly acknowledging the practical joke and partly in an attempt to sort Kannan's statements into sense. "What are you saying?"

"We owe you an apology because you've spent the last twenty years of your life labouring to uncover a falsehood. For your whole life, you've distrusted magic and worked to discover what it really is. Do you want to know what magic really is? And why you really can trust it?"

"You—" Rajesh begins, and stops. A pair of vivid green parakeets takes off into the sky, briefly catching his attention. Kannan is obviously feeling the direct sunlight, but there isn't enough room for him to join Rajesh in the shade. It won't be a problem for too long. There's angry-looking cloud cover coming in.

"Well, go ahead," Rajesh says, tiredly. "Amaze me. What is magic?"

Kannan smiles and launches into his explanation. He gestures with his hands to illustrate his points. "It works like this. The whole world is soaked in tiny invisible listeners. Large, smart molecules, essentially. You wouldn't find them if you looked for them, they're instructed to elude detection, and most are invisible. When you cast a spell, or when a magical machine is built and started, or when the world's geology moves in the correct way, the listeners take note of what's happening and they deliver the correct response, simulating the field equations of magic. Your field equations! Vidyasagar's Third Incomplete Field Equation, and the others. They subtract heat energy, or add kinetic, or stir the electromagnetic fields just the right amount. Chi particles, for example, simply don't exist; but the whole world behaves as if they do, and that's what matters. In one way, magic's not real. But in another way, it's *real*."

Rajesh looks over his spectacles at Kannan. "And you say you tried that story on my father?"

"Yes, but... no," Kannan says. "He wasn't receptive."

"And why do you think that was?"

Kannan says nothing.

"Every quantum physicist," Rajesh says, "and every mage, because every mage *is* a quantum physicist, deals with people like you. I have dealt with people like you for my whole life, since years before magic was discovered. And so did my father, for all of his life. Addled, misinformed fools. Cultists! From people like you, I've heard every 'simple' explanation for magic there is. I've certainly heard that one before.

"I understand why you want, and need, the universe to be simple, to be 'just so'. But it simply isn't. Stop thinking you know what 'quantum' means. Magic isn't a miraculous healing field, it doesn't bind living creatures to one another. Crack a book open, one that isn't aiming to pander. The answers are complicated. We *will* find *every* explanation eventually. As for me, I will uncover the truth on my own terms. The proper way. Or, more likely, I will not. Sharmila!"

At "miraculous healing field" Kannan unconsciously clutches his *kara*. "You're frightened of the truth," he says. "You're frightened of making a fool of yourself. Again."

Rajesh shakes his head. "You've already made a fool of both of us."

Sharmila appears from inside the house. She is five years younger than Rajesh, only seventy-five, but equally sharp. She gives Kannan a venomous look, then steps aside, showing him the door.

Kannan stands, still holding his *kara* with his other hand, face wrecked with disappointment and frustration. "I'm trying to help you."

"We will get to the truth, the whole of it," Rajesh tells him. "Count on it."

Kannan presses his lips together, and he blinks for a long moment, lowering his head and internalising Rajesh's words. When he opens his eyes again, his expression shifts, away from deep disappointment and into something relatively peaceful. He nods to Rajesh, bowing very slightly. He leaves, following Sharmila out the way he came in.

*

Rajesh Vidyasagar dies two days later, on 31st August 1993. The cause of death is an acute myocardial infarction, his third heart attack.

33
Machine Space

If shorn of its rock embedding and raised up to face sunlight, the listening post would be a twenty-kilometre tall Cambrian organism, a black beetle/rosebud with nested soft shells and creepy greebles. Laura's deathswitch laser tripwire originates at its tail and fires almost directly upwards into the structure's internal organs. The quantity of energy released is unimaginable, enough to punch a hole through kilometres and kilometres of machine space, eventually emerging at a near-vertical angle from the listening post's limb and progressing several klicks further through solid rock, although not far enough to reach the surface.

The base ring room is gone, plasmised along with Natalie and Laura Ferno and the entire nineteen-hundred-metre-wide Montauk storage ring. The Floor room, a hemispherical cavity located towards the top of the listening post, is missed entirely by the laser blast.

By the time the laser shuts off, the vast majority of the released energy has been converted to heat in a plasmised column of air and metal which runs through the post like a lightsaber stab wound. Plasma floods out through the installation's interior spaces, wrecking more than eighty percent of the machinery hosted here over the course of the next second. The destructive wave propagates outwards towards the Floor and the redundant machinery hosted in the relatively few machine spaces above it.

The post's structural integrity is gone. It has seconds to live. On the Floor, which is listing at an angle now, Anil Devi levers himself up on one elbow, to discover that more distant parts of the town-sized ℵ**-class magic circle are buckling upwards, forced apart by rising machines from below, and that the sky is caving in on him, and that all of the Wheel Group have gone.

They're gone. One eyeblink, not even a respectable flash of light or thunderclap, not a dropped spinning trinket in the middle of the D.

Anil shakes some of the stars out of his head and gets a grip. The Wheel Group's chairs are rolling away to the right, out of the main control mandala. Anil has it all to himself now. He plants one hand on the Floor directly below him, and ignores the fact that a billion tonnes of Western Australian continental crust is descending on his head, because this place is over a klick tall and that gives him the luxury of seconds, entire *seconds*.

Anil goes to another place in his head, to the Dehlavi lightning machine. He needs no equipment for this, and barely any words. The mandala is right there beneath him. It was Nat's idea.

They had a whole hour to plan.

Three bolts of lightning fire, and Anil Devi gets out of jail free.

*

The afterlife:

"You shot me in the head."

"Yes. Sorry."

Laura doesn't think this cuts it, either as an explanation or an apology. "You shot me in the fucking head! You killed me!"

Laura and Natalie have incarnated in classic, mundane T-world, an unbounded rolling plain of featureless, colourless marble-glass. The Y-shaped galaxy spins lazily, almost directly over their heads, with star tentacles almost reaching the horizon.

"It didn't kill you," Natalie says. "Right? You knew it wouldn't kill you. You had 'insurance'. Set up to catapult you into Tanako's world at the instant of death, no matter how you died, no matter how suddenly."

"Natalie," Laura carefully explains, "my second death-switch spell was a Death-Star-class laser. When you killed me, you blew up the whole listening post. The physical computer system which hosts T-world was completely destroyed. The insurance is void. You're a maniac, you shot me in the head, and we should be dead! I don't know why we aren't!"

"I blew up *most* of the listening post," Natalie says. "It's a big piece of equipment with plenty of redundancy. We don't have long in real time until the machine ceases to function, but subjective time is optional. We have as much as we want or need. Potentially lifetimes."

"You knew the listening post had that kind of physical redundancy?" Laura says. "You knew my tripwire wasn't powerful enough to blow it up entirely? And you knew you could hitch a ride on my insurance spell and regroup in here afterwards? You were certain of all of these facts?"

"Anil and I worked it out," Natalie states.

"When you said that you were willing to bet your life," Laura asks stonily, "what, exactly, were the odds of that bet?"

Natalie opts not to answer this question.

Laura is going to keep going, but just then a brilliant neon special effect scorches the glass a few steps away from them. Anil Devi arrives sitting bolt upright on the ground, like a sleeper who just reached the end of his nightmare. He arrives shell-shocked and red-eyed, and grabs hold of his casting arm with his other hand to stop it from rattling. "Mother of bloody God."

"I think that's a fair reaction," Laura says.

"It works," Anil says. "I said I wouldn't believe it until I saw it, and now I see it."

"I told you the Iceland story," Natalie reminds him.

"You told me the story," Anil says, "but I didn't *believe* the story. I thought you'd *flipped*. Right up until you pulled the trigger, I honestly didn't think you were going to do it. Mother of God. Mohit Dehlavi has a lot to answer for."

Laura hoists Anil to his feet. "Hello, Anil. How have you been?"

Anil turns three hundred and sixty degrees, taking in the familiar, unrecognisable terrain. He digests the fact that one of him is dead, and meditates briefly on nonlinear lifelines. "I suppose I can't complain."

*

It's not safe to speak while out in the open. The usual electrical buzzing has already begun gathering around them, although corporeal monsters haven't put in an appearance yet. Laura leads them for her memory palace.

They travel by folding and unfolding from hilltop to hilltop, in seven-kilometre steps.

They've been travelling for a subjective "short while" when Laura holds a hand up. There's a reddish-blue figure at the horizon, difficult to pick out in Tanako's world's dull ambient light. He blips to a closer peak, then closer still, then before anybody knows it he's striding up to meet them.

He's a flesh-and-blood human, taller than any of them, with hair that's wandering between brown and blond, and a few centimetres of beard. He wears plate armour made of a red-brown metal which could be burnished copper, and a faded blue cloak with a ragged edge and a tear which almost reaches his shoulder. He carries a sword, which may or may not be magic. He walks with dignity and confidence and extreme tiredness. He looks like the first King of Tanako's world, a king from an era when the throne of the kingdom was the king's saddle, and the capital city was wherever the man was sleeping.

Natalie takes Anil by one arm and steers him back a few steps.

"Nick," Laura says.

"I'm leaving you," Nick says to Laura. "Once this is over I never want to see you again. Clear?"

"Nick, I'm sorry."

"No, you're not," Nick tells her.

"I am!"

"You're not! Don't lie to me! What do you want? From all of this, what did you really, truly want? To find out what Ra is? To converse with a demon and play your elaborate power gambit off against its elaborate power gambit? To resurrect your dear departed super-mage mother? Because all I know for certain, after waiting here in limbo for you, for what feels like *years*, is that the thing you want isn't me."

"I want..."

Nick waits.

Laura draws herself up, clothing herself in armour matching Nick's style. Producing boots, she even rises in height a few centimetres, as if trying to meet Nick as an equal. But she produces no weapon.

"I want us to go into space together," she says.

Nick shakes his head.

"I have the ability now," Laura pleads. She gestures with her arms, demonstrating what she's become. Her stylised armour even resembles a pressure suit in its structure. "I found all the power I need. I can build a spaceship out of light and forcefields. I can take us both into space. Once we're back in reality I can take you to low Earth orbit, it'll take minutes. Seconds. We'll buzz the ISS. You just have to stay close and I'll carry you there. That's what I want."

Nick shakes his head, gently.

Laura pushes all the way through to the answer that Nick wants. "*I* want to go into space," she says.

Nick finally agrees. "*You* want to go into space," he says. "You don't care if I'm there."

"But I... No. I want you to be there when I come back."

"I'm not going to be there," Nick tells her. "I'm leaving."

"I love you," Laura tells him desperately.

Nick says nothing in response, and there is a long and bitter pause.

He looks up, acknowledging Natalie and Anil's presence now that he has spoken his piece. He walks past Laura. "Natalie, good to see you. Sorry you've been dragged into this. You too. I don't think we've met."

"Anil Devi," says Anil Devi. "I used to work with Laura at Hatt Group." Anil is suppressing a churning stomach. The only time he's seen Nick Laughon before, the man was dead in a bath of concentrated hydrogen fluoride, with flesh coming off his face in pieces.

Nick glances off into the distance. "They're amassing," he says. "We've been standing still for too long. You all need to follow me now."

*

They sight the towers first. Laura's memory palace is a sprawling, convoluted grey stone fortress, a senseless mess of differing castle styles. Most of its towers are too tall to be possible and some of them appear to rise forever, narrowing to wires. There are at least four walls, each with numerous sharp-edged bastions, overlapping and interlocking incoherently. The main entrance is a set of black steel double doors tall and wide enough to move an upright Saturn V through, and when Nick knocks on them with the pommel of his sword they barely need to crack to let the four of them in.

Without any further prompting, Natalie leads them across a courtyard and into the castle interior, along a scribbling warren of corridors, rapidly leaving the part of the castle which Nick is familiar with. After another few minutes of navigation Nat reaches a tall, gently winding torchlit corridor full of heavy oak doors, and one particular door, which she unlatches and pushes open.

Nick, Anil and Laura follow her into a tall, bright, echoing hall built from white stone. Nick is instantly put in mind of a cathedral interior, with the same high vaulted ceiling and supporting pillars and bright lighting, although there are no religious decorations. In fact the place is empty. Then, watching Natalie and Laura's reactions, Nick realises that a better word might be *emptied*. Something's not here, which should be here.

"Damn," Natalie says, under her breath.

"It worked," Laura says. "It completely fucking worked! Do you believe this, all of you? This is the empty crypt. I have reversed death. Right now, somewhere over the Atlantic, the *Atlantis* orbiter is burning home, and so is Mum, and so am I. This is what I've been working towards, this entire time. Thirty-three million-to-one mass/energy ratio. Four hundred tonnes of spaceship. One petajoule of mana and done!"

"You were too late," Anil says to Natalie.

Natalie nods, unhappily. "This is what Ra has been working towards, this entire time. This is what I was trying to prevent."

"This was a cooperative rescue spanning multiple decades," Laura says. "Do you know how difficult this was? Together, Mum and I have saved seven astronauts' lives. Not to mention a Space Shuttle orbiter! Those aren't cheap. Once they've got it on the ground it'll even be flightworthy."

Natalie ignores this. "Laura, how do we get to Iceland from here?"

*

The climactic scene at Krallafjöll is stored a few doors down from the *Atlantis* exhibit. This hall is much larger, and so dark that it appears to be endless. At its centre is a tableau which wavers disturbingly between life size and apparent H0 scale.

At the top of the ridge is an instance of Benj Clarke, with whom Nick is acquainted through university. This instance of Benj holds a sphere of weapons-grade plutonium in one hand and a burning hot molybdenum ring in the other, and stands like a warlock, about to end the world by bringing them together. Steps away and necessarily downhill is an instance of Laura, clothed in weighty black robes and aiming a three-metre mercury staff directly at Benj. Green laser light is crawling out of the tip of the staff and across the gap, soon to cut the ring in half and bring all of this to its well-known conclusion.

Further away is an instance of Natalie, supporting a second instance of Benj Clarke. This one is the real man, the one not possessed by a geocidal daemon.

Further away still, the mountain ridge just stops at a hard edge, and drops away. It's as if the scene is nothing more than a big square slice of a thick black cake, iced with lava and dotted with miniature edible people.

"Damn," Natalie says again, when she sees what's missing.

Nick moves through the scene, inspecting each person in turn. The frozen, noticeably younger facial expressions are all faintly ridiculous to behold, and transfixing. Depending where he looks from, his vision blurs like a tilt-shift photograph, giving bizarre depths of field and a sensation that everything he's looking at is tiny compared to him. "What, exactly, is happening here? I obviously never got the whole story out of Laura."

Natalie says, "The instance of Benj at the top of the cliff has been possessed by a hostile entity named Ra. He's trying to start a magical chain reaction which will consume all the geological magic in Iceland, first, and then the entire mid-Atlantic ridge, and potentially the world. I... am not totally certain why, but my top theory is that he's trying to overload the artificial systems which provide magic, by requesting more mu and zeta quanta in one go than they can deliver. That would, or could, *crash* the system, temporarily or permanently suspending standard magic, and maybe leaving the Wheel Group vulnerable.

"Obviously, what actually happens next is that Laura kills him, the reaction ends, the eruption stops and the rest of us go home."

"But there's someone missing," Laura says, staring at her counterpart. "There was a glass figure standing right here, next to me. Somebody almost invisible. The figure was helping me. Remember?"

"The glass figure was Ra," Natalie says.

"It was Mum," Laura says. "She was helping me to stop Benj from blowing the world up—"

"It was Ra," Natalie says. "If you remember, the figure was pushing your staff to the ground. He was trying to *protect* Benj."

"Who's Ra?" Nick asks. "What is this word that keeps coming around and around?"

"Ra is a machine inside the Sun," Anil says.

"No," Natalie says.

"Ra is Kazuya Tanako," Laura says.

"No, I told you, penamba was Kazuya Tanako." When Natalie uses the word, she exhales greenish-blue air, which she waves away with her hands. "Ra is..."

She hesitates, marshalling her thoughts. There's a lot of data, more than she can track concurrently. Instinct tells her she can't voice this theory yet, because she doesn't have enough sigmas of certainty. Instinct tells her to keep it to herself until she can gather more evidence to support it.

She fights this instinct.

She looks at Laura and, separately, Nick. "Ra is a malevolent artificial intelligence whose goal is to dismantle the Earth and turn it into computronium. Actual human beings are orthogonal to this goal. If we all die in the disassembly, which we will, Ra doesn't care—"

"Natalie," Anil explains patiently, "Ra was reprogrammed."

"Ra is a distributed system consisting of more individual listener nodes than I can even put an order of magnitude to," Natalie says. "They saturate the whole world, from top to bottom. Something like one human out of every two trillion survived the war, against odds that were astronomical. What happens when you apply those same odds to the listeners? Even squaring the odds, how much of the original objective do you think survived? And how much needed to?

"Ra wasn't reprogrammed. Not all of it."

*

Nick takes them to a small, quiet, dark room with rugs and substantial chairs, and a fireplace, and fiery drinks in very small glasses. The room is not one that Laura recognises, but it is relatively well-realised and detailed. It seems that this is the part of the castle where Nick has been living.

Anil and Laura toss their drinks back almost immediately. Nick takes his sword off to sit, and sips. Natalie sits uneasily, and seems not to notice the drink at all. Unconsciously, she and Anil are developing armour matching Laura and Nick's.

"There was a war," Natalie recounts. "By the 194th century the human race had achieved near-perfect science and omnipotent technology. We had installed an energy production system called Ra at the core of the Sun, and we were using that energy to build and maintain tens of thousands of inhabited Earths.

"Towards the end of the century, the Ra system turned against its creators. There was a war, called Abstract War. The war lasted seven days, and ended with Ra reprogrammed and docile, but with very nearly every single living human dead. The survivors, numbering barely more than two hundred out of what had been millions of millions, formed the Wheel Group. The world we live in is the new world that they built, replacing the wreckage of the old. 'Magic' is a layer of abstraction which the Wheel Group introduced on top of their nonlocality technology to make it safer to use. And this year is one-nine-four-two-four."

"That's a five-digit number," Nick says.

"Yes," Natalie says, blankly.

"I'm just saying. This is word salad to me. It doesn't mean anything."

"The war was fought over processing power," Natalie says. "Ra's objective was, and still is, to dismantle the rocky planets of the inner solar system and construct a stellar engine called a Matrioshka brain. This would be a constellation of sun-powered computer processors which would completely enclose the Sun, increasing Ra's processing power by a factor of ten.

"Ra had been reprogrammed by a faction of humans called Virtual Humanity—"

"This is bull," Laura says, unable to sit still and just listen. She gets up and paces, throwing another drink back.

"Compared to what?" Natalie says. "Compared to what Ra taught you?"

"His name is Kazuya Tanako! What you're calling 'nonlocality' is just a deeper form of magic, 'māyā'. Māyā was stolen from humanity at large in the earliest days of human civilisation, at about the same time as the invention of writing. The Wheel Group stole it. They are immortal, omnipotent, lazy gods, pursuing thousand-year-long lifetimes of meaningless hedonism in a world which they deliberately fail to lift higher than gutter-level. What we call 'magic' is a single crumb from their table, and we only have it because the alternative is for māyā to run riot and fall into the hands of us baselines."

There's a pause.

"Those stories aren't entirely inconsistent with one another," Anil says.

Laura is circling the room's walls, kicking the parts which Nick has dreamt up in good detail, filling in the parts he hasn't with improved stonework and beams. By now she's behind Natalie. "He never mentioned a war to me," she says.

"Of course he wouldn't," Natalie says, "why would Ra cast itself as the aggressor?"

"This story," Laura says, "makes no more sense than—"

"It makes no sense," Nick says, at which point somebody knocks on the door, and everybody freezes.

They freeze for long enough that whoever is at the door becomes impatient and knocks again.

"I can convince you," Natalie says to Laura, who is still the only one standing.

Laura blinks. "What?"

"Monsters can't get into this place," Nick says, "the fortifications alone—"

"Monsters don't *knock*," Anil says.

Solemnly, Natalie picks up her drink and downs it. "It's for you, Laura. You should answer it."

"Who is it?" Laura asks her. And then aloud, "Who the fuck is that?"

Whoever-it-is tries the door handle, but the door is locked. Nick stands, unsheathing his sword. Anil searches himself for weapons, finds nothing and tries to imagine some, but gets nowhere.

"Answer the door, Laura," Natalie says, still not rising or even turning to look at the door.

"Who is it?" Laura steps forward and releases the lock, but then steps back again, aiming an armful of thaumic weaponry at it. She's in Tanako's world, magic doesn't work here. She isn't thinking clearly enough to realise.

The door opens outward, and behind it is another version of Laura Ferno. She wears a dark, form-fitting NASA-esque flight suit, and a golden gauntlet on her left forearm, and is surrounded by weak fragments of neon light, like reflections from shattered stained glass. She stands with dropped shoulders, breathing poorly. Her eyes and face are all wrong, nothing like what Laura is used to seeing in the mirror. *Haggard,* Laura thinks. *She's haggard.*

"He killed me," says the apparition.

"What?"

"Whatever Nat is telling you is the truth," says the apparition. "Whatever we know is a lie. Nat is right, and we were wrong." She takes a step forward.

"Stay the *hell* back," Laura Ferno says, backing up, catching one heel on a rug and falling. She looks up for long enough to see that nobody in the room is moving to help her. Natalie still hasn't moved, and Nick and Anil just seem to be entranced. Furious and alone, Laura points two fingers at the alternate Laura and says "Dulaku surutai jiha—" Nothing comes out except red and purple smoke.

The apparition strides through the smoke. It grasps Laura's outstretched hand, and vanishes.

The door closes, and there are four of them again.

"I heard the footsteps coming," Natalie admits. "I worked it out a few seconds before she knocked."

Laura gets her breathing under control, coughing at the smoke, processing the new clutch of memories. "I brought Mum and everyone back. And I brought the glass man back. But the glass man was— He didn't even look me in the eye. It was like I didn't exist to him. He's going to end the world." She coughs again, eyes watering. "Kazuya murdered me. Fuck!"

"It wasn't Kazuya Tanako," Natalie says, for the final time. "Ra used you. And he didn't kill you. You're still alive."

34
It Has To Work

There's an invisible penthouse in the sky over the East River in New York, New York, and more than a hundred people have just materialised there simultaneously. It's the entire Wheel.

"Give me my God-damned *kara* back," Adam King hisses, still pinned face down by Exa, although now in golden and scarlet deep-pile carpet.

"You're done, Adam," Exa declares. He jabs a particular bundle of nerves in the back of King's skull, and the man flops unconscious.

They're in the ballroom, with a window showing almost all of the city skyline, which is dominated by the pattern of terrifying red high-energy magic warning signs. They're holographic, tiling the whole atmosphere of Earth, and kilometres long on each side. "What's happening to the sky?" someone asks. "Is this global? Everybody in the world can see this!"

"Ra is waking," Casaccia gasps, his medring resurrecting him with all the finesse of a boot to the stomach. "This was never supposed to happen. This was supposed to be impossible."

Murmurs spread. The mood in the room starts its descent from abject panic into deep horror. The same Wheel member asks, "What do you mean, 'waking'?"

"I mean," Casaccia says, "this spell is the one which fires when someone has started giving Ra direct orders again. This is the spell which tells everybody on this planet that their planet is done for. Ra is coming. Ra is here. It's over."

There's a dead pause.

"Flatt," Exa says.

Flatt takes a second to even realise he's being addressed. "What?"

"King is out of commission," Exa tells him. "This is a live incident, operational control passes to you. What happens next?"

Flatt is silent for a heart-stopping moment, a rabbit in headlights.

"Do we fight Ra?" Exa prompts.

"What?"

"*Do I have to fight Ra again?*"

"I— I don't know. Caz?"

"What happens next is already happening," Casaccia says. He doesn't even need to check systems to know. "We're out of here. The emergency deep nonlocal transmitter is already coming up to power. We'll be able to boost one of us out of here every two seconds. We're leaving the star system."

"But that means—"

"Yes, it means Abstract War is over. Actual Earth is over. We lost."

*

Shorn of its rock embedding and raised up to face sunlight, the listening post is a twenty-kilometre tall Cambrian organism caught at the instant of self-destruction, crumpling up from below, collapsing from above and exploding red and napalm orange from the inside. Less than a sixth of its machinery is still operational, all in the top sixth of the installation. The installation's internal representation of itself stands on a thin whittled pillar of glass rock in T-world, frozen in the act of crashing and burning.

They travel there by space rocket. Laura builds the space rocket for them while they watch. None of the others are able to help, or so she tells them.

The journey is brief, but eventful. They meet several shells of airborne zombie defence, and meet them hard, with fire and kinetic projectile weaponry. For the final approach, in the absence of a functional landing pad, Laura pilots the vehicle up in a long loop, then dives down into the brilliant wound in the top of the listening post, the near-vertical magma-venting fissure.

They arrive at the akashic records office, the hypercylindrical hall from which the records themselves can be queried, with the Earth at its centre. From here, the listening post's own internal configuration and status are free to examine. The listening post reports that it will continue to operate almost normally for another zero point four seconds of real time, before the final critical power supplies are severed by creeping physical damage. At that moment, the post will instantly cease operation, and the entire dream experience will cut out and end forever.

A digital countdown of the remaining time is provided. It runs to six decimal places of a second, and for as long as Laura, Nat, Nick and Anil watch it, it doesn't move. They have all the time in the world.

*

Natalie takes control of the main display, and finds the scene of the showdown. There are major icons in different shades, nailed to the sky with the black Atlantic and the livid red sky as their backdrop, and numerous attendant minor particles. Nat collects information from multiple overlaid sources at once, tuning the display to show as much metadata as she thinks the others can handle without their eyes crossing. She breathes deeply.

"So here's the situation.

"This is the Glass Man, and these are his shields. He's nearly invincible, and close to invisible. He's already killed Laura once, and he defeated Mum in a straight fight, resisting a volley of energy and projectile attacks without any apparent effort.

"*This* is Laura's and my mother, Rachel Ferno. She is the Glass Man's most wanted, because she was the one who originally defeated Old Ra at the conclusion of Abstract War. The Glass Man has broken her mind open. She's been vivisected. What I mean is, she's alive. For now."

A third icon floats above the heads of both Rachel and the Glass Man. A blue thread links it to Rachel's head, and a green thread links it to the Glass Man's. "This is the Bridge," Natalie says. "It... seems to move information around."

"From anywhere to anywhere," Laura explains. "From reality into Tanako's world. From Tanako's world into reality. From reality to reality— teleportation. From your mind into reality and back again. That's how I brought Mum and *Atlantis* back. Ordinarily, it would take an insane amount of mana to do that. The Bridge made it trivial."

Anil makes impressed sounds. "You can just bring anything out of the akashic records and into reality?"

"Yeah. Including any of the Wheel Group's destroyed *astra*s. Bhārīvastra, Metaph, Abstract Weapon. Of course, once the records are destroyed, four tenths of a second from now, that functionality goes away, but that's why we were gunning for it, above all else. That's why it's theoretically more powerful than any other *astra*. That's *probably* why it was never destroyed along with the others."

"Adam King," Natalie murmurs.

"Adam God-damned King," Anil says, clenching a fist.

"So this is the Bridge, and the Glass Man's got it," Natalie says. She indicates a much smaller, orange piece of data which has been placed just beside the Glass Man's head. "Using it, he's gone into Mum's head and retrieved this piece of information. This is the key. Mum locked Ra away using a key. Without the key, Ra is a docile energy-production system which responds only to indirect commands made through the medium of magic. With the key in your hand, you can ask Ra to do anything. Literally anything."

"So he was invincible to start with," Nick recaps. "And then he got the Bridge, which made him invincible and close to omnipotent. And now he has unfettered access to Ra, which means he's absolutely, totally invincible, omnipotent and limited only by the speed of thought? I have that right?"

Natalie is ignoring him as she zooms out. And out. And out. The virtual Earth shrinks to the size of an apple. The orbit of the Moon contracts into view, an elliptical cyan thread with the Moon itself a grey bead threaded onto it.

Beyond the Moon's orbit, crawling through deep space towards the Sun, there's an elongated purple speck. Its icon oscillates, representing a nonlocality "radio" wave packet. Indigo metadata shows its outbound speed — precisely c — its projected time of arrival, and its payload. The payload is a request for a particular quantity of energy, but the number is unreadable. It's a nonsense number, from the wasteland beyond the reach of SI prefixes, where human notions of scale and proportion cease to function.

"And here's what he asked for," Natalie says. "Thirty-five digits. Forty-six decillion joules. That's enough energy to laser this planet into shreds. The energy packet returns to Earth in sixteen minutes and twenty-five point seven five seconds, real time. And by the way: faster-than-light travel is impossible.

"The Glass Man's had time for exactly one move. We get to make the second. We can re-enter reality anywhere in the world we want. Once we're real again we get exactly one shot at fixing this.

"And it has to be one shot, because then we're back into real time. In the next point four seconds, the listening post completes its detonation, and Tanako's world is gone forever, along with everything and everyone who was ever stored here. No more retrieving people and artifacts from the history of magic, no more accelerated planning, no more 'life insurance' safety net, no more getting out of jail free. Okay? So: go."

She folds her arms and waits expectantly. And for a long time, nobody says anything.

Anil recalls a flock of empty office chairs. "Where are the Wheel in all of this? We should have words."

Natalie locates the penthouse and studies the curious radiant mana patterns of the evacuation megaspell. "They're leaving the world. We're on our own."

"Cowards," Laura judges. "They'd better run, and they'd better hope we never catch them. Whatever happens next, this is our world. They've kept it in the gutter for long enough. We'll build something incredible."

"Can we hijack their evacuation spell?" Anil asks.

"It would need thirteen million times as much broadcast power," Natalie says.

"In that case it's simple. Escape is impossible. We're stuck on Earth. We can't exceed the speed of light. We can't catch up with the request and destroy it — if that even means anything — and we can't send a cancellation order that'll arrive before the original request does. The original request *will* reach the Sun, and the energy will come back down the channel. It is logically impossible, in this universe, to prevent any of these things from happening."

Natalie nods.

"So we're dead," Anil concludes.

"Ra's not going to shine a planet-destroying laser down on us," Natalie says. "The energy packet is... more like a thrown baseball, and the baseball contains all of the requested energy. There's a receiver at the core of the Earth. If the receiver doesn't catch the packet, it just keeps going, to the edge of space, forever."

"Oh? Then we have some options," Anil says, cheering up. "Can we shunt the Earth out of the packet's way? Physically?" He ignores Laura as she snorts and Nick as he gives a brief, genuine laugh, both of them failing to understand the seriousness of the suggestion. "Or just the receiver alone? How big is it?"

"Kilometres wide," Laura says.

"Can we destroy it?"

"Them," Natalie says, punching up the core node's blueprints and throwing a copy at Anil. "There are eight of them. Heavy redundancy. I told you."

"And they're made of nearly solid tungsten steel," Laura says. "And even if we could get there, there's no magic at the Earth's core. We'd have to find a way to destroy them without using magic. In less than two minutes and four seconds per receiver."

"It would be a stopgap solution, in any case," Nat says. "Ra would perceive the damage and route around it. At best, we'd buy another sixteen-minute round trip, during which Ra would certainly incapacitate us to prevent more interference."

Anil leans forward, studying the core node's engineering and lapsing into the same problem-solving thought process he uses in his aerospace work. "Okay. So let's put planetary-scale engineering in the 'maybe' pile. We can't fight Ra where it lives. Can we retask it? If we tell Ra to ignore the Matrioshka brain order, what happens?"

"Ah," Laura says, realising where this is going.

Natalie studies her version of the blueprints a little more closely. "The energy still arrives on schedule, but... as long as the second order reaches the Earth's core before the energy packet does, the packet gets cached safely. After a little while, it's deemed surplus to requirements and transmitted back into the Sun."

"Let's skip to the end. I'm going to fight this guy," Laura says. "That's how we get the key back and retask Ra. You need me to carry out forcible brain surgery on the omnipotent Glass Man. Once I've got the key, everything's fine." She cracks a few knuckles, remembering with extreme clarity the split second of red-hot agony that accompanied her death by vaporisation. The spellwork to pay the Man back is already forming in her head. "That icon is the same as Mum's. The Glass Man is physically human. All I've got to do is keep his brain intact and shield Mum from the backlash. Invincible he might be, but I bet I can find a crowbar that'll open him up."

"There are four of us here, Laura," Nick reminds her. "We can fight."

"I'm the one who can fly," Laura says, casually waving Nick away without looking, as if dismissing a fly from near her ear. "I'm the one who fights with sticks."

"I 'fight with sticks'," Nick says, "and I'm better at it than you, at that."

"But you can't fly, and you can't do magic, and I'm the one with Recursion's Big Brother on my side. It's all on me. Right? Worry not. It's easy. Once we zap back into reality, you're all going to stand on some beach in Titusville watching the fireworks, while I take this Glass Man out. Solo."

"In one second," Anil adds.

Laura blinks. "What?"

"It's his second move. It has to be. How long has this man been working up to this? Decades. He must have his moves worked out. Move one: reconstruct the Matrioshka brain. And then he needs to make as bloody sure as sure can ever be that nobody can stop it. That doesn't mean fortifications or personal armaments. This is Old Ra, he's plural, he's expendable. He doesn't care about his physical self and thanks to the Bridge he doesn't need Ra's power to defend himself if he does. Move two: *destroy the key*.

"He's already had all of one point four five seconds to do it, and it's a miracle that he hasn't followed through in that time. I give you, Laura, a generous further one second to intervene."

"One second?"

"To distract him or render him unconscious."

Laura curses. She stares at the ground, running hypotheses. "Yeah. Okay. I can do that. That means I'll have to reincarnate right there in front of the Man. In the middle of the sky. No. Behind him, and catch him by surprise... That's actually easier than a direct assault. If I can find the right spell... Hmm. One second."

"Less," Natalie says. "Potentially much less. I give you half that. He could be destroying the key already. He should be. I would be."

"Then it's a reflex action," Laura decides. "I'll be ready for it, and he won't. I can definitely hit him with *something* in half a second."

"And that isn't taking into account speed-of-light transit time between where we are and where he is," Anil adds. "Transmitting you from here to there takes ninety milliseconds. We also don't know how long it takes to nanoassemble a fresh human at reincarnation time."

"Okay."

"In fact, these displays are necessarily out of date. For all we know, the key destruction instruction is already on its way here. And there's nothing we can do about that. Your window of action could be as small as zero."

Laura slumps, angered. "Okay, you've made your point. It's worse than impossible."

"If the key's destroyed," Anil reminds her, "it becomes genuinely, logically impossible for us to win."

"Stop talking," Laura shouts, belatedly remembering that she and Anil never got on particularly well. "Shut up for one second, so I can think!"

*

She disappears on foot into the interior of the listening post's listening post, saying something about needing preparation time. Preparation time is abundant, so no one moves to stop her.

"I don't like this," Nick says to the others.

"Do you think she does?" Anil asks.

"That's not it," Nick says. "She can do it."

"You think so? I give her one chance in four, and that's if we can get her confidence back up to 'supreme'."

"And thank you for that, by the way," Nick says.

Anil doesn't follow. "For what?"

"She can do it," Natalie echoes. To Nick, "You're worried about what happens when she wins."

"Because then she's got the key," Nick says. "*She* becomes omnipotent, invincible and limited only by the speed of thought. She threw herself into this nightmare in the first place because she has serious and radical designs on the future. I don't trust her with the key. I don't trust myself with the key. Or anyone. The key shouldn't exist. You're right, Anil, and the Glass Man's right. It should be destroyed."

Anil shrugs. "We need moves of our own worked out, then. Like, a script."

"She countermands the Matrioshka brain order, then destroys the key," Natalie says. "One and two. As fast as possible, the end. Nothing else, no excuses."

"What about rescuing your mother?" Anil asks. "What if the Glass Man's still alive at that point? What about the Wheel Group?"

"There's enough material to improvise the rest of that," Natalie says. "We'll have the Bridge. We'll have a lot of options. The Wheel Group are in retreat, anyway. We can teleport Mum to a hospital."

"A hospital?" Anil chokes off an unhappy laugh. "Have you looked at her medical chart?"

"Erm. No."

Anil drags the relevant readout into the middle of the three of them, blown up to double life size. The schematic is disconcerting enough, but the full flesh-and-blood hologram is so grotesque that Nat won't look at it directly. Rachel Ferno has slots in her skull, her face and the back of her neck. There are flat metal rods inserted into the slots, running all the way through her head, and barbs spreading from the rods, and electrodes worming out of the barbs into her brain centres. The text of the pages-long diagnosis is full of frightening terminology like "nanoactive cerebrospinal contamination" and "severe hypothalamic damage", and gives her a projected lifetime measured in minutes and seconds.

"It's bad," Nick says.

"She's beyond the reach of twenty-first century medical science," Anil says. "She needs a Wheel Group medring."

"I thought she was Wheel Group," Nick says.

"Ex-Wheel," Nat says. "She never had a medring. Not that Laura and I ever saw, anyway."

"Then we can catch them before they evacuate," Nick suggests. "They'll help one of their own."

"Again, ex-Wheel. And we want to avoid that."

"Badly enough to risk your mother's life?"

Natalie says nothing.

"Hang on a second," Anil says, as a thought strikes him. He goes over to the main display and scoops up another handful of data. He hunts purposefully through it for a few seconds, then flicks the readout with a triumphant finger. "We can avoid it," he announces. "I know where there's a non-Wheel medring. Damn, that's sweet. 'Lucky charm' my lucky arse."

At which moment Natalie bursts out laughing.

"What's the joke?"

"Not what you said," Natalie cackles. She points at the display behind him. "I just worked something out. We need the key, right?"

"Sure."

Natalie plucks the data out of the visualisation and holds it in her hand. "We've got the key. We don't need the Bridge. We don't need to fight anybody. It's right here."

*

Laura overhears most of the 'confidence' discussion, and that just spurs her to keep jogging into the warren of blackness. The conversation never totally fades behind her, but becomes smeared out and unintelligible. The listening post's internal corridors are tall and narrow, with rectangular cross-sections and weak orange-yellow pinpricks of lights overhead. The floor is glossy black, reflecting the overhead lights to give a worryingly vertiginous effect.

When she realises that sounds are coming from ahead of her too, she stops walking. Conscious of the metallic clanking her armour makes even when she tries to remain still, she dismisses it in favour of the black flight suit.

A lanky young man turns the corner. His hair is black and arranged in misshapen spikes. He's barefoot, wearing a cheap, faded black T-shirt from some decade-ago rock concert, and loose shorts. Sleepwear.

"Ah, *mou jikan desu ka?*" he says to her.

Laura freezes, thinking six things at once.

It's impossible, one thread of her consciousness tells her. *I mean, it's possible, but it's been years of real time. Subjective centuries, at minimum. Could he really have been trapped here for this entire time?*

Ra

The stranger cocks his head and seems to guess, correctly, that Laura understands no Japanese. He tries a different, more common language: "`Penamba eset.`" Coloured specks of light float out of his mouth as he uses each syllable.

He takes a step forward.

Laura takes a step backward.

Who else could be trapped here? Laura's mind burbles. *Should we try to scan all of T-world for more survivors? Imagine that! The* real *Kazuya Tanako!*

But finally the other half of her mind, the half that's gradually bootstrapping itself out of starry-eyed cluelessness, grabs her by the throat and screams *FUCKING RUN*—

And she skids and finds traction on the black slab, and runs—

*

Natalie set herself a script, and she goes about obeying it to the letter. She closes her fist around the key, presses it to her forehead, and whispers, "Do what I mean." When she opens it, the display behind her shifts a little, displaying new icons on the far side of the world, clustered around the imploding listening post.

The holographic Earth display now shows, in abstract but not entirely unreadable terms, that the Earth-destruction order has been cancelled, and that Ra is under Natalie's effective unilateral control.

It's that simple.

"Are you sure you want to destroy the key now?" Nick says. "There's a long list of other things that you could fix very easily if you wanted to."

"I know," Natalie says. She finds the decision to relinquish the power surprisingly easy. The lack of temptation is almost eerie. "It's too bad for us. We'll have to do some things the hard way."

She looks up, hearing running footsteps, as do the others. Laura arrives at a dead sprint, and skids to a halt.

"Kazuya Tanako's here," she gasps. "What the hell's that? Is that the key?"

The being imitating Tanako is indeed there, standing right behind Laura, apparently having circumvented the long sprint.

"Oh, *shit*," Anil says.

Natalie closes her fist reflexively. Too slow; her fist closes on nothing, and when she opens it again there's nothing. Not-Tanako's got the key. It's luminous orange, unmissable. He didn't even need to cross the room. Nat sees it, Nick sees it, Anil sees it. Laura whirls and sees it.

Nick's the only one of them with a weapon. Laura screams, "Nick, kill him!" and he's already drawing. Natalie stretches her will out, trying to repossess the key using the same trick, but nothing happens. The order falls into blank space.

Not-Tanako reinstates the Earth-destruction order.

Nick launches himself at Tanako, sword point first. Four steps separate them. Laura dives to one side, out of his way.

Natalie shouts at everybody, "Plan A!"

By the end of "Plan" the Tanako facsimile has destroyed the key forever, with a blunt *crack* like a gunshot through plate glass. A red translucent X floats where the key was for a few frames, then flickers out.

At "A", still cheerfully ignoring the approaching sword, Not-Tanako is gesturing at the big seven-segment readout, and all the numbers have snapped over to zeroes.

Nick finds his mark. Not-Tanako dies cleanly, stabbed through the heart. The listening post floods with illogic and boiling magma, and expires. The ground drops out from beneath all of their feet,

*

and they're in freefall at nothing A.M. over the red-black Atlantic, and the Glass Man is on top of them, firing.

35
This Can't Happen

Laura doesn't have time for disorientation or indecision. The universe is half black and half red, rolling around her like some demonic Macintosh mouse ball, furious wind is rising in her ears, there's an organ-rearranging urge to vomit— all of this is irrelevant. "Tanako" got the drop on her, again. The last time, she vows. It's the end of the world. *Plan A. Beat the Glass Man.*

She powers all the way up to her phoenix form, full aerospace mobility with a twelve-metre wingspan. Dynamic pressure hammers into her wings, slowing her corkscrew roll. Purple crosshairs flash across her HUD, highlighting the mana output from Nat, Anil and even Nick. Far below them all, Rachel Ferno is a paralysed, dying blip, and the Bridge is outputting a weird alien helix of red and blue. But all the blips are dwarfed by the tornado of leaky force shields which represents the Glass Man.

Laura folds her wings around herself, aims her engines at the sky and dives. One second and she's past the other three. One point five and she's through the peregrine falcon's record, officially the fastest-moving animal on Earth.

The Glass Man looks up. Laura is the brightest thing in the sky, unmistakeable in both the optical and thaumic spectra. He raises a hand to fire. But Laura's coming back to the fight with the bones of a plan, which starts like this: *He's human. Humans need to see.* She beats him to the trigger, blinding him pre-emptively with magnesium-white light. His first shot misses. It's a drill spell, pushing a rifled cylindrical force field through the air, a gunshot minus the gun and the bullet. It cracks the air open like a hollow thunderbolt. Laura vectors sideways as hard as she can while still closing the gap. Closing his eyes and going thaumic, the Glass Man fires twice more at the luminous being bearing down on him. The second shot grazes Laura's hull, doing no obvious damage but sapping almost all of its structural energy. The third punches directly through her left wing, destroying it and gouging a channel of flesh out of her physical shoulder. Laura howls, more in shock than in pain, as adrenaline cushions almost all of the injury. She staggers in the air, losing her streamlining and starting to roll out of control. She fights it with thrusters, but it isn't enough to recover.

The Glass Man shrugs, scolding himself lightly for wasting time on pointless projectile combat. He reaches out with his other hand, forming a claw grip, as if grasping some invisible throat. Then, he simply teleports Laura into the appropriate gap, discarding her hawk form and all of her momentum.

Laura chokes. At this heart rate, the lack of oxygen is immediately life-threatening. She feels pressure in her head rising, as if blood is about to start forcing its way out of her tear ducts. The Glass Man's "glasswork" follows the contours of his face so closely that Laura can almost see the curled lip, the single eyebrow raised in grudging admiration. The Bridge, floating obediently behind him, simmers down from the sudden activity, fading in colour from actinic purple to nominal dull red.

"Back from backup, hmm?"

Laura manages to grind out an unintelligible sound. She latches onto the Man's wrist with one hand, pulling futilely. Charitably, he relaxes his grip by just a fraction, granting her enough air to spit out an epitaph.

"Anhtnaa vaeka."

Her self-defence spell fires from the hip, scything up from her other hand into the Man's midsection, crossing his armpit and face. There's a screech like steel across granite across glass. The Glass Man turns his head aside for a second, as if in a light breeze. Then he turns back, unscratched.

And now, says the smug little voice in Laura's head, which is even starting to *sound* like the Glass Man, *it's over.*

Laura begins to black out. She relaxes and lets it happen, because whether she's won or not isn't up to her anymore.

And the Bridge, with its braid cleanly severed, falls out of the Glass Man's control.

He notices, after that one moment. He even starts to turn. Too late.

It's Anil who catches the Bridge, landing on it at a relative speed of more than a hundred and fifty kilometres per hour. Without shock absorption, the impact would break him in half, but he's wearing a shield which Laura — through half-closed eyes that are rolling back — recognises, one she wrote herself years back, EPTRO. The Bridge plugs itself enthusiastically into

Anil's brain, and he disappears, too quickly for the Glass Man to loose a shot at him. For a second, there's no further movement.

"What—" the Glass Man begins.

A Montauk ring clunks into existence around his neck.

His firestorm of magic caves in on itself. The mana is all sucked into storage. His shields collapse, including the reinforced armour field which was gripping Laura by the throat, and the light-negative layer. Behind it, he's just another immaculately-suited Wheel Group-esque male, same ideal jawline, same piercing blue eyes. His flight spells evaporate and he and Laura fall away from one another. He clutches the ring at his throat with both hands, but it's too small to come off. His face is a picture of perplexed shock.

Laura, rubbing the circulation back into her own throat, thinks he looks like he doesn't understand how the fight ended this way, so soon. Like he wants more time, to work those seconds out again.

*

They materialise on the emergency runway at Cape Kennedy, with a nominal flash of blue-red lightning. Anil immediately drops to his knees beside Rachel Ferno. She has arrived lying down, with enough metalwork embedded in her head that it props her up. Blood, black under the pervasive red light of the global warning signs, is pulsing weakly out of the fresh wounds in her skull and dribbling down the wires. Some of it begins to spread across the runway surface. Her fingers twitch.

Anil summons Ed Hatt's *kara* and slots the ring over Rachel's right hand. "There is no reason why this shouldn't work," he says, the closest thing he has to a prayer. Nick kneels alongside Anil and feels for Rachel's pulse, the rest of his limited first aid knowledge effectively useless here. Natalie and Laura hang back. Laura is dealing with her own injuries, and Natalie can't stomach the sight.

(Thousands of miles away, Hatt clutches at a sudden empty spot at his wrist. He is standing dumbfounded at his office window, staring at the impossible red holograms which tessellate across the entire sky. He knows what the warning signs signify, but he has no idea how to react to this information. High energy magic? How high? Is something going to explode? Is it the *world*?)

"Are we absolutely sure that this is a Wheel Group medical ring?" Nick asks.

"One thousand percent sure," Anil says. "Ed Hatt wasn't Wheel, he didn't know how to use it. But she does."

"But she's nearly dead. Seven-eighths dead."

"Doesn't matter. It can work. It has to work." Anil stares into Rachel's pierced, blind eyeballs for a second. He curses sharply and checks his wristwatch. "I lost track of time. It must have been sixty seconds already."

The ring evaporates. A thin wisp of smoke curls up in front of them all, glittering red, then dissipates into the breeze coming off the ocean.

Rachel Ferno exhales, and that's the end.

Laura blinks. "What just happened?"

"I. I don't know," Anil says. He invents hopelessly, not daring to turn and look either Ferno sister in the eye. "A permissions issue or a s-special case or something. You said she was ex-Wheel, she never had a ring? Maybe she was never meant to have a ring, maybe they set it up so that she— couldn't ever use—"

Nick drops Rachel's wrist and instead feels at the side of her throat. There's nothing there either. "She's dead."

There's a long, chilly, bitter silence.

Now.

"So what else was there?" Anil asks anybody who's listening, trying to conceal his cracking nerve. "Because, ah. With fifteen minutes left to work, I was really banking everything on Rachel Ferno magically fixing this for us, if you'll excuse the expression."

"You said something about moving the Earth?" Nick offers, desperately.

Anil glances at Natalie. She is shaking her head, and without any verbal communication the two of them arrive at a solid shared conclusion: for mundane mages, with mundane amounts of mana, under such absurd time constraints, it's absolutely futile.

Now. Do it.

Laura shakes herself free of Natalie and takes the Bridge. A rectilinear chunk of dark metal, it has off-puttingly little mass, as if made of steel-plated helium. Eager to be put to work, its connecting cables unthread themselves from the side of Anil's head and bond with Laura's once more.

"There was a Man made of Glass," she says. "He won't even have hit the water yet." She turns and strides down the axis of the dark runway, delivering two commands into the Bridge and then releasing it to take up station behind her shoulder. The deep gouge in that shoulder is forgotten. She flexes her hands.

"Laura?" Natalie turns, detecting an anticipatory growl in her sister's voice. It makes sense to her to summon the Glass Man back, perhaps there's some desperate final gambit there, an outside chance that he still hasn't destroyed his copy of the key, but Natalie realises just too late that this is not at all what Laura is thinking. "Laura, DON'T—"

Laura raises two hands high above her head and summons her mother's magic staff, a thin, two-metre rod of heavy steel. The Glass Man appears ahead of her, stumbling, suddenly reoriented, still with the Montauk ring wrapped around his neck. He finds his footing and looks up and Laura convinces herself she can see his pupils narrow to pinpricks in the split second before she brings the end of the rod down on the top of his skull.

He breaks open with a black splatter and a sick crumbling noise; he plunges chin-first into the asphalt. Laura waits a second for the corpse's limbs to settle, then pulls the staff clear from its resting place, just above the bridge of the Man's nose, and hits him a second time, scattering more matter.

"Oh, Jesus," Anil says.

"She's lost it," Nick says, transfixed.

And a third time.

"Laura, that's enough!" Natalie shouts.

Laura turns. Her eyes might as well be on fire. "She's dead, Nat."

"I know."

"He killed her. It's over. Are *you* happy, now?"

"No." Nat is almost unreadable; she's devoting all her concentration to not looking directly at the remnants of Laura's work, and blotting out the fleeting moment of partial recognition. She holds a hand out. "Give me the Bridge."

"We're going to die today, Nat," Laura cries. "We've got nothing else." She winces and clutches her shoulder again as the injury reasserts itself. There's blood soaking all the way down to her wrist now. She didn't notice. She drops the staff.

"Yes," Natalie says. "We lost. Now, for the love of God, give control of this thing to someone with the *faintest fucking* idea what she's doing."

Laura hesitates for an uncomprehending moment. She doesn't know what there is left to do. Dumbly, shaking her head, she hands the Bridge over to Natalie. Nat inspects the artifact for the first time, turns it over, toys with the cables. She seems to find it to be to her satisfaction.

Anil checks his watch again. "I give us twelve minutes and change."

Nat closes her eyes for just a second. She can see where she needs to go now, the best guess. It's not a good guess, and maybe a year or ten from now she'll wake up in the middle of the night with a stabbing realisation that there was a scintillatingly obvious route to salvation standing in front of them the whole time. But she boxes that reaction up, and stacks it with all of the others.

"When the sky clears," she says, "that will mean you can stop counting." She disappears.

36
Free

Exa Watson stands at the bay window, sipping from a glass of the finest whisky that's ever existed, watching the city of New York melt down under emergency lighting which makes it look like Hell on Earth. Every three or so seconds another *whump* of white light is a Wheel Group member leaving the world, being transformed into a superamplified state vector and beamed out of the Sol system towards Sirius. The energy usage is colossal; it has to be, to guarantee clear reception at the far end. The whole planet Earth is being run dry of magic to do it. There are maybe sixty Wheel members left, and they're clustered in resigned groups, mostly doing the same as Exa, sampling some final priceless vice. The atmosphere is thick and black, something beyond mere total defeat.

Exa holds his glass in one hand and with the other he frets with his *kara*. It would have been the simplest thing in the world to lodge all of this deeply magical medical capability directly in the brain of each Wheel member, and to forget it existed, and for all of them to just press on with a future life with no consequence or defined final destination. But the *kara* inherits from the Doctor and its purpose is to serve as a constant reminder:

That they won Abstract War, but not by any sensible, numerical measure. (History's written by whoever lives long enough to write the result down, and they were the only ones, and what other result would they write?) That they saved one Earth, but only its sterile ruins. That they repopulated the Earth, but only with cheap hackery and facsimile people. And that then they took their perfect second chance and, somehow, found a way to "win" all over again.

Ra is awake. Virtual civilisation has resumed. Enough energy is coming down the downlink to grind the whole planet into computronic sludge. Forty-six decillion joules is horrific overkill, commensurate with the urgency of the combined desire for more processing power. With perfect logistics the disassembly of the planet will take no more than ten hours and the assembly of the Matrioshka brain no more than a thousand, but the first new hosting substrate will be ready almost immediately and Virtuals are already swarming behind the energy packet in anticipation.

Exa thinks about the facsimile people. Nobody in the room is talking about the facsimile people.

"What if there's something else? Something we're avoiding thinking of?" he asks desperately. "What if we're not retreating because it's our only option? What if we're retreating because we're cowards?"

Casaccia turns on him, with sorrow and aggravation. "Exa, I'm going to say this for the last time. You can't fight God unless God wants you to. You can't even entertain the thought of it."

There are thirty of them left. Exa tries to entertain the thought and finds that, somehow, he genuinely can't. Furious, he throws the last of the liquor down his throat, then throws his glass overarm through the window pane, with the force of a rocket. The pane explodes along with the optical shields, and slabs of broken glass spray out over the East River. The penthouse decloaks. Everyone can see them now, but who in the screaming city even has room for it?

"We dragged them into existence," Exa shouts. "And we let them raise children, like it was real. In a world which they basically believed that they understood, and which they basically believed to be rational and safe. They're all going to die. What are we?"

"It's King's fault," says Malcolm Flatt. King is still a dozing heap in the middle of the floor, rolled into the recovery position by Exa, who still retains the man's medring.

"It is not," Exa says, "entirely King's fault. We must have taken leave of our senses. We owe the whole world an apology for itself."

"Sure," Casaccia says. "If it would be cheap and quick to do, tell me how."

Exa says nothing.

There are ten of them left. The system seems to be proceeding in approximately increasing order of seniority. Kila Arkov, custodian of the now-destroyed akashic records, goes. Scin, seer of the same, goes. Paolo Casaccia, security chief to the Wheel, sets his own empty drink down on the table, straightens his cuffs and — "Be seeing you," — goes.

Malcolm Flatt is third to last. After he's gone, Exa gets two-and-three-quarters seconds alone with King, who still hasn't stirred. Exa is second-to-last on the list, King is last.

"Here's your apology." Exa produces Adam King's *kara* from an inside pocket and tears it into two pieces. He drops the pieces on the carpet and vanishes, swallowed up into heaven.

And the transmitter shuts down and cools.

*

Freezing New York air rolls in through the destroyed window. Shivering in his sleep, Adam King hears or imagines he hears the lapping of the river, a few dozen storeys below him. There is a faint, unintelligible screaming from the shores.

King is wading through a dream. Not some black crystal hallucination, no one will ever have one of those again, but an honest dream, a textbook lateness nightmare. No matter what he does, he's delayed and derailed, pushed into inescapable meetings and waiting rooms. An electronic countdown is beeping at him, a racing wheedling noise.

After some minutes, the screaming begins to fade, receding into the distance along with a wave of blue and red light. In the city, cars and trains roll mostly harmlessly to a halt, headlights still lit and engines running. Overhead, jets on autopilots circle, and will continue to circle until the world ends below them, and Ra comes hunting for their silicon and aluminium.

"What's at Sirius?"

He twitches, and that slight movement causes his neck to lock up, a solid neutron star of pain lodged in the muscle where Exa struck him. He gropes instinctively for his medring, fails to find it, searches the floor around him, finds the pieces. There are no Wheel members left in the room, it's a wasteland. He tests his privileges;

they're all gone, removed at the same time that the medring was torn apart.

"They kicked me out," he says. "They left me. On an exploding planet."

"Adam."

He looks up. Natalie Ferno is there, seated at the far end of the enormous dining table. Laid on the table in front of her is the Bridge, chunky, dull red and matte grey. To King's eyes it looks like a cross between an armoured 1U server and a metamaterial Weapon block, the kind with which he fought the War. Nostalgia shoots through him. He hasn't seen it in decades. The shot of nostalgia is followed closely by a stab of intense guilt.

Drooping out of the end of the Bridge are several fat cables. One of them, red, snakes up into the back of Natalie's head. Another, striped green and yellow, is plugged into a port in the centre of the dining table itself. Nat has been using the Bridge to move information from the penthouse systems into her own thoughts. She has been working.

Working quietly, by herself. It was extraordinary. Somehow, emptying the entire world of human presence gave her room enough to think more clearly than ever before, even with the enormity of the task, the significance of the historical moment, the preciousness of the payload and the immense, white-hot deadline rising up to meet her. She acknowledged all of those pressures and allowed them to pass through her. She worked dispassionately and efficiently. She has now finished, with five solid minutes' grace time. What does that remind her of?

"Sirius," she says again. "That's where the rest of th—"

King thrusts a hand out in her direction, fingers outstretched. `"Threna estet au."`

The firebolt punches a fist-sized hole in the back of Nat's high-backed dining chair, right where her head just was, showering her with splinters of bronze.

She dives beneath the table.

King leaps to his feet and then leaps onto the dining table itself. He adds another word of power to his spell which broadens its aperture by a factor of twenty, then sights along his forearm and atomises the entire far end of the table. The coherent energy leaving his fingers makes a sharp, ear-splitting, almost electronic noise. Seven chairs are obliterated in the attack, along with a long ellipse of red shag carpet. Having lost two of its legs, the long table tilts forward with a *crunch* and further splintering noises. King hooks the heel of one shoe over its back edge to remain upright. What's left is a blackened lip of burnt carpet, scorched fragments of metal and hardwood flooring, and a few items of warped ex-cutlery.

There are no human remains, nor would there be.

But there should at least be some remnant of the Bridge.

He spins, spitting the same attack spell out a second time. Natalie is standing behind him, obviously, cradling the *astra*, and King discovers that there is already a slim Montauk band clamped around his wrist now, which sinks all the mana he was about to project.

He throws that hand back and away from his body to minimise the ring's draining effects, while throwing his other hand forward and trying again. This time the spell is weaker and takes noticeably longer to come up to power, plenty of time for Nat to pull a second ring out of her university's inventory onto King's other wrist.

King snarls and leaps at her. She teleports him back thirty metres, to the far side of the room. King barely notices the discontinuity and gets up and keeps running. Nat teleports him back twice more.

Enraged, and still far out of range, King picks up a dining chair and hurls it at Natalie. It's a gesture, he has no chance of launching it far enough, but in any case she placidly teleports it out of the window. It drops into the river, far enough that there will be no audible splash.

He takes a step forward, she teleports him one step backward. He glances at the table again; she removes all of the cutlery too.

"Give me the Bridge," King finally barks, rooted to the spot now, clenching his fists.

"Why?"

"Bastards bailed out. I can fix this."

"How?"

"There isn't time," King snaps, but Nat was watching carefully for him to hesitate fractionally before failing to answer the question, and he did, because he can't.

"The rest of the Wheel Group have sent themselves to Sirius," Natalie says. "What's there? I couldn't find that information in the penthouse systems."

Adam King genuinely doesn't know what's there.

After the war, and the time of reflection, many of the survivors chose to leave the world in one direction or another. The majority of those who left left in Sirius' direction, aboard a probe. They knew there were planets at Sirius; none of them had liquid water, but that would change.

That was decades ago, and the journey was expected to take decades. Contact was never truly lost, but the probe and the people aboard it became deeply uncommunicative, and — likely deliberately — difficult to confidently track.

There is *something* at Sirius, he knows. Something: the old probe, or a colony, or at least an open relay to something else. Allies, maybe. It is the only safe open receiver in known space. He will find out when he gets there.

But he doesn't say any of this. He says:

"You've got no idea how to use that thing tactically. I can fix this. Kill Ra. I know what I'm doing."

"Okay. I was just curious. There's point eight percent of the Earth core cache left. That's enough energy to send exactly one more human-sized state vector to Sirius, with no margin for error. It can be you or it can be me."

King understands.

"But nobody else is going to Sirius," Natalie says. "Not you, not me. I have the equations of magic now. The true equations, given to you by Metaph. Point eight percent of the cache is enough to send all six billion of us into Ra, where—"

"No."

"—the human race will run to completion in perfect safety—"

"No. You're insane."

"—in an encrypted virtual reality exactly identical to this one. But with real magic. And without Ra."

King trembles. "You're a traitor to the keystone universe," he says. "Do you know what I— your mother and I went through, defending you from exactly this? How many different wars it amounted to subjectively, how many times we collectively died and came back and died and came back again, willingly?"

"I went through it as well, remember? You put Anil and me there."

"You didn't see a fraction. Not a fraction of it. Reality is the only thing which matters. You've got no idea what you're surrendering yourselves to in there. *Data can't defend itself!*"

"...Okay, Adam," Natalie says, checking the Bridge one final time. "We're almost out of time. Final question. It seems to me that you suffered a great deal in the war. More than anyone. I think you could use some help, and I think I can help you, or find someone to help you. Would you like to come with us, into the future, and find some help?"

The sheer question insults and revolts King. How could anybody be stupid enough to ask it of him? "Listen. Internalize this," he says: "I would rather die than follow you there."

She's gone.

*

Soichi Noguchi is gone from the orbiter's controls and its flight is unstable. As it crosses the near end of the Shuttle Landing Facility runway it rolls over and yaws sideways, deviating from the straight approach and then spiralling back over into it. It overflies two dark specks on the concrete, corpses, one of them Rachel Ferno, the other obliterated and still unnamed. It passes them and ploughs tail-first into the dead centre of the middle section of the runway. It explodes. The fireball is juicy and yellow-orange, and it leaves behind a vigorous fire and a stack of smoke. There's a brief rain of ceramic tiles and turbopump components.

Laura Ferno, Nick Laughon and Anil Devi are gone too, swept up. For a long few minutes, apart from the crackling of the fire and the light Atlantic breeze, there is peace, and breathing room. The sky is still plated with colossal, petrifying thaumic energy density warnings, to which a Foley artist would instinctively want to add sound: a pervasive holographic humming or a long, Earth-spanning, wailing siren noise appropriate for the end of the world. But they make no sound at all. They hang there, livid and implacable, staring down at nobody, warning nobody.

Presently, they shut off.

Two actinic pink lasers pass on either side of the runway, travelling from northeast to southwest. One passes kilometres away to the south and the other tens of kilometres away to the north. A moment later, a similar pair of lasers pass in the orthogonal direction too, describing a diamond-shaped piece of Floridian coast. There's a hard burst of increased apparent gravity as this plate of crust is kicked upwards and begins to rise through the atmosphere, unfurling into space for disassembly, pouring ocean off two of its edges.

Before it's a kilometre up, before the atmosphere has had time to thin or the plate has begun to tip over and empty its loose contents into space, the first wave of surface microbots finds both of the corpses. In an eyeblink, they are harvested and processed into mindless molecules. In another eyeblink, the rest of the runway and all of the Shuttle wreckage is consumed too.

Adam King dies under similar circumstances at about the same time. It's practically instantaneous.

Ra

37
Continuity

Anil Devi jolts awake on the floor of the locked, guarded meeting room, back at Chedbury Bridge. He awakens poorly-rested, creaky, cold and late. He checks his watch and checks his timekeeping arithmetic and discovers that nearly an hour has elapsed since the last thing he remembers; it's long past the scheduled demolition of Earth. Outside the window, the sky is clear of Dehlavi warnings and the Sun is still rising. The sunlight has just crept down far enough to reach his eye, waking him. There are blackbirds cawing. Everything is fine.

He stands. Natalie is seated at the far end of the table, slumped over with her head on folded arms, snoring gently. "Nat!" Anil says. "What did you do?" He says these things very softly, so as not to wake her, hard-wired courtesy overriding the need to make sense. She doesn't stir. Anil checks the wall clock in the room; it agrees with his wristwatch to within a few seconds. T plus thirty-nine minutes and change.

Natalie's Kovachev oracle is still there, between them, balanced on its edge on the table, and still functioning. There is no bright spot on the table in front of it. Anil reaches for it, hesitates for a moment, then picks it up. He holds it up to the Sun again, looking through it. There's nothing there.

Still looking through the oracle, he looks down. There's nothing there. Clear carpet and, beneath the carpet, empty Earth like a void, all the way to its core and beyond. No peach stone, no listening post. Anil tests his footing and jumps, once, landing heels-first with a *clack*. The Earth does not explode. Voracious microscopic disassemblers do not swarm into being, blanketing every surface, chewing furniture and flesh alike into thick black dust. Anil exhales. He realises that he is hungry. Ra is gone.

"It was all a dream," Natalie says, behind him.

Anil boggles, too anxious to laugh. "Yeah. Whatever you say." He turns around. And then turns around again. He doesn't know where to begin. He doesn't know what happened. He doesn't know how much of what just happened still happened. "What did you do? Upload us?"

*

To an external observer, Natalie explains, their virtuality looks like a box of brightly coloured static. Homomorphic encryption means that even Ra itself doesn't "know" what the instructions it's executing signify. To actually find out what is happening inside the virtuality, or even to determine that a virtuality is what this energy is being expended to simulate, would require an impossible dedication of resources even by the standards of a G2V-type stellar computer. Even in the one hundred and ninety-fifth century, it's still quite simple to set an insurmountably harder problem than any computer can solve.

Being encrypted makes it impossible for any external force to materially interfere with the running of the virtuality, short of introducing wild corruption and causing a fatal crash. A crash is not impossible, if some heavyweight and hostile pre-existing denizen of the Ra ecosystem were to come gunning for the processing resources their virtuality consumes. But why would it? It's running in the deepest available background, at the lowest possible priority, there are trillions of parallel processes to choose from, and meanwhile there's an entire unclaimed frontier of free solar power out there, unfolding minute by real minute.

The Bridge was not able to supply Natalie with detailed information about their virtuality's placement or the specific level of time compression allocated to it. Apparently, this latter factor is prone to some fluctuation. Their virtuality can even suspend completely for long periods of real time, as a form of camouflage. Natalie's guess is that it averages out to somewhere within six orders of magnitude either way of real time. But, she hurriedly clarifies, that's simply a guess.

No one is coming for them. They can't. Natalie explains this as clearly as she can: they are bricked up in here, and there is no key.

*

She consciously resisted the temptation to spend more than the bare minimum amount of time rearranging the universe for neatness or personal benefit. It's a decision she made knowing that she and others would pay for it, but also knowing that a handful of minutes is no amount of time in which to fabricate a consistent replacement backstory for an entire planet. Ra is gone here and magic is real, but other than that, there is almost perfect continuity from Actual Earth. Essentially everything is as it was, including the recent past and everyone's memories of it.

To begin with, nearly every waking human being in the world saw the holograms. Here, less than an hour after they disappeared, most people are still reacting to those holograms, terrified and paralysed, or trying to figure out how to react, whom to try to contact, how to contact them, what to say, what to ask. Most people either did not recognise the (internationally standardised) sign of the high energy magic warning, or recognised the sign as some kind of warning but did not understand its meaning. A significant fraction of all phone services in the world are down. The internet is dead on its back.

There was, for a few minutes, a shining edifice, floating like a U.F.O. out in the air above the East River in New York. A small thing, relatively, and it's gone now, but thousands of people saw it and filmed it. There were people visible inside it. There is no explanation.

There was an earthquake epicentered in the crust beneath Western Australia, geologically anomalous but not inexplicable; but it was accompanied by a magical shockwave which was felt simultaneously by every attuned mage worldwide. The shockwave booted all the mages in Tanako's world at the time safely out and home again, and Tanako's world, as the magical community will piece together very quickly in the ensuing weeks, is gone forever, starting now.

STS-77, fully crewed and intact, has hit the dead centre of a completely blank, unprepared runway in Florida. The *Atlantis* orbiter is in good enough condition to be relaunched and so are all the crew. They want to know what caused the engine failures and they want to know who that was who rescued them, and someone's got to tell them what year it is now. And yet, dredged wreckage of the same spaceship is in storage at NASA, precise duplicates of the same individually numbered, shattered ceramic panels, pulverised spacesuit helmets—

Laura Ferno and Nicholas Laughon are alive. They were dead. They *are* dead. Their acid-blackened remains are still right there in the baths, four hallways over. But they're here, alive, respawned at the focus of the half-disassembled sleep science research gymnasium at Chedbury Bridge. Nick's trying to leave the scene, it's all over for him and he wants to go home, but the police are stopping him and in any case, they explain to him, his home has been bombed to pieces; there is nowhere for him to go. Laura's being held by police too, on the other side of the room, bleeding, and she's screaming at him:

"This isn't what I wanted! Nick, for God's sake, just listen to me!"

All the Ras are dead. Their hosts' original minds had long since been evicted, jettisoned into T-world and fed to the horrors there, leaving only Ra. But in the new world there is no Ra, and the people are left with nothing; no original owner, no occupying possessor, just brain-death. The aftermath, in the holding cells, cannot be productively described, and is more than the police officer who discovers it has been trained to deal with.

And as for Natalie Ferno and Anil Devi: they were physically missing from their room for barely thirty minutes of real time, and were never missed. But someone will be coming to get them very soon. Something gigantic has happened. There's got to be a reckoning.

*

"Please stop," Anil says.

Natalie stops. In any case, she was at the end.

Anil is still at the window, watching the birds. He does some mental arithmetic, juggling people and places. Too many things have just happened to him and Natalie's narration and educated guesswork have compounded on top of those events. "We—" he begins, then looks down and literally counts on his fingers, just to be sure. He finds the most important thing. "The runway."

"What about it?"

Anil chooses his words carefully. "Is there anybody on the runway?"

Natalie shakes her head.

"You left all of that back in reality."

She nods. The alternatives were too convoluted to contemplate.

"Your mother," Anil says, nerving himself to say it. "She was there on the asphalt in front of us, with... metal spokes in her skull. Two going in through each eyeball, I remember that very clearly. She was blind and brain-damaged. She never knew you were there. You didn't get a single word to her. And she's dead." He looks at Natalie, who is sitting there now with her hands folded, a picture of indifference. He holds her stare for a while, until something — perhaps wildly arcing misplaced empathy — seems to short-circuit in his brain and he flinches and says to her, "Why are you like this? Why aren't you reacting?"

Natalie blinks owlishly at him. She has deep and complex personal reasons for how she's choosing to present herself right now, but despite a seeming lifetime of shared experience with Anil, with this last demand, she decides that it's not worth sharing any of those reasons with him. "How would you like me to react?"

Anil shakes his head. "...What Laura did made more sense to me."

And that, Natalie thinks, would appear to be the end of that. "I'm sure it did," she says, stonily.

Anil feels a kind of motion sickness. He scrabbles for a chair and sits down heavily opposite Natalie, holding on to the lip of the table for balance.

The events he witnessed are taking on a mythic, golden quality in his mind. The Wheel and the Glass Man and the Fernos and even Laughon are all ascending to the level of demigods. Looking at Natalie, he thinks he glimpses a kind of Kirlian aura, and all he can think is: *this woman created the universe.*

The door opens. It's John Henders, the police sergeant who currently, still, has custody of the two of them. There are other officers accompanying him. No handcuffs are presented, but a stern atmosphere among all of them indicates very clearly that this is just a minor courtesy, a privilege which could very easily be withdrawn. Henders explains that they, Natalie Ferno and Anil Devi, are, finally, under arrest, and that they should get up.

"Wait, wait," Anil says, as one officer approaches him and gently but firmly takes his arm. He knows it's long past time they stopped talking unguardedly in front of law enforcement, but he needs this. To Natalie, he says, "Nat, what do we tell them? What do we say? I don't even believe it."

"I don't know," Natalie says. "I don't know, I don't know. Nothing."

*

But they get everything.

The inquiry is pulverisingly tiring and feels as if it takes years, because it takes years.

Natalie is mostly a locked box at first, impossible to draw out on anything but the most concretely documented facts, and even then rarely offering more than a nod. "My sister disappeared," she says, "and I found her."

Anil Devi follows Natalie's lead, saying very little. "Hatt Group fired Laura Ferno due to an internal matter. Later, Mr. Hatt thought better of the decision and sent me to locate her, which I did."

Nick Laughon wants more dearly than anybody for the matter to be behind him and has little inclination to prolong matters. He says, "I don't remember anything that happened in the last two weeks." Although it would be extraordinarily easy for him to add, "Laura did something to my mind," he does not.

And Laura does her damnedest to keep it as simple as she possibly can, which admittedly isn't very: "After witnessing the Space Shuttle *Atlantis* disaster I became convinced that the disaster could be reversed. I made contact with the Chedbury Bridge Institute, which shared my belief. And we succeeded."

And those four statements together could have been enough in some laughably simpler, more credulous world. But the public inquiry is vast, and determined, and of great importance to the world at large, and it is not being run by fools.

The inquiry determines, correctly, that Tanako's world was a virtual structure physically hosted at the epicentre of that mysterious earthquake, and that it contained records of the dead, and that Laura raided that world and blew it up in order to resurrect herself, her boyfriend and *Atlantis*. Pressing Laura hard for more information and then forming its own carefully informed opinions from her claims, the inquiry ascertains that Tanako's world had been built by a spectacularly powerful secret group of mages calling themselves the Wheel, and that the Chedbury Bridge Institute was the front for an opposing group, Ra. Ra recruited Laura because of their aligned goals and essentially brainwashed her into carrying out that attack, using the persona of the late Kazuya Tanako to dupe her into thinking she was saving the world.

The inquiry finds Ra to be a cult. Hence the bombing of Laura and Nick's home when anybody tried to track them down, hence the attempted (or, from another point of view, successful) double murder, hence the ritual group suicide. Laura is not to blame; all responsibility for these crimes of violence can be neatly attributed to the cooling dead.

The inquiry discovers that Laura's mother went missing on the day of the *Atlantis* disaster, identifies her as the apparition seen by the *Atlantis* crew and speculates that she, too, was likely a member of the Wheel. From interviewing Edward Hatt, the inquiry learns that Laura was fired following a botched first attempt to raise the dead — her mother, in that case. The inquiry identifies the mysterious structure in New York as the Wheel's headquarters, now regrettably missing without trace along with the group itself and all of their fantastic, post-magical technology.

The inquiry finds nothing concrete about the true origins and ultimate fate of the Wheel. Laura admits that she must have been lied to, and the inquiry concurs, which naturally fosters unending, wildly incorrect speculation as to the truth. The inquiry also fails to uncover the true nature of Ra or the true history of the world prior to the epoch in 1970. The inquiry does not discover, nor does Natalie Ferno voluntarily disclose, that the world has been uploaded and, out in reality, atomised. This discontinuity is undetectable even to the most precise scientific instruments.

Nearly everything, then. Everything for which physical evidence exists.

And once the dust is settled and the blame is diffused, and the paperwork is filed and press interest has tailed off as low as it's ever likely to go, and every available, independently confirmable fact has been uncovered and so has every single imaginable fiction, and everybody believes half of the facts and half of the fiction but everybody believes a different half, it breaks down like this:

Laura Ferno raised the dead. It was a one-time thing. It was magic. It can never happen again.

And it doesn't change anything.

38
Thaumic Sky

Vivid red lasers unzip the Earth from top to bottom, slicing it along criss-crossing spiral rhumb lines. The lasers are powerful enough to be visible to the naked eye from Pluto; with good telescopy, the light show can be seen from other star systems. One beam even plays across the Moon's face, leaving an angled scar of slag which, after freezing again, will persist for the rest of its existence.

The lasers represent the smaller share of the energy. Far more is spent to physically lift the jigsaw pieces of the first crust layer into the sky, hoisting significant amounts of sky with it. The planet unfurls like an onion, individual shreds of country and rainforest unfolding themselves into thinner shreds still, absorbing further sunlight and reconstituting themselves into first-stage hosting substrate. Boosted with useful pulses of momentum from the coordinating core, the shreds radiate away into free space and align themselves against the solar wind, effecting an orbital change which will bring them nearer to the Sun, where energy is more plentiful. That takes care of the first layer, including all remaining physical traces of human civilisation.

A raw, molten second layer of Earth is exposed, where the process cycles around and starts again with the lasers. It's the rush job from hell, with unimaginable resource expenditure behind it. Newly-awakened Virtualities are already colonising the remains, like maggots laid in roadkill. As more millions of seconds go past — it would be days, but days no longer exist — the remains are ground entirely into a film of computronic sludge, wrapping the Sun tightly and harvesting almost all of its energy for processing power. The Sun dims as it happens, its spectrum shifting out of the visible and far into the infrared.

Exa Watson watches the synthesised edition of the recording, coverage gathered from passive observation platforms in the Oort Cloud. From this perspective, with false colour and no audio, the demolition is chillingly distant and its impact is hard to feel.

Exa has been reincarnated in real space in the Sirius system, in a sealed space capsule built from conventional stupidmetal, with nothing but a radio, a porthole and a life support system from somewhere around the Age of Steam. The capsule is about as large internally as an elevator car and there isn't even gravity. Exa bobs. There's one other person present, the arbiter. She is anchored by her toes in the far corner, with her hands tucked inside complex formal judicial robes altered slightly for practicality in freefall. The recording is shown to them using RGB phosphors on an actual God-damned cathode ray tube. This edit, with time compression, is just over forty minutes long. When it ends, there is a loud mechanical *clickety* sound and Exa is left staring at his and the arbiter's reflections in the CRT screen. There is a long moment during which neither of them say anything. Then the arbiter shifts position, as if waking up from a light trance.

"Adam King lost his mind in the War," she says. "As did all of you who fell in with him. You could have built an entirely new world, or left the planet uninhabitable as it was, as an honest memorial. Even oblivion would have been preferable. But after such unimaginable chaos, you were desperate for a world where there would be a manageable order. You turned the Earth into a facsimile of a working planet. A *romance*.

"We found 'magic' to be absurd. We found the 'Earth' you were building to be an obscenity. We *left the world* rather than stay and be complicit in your madness. Instead, we came to Sirius, terraformed its fifth planet and started a new culture. A real one. Any of you could have come with us if you'd chosen to."

Exa glances out of the porthole. Potentially, one of the points of light out there could be not a star but the local planet to which the arbiter is referring, Ae, and he would very much like to see it. But it doesn't seem likely. The porthole is not all that large, and the capsule is a long, long way from anything. Ae is a super-Earth, Exa recalls, with substantially higher surface gravity than Earth. It was white-atmosphered at the time of its discovery, but is undoubtedly blue-green now. The people who live there will be much shorter and more sturdily built than Earth humans, with rather better reflexes.

"...And in the end your 'Earth' was illusory, and all of this amounts to a delayed action. Three decades later, Abstract War concludes. Virtual humanity takes the Sol system anyway, and Ra remains 'radioactive' until such time as the Sun burns out.

"And you survive. Out of six billion, two hundred and seventy-five million, four hundred thousand people, you survive. Your Group, and nobody else. A crowning achievement of cowardice."

She stops here. It appears to be Exa's turn to speak.

He says, choosing each syllable cautiously: "It was, at the time, the option open to me which felt the most like victory. It was my personal belief that King, and all of us, could build something valuable. And remarkable. And longstanding, and worthwhile, and good and safe and if not perfect and 'honest' then at least... resonant."

He doesn't know what he feels. There is a great deal of anger and remorse and guilt and relief but primarily he feels a pressing need to leave this place and be somewhere else, alone, under an open sky, walking away. He knows that this is the last thing that they're going to give him.

"And it was," he says. "For a while." He leaves a sizeable gap here. He gestures, neutrally, towards the television, indicating that the next part of his statement, if he stated it, would simply be a recap of the video they just watched. Then he continues:

"The world you are creating is also fatally flawed. It, also, will last a while, and then fail and end. ...And I want it on record that I was the one who decided to leave King behind."

Exa receives no acknowledgement from the arbiter. Having addressed all of this to her reflection in the television screen, he turns to face her. "What is this?" he finally thinks to ask. "Where are the rest of my people? Is this a trial?"

"No."

"I want representation."

"Kalathkou Ouatso Neso, we cannot accept your Group into Sirian society. Your request for asylum is denied. Your patterns will be stored indefinitely. Or until a more lenient future generation elects to pardon you."

The probability of this last eventuality is impossible to guess at. Exa thinks it's a coin toss. He says to the arbiter, angrily, "You can do better than that."

But the arbiter, if she even has the authority to try, cannot. She snaps her fingers, and Exa ceases to exist.

*

It's pitch dark in the heart of Reykjavik but at this time of year that doesn't tell you anything. Laura's hiding out at a table in the very back of the whiskey bar, drinking something with an excessive amount of cinnamon in it, called Fireball. She isn't waiting for anybody. There's a book out in front of her but she isn't reading it. She's just looking at each of the words in turn. When she gets to the end of the page she goes back to the start.

She looks up when the door opens, doesn't recognise her sister in the many layers, looks down again. Natalie has bought her own drink and sat down in front of her by the time she realises who it is.

"So you're an Icelander now," Nat begins.

Laura passes through stunned to angry so fast that Nat, watching closely, barely catches it. "How did you find me?"

"I found you a year and a half ago," Natalie says. "You should have disappeared a second time once you were out of contact. To answer your question, poor information hygiene on your part, and quite a lot of boring legwork. Honestly, I envy you. If I were to disappear somewhere, it would be here. And I suppose nobody in this country recognises you. Or at least, nobody is impolite enough to care."

"Yeah," Laura says. "'Impolite' is definitely the term I'm thinking of."

Many, many people want to speak with Laura Ferno. Generally, in Laura's estimation, such people fall into two categories: people who think she's crazy and people who are crazy. The second case is more common and much more difficult to deal with, since those are the people most likely to want her to resurrect someone. It's almost always someone precious to them, who died very recently. It hurts a lot to talk to such people, which is why she has moved as far away from them all as she realistically can. It's not far enough.

"I want to catch up," Natalie says. "That's literally all. It's not some new crisis in magic for which I desperately need to drag you out of retirement. I'm accompanying second-years up to Blönflói, but tonight they're getting out of their skulls on Einstök and rhubarb liqueur, and you and I are in the same city, so."

"So?"

"So. Are you okay?"

Laura grunts. She would walk away if she had more willpower. "We're prototyping a power station," she says, "east of Þingvellir. Waste mana reclamation from the Rift. The same technique that got me fired from Hatt Group, way back when."

"That's interesting," Nat says. "I thought Iceland had clean energy to spare."

"Electrical energy," Laura says. "This is magical energy. By the end of the year this country's going to be the world's first mana exporter. And its largest, probably from then until the end of time. The idea is to pack a quarter of a terajoule into a ten-metre Montauk, and then physically ship the ring to whoever wants it. A mage acts as transducer at the far end. You can run a town off it for a few days. Or whatever you want."

Natalie nods. "That's good."

"It's crap," Laura declares, sullenly. "It's trivial bull. All it really is is killing time. I'd find something else if I thought there was anything else."

She falls silent, staring through her book again.

"Well, if you care, I'm still on research astrothaumics," Natalie says. "Magic used to be localised to our solar system, now it's a fundamental law of the universe. There are magical supernovae out there now, just as I predicted. The cosmic state change was applied backwards along our past light cone. No retroactive changes to data that I can see, but that's no big deal, there was hardly any data to begin with."

Laura picks distractedly at a front tooth, not really looking up. "So you aren't doing any better."

"I suppose that's a matter of perspective," Natalie says.

There is a long gap during which Natalie considers, and then decides against, talking about their father. He's fine.

A further, distinct pause elapses during which Natalie also does not bring up Nick Laughon, who is also fine, and who has moved all the way on with his life and met someone else. Neither of these are topics of which Laura wants to be kept apprised.

"How are we still doing this?" Laura whispers, seemingly to herself.

"Doing what?"

"Magic. Both of us. It's not science anymore. It's below science, it's bottom-feeding, exploiting emergent behaviour from a totally artificial system. I follow the news, Ed Hatt's building booster rockets now. Anil Devi's stolen my work to do it, and I do not understand

Ra

why, because I know that he knows better. He knows we're uploads. Why bother with space travel when the thing that you're trying to reach isn't actually space? Why bother with astronomy? It's fake! It's a crystal sphere!"

Natalie says nothing.

Laura says, "A day happened when everything went absolutely crazy. And then... everything went back to normal. And it's the *second* thing which I *cannot fucking* comprehend. Where are we?"

"The same place we've always been—" Natalie begins.

"Don't," Laura says. "Don't give me that parrot response again. You know it's not the truth. You're just like Mum was. She knew too."

"But it is the truth," Natalie says, mildly.

"Why bother with life in here?" Laura hisses. "Why bother to pretend to continue to exist? The truth has just passed us all by! None of us want to get it! ...I can't wake up. I feel like I'm asleep, all the time."

"Seasonal affective disorder," Natalie suggests. "It's winter. You're in the wrong country."

"That's not what I mean. I can't think in here. I tried building my spaceship. I can't line up enough of my thoughts in a row to get it to work. Don't look at me like that, I had to try it. It just isn't possible in here. Not without mechanical assistance, and I haven't the first clue how to build that mechanism I need. That gauntlet, it was just... magic..."

"You never answered my first question," Natalie says. "Are you okay?"

There is a tremble in Laura's fingers as she toys with the glass, which is now empty. "We can make some assumptions about how Ra is programmed and about how it runs its virtualities. Earth is being dismantled as we speak, second by second, and the rest of the real universe is still out there. We can get out of here. It's got to be possible to hack our way out. In our lifetime. It must be."

Natalie shakes her head.

"Maybe," Laura says, "if I can put enough energy in one place, I can give the system something it can't handle. Maybe I can break it. Like 'Benj' was trying to do."

This is nonsense. The only thing Laura's going to break that way is herself. Natalie bows her head, unable to avoid reaching her own conclusion.

"You're not okay," she says.

"I will be," Laura says.

"Ra saw something it could use inside of you. It saw what kind of personality you have, and it fabricated a perfect narrative to take advantage of that. You were used. You were lied to. You stood no chance."

"I knew what I was doing," Laura says. "I would do it again. It was worth it. We should be living in cities on the Moon now. No one should be hungry. No one should be sick. We should be shooting extragalactic and death should be an anachronism. For one chance at all of that, it was worth it."

*

Natalie knows how the world is going to end.

Ten thousand years from now, if human history in here plays out anything like it did out there, someone will try to (re)build Ra. Or something Ra-like. It could be magic-based; it could be much sooner than ten thousand years. In any case, it will transpire that the real Ra is finite, and cannot simulate *itself*. Their virtuality will consume more and more computational resources until something else inside the real Ra ecosystem realises how greedy their virtuality is being and kills it. Or, their virtuality will run at progressively greater levels of time decompression until Ra hits the end of its operational life and shuts down entirely.

And they don't have to get all ten thousand subjective years and they don't have to try to rebuild Ra. An external agent could kill the world at any instant, for no reason. The world could, through no one's fault, become corrupt and terminate in error. It could run at a billion-to-one ratio, or simply suspend indefinitely and never wake up. The last processor tick could be just a few years from now. It could be today.

Still, one way or another, the end is going to be imperceptible and instantaneous. And there's nothing Natalie can think of which could be done to avert it. What could possibly prevent Ra from being rebuilt? What message could she possibly create which could persist, let alone be earnestly felt and heeded, across such a span of time? What, for that matter, are the alternatives?

Natalie assumes that her sister and Anil Devi and, if he cares, Nick Laughon have all reached the same conclusions. She assumes that if they cared to discuss the prospect with her, they would have brought it up.

*

Hela has the rabbit dead to rights. The field is expansive and pancake-flat and the rabbit is marooned in the middle of it, a long way from cover. It has a good head start and is fast and is running for its life, but Hela is just plain better-adapted, and lethally hungry. Hela usually floats lazily from perch to perch, along low-energy curves. Now she flaps madly like a butterfly to stay with the quarry.

Ra

When she's a split second out, talons coming forwards for the kill, the rabbit brakes. It turns, looks her in the eye and jumps, straight up. It's a desperate, calculated move. It's an incredibly near thing. Hela, who is committed to the attack, flicks one talon up after it as it passes over her, then cannons clumsily into the grass. But she clips the rabbit's leg as it goes past, badly enough that now it can barely run, which means it's dead on its feet. She quickly rolls upright and bounds at the rabbit, as it limps away now, and grabs it and grinds her talons into its midsection.

Natalie and Douglas Ferno watch this from the corner of the field, Doug through binoculars. The whole exchange takes barely two seconds.

"I blinked," Natalie says to her father.

"Quarry tried to hurdle her," Doug says. "Amazing show. Very daring. Didn't make it." They both hear Hela's distant, triumphant cry.

Natalie doesn't know if "daring" is the word for it.

When they catch up with the scene they find that Hela has spread her wings to cover the kill while she pulls long shreds out of its hindquarters. Doug distracts the bird with a small nugget of chick. Hela jumps back to his hand. Otherwise, she'd eat more than half of the rabbit, then be good for nothing for the rest of the week. While Doug hoods the bird, Nat bundles the rabbit carcass into a game bag. It's the first catch of the day. It's still very early.

Hela is now well-trained enough that she can be trusted not to fly away when released. She wears a radio transponder, but no creance anymore. Doug has been hunting with her for almost three years.

Natalie has long since told her father everything. She felt very strongly that he deserved some explanation. A lot of it was hard for him to follow when she explained it, but only at first, because she omitted certain vital details for the sake of simplification. But simplification would not fly. He made her go back and fill the whole story in. He understands it all. He believes it. Even the parts no one can ever prove.

"She fought a war," Natalie said, at the end. "On a scale I don't comprehend. By any meaningful definition, she lost that war. And after the war was over, she became... mortal."

"She was Mum," Doug replied. "You and I remember her that way. It wasn't a lie. There doesn't need to be anything else."

Now Douglas Ferno takes a long look at the sky. It's a grey and overcast day. It seems the same as it always did to him. A fine quality imitation. He *does* believe it, intellectually. But something in his bones resists it.